Where was her name? Belle's ⟨...⟩ ⟨...⟩st. Becoming ever more franti⟨...⟩ — *Jack Thorne.* Jack had a due⟨...⟩ ⟨...⟩ ⟨...⟩ and looked again . . . Could they really be singing together?

No, they couldn't!

Jack was paired with Ruby Drew! Jealousy bit as hot and sharp as a wasp sting. Belle knew Ruby from advanced singing class and had always got on well with her. But suddenly she couldn't bear the thought of Ruby Drew singing the sweet, romantic duet *Let's Play a Love Scene* from *Fame* with Jack. It was so-o-o unfair!

Then, at last, she saw her name . . .

Fans on *Superstar High*:

'This book was amazing! There is not really much more that I can say about it except WOW!'
Beth, 13

'I read it all in one weekend because
I enjoyed it so much'
Georgia, 10

Also available in the Superstar High series:

Nobody's Angels
The Time of Your Life

Or get the first two Superstar High books in one!

Star Friends

✸ SUPERSTAR HIGH ✸

DON'T STOP BELIEVING

Isabella Cass

CORGI BOOKS

With special thanks to Helen Moss

SUPERSTAR HIGH: DON'T STOP BELIEVING
A CORGI BOOK 978 0 552 56092 4

Published in Great Britain by Corgi Books,
an imprint of Random House Children's Books
A Random House Company

This edition published 2011

1 3 5 7 9 10 8 6 4 2

Series created and developed by Amber Caravéo
Copyright © Random House Children's Books, 2011

The Random House Group Limited supports the Forest Stewardship Council
(FSC), the leading international forest certification organization. All our titles
that are printed on Greenpeace-approved FSC-certified paper carry the FSC logo.
Our paper procurement policy can be found at www.randomhouse.co.uk/environment

Mixed Sources
Product group from well-managed
forests and other controlled sources
www.fsc.org   Cert no. TT-COC-2139
© 1996 Forest Stewardship Council

Red Fox Books are published by Random House Children's Books,
61–63 Uxbridge Road, London W5 5SA

www.**kids**at**randomhouse**.co.uk
www.**totallyrandombooks**.co.uk

Addresses for companies within The Random House Group Limited can be found at:
www.randomhouse.co.uk/offices.htm

THE RANDOM HOUSE GROUP Limited Reg. No. 954009

A CIP catalogue record for this book is available from the British Library.

Printed and bound in Great Britain by CPI Bookmarque, Croydon, CR0 4TD

CONTENTS

CHANCE TO SHINE

Isabella Cass

For Mum and Dad

CHAPTER ONE

Holly: No Time for Wobbles

Holly Devenish had never felt so nervous.

Peeping out from the wings of the Redgrave Theatre, she could see the dancers on the stage coming to the end of the Cossack Dance. Only twenty seconds until her big solo. Her heart was thrashing about like a wild animal caught in a trap and her lungs had forgotten how to breathe. Now her knees were joining the mutiny and turning to marshmallow.

Her body was definitely trying to tell her something!

Something that sounded a lot like: *Run away!*

Fifteen seconds to go . . .

Holly had danced in hundreds of shows before, of course. But this was no ordinary performance; it was the Dance Department's special ballet recital at the world-famous Garrick School for the Performing Arts. They were dancing *Nutcracker Sweeties* – a jazz ballet based on *The Nutcracker*, and Holly had been thrilled to be selected for the role of Sugar Rum Cherry. She was one of the very few Year Eight students to land a major part.

Ten seconds to go . . .

Six weeks of intensive rehearsals had all led up to this – the Big Moment! Most of the school was watching, including her best friends, Cat and Belle, and her boyfriend, Ethan, plus her mum and stepdad, and her old dance teacher, Miss Toft – not to mention mega-important visitors from talent agencies and dance magazines, all eager to see whether the latest crop of Garrick students lived up to the school's reputation for producing super-talented mega-stars; so many, in fact, that it had earned the nickname Superstar High!

Holly's mind was racing. *I'm no superstar. I'm just an ordinary girl from north London. I'm in the wrong place, the wrong school, maybe even the wrong planet . . .*

I can't do it . . .

Down in the orchestra pit, the Garrick jazz band were starting to play her music.

Five seconds to go . . .

'Holly Devenish! That is your cue!'

She jumped as she felt her ballet teacher's bony fingers dig her sharply in the ribs. Miss Morgan, tiny, and dressed entirely in black as always, was hopping about like a demented crow, her wizened face ablaze with the excitement of the show. Holly smiled bravely. Clearly not quite *bravely* enough to convince Miss Morgan, who gripped her by the shoulders and propelled her firmly towards the stage. 'You are a great dancer, *si*?' she yelled. 'This is no time for the *wobbles*! *ALLORA!* OK!'

One second . . .

With a deep breath, Holly summoned up every ounce of courage in her petite frame, lifted her chin and stepped into the hot dazzle of the stage lights. *I can't let everyone down . . .* She forced her legs to carry her to centre stage, her arms to extend, her mouth to smile — *but what if I mess up?* — forced her shoulders down and her head up, even though her heart was hurtling around at a hundred miles an hour . . . *What if I make a complete fool of myself . . . ?*

But then, suddenly, Holly wasn't thinking about *anything* any more . . . Without knowing quite how it happened, she felt the slow, sinuous jazz rhythm take over. She was dancing! Her body had changed its mind about running away!

Now it wanted to be on this stage for ever!

The music carried her like a magic carpet. She was

Sugar Rum Cherry, the sultry, flirtatious nightclub dancer.

It was as if someone had suddenly turned the dimmer-switch on life up to full brightness. This was her chance to shine!

Holly wished it would never end!

CHAPTER TWO

Cat: Dancing Bees

Cat could hardly believe her eyes!

Sugar Rum Cherry shimmered with confidence in her sparkly red dress and long red gloves. Cat was no expert on ballet – but you didn't have to be an expert to see that Holly was very special. You only had to be *conscious* to see that!

Next to her, Belle shook her head in amazement with a swish of her long blond hair. 'Wow!' she breathed, her perfectly shaped eyebrows nearly rocketing off her forehead.

Double-wow! Cat thought. They both knew that Holly was a great dancer, of course, and they'd seen her in the core dance classes which all students took. But neither Cat nor Belle took advanced ballet or jazz dance – Cat's speciality was classical acting and Belle was a singer – so they'd never seen Holly perform at the highest level before.

Now she was gliding around the stage, every step

perfectly timed, every movement smooth and flowing.

Can this really be Holly? Cat marvelled. *The girl who can't cross a room without bumping into the furniture!*

Suddenly Cat had a flashback moment to their first day at Superstar High last September: somehow Holly had catapulted her backpack into a giant puddle in a bizarre accidental reverse-hammer-throw manoeuvre, spattering mud all over Bianca Hayford's designer suitcases. Belle and Cat had come to Holly's defence. The results of this unfortunate episode were mixed. On the up-side – and it was a *very* big up – Holly, Cat and Belle had been best friends ever since. On the down-side, Bianca had turned out to be the Chief Mean Girl of their year and she'd *never* got over it; to say Bianca held a grudge would be a serious understatement; she'd built a gold-plated carry-case for that grudge and hadn't put it down since.

When *Nutcracker Sweeties* ended, Cat clapped so hard her palms tingled. The dance teachers all filed out onto the stage to congratulate the dancers, followed by the principal, James Fortune – crinkling his blue eyes at everyone and handing out bouquets of flowers like a film-star Father Christmas.

'Let's go backstage and see Holly!' Cat urged, tugging Belle's arm. 'You guys coming?' she added, turning to their friends Nathan Almeida, Nick Taggart and Jack Thorne, who were sitting with them.

Nathan nodded enthusiastically, his black fringe flopping over his wire-framed glasses. Nathan was so shy that *enthusiastic nod* was his equivalent of punching the air and screaming '*YAAAAY! WAY TO GO!*'

Nick, on the other hand, was the opposite of *shy*. 'Try and stop me!' He laughed and began to sashay down the aisle towards the backstage door, singing, '*She is our Dancing Queen . . . oh yeah . . .*' in a piercing falsetto voice.

'Er, people are *staring!*' Belle whispered. Cat laughed, joining in with Nick's disco-fever routine just a *teensy* bit as she followed him to the door, even though Belle was shaking her head and shooting her don't-encourage-him looks.

'Gotta see the Zakster too!' Nick called back over his shoulder. 'He wasn't bad either!'

'*Wasn't bad?* Zak was brilliant!' Cat protested. Zak Lomax – Nick's best friend and room-mate – was the only Year Eight student apart from Holly to have been given a major part in the show.

The friends were soon crowding into Holly's dressing room, hugging and congratulating her. Holly – usually so down-to-earth and unassuming, the kind of girl who said sorry if she trod on an ant – was zipping around on such a high, she was in danger of spinning off into orbit. Her smile grew even wider as Ethan Reed squeezed into the room, bearing a garden-sized bouquet, and engulfed her in a big swirly hug. Holly and Ethan were *officially* the sweetest couple at Superstar High; Ethan Reed was two years older than Holly, a brilliant actor, swimming champion and captain of the football team. Oh yeah, *and* he was gorgeous – with dark hair, chiselled jaw and green eyes. *In fact, if Holly wasn't my best friend and all-round adorable person, I'd hate her!* Cat thought. *And Belle too, for that matter!* Since Christmas, Belle had been going out with Jack Thorne – who also scored pretty high on gorgeousness points, and was generally agreed to be the coolest guy in their year.

Yep, Cat thought. *A girl could get a serious odd-one-out complex here.*

There was a cheer as Zak Lomax burst into the dressing room. He'd already combed out the gel that'd been slicking back his long, sun-streaked hair, and changed into his usual baggy T-shirt and surfer shorts – even in February. 'Yo-o-o, dudes!' he laughed, high-fiving everyone within reach. 'Totally psyched, man!'

'*Bravo!*' Miss Morgan cried, elbowing her way into

the packed dressing room. 'Now, we have a little supper party in the Dance Department to celebrate!' She clapped her hands briskly. 'Chop, chop!'

'Come on!' Cat shouted over the noise. 'We're in danger of missing a *party* here, guys!' She threw her arms around Holly and Belle and steered them out of the Redgrave – the Garrick School's purpose-built theatre – past the sports centre and across the central courtyard. Along the path, rows of lamps glowed cheerfully in the winter darkness.

The Dance Department was in one of the modern wings that flanked the courtyard. A buffet supper had been laid out on a long table in the bright, spacious foyer, and lively *Nutcracker Sweeties*-style jazz music was playing in the background. The party was *meant* to be just for the performers and one or two guests each, but somehow it seemed half the school had come along, and everyone – even the usually ferocious Miss Morgan – was far too jubilant to object to a few gate-crashers.

Cat helped herself to a plate of sandwiches and joined her friends at their table.

'I can't *wait* for the Rising Stars Spectacular!' Belle was saying, her lavender-blue eyes sparkling with excitement. 'Mr Garcia told me it's the most ambitious show in the history of Superstar High!'

Everyone agreed. The musical theatre showcase at the end of term was the next major school event and it was a *goosebumpily* thrilling prospect. All the Year Eight students were taking part – and with all sixty of them on stage together in the ensemble numbers it was going to be Seriously Big! *Bigger than the London Olympics and Beyoncé all rolled into one*, Cat thought.

'Yeah, we didn't have anything like it when I was in Year Eight,' Ethan said.

'But then you didn't have *electricity* or *penicillin* in those days either . . .' Nick teased.

They all laughed. 'Ethan's only in Year Ten,' Holly objected, flicking Nick with her napkin. 'He's not exactly prehistoric!'

'Thanks, Holly!' Ethan said, smiling at her.

Like I said, Cat thought. *Swe-e-e-t or what!*

'It's only seven weeks away!' Nick added, clutching dramatically at his sandy hair – making it stick up like a halo of electrified Shredded Wheat around his freckled face.

'Er, *six*, dude, not counting half-term next week,' Zak pointed out.

'*Technically*,' Nick countered, putting on a pompous science-nerd voice, 'time doesn't actually *stand still* when we're not at school, so it's still seven weeks away, I think you'll find.'

Zak grinned. 'Yeah! *Whatever!*'

'Stop squabbling, you two!' Belle told them. 'The cast list is going up tomorrow for the solos and duets – it's so exciting.'

'Ooh yeah!' said Holly. 'But they won't have given me much. I've had my turn already with *Nutcracker*.'

'I'm not expecting anything either,' Cat added, 'after playing Lady Macbeth last term.'

'As long as I get to be in the main dance numbers, I don't mind!' Gemma Dalrymple said as she and Lettie Atkins joined the group. Gemma, a tall, athletic Australian girl, was Holly's room-mate. She and Lettie had both danced in the chorus of *Nutcracker Sweeties*.

'Hey! What *is* this?' Belle wondered. 'A modesty competition? Well, sorry, guys, but I for one am secretly hoping for the biggest, fattest solo in the entire show!'

'Ambitious, Belle?' Nick joked.

Everyone laughed. 'You go for it, girl!' Holly told her.

Cat couldn't help hearing Jack whisper to Belle, 'I know you'll get a solo! You're the best singer by miles!'

To the untrained eye, Belle appeared as cool, calm and collected as always, but Cat could tell that she was hiding just the *tiniest* hint of a flustered blush as she nibbled her smoked salmon sandwich. Jack was the only person who had that effect on her – the flustered blushing thing, that was, not the nibbling-smoked-salmon-sandwiches part!

Suddenly Holly, Ethan, Gemma and Zak jumped up and started pushing back the tables to create an impromptu dance floor.

Cat would usually have been first up for a boogie, but tonight she stayed at the table. It wasn't that her party-animal spirit had deserted her; but since practising the *Flashdance* number for the Spectacular in yesterday's dance class, her legs felt as if someone had borrowed them and used them to run the London Marathon!

'Whoa!' Jack whistled, leaning his chair back to watch the dancers jitterbugging to the jazz music. 'Those guys can *really* dance! But . . . I have to admit' – he snapped his chair back to the table and lowered his voice as if about to reveal something truly scandalous – 'I've never quite got the *point* of dancing . . .'

Cat gasped in mock-horror.

'Steady on there, old boy!' Nick exclaimed in his best upper-class-twit accent. 'Next you'll be telling us that you're not terribly keen on all that *singing* malarkey either. Then Belle would stop speaking to you – and who knows *where* it will end!'

Jack grinned and put his arm round Belle. 'Don't worry, I *love* singing! And acting. It's just the *dance* thing I don't get. It's not really *about* anything, is it?'

Before Cat could protest, Nathan piped up, 'It *is* for bees.'

'*Bees?*' Cat said incredulously. Nathan was one of her closest friends, a super-talented actor and all-round brainiac, but sometimes she had no idea where he was coming from.

'Er, yeah,' Nathan mumbled, shy again now that everyone was staring at him. 'Dance is how bees tell other bees where to find the best flowers . . .'

'Hey, I've heard of that – it's called the Waggle Dance, isn't it?' Nick laughed. 'They wiggle their butts – like, three waggles to the right, epic patch of buttercups in the park . . .'

Nathan grinned back. 'That's right! Two wiggles to the left, check out the geraniums in next-door's garden . . .'

'Uh-oh! I think I know where this is going!' Belle groaned, clasping her palm to her forehead.

'Me too!' said Cat.

They were right. Nick was off, waggling onto the dance floor. 'You are a Dancing Bee!' he warbled, to the tune of Abba's Dancing Queen.

They all watched, laughing, as people started joining in – until the dance floor was *buzzing* with waggle-dancers.

'Like I said,' Jack repeated, holding out his hands in an I-rest-my-case gesture. 'Dance? *What's it all about?*'

CHAPTER THREE

Cat: Red-carpet Fatigue

Suddenly Cat felt Belle nudge her elbow. 'Wow! It's Stella McCartney!' Belle murmured, staring across to the other side of the room.

'Where?' Cat asked excitedly, craning her neck to see. 'What's such a famous designer doing at our party?'

'No, the *dress*! Bianca's wearing Stella McCartney. Spring collection . . .'

Cat was impressed. Belle could identify a designer garment at fifty paces – like a bird-spotter picking out a pied flycatcher or a reed warbler.

In her flowing white dress Bianca Hayford looked like a statue of a Greek goddess sculpted from pale marble. Next to her, her best friend, Mayu Tanaka, was resplendent in bubble-gum pink, her long black hair piled into an up-do so enormous and complicated it must've come with an instruction manual. Both were fully accessorized with matching jewellery, clutch bags and killer heels.

'And Alexander Wang,' Belle commented.

Cat guessed she was referring to the designer of Mayu's outfit and not a new boyfriend she'd brought with her, and nodded wisely. 'I think those two have over-dressed for a school party just a *fraction*,' Cat whispered. 'Especially since they didn't even *come* to the recital!'

'Yeah! *Some friends!*' Belle muttered darkly. 'Poor Lettie was expecting them to turn up and watch her . . .'

Cat shook her head in disbelief. It didn't surprise her that Bianca hadn't bothered to show up to watch her room-mate dance. What she *couldn't* get her head around was how an apparently *sane* human being like Lettie Atkins – a shy, serious musical genius – could be friends with Bianca in the first place, even if they *had* known each other since they were four years old.

And now Bianca and Mayu were heading straight for their table! Cat exchanged puzzled looks with Belle, Jack and Nathan. Bianca disliked Cat, she loathed Belle, and she wasn't exactly Jack's number-one fan either – ever since he'd seen through her trickery last term and turned her down in favour of Belle! As far as Cat knew, Bianca didn't have anything against Nathan, but that was only because she'd never even noticed his existence. So the fact that Bianca and Mayu were steaming towards them – wearing matching fake smiles under their lipstick – couldn't be a good sign.

'Oh yeah, we've just got back from Leicester Square,' Bianca announced loudly, to no one in particular. 'The premiere of the new Zac Efron movie, you know. My cousin, Tamara, runs their marketing campaign – she got us tickets. *And* she gets to borrow all these designer dresses . . .'

'Oh, was it good?' Cat asked, forcing herself not to sound *too* interested. *She was dying to see that film!*

'Oh, we didn't actually see the film!' Bianca giggled. 'We couldn't get away from the photographers . . .'

'It's so *exhausting* – all that waving and smiling,' Mayu gushed. 'They call it *red-carpet fatigue*, you know . . .'

'I don't know *how* Britney and Paris and Miley do it!' Bianca agreed.

Cat suppressed a giggle. *One film premiere and Bianca's on first-name terms with half of Hollywood!*

'Anyway, thought we'd swing by on the way back,' Bianca continued, 'and see how the ballet recital thingy went.'

Not to show off your dresses at all, then? Cat thought, biting back the words.

'Lettie danced beautifully,' Belle said. 'Everyone did.'

'Where is she, anyway?' Bianca asked.

Cat pointed to the dance floor.

'*Oh! My! God!*' Mayu squealed. 'What on *earth* is she doing?'

Cat had to admit Mayu had a point. Everyone else had gone back to swing-steps, but Lettie was still gamely doing the Waggle Dance with Nick Taggart.

'It's called *dancing*, I believe,' Jack said in a matter-of-fact voice.

Bianca sneered at him. 'Yeah, ri-i-i-ght!' Then she rolled her eyes at Mayu and pulled her arm. 'Let's get out of here. It might be catching!'

'Surely you've heard of *waggling?*' Belle said quietly, looking up at Bianca. 'It's *only* the hottest new craze in New York and LA.'

'Do I *look* stupid?' Bianca snarled.

'As if!' Mayu added, in her lisping little-girl voice.

Belle shrugged in a like-I-care-whether-you-believe-me kind of way.

Doubt flickered across Bianca's face. If *anyone* was up to date with all the latest international fashions it was Belle; her mum *was* Zoe Fairweather, the super-model, after all, and her dad was Dirk Madison, the famous film director. Not that Belle made a habit of trading on her parents' A-list celebrity status. In fact, Cat knew she was so worried that people might think she was bragging that she rarely mentioned them; she'd probably be happier if she came from a long line of bank robbers . . .

There was a tense Moment of Silence as Bianca grappled with the possibility that Belle was telling the truth and there really *was* a cool new dance-craze called *waggling* that she – Bianca Hayford, Girl About Town and Red-carpet Diva – had *somehow* missed.

'Hmph!' she snorted eventually, and with a defiant am-I-bothered? expression and a rustle of white silk, stomped a high-heeled stomp out of the room. Mayu scowled at Belle and Cat and then followed her out.

'Er, *waggling*?' Cat wondered.

Jack laughed. 'The hottest craze in New York?'

'Belle Madison, you should be ashamed of yourself!' Cat teased.

Suddenly Belle looked serious. 'I guess I shouldn't have done that. But it just slipped out. They were being so mean about poor Lettie . . .'

'You were right to stand up for her. Bianca shouldn't get away with it,' Jack told her.

Cat couldn't agree more. But secretly she wondered

if Belle's remark had just opened the door to a whole heap of trouble.

Bianca Hayford was *not* the kind of girl who liked to look foolish in public.

And she was *certainly* not the kind of girl to forgive and forget!

It was almost midnight by the time the girls made their way up the sweeping staircase that led from the elegant wood-panelled entrance hall in the eighteenth-century main school building to their bedrooms on the upper floors. Although they were tired, they lingered in the corridor, chatting, until Miss Candlemas, the housemistress, emerged from her room dressed in one of her voluminous purple and orange kaftans and shooed them all towards their beds. Holly and Gemma hugged Cat and Belle goodnight before disappearing into their room. Cat followed Belle into the cosy turquoise and blue study-bedroom they shared on the opposite side of the corridor.

She might not have been battling with the paparazzi on the red carpet all evening, but Cat was exhausted. She pulled off her sparkly black mini-dress and fluffy mohair cardigan, flopped onto her bed and snuggled into her duvet. Bliss!

She could hear Belle setting her alarm clock. 'But it's Saturday tomorrow!' she groaned.

'The cast list for the Rising Stars Spectacular goes up first thing,' Belle pointed out.

'Don't wake me,' Cat murmured. 'I'm not expecting anything!'

'Ooh, and it's February the fourteenth tomorrow! Valentine's Day!'

'Ugh – definitely don't bother waking me!' *I'm not expecting anything for that either!* Cat thought as she drifted off to sleep.

CHAPTER FOUR

Belle: I'm Not That Girl

D-D-D-DR-I-I-N-G!
D-D-D-DR-I-I-N-G!
Belle sat bolt upright in bed.

Please, please, please, let me get a solo! she prayed silently as she cleansed and moisturized her skin before slipping into the Calvin Klein jeans and sweatshirt she'd left folded at the end of her bed. She'd never wanted anything this much! Belle glanced across at Cat, tangled in her duvet as if she'd been wrestling with it all night. Cat was still wearing her underwear from yesterday and − Belle could hardly bear to even think about it − *her make-up!* Belle couldn't understand how Cat's complexion was always flawless. And her long red curls were always glossy, even though she blasted them with the hairdryer *on full-heat!*

'Whassup?' Cat murmured groggily.

'The cast list!' Belle whispered.

Cat rubbed her mascara-smudged eyes. 'I'll come with you.'

'Thought you weren't expecting anything?'

'Well, I'm awake now . . . and it feels like a lucky kind of day!' Cat rolled out of bed, wriggled into a little black dress that was hanging on the radiator and combed her fingers through her hair. 'Come on,' she said. 'What are we waiting for?'

As Belle and Cat opened their door, they bumped into Holly and Gemma, hurrying out of their room. 'Good luck! I'm crossing my fingers for all of us!' Holly said.

'And toes!' Gemma added.

'And eyes, of course,' Cat said, turning to face them with her pretty grey eyes crossed so far they almost met at the bridge of her nose.

Gemma giggled. 'Eugh! That's gross!'

Belle smiled happily. The best thing about Superstar High was having such awesome friends. All the Garrick students were reaching for the stars, but they didn't step over each other to get there! They were all always there for each other. *Well*, almost *all of them!* Belle thought as the door behind her crashed open.

'No point trying to sleep with this bunch *yakking* right outside my door!' Bianca was muttering to Lettie as she stormed out of their room. 'May as well go and look at this list now I'm up, I suppose.'

Belle smiled. Bianca was trying to sound oh-so-casual, but Belle knew that if there was anyone else at Superstar High who wanted a solo in the Spectacular even more than she did, it was Bianca Hayford!

The girls clattered down the stairs and across the entrance hall, and by the time they arrived at the notice board, their numbers had snowballed into a large, exuberant crowd.

There were shrieks, groans and cheers as everyone started to read the names on the list.

'Yes!'

'No!'

'Way-hay!'

'No way!'

Heart pounding, Belle pushed her way to the front of the scrum. This was no time for style or grace! Somehow Bianca had got there ahead of her. 'Oh, sorry,' she said, turning to Belle with a toss of her ice-blonde bob. 'The best solo's already taken. *Popular* from *Wicked*. It's so-o-o-o *right* for me!'

Belle gulped, trying to hide her bitter disappointment. *Wicked* was her favourite show, and

Bianca was right, *Popular* was a fantastic song. *But, if they've given* Popular *to Bianca, what's left for* me? Belle despaired – her brain, now spiralling into panic-mode, somehow forgetting about the *thousands* of other great musical theatre hits in the universe.

Where was her name? Belle's eyes darted wildly over the list. Frankie Pellegrini was down for *Razzle Dazzle* from *Chicago*. Gemma Dalrymple was lead dancer in *Disco Inferno. As Long as He Needs Me* had been given to Darya Petrova, a pretty Russian girl Belle knew slightly. Becoming ever more frantic, she spotted another name – *Jack Thorne.* Jack had a duet. Belle held her breath and looked again . . . Could they really be singing together?

No, they couldn't!

Jack was paired with Ruby Drew! Jealousy bit as hot and sharp as a wasp sting. Belle knew Ruby from advanced singing class and had always got on well with her. But suddenly she couldn't bear the thought of Ruby Drew singing the sweet, romantic duet *Let's Play a Love Scene* from *Fame* with Jack. It was so-o-o unfair . . .

Then, at last, she saw her name!

BELLE MADISON – I'M NOT THAT GIRL (*WICKED*)

And what a solo! *I'm Not That Girl* was a haunting love song, full of jealousy and longing – way more interesting than *Popular*! It was all Belle could do not to jump up and down, screaming *YIPPEEE!* She managed to keep her cool – just – but inside, her heart was dancing the hokey cokey and singing *Celebrate!* at the top of its voice.

'You did it!' Cat shouted, enveloping Belle in an enormous bear hug. Keeping her cool was not a concept Cat really went in for!

Suddenly she stopped. 'I can't believe it!' she stammered, staring at the cast list. 'Does that say what I think it says?'

Belle looked where Cat was pointing:

CATRIN WICKHAM – WOULDN'T IT BE LOVERLY? (*MY FAIR LADY*)

'How did they know *My Fair Lady*'s my favourite musical?' Cat cried. 'I love Audrey Hepburn and I'm actually getting to play one of her roles! I know I said I was feeling lucky, but this is *stupendous*!'

'Not bad for a girl who *wasn't expecting anything*!' Belle said, returning the hug.

She felt a tug at her sleeve and turned to see Holly

squeezing through the throng. She looked back at the list – and then all three of them saw it at once:

HOLLY DEVENISH & ZAK LOMAX – TIME OF MY LIFE (*DIRTY DANCING*)

'*No way!*' Holly screamed in amazement.

Suddenly Zak was at her side. '*Way!*' he yelled, scooping her up and swinging her round – causing chaos amongst the press of students still gathered about the notice board. Laughing, the friends struggled out of the crowd to the seating area on the other side of the entrance hall.

Belle sank down onto the leather sofa with Cat and Holly. She had never felt so happy!

'*Time of My Life*! It's *legendary*, dude!' Zak whistled, flopping into an armchair. 'It's got that *intense* overhead lift at the end. *Bru-u-u-tal!*'

'And Tory King's going to be working on the choreography with you!' Belle said. She'd had a chance to skim through the full details on the board while Zak was spinning Holly round.

'*The* Tory King!' Holly gasped, her dark eyes as big as frisbees.

Everyone smiled, happy for Holly and Zak's good

fortune. Tory King was a mega-famous ex-Garrick student – Belle had seen her photograph in the Hall of Fame in the common room – and she was currently starring as Baby in *Dirty Dancing* in the West End.

But Holly had gone very quiet, nervously tucking a braid behind her ear. Belle exchanged a worried glance with Cat. 'What's wrong?' she asked.

'Miss Morgan practically had to push me onstage with a bulldozer last night,' Holly said. 'And this is much bigger than *Nutcracker Sweeties*. What if' – her voice dropped to a whisper – '*I stuff it up* . . .'

'You'll be brilliant, Hols!' Cat reassured her, putting her arm round her shoulder.

'But I'll have to sing . . . and act as well as dance . . . you know I can't act!'

'Er, *can't act*? So, last night onstage you weren't acting? We all just *imagined* that foxy Sugar Rum Cherry character, or what?'

Cat was right, Belle thought. 'You just have to *believe* in yourself!' she said firmly. 'You were awesome last night. And you will be again!'

'Thanks . . .' Holly said slowly. 'Yeah! Of course I can do it! Of course *we* can do it, I mean!' she corrected herself, grinning over at Zak.

Zak grinned back but his smile turned into an

'Ooomph' of surprise as Nick Taggart crashed over the back of the armchair and landed on top of him.

Nick laughed. 'Sorry! Too much momentum there!'

'Er, what's with the sky-diving off the furniture?' Cat asked.

'*I Am Sixteen, Going on Seventeen!*' Nick replied.

'I thought you were thirteen and a half!' Cat said.

'Mental age, five and three-quarters, dude!' Zak grumbled, extracting himself from underneath Nick and bombarding him with cushions.

'Ha ha!' Nick replied. 'The duet from *The Sound of Music*. I've got the part of Rolf! I was just practising a couple of moves. You'll never guess who it's with . . .'

They all thought for a moment. *Who could be playing the sugar-sweet sixteen-year-old Liesl von Trapp?* Belle wondered.

'Only Mayu Tanaka – who, without doubt, is the most . . .'

Suddenly Belle noticed Mayu standing behind Nick. 'Ahem! Hello, Mayu!' she said loudly.

'. . . the most . . . talented and utterly gorgeous girl in the whole year . . .' Nick continued, hardly missing a beat, although Belle had a sneaking suspicion those weren't the *precise* words he'd had in mind!

Mayu shot Nick a look as deadly as a poisoned dart.

Doing a duet with Nick 'Court Jester' Taggart had clearly not been top of her wish-list. 'I'm going to see Mr Garcia,' she muttered. 'It must be a mistake . . .'

Belle bristled with anger. OK, Nick was an annoying, goofball joker, but he was her *friend*, the annoying, goofball joker! He also had a great voice and was a pretty good dancer too. '*You're* the one making a mistake, Mayu . . .' she began hotly. But her voice trailed off as she noticed Jack sauntering towards them, hands thrust in his jeans pockets. Although they'd been dating since Christmas, Belle's stomach still did a little tap-dance whenever she saw Jack. She smiled back at him as he leaned across the sofa and planted a kiss on her cheek.

'Congratulations!' he said, addressing the group. 'I heard you guys all got great parts.'

'You too,' Holly said. 'You've got that cute duet from *Fame*.'

Suddenly Belle remembered: *Jack's duet with Ruby Drew!* It had flown out of her mind the moment she saw her solo part, but now it was back – like a small black cloud in a perfect summer sky.

'Yeah!' Jack winked at Belle. 'You know, for one *terrible* moment I thought they might've given *us two* that song!'

The cloud burst and poured down on her parade. Had she heard right? Did Jack really just say he'd rather sing with Ruby than with her?

'Imagine!' he continued. 'Doing a schmaltzy romantic duet with someone you *really like* in real life! *How embarrassing would* that *be!*'

It took a moment for Jack's words to sink in. He didn't want to sing with Belle because he *liked her too much*! Suddenly the sun was shining again. Which was fortunate, because at that moment a stocky girl with heavy Goth-style make-up, dressed in layers of black lace and velvet, came hurrying over. It was Ruby Drew – and she'd just found out about her duet with Jack.

'I'm so-o-o excited!' she gushed in her musical Welsh accent, jigging up and down on the spot. 'I've always loved *Fame* . . .'

Jack smiled. 'Yeah, me too! It's going to be fun!'

'It's my all-time favourite, it's so romanti—' Suddenly Ruby broke off as she noticed Belle sitting on the sofa. Her blush was visible even under her thick white foundation. 'Oh, er, I – sorry – you . . .' she babbled.

'Hey, don't worry,' Jack laughed. 'Belle's way too cool to go off on a jealousy trip!'

'Absolutely!' Belle said – trying not to catch Cat or

Holly's eye, just in case either of them had noticed her initial ever-so-slightly-jealous reaction. 'You two will be great together!'

'Thanks, Belle!' Ruby said, grinning with obvious relief.

'Hey, has everyone forgotten?' Nick shouted, jumping up from the armchair, scattering cushions in his wake. '*It's Valentine's Day!*'

Belle hadn't forgotten. But suddenly she had a moment of doubt. *Is the gift I put in Jack's pigeon hole last night too soppy? Or too cheesy? Or both?*

Jack was so chilled, maybe he didn't even *do* Valentine's Day.

But he was already on his way to his pigeon hole.

It was too late to snatch the envelope back now!

CHAPTER FIVE

Cat: Martian Chocolates and Secret Admirers

Cat groaned to herself as she walked slowly across the hall to the pigeon holes. Everyone was ripping open Valentine cards, and there were so many red roses flying around, their petals were scattered across the wooden floor like splashes of blood. It was like a feeding frenzy in a cage of lovebirds!

Cat reached into her pigeon hole and took out the single envelope. Maybe it really was her lucky day! She opened it, trying – in vain – not to get her hopes up.

Dear Miss Wickham,
Your mathematics homework is now three days overdue.
Please report to my office for lunch-time detention the first
Monday after half-term.
Yours,
Dr A. E. Norris

Or maybe not!

And a Happy Valentine's Day to you too, Doctor Norris, Cat thought.

'Oooh, look at this, Cat!' Holly said, tearing pink wrapping paper from a box of Love Heart sweets the size of a small caravan. 'From Ethan!' she explained, glowing as if she'd just been appointed principal dancer with the Royal Ballet.

'I think I could have guessed that!' Cat told her.

And now Belle and Jack were opening their envelopes.

'Tickets for the new Royal Shakespeare Company production of *Romeo and Juliet* in the West End!' Belle laughed.

'Snap!' Jack grinned, waving his tickets in the air.

'We've given each other exactly the same present! Now we've got *four* tickets,' Belle realized. 'Holly, Cat, why don't you come with us? It's a Sunday afternoon, the week before the Easter holiday.'

Holly shook her head. 'Sorry, I'm going home to help Mum with my little brother's birthday party that weekend.'

'Cat?' Belle asked.

Cat smiled. 'Thanks for the offer . . . but tagging along on your special Valentine's date with Jack *might* just hint at advanced gooseberry syndrome.'

'We wouldn't mind . . .'

'No, but I would!'

Holly offered the Love Hearts round.

'*Ever Yours*,' Belle read out before popping a sweet in her mouth.

'*Be My Love*,' Holly read from hers.

Cat picked an orange one and looked down at the message: *Dream On*.

Yep, lu-u-u-rve is definitely in the air, Cat thought. *Just not the bit that* I'm *breathing!*

Soon all the bouquets had been claimed, apart from one enormous arrangement of velvety red roses – which was still sitting on Mrs Butterworth's desk. The school secretary sat in the entrance hall, midway between the notice board and the pigeon holes, where she commanded the best view of all the school's comings and goings. She looked up and placed her gold-rimmed glasses on her nose as she saw someone coming in through the front entrance. 'Ah, Elizabeth,' she called, pointing at the roses. 'These appear to be for you!'

Everyone turned to stare. Who was this mysterious Elizabeth?

Cat felt her chin drop several miles. The woman walking across the hall was Mrs Salmon! The science teacher from Hell! She was huffing and puffing, rain dripping from her black mackintosh and umbrella;

she looked like a cross between Mary Poppins and a stranded walrus.

'Mrs Salmon has a *Valentine*?' Cat gasped.

'Her husband, I guess,' Belle said.

'*Mrs Salmon has a husband?*'

'Er, the *Mrs* part is kind of a clue,' Holly giggled.

'Yeah, but I always thought that was just like a *stage name*. You know, like Batman or something. He's not *actually* a bat. I didn't think Mrs Salmon was *really* married!'

Holly and Belle laughed, and Cat held up her hands in surrender. She had to admit she wasn't making much sense! She'd been so elated about getting the *My Fair Lady* solo, and now suddenly she was feeling a little sorry for herself.

Even Mrs Salmon had a Valentine! Somewhere out there, female Martians were probably opening heart-shaped boxes of Martian chocolates. *I must be the only single girl in the solar system*, Cat thought tragically. *I should be in a nunnery, not a stage school.*

'OK, you rowdy rabble, *scram*!' Mrs Butterworth shot out from behind her desk on her swivel chair and shouted at the students still loitering around the pigeon holes. 'Go and have some breakfast!'

Even in the dining room there was no getting away

from Valentine's Day. First, Mrs Morecambe, the cook, was serving heart-shaped pancakes. Second, Lettie was trying to hide a card under her plate. But, given that the card was the size and shape of the photo album Cat's parents kept their wedding pictures in, it would've been easier to hide a hot-air balloon about her person.

'What's that?' Cat asked as they sat down to eat.

'What's what?' Lettie asked innocently, trying not to look at the ornate padded card. Lettie was a gifted cello player and songwriter, but she was a truly hopeless liar.

Cat silently pointed to the card.

'Oh, this?' Lettie said, picking it up. She hesitated, then nervously opened the card and placed it on the table. 'I've no idea who it's from . . .'

Belle read out the greeting: '*To Lettie, from a Secret Admirer . . .*'

'Nick Taggart!' Cat said instantly. Holly and Belle both nodded.

'How can you be so sure?' A hopeful gleam shone in Lettie's serious brown eyes.

Holly smiled. 'Er, he *obviously* has a massive crush on you. You were doing the Waggle Dance for ages at the party last night!'

'It's Nick's writing,' Belle added.

'And look at his face . . .' Cat glanced over in the

direction of a nearby table. Nick quickly stopped staring at Lettie, blushed to the roots of his straw-coloured hair, and started studying the special offer on the back of the Weetabix box.

Lettie smiled shyly as she drank her orange juice.

The third contributor to the Remind-Cat-She-Doesn't-Have-a-Valentine conspiracy was Gemma. She and her best friend, Serena Quereshi, joined the girls at their table. On Gemma's breakfast tray was a home-made card, featuring a beautiful photograph of a sunset over a deserted beach. *It's so unfair*, Cat thought. Not only did Gemma have a Valentine, she had one who was romantic enough to *make* her a lovely card.

'Ooh, who's it from?' Holly asked.

Gemma flipped open the card to show them the writing inside.

TO GEMMA, FROM ??? XXX

'It's been printed, so we can't identify the handwriting,' Serena sighed.

'How dumb is that?' Cat said. 'What's the point of sending a mystery Valentine if you don't want to be found out? Isn't that right, Lettie?'

But Lettie wasn't listening; she was too busy feigning

an interest in the calorie content of Coco Pops, while peeking at Nick over the top of the box.

'So, any guesses?' Belle asked.

Next moment, the girls' table was surrounded by boys. Nick, Zak, Nathan, Frankie, Jack and Mason Lee were all eager to join in the speculation about Gemma's mystery card.

'There was a stamp on the envelope,' Serena pointed out. 'So it was sent by someone outside school.'

'Nice try, Nancy Drew!' Nick said. 'But Mr Romantic could have just gone out to the postbox so it didn't *look* like an inside job . . .'

'Do you have, like, you know, *a guy* back home in Oz?' Zak suggested.

'Good thinking, mate!' Nick chimed, in an exaggerated Australian accent. 'I'm seeing a lonely kangaroo farmer, wandering through the outback, abandoned by his Sheila—'

'You may be, but *I'm* not!' Gemma prodded Nick's arm with her fork. 'It wasn't an *Australian* stamp anyway!'

'Maybe it was Prince Harry!' Mason joked. 'Or Shia Labeouf?'

'Or Harry Potter!' Jack said.

'This is getting silly now!' said Belle. 'Gemma did *not* receive a Valentine card from a fictional character!'

'Yeah, Harry Potter's not my type anyway!' Gemma grinned and shook her head, her short blonde hair bouncing like a shampoo advert. Cat wondered for the millionth time how Gemma looked so healthy and tanned in the middle of winter in London.

Suddenly Jack glanced at his watch. 'Yikes! Football match. You guys coming to watch?'

'Of course!' Belle replied.

'I'll be along in a minute. I promised Ethan I'd be there,' Holly said, starting to clear away. Everyone flinched; Holly had the same effect on a pile of plates as a bull in a china shop.

'Can't wait!' Cat added, forcing brightness into her voice. She didn't even *like* football but there wasn't much else to do on a rainy Saturday in February. By herself.

And Emo-Girl just wasn't her style, anyway.

I wish I had a secret admirer like Gemma, she thought as they all filed out of the dining hall. *Or even a not-very-secret admirer, like Lettie! Maybe I'm destined to be one of those crazy old ladies, sharing my tinned tuna with a houseful of cats.*

Right on cue, Shreddie, the school cat, sidled up and wound himself around her shins.

She picked him up and cuddled him.

'At least *you* love me, don't you?' she mumbled into his marmalade fur.

CHAPTER SIX

Holly: Love Hearts and Zero Gravity

Holly was feeling slightly sick – and it wasn't entirely due to the excitement of the big match. The Garrick All-Stars had to defeat the Kensington Crusaders to progress to the semi-finals of the London Schools Cup. The over-stuffed feeling was more to do with Ethan's Love Hearts. Somehow, she, Cat and Belle had got through the entire box when they went back up to their rooms to pile on layers of thermal underwear and waterproofs.

And that was on top of three heart-shaped pancakes.

Still, Holly thought, *all that food will keep us warm!* The three girls were huddled at the side of the pitch, along with most of the rest of the school; even some of the teachers had braved the horizontal sleet to watch the match. The Crusaders had brought along a coach-load of supporters too, and already the air was full of competing cheers and chants as the teams filed out onto the pitch.

The referee blew the whistle and the game started.

'Go on, Ethan!' Holly yelled as Ethan headed the ball.

'Go, Jack, go!' Belle whispered as Jack evaded an aggressive tackle.

'Go on . . .' Cat bellowed, then paused. 'Go on, rest-of-the-team!' She looked at Holly and Belle. 'I'll just fill in with general back-up cheering for the other nine boys. I don't have my own personal Ronaldo or Beckham to support like you two.'

Cat was laughing, so Holly joined in, but she noticed that it wasn't Cat's *usual* laugh. Normally when Cat threw her head back and roared with bubbly laughter, it was so infectious you couldn't help laughing as well – any more than you could *choose* not to catch chickenpox. But this time, Holly had to *think* about joining in. Something was wrong with Cat. Maybe she'd eaten too many Love Hearts too!

A huge groan from the Garrick supporters interrupted Holly's train of thought. Kensington had just scored, to go 2–0 up. The half-time whistle blew. She stamped her feet to ward off frostbite.

'We'll come back strong in the second half!' Nick was saying as he came over.

'Yeah, dude,' Zak replied. 'It's not over till it's over!'

At that moment a group of Kensington supporters swaggered towards them. 'We're just *owning* you guys!' the one in front jeered.

'Garrick All–Stars? Garrick All–*Tarts* more like!' one of his mates chortled.

'Bunch of *girls*!'

'Bunch of *ballet dancers*!' The Kensington fans all guffawed – as if the single thing in the entire world that might just possibly be worse than being a *girl* was being a *ballet dancer*.

Hel-lo! Excuse me! Holly fumed silently.

'*OH YEAH, BRO! AND YOU, LIKE, KNOW ALL ABOUT BALLET, DO YOU?*' Zak yelled, stepping in front of the Kensington fans and blocking their path.

All the friends stared in amazement; this was Zak Lomax – a boy so laid-back he could take gold at the World Limbo Championships – squaring up for a fight, the fog-cloud of his breath puffing out as if he were breathing fire.

The Kensington crew sniggered. *Uh-oh*, Holly thought. *If this gets physical, we're going to get flattened!* These guys were all heavyweights!

But Zak wasn't backing down. 'If ballet dancers are so *lame*, you try doing this!' he said.

By the time Holly was halfway through the thought

I wonder what he means by 'this'? she was already high in the air above Zak's head – and the question had already been answered. She stretched out her arms and pointed her toes as Zak spun through 360 before planting her safely back on the ground.

The Garrick supporters clapped and whooped in admiration. Even the Kensington posse couldn't help looking impressed, although they tried their best to conceal it.

'*Oo-ooh, very* Strictly Come Dancing*!*' one of them mocked, stepping towards Holly. 'Let's have a try then!'

Horrified, Holly leaped away. The Kensington boy hesitated. The rest of his mates were already drifting off. He snorted dismissively and shrugged his shoulders, as if to say, *Obviously I could do that, I just don't feel like it right now*, before sloping after them.

Holly grinned at Zak. They were both breathless and elated by the incredible dance move. 'Wow!' Holly gasped. 'That felt like zero gravity!'

'Joyous! You caught some serious air there, dude!' Zak panted. Then his face dropped. 'Uh-oh! Miss Morgan's droppin' in! Bummer!'

Holly's heart shrivelled with dread as she saw her teacher beetling across the pitch, her black cloak billowing behind her. She must have seen them doing that lift! They were going to be in major-league trouble!

'What, *precisely*,' Miss Morgan shrieked as she approached them, 'do you two think you were doing? No warm-up! No safety mats! You could have been seriously injured! *E pericoloso!*'

Holly and Zak started to mumble their apologies, but there was no stopping Miss Morgan in full flow. 'You are two of the most talented dancers we've had at the Garrick in a long time! You should know better than to be this . . . reckless . . . irresponsible . . . *stupido*! I've half a mind to . . .'

Holly couldn't bear it. She knew that Miss Morgan was going to say *to take your dance out of the Spectacular* . . . She felt as if she were going to faint. They were going to lose *The Time of Your Life*!

But suddenly there was a tumultuous cheer. Miss Morgan's voice faltered and then she fell silent. Holly looked up in surprise to see her ballet teacher staring open-mouthed at the pitch.

Jack had the ball and was running down the wing. He was dancing past defender after defender with lightning-fast footwork. He shimmied around the last player with a perfectly timed sidestep. He picked his spot and slammed the ball into the back of the net, dummying the goalkeeper with a clever little twist of the shoulders.

The Garrick supporters went wild as Jack did a double backflip and ran around the pitch in triumph. Belle was jumping up and down, barely able to contain her pride.

'Has she left us for another time-space dimension?' Cat whispered, nudging Holly in the ribs and tilting her head towards Miss Morgan.

The elderly ballet teacher was still staring at Jack Thorne with a strange, mesmerized look on her face. '*Mamma Mia!*' she sighed. 'Who *is* that boy?'

Before anyone could answer, she'd turned and walked away, her cloak flapping in the wind, in the direction of the sports centre.

'I think you've got some competition there, Belle!' Cat joked. 'Miss Morgan looks as if she's just fallen in lu-u-u-r-ve!'

Holly and Zak gazed at each other. 'Phew! I reckon Jack just saved our dance-number!' Zak breathed.

Holly nodded slowly.

They'd had a very narrow escape!

CHAPTER SEVEN

Belle: Magical Mermaid Powers

Belle's day just kept getting better and better!

First there was her *Wicked* solo. Then the Valentine's gift from Jack — Belle could hardly believe that he'd bought *Romeo and Juliet* tickets too! — and now, the Garrick All-Stars had beaten the Kensington Crusaders 3–2 in their Cup match! After Jack's fabulous goal, Ethan had scored from a corner. And then, seconds before the final whistle, Felix Baddeley — his ankle fully recovered from last term's injury — sprang up like an antelope and headed the ball into the net.

In fact, Belle thought, *there's only one thing that's falling a teensy bit short of perfection right now. My outfit!*

Truth be told, she was having a fashion *nightmare*!

Her beautiful new powder-blue waterproof jacket had just one tiny design-fault: *it had remained waterproof for precisely three and a half minutes!* It must have been tested in a light California shower, not London-in-February sleet, which seemed to be ninety per cent wetter than ordinary water. And beneath the jacket, Belle's thick white mohair sweater was so waterlogged it felt – and smelled – as if she were carrying a dead goat.

And as for her hair! It was clinging to her face like strands of seaweed. *Strange*, Belle thought. *When you see mermaids in films, they always have beautiful, flowing, dry tresses. How does that work? Maybe it's one of their magical mermaid powers?*

Her only consolation was that she was not alone! Cat's hair had frizzed like candyfloss. Holly's long micro-braids were safely tucked under her wide hairband, but her jeans had soaked up so much water they looked as if they'd been dipped in black dye.

The match was over and the players ran across the pitch to celebrate with their supporters.

Jack scooped Belle up in a hug. 'Eughh!' she cried, looking down at the thick stripe of mud that had been transferred from his football kit to the front of her non-waterproof waterproof. 'Now my look is truly complete!'

Holly tried – and failed – to dodge a similar hug from Ethan 'Mud Monster' Reed. 'Let's all go to Café Roma and thaw out with hot chocolates,' she suggested.

Holly's suggestion was greeted with a roar of approval. Café Roma, a cosy Italian pizzeria and coffee bar on the other side of Kingsgrove Square, was a favourite with the students at Superstar High. The owner, Luigi, always made them welcome. Luckily he was passionate about football too, and didn't mind the team descending on the café on Saturday mornings . . . *Although*, Belle reasoned, *he'd probably appreciate a slightly lower mud-to-student ratio.* 'I think *some* people need to shower first,' she hinted.

'Oooh, picky!' Felix teased.

'Mud *is* the new black you know, darling,' Nick added.

'Come on! Let's go before hypothermia sets in!' Cat urged.

'OK,' said Belle. 'We'll go on ahead and save a table and the players can follow.'

A few minutes later the friends were settling into a large booth in Café Roma. Steam was rising from their damp clothes. 'I'm liking that dead-sheep look on you *a lot*!' Nick joked as Belle struggled out of her coat to reveal the soggy jumper. She caught sight of her reflection in the glass of a print of Rome on the back wall. Normally she'd have stuffed her head into her Gucci tote bag and crawled under the table rather than be seen in public like *that*. *But*, she suddenly realized, *it doesn't matter!* She was with her friends and having so much fun – who *cared* if she was more Creature from the Deep than Mermaid Princess!

'Hot chocolates all round?' Luigi asked.

'Let's go cra–a–a–a–zy and have extra whipped cream on top,' Nick suggested. 'We've got a lot to celebrate!'

Now the players were starting to arrive and the friends shuffled round to make room. They were in high spirits after their win, still reliving every detail of the game. 'Trust Felix to leave it to the last second to score the winning goal!' Ethan joked. Belle knew what he meant. Punctuality wasn't *exactly* Felix Baddeley's strong point.

'Better late than never, eh?' one of the other footballers teased. Belle recognized Danny Adu, a Nigerian boy she knew from her advanced singing class.

'Hey, that was split–second timing!' Felix protested. 'And I'll have you know, knocking in that header has seriously squashed my dreads!' He patted his dreadlocks lovingly.

But Belle's attention was wandering from Felix and his hairstyle crisis. Where was Jack? All the rest of the team had now arrived, overflowing into a second booth. 'Do you know where Jack went?' she asked Ethan.

'He left the changing room before me,' Ethan replied. 'I thought he'd have been here ages ago . . .'

But just as Belle was starting to put in some serious worrying (*Knocked over by a bus on Kingsgrove Square? Mugged? Or – possibly even more terrible thought – so horrified by her dead-sheep look that he couldn't bear to see her again?*), Jack finally appeared. He squeezed in next to her – seemingly uninjured and unfazed by her appearance – although a thoughtful frown was furrowing his forehead. But when Belle asked what was the matter, he shook his head and smiled.

'Oh, sorry, nothing – shattered, that's all,' he mumbled, flicking his shaggy brown hair out of his eyes. Suddenly he grinned and jumped to his feet. 'Let's have a toast! To the Garrick All-Stars!'

'Not bad for a bunch of ballet dancers!' Zak chipped in. Everyone cheered and raised their mugs of hot chocolate.

'And to the Rising Stars Spectacular!' Nick Taggart shouted, holding up his mug again. 'And all who sail in her!'

There was another cheer. The thought of her solo in the Spectacular sent a jolt of happiness pulsing through Belle's veins. She clinked her mug with everyone at the table. Jack seemed fine now too. *I must have imagined that there was something wrong*, she thought, making a mental note not to worry so much in future!

The toasts were coming thick and fast now. 'To Holly and Zak and their amazing performances in *Nutcracker Sweeties* last night!' Cat proposed. They all cheered. Holly blushed and almost knocked her hot chocolate over.

'To Valentine's Day!' Ethan added.

'To Superstar High!'

'To all of us!' cried Belle as they drained the last dregs of hot chocolate from their mugs.

I was right, she thought. *Today really does keep getting better and better!* And there was so much to look forward to as well. Next week was the half-term holiday. Belle's parents were in their usual jet-setting mode – Dad in Hong Kong directing a new film and Mum doing a fashion shoot for *American Vogue* in Hawaii – so Belle was going to stay with Holly in north London for the week. It was going to be so much fun! They already had lots of plans: re-decorating Holly's old bedroom, a day trip to Cambridge to meet up with Cat, shopping in Harrods . . . And when they came back after the holiday, they would have the Spectacular to work on. Belle couldn't wait to get started!

But first, there was something she was looking forward to *even more*.

A very long, very hot soak in the bath!

CHAPTER EIGHT

Cat: Other Things That Would Be Really Nice

The half-term holiday had flown by.

Cat spent a lovely lazy week at home, lying on the sofa watching *My Fair Lady*, immersing herself in her role as Eliza Doolittle. She was a poor flower-seller, trying to make a few pennies to support her alcoholic father, cold and hungry . . . It would've been easier to imagine if she hadn't been snuggled up with her little dog, Duffy, in front of a roaring fire, with a constant supply of snacks. Mum had totally forgotten their civil war over the *Oliver!* and *Bugsy Malone* auditions last term, and was so pleased Cat was finally performing in a musical that she was spoiling her rotten.

Not that I'm complaining, Cat thought, tucking into a piece of fruit cake.

She'd made it off the sofa long enough to show Holly and Belle round Cambridge. They browsed through the market and second-hand shops for cool accessories for Holly's bedroom makeover, and –

remembering that Belle had a bit of a thing about the Tudors – Cat took them to King's College Chapel to see Henry VIII and Anne Boleyn's initials carved on the choir screen. Belle thought it was the most romantic thing she'd ever seen.

Then, suddenly, it was Sunday and time to pack. Cat hated saying goodbye to her family – especially her younger sister, Fiona – but the moment they pulled into the drive and she saw the familiar soft red-brick façade of the Garrick School and those wide stone steps bordered by little star-shaped trees, her heart skipped a beat.

This was where she belonged!

That wasn't to say she loved *every* minute at Superstar High. For example, there were thirty minutes of Dr Norris's lunch-time detention tomorrow that she could have happily fast-forwarded past. She was never going to grasp the difference between a sheet of linear equations and a shopping list written in ancient Egyptian hieroglyphics.

Now it was Wednesday morning and Cat was in geography, researching soil erosion with Holly and Belle. Bianca, Mayu and Lettie were 'working' at the next computer. While Mrs O'Brien was sorting out a keyboard malfunction on the other side of the classroom, Bianca pulled a magazine out of her bag. Cat couldn't help overhearing as she flicked through the pages.

'Here it is! Look, Lettie!' she crowed. 'Our photo's on the Celebrity Round-Up page. *Miss Bianca Hayford (thirteen) of the Hayford Baby Food Empire,*' she read out, '*and Miss Mayu Tanaka (thirteen), daughter of Japanese businessman Sonny Tanaka . . . photographed at the London premiere . . .*'

'You both look lovely,' Lettie replied dutifully. 'Ooh, this website has got loads of information about soil—'

'*OH MY GOD!*' Mayu squeaked, grabbing the magazine and peering at the picture. 'They've made my legs look so-o-o short!'

'Well, they are a bit, compared to mine,' Bianca answered, tugging the magazine back.

'*Causes of soil erosion include rainfall, wind . . .*' Holly read out from the computer screen, attempting to ignore Mayu and Bianca's conversation.

She may as well try to ignore a Nickelback concert, Cat thought.

'Listen, there's more,' Bianca was saying. '*Miss Hayford and Miss Tanaka are both* star *students at the prestigious Garrick School for the Performing Arts . . .*'

Cat exchanged glances with Belle and Holly. *Star students?* Holly grinned and Belle did that thing with her eyebrows. 'Causes of *brain* erosion,' Cat whispered, 'include Bianca's *red-carpet experience . . .*'

'I've so-o-o got to put the link to this on my Facebook page,' Bianca said.

'*Further causes of severe soil erosion,*' Holly continued doggedly, 'include poor farming practices, deforestation . . .'

'*Further causes of severe brain erosion include Bianca's Facebook page . . .*' Cat whispered. '*This is predicted to become an increasingly damaging factor in future . . .*'

Belle and Holly giggled.

'Are you girls doing any work over there?' Mrs O'Brien shouted.

'We're trying our best, miss,' Mayu replied innocently, 'but Cat, Belle and Holly keep messing about.'

Cat was fuming as she was split up from the other two and sent to work with Mason and Frankie instead.

After lunch, Miss LeClair's core dance class was devoted to rehearsing the opening number of the Rising Stars Spectacular. The entire year-group was performing *You Can't Stop the Beat* from *Hairspray*, and that included the *non*-dancers as well as the dancers. Luckily Miss LeClair couldn't have been more different from Miss Morgan. She was young and pretty, with a mass of blond curls, she wore parrot-bright green and orange sweats rather than a raven-black leotard, and she had seemingly infinite reserves of patience. She stood at the front, clicking her fingers to count the class through the steps, as the rehearsal pianist, Mr Piggott – a nervous young man whose most prominent feature was a nose so large it needed its own postcode – started to play the introduction. '*And one, and two, and reach with the right arm, and hop left – LEFT . . . Nathan Almeida . . . that's your RIGHT! OK, let's start again . . .*'

Poor Nathan. He was a gifted actor – he'd been exceptional as Macduff in their *Macbeth* production last term – but dancing was a different matter. He didn't know his *chassé* from his *shimmy* and his feet didn't speak the same language as the rest of his body. '*And kick to the right . . . the RIGHT, NATHAN . . .*' Miss LeClair shouted as Nathan swam against the tide yet again and hoofed Jack Thorne in the thigh.

But for Cat and the other students the vibrant feel-good number was exhilarating. 'I can't wait till we get our costumes!' Cat said as they gathered in the corner of the studio at the end of class, pulling on their sweat pants and changing their shoes. 'All those bright swishy nineteen-sixties skirts will look fantastic!'

'Er, Cat, can I ask you something?' Nathan whispered, pulling her to one side.

'Oh, don't worry, Nate,' Cat joked. 'I think those skirts are only for the girls!'

Nathan laughed but he looked tense. 'Could you help me practise my dance steps? I just can't get the bit where . . . well, any of it really.'

'Of course!' Cat replied. 'I'll ask Holly to help. She's the expert!'

'No, please, just you!' Nathan gulped, looking as terrified as if Cat'd suggested Holly advise him on his choice of underpants.

She grinned. Nathan was so shy that she was the only girl he really felt comfortable around. 'No problem, Nate!' she said. 'It'll be a private Cat Wickham master class!'

After all, Nathan's helped me with my science homework so many times, how could I refuse?

Dinner was over and Cat was looking forward to a quiet evening in her room chatting with Holly and Belle. But first, Ethan asked Holly to go out for a walk, and then Belle vanished into the music library with

Jack. Cat drifted aimlessly into the common room. Some of her friends were settling down to watch a film. 'Come and join us, Cat!' Gemma called, making space on her beanbag.

'What about the Jonas brothers?' Nick said.

'What, *all* of them?' Lettie giggled.

'Excuse me?' Cat asked, confused. She was used to Nick making very little sense, but this was even more random than usual!

'We're still trying to work out who sent Gemma's Valentine card,' Serena explained.

'What kind of guy would send an *anonymous* Valentine card, I wonder . . .' Lettie mused, glancing shyly at Nick, who was sitting next to her on the sofa.

He fiddled busily with the remote control for the DVD player. 'Dunno . . .' he mumbled.

'So-o-o, what film are we watching?' Cat asked, quickly changing the subject. She'd been trying to put that whole feeling-sorry-for-myself-because-I-don't-have-a-Valentine episode behind her.

'*Titanic*!' Gemma said. 'I just love it, don't you? It's so-o-o romantic!'

'Yeah, love it!' Cat sighed.

Why was the entire world ganging up to remind her she was deficient in the romance department? It wasn't such a big deal! She was perfectly happy with her life – her family, her friends, her acting . . . Having a boyfriend wasn't exactly her number-one priority. It probably wasn't even in the top ten. *It's just*, Cat thought, settling into the beanbag, *somewhere on my list of Other Things That Would Be Really Nice.*

Along with a secret recipe for calorie-free chocolate and understanding linear equations.

CHAPTER NINE

Belle: A Sense of Urgency

Belle glanced at her silver Gucci watch again.

She couldn't wait for the Thursday-morning history lesson to be over, even though it was one of her favourite subjects. Usually she'd have stayed behind after class to ask Miss Chase-Smythe some further questions, but today she had something even more important than the French Revolution on her mind. She'd borrowed the sheet music for *I'm Not That Girl* from the music library and booked a practice room for half an hour over lunch to run through her solo before the afternoon's advanced singing class with Mr Garcia.

At last the midday bell rang. She scooped up her books and rushed to the dining room to grab a quick snack. The only free slot in any of the practice rooms today was 12.15 to 12.45 and she wanted to make the most of her time. Impatiently she queued for an orange juice and a chicken wrap to eat on the way. Stopping only to pick up the key to the practice room from Mrs Butterworth, she began to jog across the courtyard.

'Hey, Belle, hang on!'

Belle turned to see Jack following her into the courtyard. 'Wait for me!' he called.

Belle waited, munching on her wrap, as he strolled towards her. *Jack didn't do hurrying*, she realized. *He did ambling, sauntering and loping*. A Sense of Urgency was an alien concept to him.

'Hey, Belle!' he said when he finally caught up with her. 'Do you have a minute?'

Belle looked at her watch. It was 12.14. 'Er, just the one?' she asked.

'Well, I was kind of thinking of a few! There's something I wanted to talk to you about . . .'

Belle instantly feared the worst. *Something was wrong!* Jack must have seen her frown, because he laughed. 'Don't look so serious. It's nothing fatal!'

She paused. She *really* wanted to warm up her voice and try out a few ideas before the singing class. And if it wasn't anything *catastrophic* . . . surely Jack would understand. 'Could we take a rain check?' she asked. 'I have to practise my song. Let's meet for a coffee later this afternoon?'

Jack held her gaze for a moment, the look in his hazel eyes skewering her conscience like a kebab. Belle was on the point of abandoning her practice session to listen to *anything* he wanted to tell her, even if it was only that he'd finally managed to beat Nick at table football, when he smiled. 'Sure! We'll talk later. It's no big deal . . . Go on then,' he urged, laughing as she hesitated. 'Get on with it!'

Belle hugged him gratefully, then turned and ran over to the Music Department. As she dashed along the corridor, she passed Mr Garcia's office. The door was open. At first she thought the raised voices coming from inside were a recording of a passionate Italian opera, but then she realized that the rumbling bass voice was Mr Garcia and the mezzo-soprano was Miss Morgan. It was impossible not to hear the thundering row between the two teachers.

'*YOU'VE DONE WHAT?*' Mr Garcia roared.

'*MAMMA MIA! HE HAS THE FEET OF AN ANGEL!*' Miss Morgan raged back.

Belle smiled. Mr Garcia was clearly trying to stand up to Miss Morgan over something. She didn't envy him. Miss Morgan might be small and about three hundred years old but she was as fierce as a piranha.

As Belle unlocked the door of the practice room a

little further along the corridor, she could still hear snatches of the argument.

'*CLEARED IT WITH THE PRINCIPAL WITHOUT CONSULTING ME!*'

'*WHY WAIT? I KNOW A DANCER WHEN I SEE ONE!*'

Then the door slammed and Miss Morgan was storming along the corridor. Belle hurriedly turned the key in the lock. Being caught eavesdropping by a furious Miss Morgan would not be a good career move! But as she opened the door and slipped into the practice room, she caught a glimpse of the expression on the dance teacher's face.

Miss Morgan was *smiling*.

Whatever that battle was about, she knows she's won it! Belle thought.

CHAPTER TEN

Holly: The One True Way

Later on Thursday afternoon Holly was in her advanced ballet class.

To her relief, Miss Morgan's excitement at watching Jack play football seemed to have totally erased her memory of the irresponsible and dangerous lift incident at the match. No more had been said about it.

The girls had been working for an hour, finishing with their *en pointe* work. Holly could hardly believe how far they'd progressed from their first shaky steps at the barre last term. Miss Morgan called Holly to the front and took them through their exercises – '*Rise and relevé, two, three, four . . . good . . . Now, we move on to tendu . . . And lovely turn-out, Holly,* bravissima! *Pull up, Gemma! Lettie,* attenzione! *Serena, you are sickling that left foot again . . .*'

Holly loved dancing *en pointe*. And she was lucky enough to have perfect feet, with strong arches and equal-length toes. She loved the feeling of all her muscles working in harmony – from the tiniest metatarsals to the core abdominals. She even loved the gentle thudding of the toe boxes on the floor and the piney smell of the rosin powder they used to stop their shoes slipping.

Finally Miss Morgan banged her stick on the floor and told them to take a break. Ballet class was over. The boys would be coming to join them shortly to work on *Disco Inferno* from *Saturday Night Fever* for the Spectacular.

The girls all flopped down on the benches at the edge of the studio, stretching out their legs and changing into their jazz shoes. Gemma, who was leading *Disco Inferno* in the role of Stephanie, was swaying with her eyes closed – as if doing some kind of strange voodoo spell – obviously running through her moves in her head. Meanwhile Serena was massaging a new crop of blisters. 'Do you think it's possible to get a double foot-transplant?' she groaned.

Holly grimaced sympathetically and carefully untied the ribbons of her beloved blush-pink *pointe* shoes. She was hanging them over the barre to dry when she heard the male dancers noisily entering the studio. She sat back down, making room for Zak and Philippe Meyer, the boy who was playing Gemma's partner in

Disco Inferno – the famous white-suited John Travolta role.

Miss Morgan clapped her hands. Holly leaped up, ready to get into position, but to her surprise, her teacher was at the door, talking excitedly with Miss LeClair and the boys' ballet teacher, Mr Korsakoff – a densely muscled man with fair hair cropped as flat as a scrubbing brush.

And then Holly noticed a fourth figure: a tall boy wearing a white T-shirt and black jazz pants hovering behind the teachers – and she did a double-take.

Wait a second!

That boy is Jack Thorne!

Holly nudged Gemma and nodded towards the door. Gemma looked. Then Serena, Lettie, Zak, Philippe and all the other students turned to stare at the new arrival like a colony of startled meerkats.

'Shouldn't Jack be in advanced singing now?' Gemma whispered.

'Maybe he's bringing a message for Miss Morgan,' Serena ventured, still rubbing her toes.

Zak looked doubtful. 'Dude always slip into his dancewear to deliver messages?'

Miss Morgan clapped again. 'Please welcome a new addition to advanced dance,' she chirped. '*Fantastico!*'

She couldn't have looked more delighted if she'd recruited John Travolta himself.

Jack stood motionless in the doorway as if held by an invisible force field.

'Come on, don't be shy!' Miss Morgan beckoned him in.

Jack blushed and tried to shove his hands into his pockets. But there were no pockets in his dance trousers, so it turned into a bizarre thigh-slapping manoeuvre. Holly squirmed, hardly able to watch Jack's toe-curling embarrassment.

Jack Thorne in advanced dance! she marvelled. She had seen Jack hiding in the back row with Nathan in their compulsory core dance classes, going through the motions with zero enthusiasm. And Cat had told her all about Jack's comment at the *Nutcracker Sweeties* party, of course! This was the boy who *couldn't see the point of dance*. Holly – who couldn't see the point of life without dance – might have taken offence at that, but she would have forgiven Jack anything! Distracting Miss Morgan at the football match wasn't the first time he'd come to her rescue. Last term he'd faked a fainting fit to save her from the total humiliation of pretending to be Cat playing the part of Lady Macbeth. *Long story!*

Jack looked as if he'd like a black hole to appear and swallow him up.

'Stretches, everyone!' Miss Morgan called with a thud of her stick. '*Cinque minuti!*'

Holly waved to Jack. 'Over here!'

Jack hurried over to her and started doing hamstring stretches while the three dance teachers conferred with Mr Piggott at the piano.

'What's going on?' Holly whispered to Jack. Zak, Gemma, Lettie, Serena and Philippe had all gathered round, eager to hear his story. They were so close, they kept banging heads as they stretched.

'You seen the light, dude? Dance is the One True Way!' Zak told him.

'Yeah, right,' Jack grumbled. 'Nobbled by Miss Morgan, more like!'

Gemma looked puzzled. 'Nobbled? Ouch!' The *ouch* part was Zak elbowing her in the ribs as he started on his shoulder stretches.

'After the football game on Saturday. She pounced on me outside the changing rooms. Told me she could always spot a dancer and I was *perfetto* for advanced dance. She kept going on and on, so in the end I said I'd think about it – just to escape. I was desperate to get inside and have a shower!'

Holly grinned. So that's why Miss Morgan had suddenly gone into a trance at the end of the match!

There was a sudden burst of *Disco Inferno* as Mr Piggott pounded dramatically at the keyboard. The dance students looked up and bounced their shoulders in time, excited to be starting work on the disco routine; all except Jack – who looked as if he were about to have his wisdom teeth out – *without anaesthetic.*

'But how come you agreed?' Holly asked.

'I didn't,' Jack said, shaking his head. 'I forgot all about it. But then I got called into Mr Fortune's office for A Little Chat. He said Miss Morgan had cleared it with Mr Garcia for me to swap some of my singing classes for advanced dance. He gave me the speech about how important it is to be an all-rounder these days – and somehow we ended up agreeing I'd try it up until the end of term. Then, if I want to, I can choose to continue after Easter.' Jack laughed. 'Like *that's* ever going to happen!'

As they danced, Holly watched Jack out of the corner of her eye. She could see why Miss Morgan was so keen: he was strong and agile, with great natural turn-out. His timing was excellent and his streetwise swagger was perfect for the disco routine.

Of course, he had no idea what he was doing and he wore a deliberately bored I'm-not-even-trying expression for the entire class. But he definitely had *something*.

Mr Korsakoff was clearly impressed with the new discovery too. As they finished, Holly heard him comment to Miss Morgan, 'I see a great future in dance for that young man . . .'

Not if Jack has anything to do with it! Holly thought.

CHAPTER ELEVEN

Belle: Smug-waves and Body-slams

Meanwhile Belle was in advanced singing class.

She sat down between Cat and Nick. Cat wasn't usually in advanced singing but was joining for this term because of her solo in the Spectacular. It had meant temporarily dropping her Latin dance class, much to her annoyance.

Belle glanced around the room. Lettie, Mayu, Bianca, Frankie Pellegrini, Ruby Drew, Darya Petrova, Danny Adu . . . they were all there – but there was a Jack-Thorne-shaped empty space at the end of the semicircle of chairs.

Mr Garcia – a barrel-shaped man with a deep rumbling voice – called the class to attention. In this lesson, he explained, the soloists would each sing their song, followed by a critique session. He was interrupted by a knock at the door. *Jack's late!* Belle thought, but when she looked up, it wasn't Jack. It was the vocal coach, Larry Shapiro, in his familiar blue suit and badly fitting hairpiece. Belle smiled at him as he came in and took a seat at the back of the class; she'd attended his workshops last term and he was one of her all-time heroes. 'Larry's joining us for the next few classes to help develop your vocals for the Spectacular,' Mr Garcia continued.

Belle couldn't wait for her turn to sing. Her practice had gone really well and she was feeling confident.

'First up,' Mr Garcia boomed, 'Catrin Wickham!'

Cat walked to the front and stood next to Mr Piggott at the piano. Belle watched, full of pride in her friend's performance as Cat began to sing *Wouldn't It Be Loverly?* Her voice quavered, and she was so wistful that you really believed that she was a poor flower girl who wanted nothing more than a room of her own. She was such an amazing actress and poured so much passion into her singing, it more than made up for the slightly husky edge to her voice.

Belle joined the applause, but as Larry Shapiro starting telling Cat how well she'd done, she couldn't help zoning out a little. *Where was Jack?* Worries began to gnaw at her stomach. He'd been trying to tell her something at lunch time. OK, he'd *said* it was no big deal, but perhaps he'd just been being brave. *He could have a life-threatening illness! Maybe he's transferring to another school! He could already be on a plane to the other side of the world!*

Now Darya Petrova was singing *As Long as He Needs Me*, which was making Belle feel even worse! *What kind of dumb, useless girlfriend am I, anyway? I couldn't even spare my guy a few minutes in his moment of need?*

'Belle Madison . . . *Belle Madison!*'

'Oh, er, that's me!' Flustered, Belle jumped off her chair, dropping her music folder. Larry Shapiro looked up from his notes and smiled encouragingly at her.

'Come on, we've got a lot to get through today!' Mr Garcia grumbled.

Belle took deep breaths, trying to think herself into her part. She was Elphaba, before she became the Wicked Witch of the West. She was in love with Fiyero, but he loved Galinda instead. In her practice session, she'd really tried to strike the perfect balance between jealousy and longing and bravery. But now she couldn't concentrate.

I bet something terrible has happened to Jack . . .

Belle launched into the song. Her intonation was perfect and her voice didn't let her down. But she was trying too hard; the emotions she tried to bring out sounded forced and didn't ring true. Her confidence was crumbling like a cookie dipped in milk . . .

and then she stumbled over a word and missed a note . . .

'*O-o-o–k-a-a-ay, g-o-o-o-o-d,*' Mr Garcia said when she finished, in a way that Belle knew meant exactly the opposite: *Not good. Not good at all.*

Belle gritted her teeth as she listened to the feedback. She tried to smile and nod in a taking-it-on-board kind of way. She couldn't even look at Larry Shapiro, who was sitting quietly at the back. She knew he was expecting much, much better from her. And she certainly couldn't look at Bianca and Mayu. She didn't have to! She could *feel* the smug-waves coming off them.

'What's wrong?' Cat whispered as Belle sat down.

'Do you know where Jack is?' Belle asked.

Cat shook her head.

Before she could stop herself, Belle suddenly heard her voice blurt out, 'Excuse me, Mr Garcia? Do you know why Jack Thorne isn't in class?'

Mr Garcia ran his hands over his bald, mahogany-coloured head, as smooth and shiny as a giant conker. He spoke ve-e-e-r-y slowly, as if he were deeply weary of the subject. '*Apparently*, Mr Thorne will be replacing half of his singing classes with advanced dance classes. At least until the end of term. Now, let's get on. Bianca, you next!'

Relief surged through Belle's veins. Jack wasn't dying or flying!

He was *dancing*! It was weird, but it wasn't *tragic*.

'Phew, that's good!' she sighed, and then clapped her hand over her mouth. 'I mean, not *good* that he's not singing, obviously. I mean, good that he's not dead or . . . well, I don't mean dead, but . . .' Belle forced herself to stop waffling. She straightened her skirt and snapped off an imaginary thread, hoping everyone would blot her little outburst from their minds and move on.

But with Bianca Hayford in the room, there wasn't much chance of *that* happening!

Bianca turned and levelled a long, triumphant look at Belle. 'I thought *you'd* have known all about it?' she said ultra-casually, pretending to flick through her sheaf of papers for her song sheet. 'Since he's your boyfriend and everything . . .'

Belle closed her eyes. *Rise above it!* There was *no way* she was going to be drawn into a brawl with Bianca. Especially not in front of Larry Shapiro, for goodness' sake!

Then Mayu joined in. 'Well, Jack *has* been spending a lot of time with Ruby Drew on their *Love Scene* duet . . .' she said, in a voice like sugar-coated sulphuric acid.

Belle could hear the blood roaring in her ears.

'Ooh, looks like you've touched a nerve there, Mayu!' Bianca giggled as she pretended to flick a speck of dust off the microphone. 'Has there been a little tiff or something, Belle?'

'*Mind your own business!*' Belle snapped, unable to bite her words back a moment longer.

'*Ooh, touchy!*' sang Bianca nastily.

'*GIRLS! GIRLS! STOP THIS BICKERING IMMEDIATELY! WE ARE NOT IN KINDER-GARTEN!*' Mr Garcia bellowed. 'Bianca, you *must* have found that song sheet by now!'

'Oh yes, here it is!' Bianca replied chirpily, with a little toss of her perfect blond hair. '*Popular!*'

Belle closed her eyes, hung her head and groaned a whole-body groan. *I must never, ever let those two wind me up again, she vowed.*

Belle had never been so happy for a class to be over. Without even waiting for Cat, she darted out into the corridor and pushed open the door onto the courtyard. She leaned against the wall and gratefully gulped down lungfuls of cold fresh air.

It was all so humiliating!

The class had run on late and she only had a few

minutes before her music theory class. Belle started speed-walking round the block, trying to march it all out of her system. Head down, hugging her books to her chest, she didn't notice the person rocketing out of the Dance Department until it was too late.

'Ooomph!' he yelped as he rebounded into a rose bush. 'Oh, Belle, it's you . . .'

In the fading afternoon light, Belle realized that it was Jack. She pulled him up and helped him brush twigs from his sweatshirt as she apologized – not only for the body-slam, but for not listening to him and for being so selfish . . . and for anything else she could think of.

Jack laughed. 'Enough apologies already! I should've told you about this whole dance-switcheroo thing earlier. It's just that I didn't take it seriously at first . . . and then it all happened so fast. Miss Morgan finally sorted it with Mr Fortune and Mr Garcia today!'

Belle grinned. 'That must be what I heard when I passed Mr Garcia's office at lunch time. Being *sorted* by Miss Morgan sounded a bit like being hit by a freight train!'

Jack laughed. 'Now you know how I feel too! I just hope Mr Garcia doesn't drop me and find someone else to do my duet with Ruby, now that I'm not in all the advanced singing classes. I really don't want to lose that song, and it'd be tough for Ruby if she has to start all over again with another partner. She's not very confident about her voice . . . In fact, I suggested you might even help her with some vocal exercises?'

Belle smiled. Bianca and Mayu had got it so-o-o wrong. She was totally *over* feeling jealous of Ruby. In fact, she thought it was *sweet* that Jack was so concerned about his singing-partner's feelings. 'Of course I'd be happy to help,' she said. Then she shivered, suddenly realizing how cold she was. Jack put his arm round her shoulders and gave her a squeeze, and she instantly felt warm again. 'So how was your first advanced dance class?' she asked, snuggling in as they walked slowly across the courtyard.

'More *Disco Disaster* than *Disco Inferno*!' Jack laughed. 'How was the singing class?'

'Hideous!' Belle said with a grimace. But suddenly it didn't really seem so bad any more. It was amazing how a few minutes with Jack had lifted her out of the swampy depths of her bad mood! She wished they could spend more time together. 'Let's meet up after dinner—' she began, but stopped mid-sentence. She had band practice this evening with Holly and Cat – and she could hardly cancel when *she* was the one always telling the other two to get organized and make time for Nobody's Angels. 'Oh, no, sorry,' she said, 'I can't . . .'

'Don't worry.' Jack sighed. 'I've got a date too. With Miss Morgan. In the dance studio. Seems like I've got a lot of catching up to do!'

CHAPTER TWELVE

Cat: Operation Romeo

There was only one topic of conversation as Nobody's Angels – alias Cat, Belle and Holly – met up in the rehearsal room later that evening.

In fact, there was only one topic of conversation throughout the entire school!

Jack Thorne, the dancer.

'Everyone was *stunned* when Jack walked into our dance class!' Holly said. 'Did you know about it, Belle?'

Belle shook her head. 'First I knew was when he didn't turn up for singing.' Then she grinned. 'But it was my own fault. He tried to tell me at lunch but I was too busy to listen.'

Cat was pleased – and surprised – at how fast Belle had bounced back from the afternoon's catastrophic singing lesson; normally even a slightly substandard performance, especially in front of Larry Shapiro, would've set her off on a marathon worry-fest.

'So,' Cat said, 'Jack's a mega-star actor, singer *and*

dancer. The all-round triple threat! Is there anything he *can't* do?'

'Don't forget he's great at football too.' Holly was adjusting the controls on the sound system. 'Although I did hear he's only so-so at neurosurgery and he's not *quite* fluent in ancient Greek yet . . .'

Cat laughed. 'Ethan's just as bad. Or *good*, should I say! Actor, football captain, champion swimmer, Saviour of the Universe . . . So where did I go wrong?'

'What do you mean?' Belle asked.

Cat hopped up onto a stool next to the mixing desk. 'You two get these good-looking, ultra-talented, top-of-the-range boyfriends. And I . . . well, I don't.'

Holly clapped her hand to her forehead as if she'd suddenly remembered she'd left the bath taps running – a feeling Cat knew only too well after an unfortunate incident last term. 'Now I get it!' Holly said. 'I *thought* you seemed a bit gloomy at the football match . . . I'm so sorry, I didn't know you were bothered about not getting a Valentine—'

'I was *not* gloomy!' Cat retorted. 'Was I gloomy, Belle?'

Belle nodded. 'Now you mention it, you did seem a little woebegone.'

'I was *not* woebetide.'

82

'Woebe*gone*!' Belle corrected.

'*Woebe-whatever—*' Cat stopped, realizing she wasn't convincing anyone. It was a fair cop! She *had* been gloomy!

'OK,' Belle said in her taking-control-of-the-situation tone as she pulled up a chair and made herself comfortable, 'There must be loads of boys who'd love a date with Cat – we just have to find them . . .'

'Like who?' Cat asked. Normally she'd be bristling at Belle trying to run her life for her, but secretly she was interested. Perhaps Mr Perfect *was* out there somewhere.

'OK, let's think,' Holly said. 'Frankie Pellegrini? He's got a great voice.'

'But he looks like he's gone three rounds in the boxing ring with Mike Tyson,' Cat pointed out.

'Zak Lomax?' Belle offered.

'Too laid-back!'

'Nick Taggart?'

'No way!' Cat giggled. '*Dancing Bees*, people! Let's leave Nick for Lettie. Some time this century those two might finally figure it out and admit they really like each other!'

'Duncan Gillespie!' Holly named the Year Ten boy who'd directed *Macbeth* last term. 'I *know* he liked you!'

Cat shook her head. 'He's going out with Lucy Cheng now.'

'This is hopeless,' Holly sighed.

'You're right,' Belle agreed. 'But we've got the whole school to pick from. We need to cast our net wider and start scouting for suitable candidates.'

Holly glanced uncertainly at Cat. 'Is this all right with you?'

Cat grinned. Holly was such a diplomat – always considering everyone's feelings. She thought for a moment. *It might just be fun to see who they come up with, and they'll probably forget about it in a day or two anyway. What harm can it do?* 'Sure, why not!' she said.

'Great!' Holly rubbed her hands together. 'I love matchmaking! Operation Get Cat a Boyfriend is GO!'

Belle took out a notebook and started jotting down some dates. 'OK, team,' she stated. 'We've got five weeks. Plenty of time to find Cat a boyfriend so they can use those spare *Romeo and Juliet* tickets—'

'Ooh! Ooh!' Holly said, waving her hands excitedly. 'We could call it Operation Romeo instead!'

'Good thinking, Holly.' Belle wrote the new heading down in her notebook.

Cat shook her head. *What*, she wondered, *have I let myself in for now?*

Suddenly Belle jumped up out of her chair. 'Come on, guys! We've only got ten minutes left to practise.'

The girls warmed up with one of their favourites, *Opposites Attract*, a romantic ballad that Lettie Atkins had written for them for the talent show last term. *That seems like a lifetime ago now*, Cat thought. Since then, Nobody's Angels had performed at the Gala Showcase, a wedding and a company Christmas party. There wasn't quite the same buzz without a gig coming up to rehearse for, but it was still fun to sing together.

But after a few minutes, Belle suddenly stopped. 'Holly, you're straining your voice!'

'Oh, it's just all the extra singing we've been doing for the Spectacular numbers,' Holly told her. 'I'm fine.'

Now Cat could hear the tell-tale catch in Holly's voice too.

'Holly Devenish!' Belle scolded, holding up her hand. 'Step *away* from the microphone!'

Obediently Holly jumped back.

'You've got to rest your voice,' Belle said firmly, 'or you'll be sounding like Bruce Springsteen by tomorrow morning. No more singing today.'

Cat and Holly both saluted and grinned. Belle was having a Bossy Moment, but they knew she was right this time!

As they tidied away, Felix Baddeley, Ben Stein and Mason Lee – aka The Undertow – arrived at the rehearsal room. They'd booked the next slot for their band practice.

Felix was brandishing an application form. 'Battle of the Bands competition at the university next term,' he explained. 'We're entering. Hey, why don't you go in for it too? Nobody's Angels would go down a storm.'

Cat, Holly and Belle stared at each other, excitement lighting up their faces. *What an amazing idea! A chance to perform together again.* They'd just need to put in some serious rehearsal time . . . Cat was already walking up onto the stage to collect her trophy, which was being presented by Simon Cowell. She was waving to the audience, looking proud – but modest at the same time, of course – and then . . .

. . . and then she came back to reality.

'We can't,' she sighed, although it took all her willpower to force the words out. 'We've got to save our voices for the Rising Stars Spectacular.' She couldn't believe that she, Cat Where's-the-Party? Wickham, was being the *sensible* one, but Larry Shapiro *had* told her she needed to take better care of her voice, and Holly was getting croakier by the minute . . .

Belle smiled, shaking her head sadly. 'Cat's right. And we're all so busy this term. It would be crazy.'

Holly looked close to tears but she nodded slowly.

'Let's go and get you a honey and lemon drink,' Belle suggested.

As they left the rehearsal room, Belle whispered to Holly, 'What about Felix?'

'Hmmm . . . good-looking,' Holly said, suddenly sounding more cheerful. 'But he'd never turn up to a date on time!'

'Ben Stein?' Belle suggested, referring to The Undertow's bass guitarist.

'Too tall,' Holly replied.

'And tall's *bad*?' Belle asked.

'OK, put him in the *possibles* column,' Holly conceded.

'Shh!' Cat hissed. 'They'll hear you!'

If those two carry on like this, she thought, *it won't just be a boyfriend I'm short of – I won't have any male friends left at all!*

But she couldn't help feeling just a tiny bit excited. Maybe Holly and Belle really could track down her Perfect Guy.

CHAPTER THIRTEEN

Holly: Trappist Monks and Hissy Fits

Miss Toft, Holly's old dance teacher, was standing at the bottom of a mountain. She hadn't noticed the avalanche approaching. Holly opened her mouth to shout *Look out!* but no sound emerged. She tried again – nothing!

Then she woke up, safe in her cosy lilac and blue room at Superstar High.

Gemma was making her bed.

'Phew!' Holly said. 'I just had a horrible nightmare . . .'

Or at least, that's what she *tried* to say.

Gemma winced. 'Youch! You sound like a bullfrog with tonsillitis. Does it hurt?'

'No!' Holly croaked, laughing at the strange sound. 'It's just my voice.'

It felt as if a big furry caterpillar had taken up residence in her throat.

★ ★ ★

Holly hurried off to meet Ethan at the pool. They usually swam lengths together several mornings a week. He was waiting on the steps of the sports centre, bundled up in a padded jacket and scarf.

'Hi!' she called into the wind. 'Brr, it's cold out here . . .'

A feeble little rasping noise came out of her mouth.

Ethan grinned. 'No swimming for you!'

'But I'm not ill!' Holly protested. 'It's just . . .' She pointed at her throat as her voice gave out.

'Sounds like you've been gargling with gravel! The chlorine'd just make it worse,' Ethan insisted, putting his arm around her. 'Come on, let's go and get breakfast instead.'

Holly was about to object when she suddenly spied a boy jogging out of the sports centre. He had a cute smile and a hunky athletic build. 'That's Paul Zhao, isn't it?' she squeaked. 'He looks quite nice!'

'Er, have I got competition here?' Ethan asked.

Holly laughed. 'Not for me, silly! For Cat. D'you know him?'

Ethan nodded. 'A bit. Year Nine. Nice guy, great singer. He's pretty shy though.'

On the 'opposites attract' principle, that could be perfect, Holly reasoned. Cat was definitely not shy! 'Could you . . . ask . . . interested . . . date . . . Cat?' she rasped. Her voice was now producing detectable sound on only about half the words she attempted.

'Ask him if he'd like to be my girlfriend's friend's boyfriend, you mean?' Ethan teased.

Holly nodded.

He grinned at her. 'Sure, anything to *keep you quiet!*'

Holly punched his arm and smiled back.

Phase One of Operation Romeo was underway.

Halfway through her second mug of honey and lemon at breakfast, Holly came to A Decision. She would rest her voice by not talking at all for the rest of the day. She could get through morning lessons with the occasional nod and grunt without anyone noticing, and, as it was Friday, she had advanced dance classes all afternoon; you didn't need to talk to dance. That way, her voice should be fully operational again by the next band practice on Sunday afternoon and for singing lessons on Monday.

How hard can it be to remain silent for a day? Holly said to herself. *Trappist monks have been doing it for years!*

But Trappist monks didn't have double English with Mrs Jeffries to deal with.

Holly took her seat next to Belle and Cat.

'Voice any better this morning?' Belle asked.

Holly nodded. She didn't want Belle to start worrying, and anyway it wasn't *technically* a lie, since she didn't say a word.

'Good swim?' Cat asked.

'Mm-mm,' Holly replied, with a so-so wave of her hand.

Mrs Jeffries was a plump, mild-mannered lady who looked as if she should be wearing a flowery apron and baking apple pies. She often brought in photos of her grandchildren to show the class. But she had a great passion for literature and was one of Holly's favourite teachers. Usually Holly put her hand up for every question, but today she kept her head – and her hand – firmly *down* as they analysed a scene from *Romeo and Juliet*. But eventually Mrs Jeffries asked her a direct question. 'Holly, can you find an example of a *simile* in this scene?'

It was so obvious. They'd done similes a million times! *Death lies on her like an untimely frost . . .* Holly screwed up her eyes and frowned as if she was totally baffled. Cat and Belle were both staring at her. Cat even pointed at the line discreetly with her pencil. Eventually Holly shook her head.

'*Simile*. It means saying one thing is like another, remember?' Mrs Jeffries explained patiently.

But a few minutes later Holly was asked to read out Juliet's part in the balcony scene. She gazed at the page, willing her voice to miraculously come back to life. After a long, long silence, she opened her mouth . . . and squeaked. She disguised it with a cough, cleared her throat and tried again. '*Wherefore . . . art . . . thou . . . Romeo . . .*' she croaked. She could feel Cat and Belle staring at her in horror. Bianca and Mayu were giggling at the desk behind.

Mrs Jeffries smiled. 'Never mind, Holly, dear! You need to rest that voice. And make sure you get an early night! Mayu, could you take over please?'

'That's it,' Belle whispered as they started writing notes on the scene. 'No more band practice until the end of term. We've got to save your voice for the Spectacular . . .'

Holly felt terrible. She knew how much Nobody's Angels meant to Belle, and now she'd spoiled it by not looking after her voice properly. 'Sorry!' she rasped.

'*No talking!*' Cat reminded her.

Belle smiled. 'We'll get Nobody's Angels going again next term. We're all so busy right now, you're doing us a favour really.'

Reassured, Holly turned back to her work. But she was interrupted by a comment from Bianca – who'd obviously been earwigging on their conversation. 'So, Belle, looks like your little band isn't working out then? I'd better call The Saturdays and tell them they don't have to worry *just* yet!'

Holly glanced at Belle. Good! She was *rising above it* – although her teeth were clenched and she was gripping her pen so tightly, her fingers had turned white!

But Bianca wasn't giving up. 'Of course, it's probably just an excuse to chicken out of entering the Battle of the Bands . . .' she said quietly, as if thinking aloud.

Belle was staring fixedly at her notebook. Her pen was almost tearing through the paper.

'Because, let's face it, you're not really up to it,' Bianca goaded her.

Belle turned in her chair. 'FYI, Bianca,' she said coolly, 'we're just putting the band on hold for a few weeks.'

'Get on with your work please, girls,' Mrs Jeffries said.

Mayu giggled.

Holly gave Belle's hand a sympathetic squeeze. She looked across at Cat – who had that dangerous about-to-boil-over look on her face. Holly shook her head in warning. One of Cat's Major Eruptions would only make things worse for Belle.

'Oh no! A few weeks without Nobody's Angels?' Bianca said in a voice as cold and sharp as an injection. 'How will we ever survive?'

'*Bianca, will you please quit bugging me?*' Belle seethed.

'Oo-ooh, Hissy Fit Alert!' Bianca whispered. 'It must be that Spoiled Little Rich Girl thing coming out again!'

'Rise above it!' Holly whispered.

But suddenly the nib of Belle's pen snapped, flicking blue ink across the page of neatly written notes. 'I AM *NOT* HAVING A HISSY FIT!' she exploded.

Holly flinched. She hated arguments – and she'd never seen Belle lose her cool before.

The whole class turned to stare. Holly could read the look in their eyes. *All due respect to William Shakespeare*, it said, *but a monster row between Belle and Bianca is* way *more interesting than* Romeo and Juliet.

'Belle Madison and Bianca Hayford!' Mrs Jeffries shouted. 'I don't know what you two are quarrelling about but it doesn't belong in the classroom! Go outside until you cool off!'

The entire class gasped. Mrs Jeffries, everyone's

favourite grandmother, had lost her temper, *and* Belle Madison, the Merit-a-Minute Model Student, had been sent out of class!

Belle stood up, face rigid with shock and hands trembling.

Bianca, on the other hand, flounced out and slammed the door behind her.

CHAPTER FOURTEEN

Belle: A Rather Disagreeable State of Affairs

'Why did you have to go and lose it like that,' Bianca spat as Belle joined her in the corridor, 'and get us *both* thrown out?'

'Me?' Belle spluttered. 'It was *you*!'

'Let's see, shall we?' Bianca said, pretending to give it some thought. '*Someone* yelled, *I am not having a hissy fit at the top of her voice* . . . and correct me if I'm wrong, but I'm pretty sure it wasn't *me!*'

But Belle had no energy left for arguing. She felt as if her world had entered a total eclipse.

She leaned against the wall and stared miserably at her shoes. They were her favourite sequinned ballerina pumps from a boutique in Barcelona – but that was no consolation.

What will Dad say if he finds out I've been sent out of class? Belle fretted. Her father was adamant that she should train for a 'proper' profession – like brain surgeon or rocket scientist. She was only allowed to stay at Superstar High and follow her dream of becoming a singer on *one* condition: that she received A grades in all her schoolwork.

She peeped across at Bianca, who was now lolling against the wall on the other side of the classroom door, looking supremely unconcerned. She was humming, tapping her toe and sending a text on her phone.

Bianca caught Belle looking and scowled back.

At least, Belle thought, *Jack wasn't there to witness my downfall* – he was in a lower set for English. But just as she was starting to feel that maybe things weren't really so terrible – and surely Mrs Jeffries wouldn't mention *this one tiny incident* on her end-of-term report – something even worse happened.

Mr Garcia and Mr Grampian, head of the Drama Department, came strolling along the corridor with a tray of coffees, deep in conversation.

Now Bianca was looking worried too. She stuffed her phone back in her pocket. They both knew that bad behaviour or poor marks in morning school could result in being banned from school performances.

What if their solos in the Spectacular were taken away?

Mr Garcia frowned at them and glanced at his watch. 'It's very early in the day to be in trouble! Have you two been bickering again?'

Mr Grampian stopped abruptly. 'Hm! This *is* a rather disagreeable state of affairs!' he muttered.

Belle was sure he wasn't just talking about the coffee that'd sloshed out all over the tray. And now that she thought about it, Mr Grampian had already heard them arguing when they were working on characterization in his core acting lesson just the other day – after Bianca accused Belle of 'looking at her'.

Belle gulped. *Now all the teachers think that I'm constantly fighting with Bianca.*

'It was Belle,' Bianca blurted. 'She just started shouting at me for no reason!'

'That's not true,' Belle cut in. 'You started—'

'*Did not—*'

'*She's always—*'

Mr Garcia held up his hands. 'I don't want to hear it!' he boomed as he and Mr Grampian turned and walked on.

Bianca tossed her hair defiantly and glowered at Belle.

Belle watched a tiny spider scurrying into a crack in the floor tiles and wished she could follow it.

By lunch time Belle had convinced herself she'd lost her part in the Spectacular *and* that her dad would be arriving by helicopter any minute to whisk her away to some Ancient Academy for Studious Young Ladies (positively no singing allowed). She sat down in the dining room with Holly and Cat, but was too miserable to eat.

Cat tried to cheer her up. 'It's not that bad! I get into worse trouble than that every day. Twice a day sometimes if we have Mrs Salmon!'

That was true, Belle realized, brightening a little. And Cat hadn't been banned from a performance yet! Although there'd been a few close shaves! 'But I just don't understand why Bianca's got it in for me!' she sighed.

Cat grinned. 'Well, let's see: you're beautiful, cool, elegant, you have an incredible singing voice, famous parents, designer clothes' – she was counting off the reasons on her fingers – 'and then, of course, you have Jack, the super-gorgeous guy *she* had her claws into until *you* came along and nabbed him!'

Holly was nodding so furiously she knocked over the water jug. She was sticking to her vow of silence but managed to croak one word: 'Jealousy!'

'And that waggle-dancing-is-the-new-big-thing line at the *Nutcracker Sweeties* party probably didn't help!' Cat added. 'I'm sure that Bianca's checked it out by now and knows that you were winding her up!'

'Oh yes,' Belle sighed. 'That probably wasn't my smartest ever move!' But as she mopped up the water, she was starting to feel a little better. Talking to Cat and Holly had really helped.

The girls were getting up to leave the table when Holly suddenly squeaked, '. . . remembered . . . something . . . tell you!'

'*No talking!*' Belle and Cat chorused.

Holly groaned with frustration. Being a monk was hard work! She pulled a pen and notebook out of her bag and started to scribble. Belle read out her words.

'Quietly!' Cat hissed, looking over her shoulder with a slightly paranoid expression.

Belle nodded conspiratorially and read out in a whisper: '*Operation Romeo. Have located suitable candidate – Paul Zhao – Ethan says he's nice. Will talk to him. Cat – permission to proceed with date plan????*'

Cat looked uncertain.

'I've met Paul a couple of times in singing workshops,' Belle told her. 'Awesome baritone voice!'

'That's a relief!' Cat said. 'I simply *couldn't* go out with a boy with a *dodgy* baritone!'

'He's not bad-looking either. And he seems like a nice guy . . .'

'OK!' Cat laughed. 'If he has the Belle Madison Seal of Approval, how can I resist?'

Belle smiled as she started stacking their plates. Finding the perfect boy for Cat was going to be fun! Then Jack popped into the dining room on his way to the library to ask her to go out for lunch tomorrow. She was really looking forward to spending some time with him. *Perhaps we could try the new sushi bar in Farleigh Place*, she thought happily.

She'd almost forgotten the terrible banished-to-the-corridor-with-Bianca episode.

In that afternoon's advanced singing class, Belle pulled out all the stops and sang her solo better than she had ever done before. After the catastrophic lesson where she'd been so worried about Jack, she had to prove to herself, as well as to everyone else, that she was Back in the Game.

And it worked!

She totally rocked *I'm Not That Girl*! The whole class was enraptured. Even Bianca was speechless for once. Mr Garcia and Larry Shapiro vied with each other in some kind of Extreme Praise Competition: '*Marvellous, superb, delightful . . .*' Mr Garcia boomed; '*Exquisite, first-rate, virtuoso!*' Larry Shapiro added. It was almost embarrassing!

It seemed Mr Garcia had forgotten the banished-to-the-corridor-with-Bianca episode too.

Belle was ecstatic! *Bianca Hayford's going to have to work a lot harder if she wants to get the better of me!* she thought.

CHAPTER FIFTEEN

Holly: Strange Boy Meets Random Girl

Later, following her afternoon of advanced dance classes, Holly met Cat and Belle in the entrance hall before dinner.

They all checked their pigeon holes and, to Holly's excitement, Cat found a note from Paul Zhao.

The girls hurried across to the big sofa to read it.

'Ooh, what does it say?' Holly asked impatiently, forgetting her vow of silence for a moment. Luckily her voice was now only slightly furry-caterpillary after its day of rest.

'It says: *Please ask Holly Devenish to stop being such a busybody and Get a Life!*' Cat said in a reading-out-loud voice.

Holly felt totally *squashed*. She'd never dreamed Paul would be offended, but he sounded *furious*.

Cat doubled up with laughter. 'No it doesn't! Holly, you're even easier to tease than Belle sometimes!'

Belle tutted and swiped the note out of Cat's hand.

'*Dear Cat,*' she read aloud. '*Would you like to go to Kingsgrove Arts Cinema with me tomorrow to see* Some Like It Hot? *If so, meet me at the front steps at 2 p.m. Yours, Paul Zhao.*'

Holly was delighted! Operation Romeo was a success. OK, so Cat still had to *accept* the invitation and then they had to go on the date and actually like each other, but those were *minor* details!

'Impressive!' Belle said, studying the note as if for fingerprints. 'He's clearly done his research into what Cat likes. *Some Like It Hot* is an old Marilyn Monroe movie, isn't it?'

Cat nodded. 'Yeah. It's part of the Classic Movie Season. It's one of my all-time favourites.'

Holly kept quiet. OK, so maybe she *had* asked Ethan to drop Paul a few hints about the kind of date that Cat might like. It was all part of her Complete Matchmaking Service!

'I'm not sure . . .' Cat mumbled, propping her feet up on the coffee table. 'What if it's awful?'

'What's not to like?' Belle asked. 'It's your favourite movie?'

'Not the *movie*, the *date*. Paul . . . What if he's some kind of weirdo loser? Think about it – he's jumped at the chance of a date with some random girl he doesn't know. He can't exactly be Mr Popular!'

Holly couldn't believe it! Cat was *actually* nervous about the date. 'You are not some random girl, Cat!' she protested. 'You're beautiful, funny and an amazing actress. *Of course* he wants to go out with you!'

'Tell him you'll go,' Belle urged, jiggling a pen under Cat's nose. 'Quick! Before you can wimp out of it.'

Reluctantly Cat wrote on the back of the note: *OK*.

'*OK?* Is that it?' Belle asked.

'Hey, do I *want* to look desperate?' But then Cat paused and added a scribbled *Thank you* before sliding the note back in the envelope. 'And thanks, Hols, for setting this up.' Then she took a short cut to the pigeon holes by hopping over the back of the sofa.

Straight into the arms of Nick Taggart.

'Nick, how long have you been——?' Holly asked.

'Lurking behind the sofa, listening in to private conversations?' Cat interrupted. 'And you can put me down now.'

'Just got here,' Nick asserted, letting Cat slide to the floor. 'Honest, guv! On me life!'

Belle gave him her sceptical eyebrows look.

'Well, OK, a couple of minutes,' he admitted.

First Bianca in Mrs Jeffries' English lesson, and now Nick! Does everyone *in this place have a Diploma in*

Advanced Eavesdropping? Holly wondered. 'I think this should be a spy school, not a stage school!' she giggled – only slightly huskily.

'Anyhoo,' Nick said, 'I couldn't help hearing that Cat's going on a blind date tomorrow with some strange boy. Do you think that's sensible?'

Holly groaned to herself. Would Nick's doubts put Cat – who had already been *seriously* wavering – off the date idea completely? But then she remembered this was *Cat* she was talking about. Cat didn't let *anyone* tell her what to think – especially not if they happened to be a boy! Suddenly she was acting as if this date was the best idea since toaster waffles. 'One,' she said, 'Paul is *not* strange. He's a friend of Ethan's. Two, *since when have you been my mother?* And three . . . well, I haven't thought of three yet but I'm working on it!' And with that she marched across to the pigeon holes and popped in the note.

'You can't be too careful,' Nick persisted. 'You should have someone there to keep an eye on things.'

'Like a chaperone, you mean?' Holly asked. 'What is this? The nineteenth century?'

'Tell you what I'll do,' Nick said, leaning over the back of the sofa. He sounded like a market trader offering a buy-one-get-one-free offer on a pair of cheap earrings. 'I'll ask Lettie to come to the film with me on a pretend *date*.' He air-quoted on *date*. 'Then, if Paul spots us, he'll never know—'

'That you're actually shameless snoopers,' Belle interrupted.

'That we're *working undercover*,' Nick countered.

'Nick Taggart – don't even *think* about it!' Cat warned darkly as she returned to the sofa.

Nick grinned. 'Got to run,' he said, dashing off. 'Toodle pip!'

Holly looked at Belle and Cat, and the three of them sank back into the cushions, laughing.

'A *pretend date*!' Cat gasped eventually.

'Why doesn't he just ask Lettie on a *real* date!' Belle giggled.

'He's shy!' Holly said, suddenly realizing that underneath all Nick's bravado he couldn't pluck up the courage to ask Lettie to go out with him – even though it'd been obvious to the entire school for months that they liked each other. This crazy keeping-an-eye-on-Cat scheme was the perfect excuse to ask Lettie out without actually *asking her out*.

'Right!' Belle said briskly, getting up from the sofa. 'Let's go and have a quick dinner. We've got work to do!'

'*Work?*' Cat echoed, with a look of horror, as if Belle had suggested they spend the evening cleaning the boys' toilets. 'Work! But it's Friday night!'

Belle grinned. 'Got to find you the perfect outfit for your date tomorrow.'

Half an hour later the girls reconvened in Cat and Belle's room.

'Stand by your beds! Wardrobe inspection!' Belle ordered.

'Er, my bed *is* my wardrobe,' Cat said, scooping up a tangle of clothes and shoes and shoving them aside.

'Hmm,' Belle muttered, throwing open the door of her wardrobe to reveal the perfectly organized contents.

Holly curled up on the bed with Shreddie to watch the fashion show.

'Can't I just wear my black mini-skirt and jumper?' Cat asked.

'Like you wear *every* day?' Belle asked.

'Yeah!'

'And what does that say to Paul?'

'Er, it says, *I like these clothes*?'

'It says,' Belle explained patiently, '*I haven't made an effort for this date!*'

'OK, what about my silver dress?' Cat asked, rummaging about in the heap.

'That looks gorgeous on you,' Holly agreed. Cat had the kind of hourglass figure that was perfect for the clingy dress.

Belle shook her head. 'Too revealing, too sparkly. On a first date, there's a fine line between *glamorous* and *trying too hard*.'

Cat pulled item after item from Belle's collection and modelled them in front of the long mirror. 'Does my bum look big in this?' she asked, twisting round to try and see the rear view.

'No,' Holly said. 'You look great. And Paul must like girls with curves,' she added. 'He wants to see a Marilyn Monroe film, after all.'

Cat wasn't convinced. She pulled off the entire outfit and tried again . . . and again . . .

'Stop right there!' Belle cried as Cat stood in a figure-hugging black and white striped top worn over jeans, with boots and a long jacket and scarf. 'That is *perfection*.'

Cat peered doubtfully at her reflection. 'Hmm,' she murmured. 'Not too bad . . . What do you think, Hols? Hols . . . *where are you*?'

Holly crawled out from under a mountain of

discarded garments to give Cat a hug. 'You look lovely!'

She felt a yawn coming on. It'd been a busy day and it was past ten o'clock.

'Can I go to bed now, please?' she asked.

CHAPTER SIXTEEN

Cat: Jelly Babies and Jellyfish

Cat stared at the pick 'n' mix selection in the Arts Cinema foyer and wondered whether there was any way she could teleport out of this date.

It had all started so well! Paul had shown up on time and immediately earned bonus points for complimenting her on her appearance. He didn't look bad himself. He had a broad, angular face with dark wide-set eyes, and his athletic build was obvious even under the thick jacket. *Promising*, Cat thought cheerfully.

On the walk to the cinema, Paul was quiet. Cat didn't mind; she knew he was shy. To break the ice she asked him about himself – after all, *everyone* liked talking about themselves, didn't they? 'Belle tells me you're a brilliant singer . . .' she prompted.

'Thank you,' Paul said. He had a cute smile with very straight white teeth.

'So . . . what kinds of music do you like?' Cat asked.

'All.'

'But what's your *favourite*? Opera? Rock? Country and Western?'

'Yes.'

Cat laughed. 'Which one? Or is it all of the above?'

Paul smiled again and nodded. 'Yes.'

She decided to change tack. 'Where are you from? I'm from Dublin originally but my family moved to Cambridge last year . . .' Perhaps if she gave him an *example* of the art of small talk, he'd get the hang of it.

'California,' Paul replied.

Or perhaps not, she thought.

But she kept trying: 'Wow! California? Cool place! But your surname's Chinese, isn't it?'

'Parents,' Paul said.

Cat made one final attempt to break through the one–word–answer barrier. 'Thanks for asking me to this film. I love Marilyn Monroe.'

'Oh yeah, me too,' Paul agreed.

Finally! Cat thought. *Four whole words! This is great. A boy who shares my passion for old movies!* 'Which is your favourite Marilyn movie?' she asked.

'Er, erm . . . well . . .' Paul hesitated.

'I know! It's hard to choose!' Cat laughed. 'I think I'd

have to go for *Some Like It Hot*, so great choice for today!'

'Yeah, me too, every time.'

Cat glanced at him. *Am I imagining things or is he just agreeing with everything I say?* She decided to put it to the test. 'Vivien Leigh is my favourite actress of all time . . .'

'Mine too!' Paul said.

'*Casablanca* was her best film.'

Paul nodded. 'Definitely!'

But, Cat thought, *Vivien Leigh wasn't even in* Casablanca!

Paul obviously didn't know the first thing about old films! *What a fake!* But just as Cat was about to confront him, they arrived at the cinema. He held the door open, insisted on paying for the tickets, and asked sweetly whether she would like something to eat. Suddenly Cat felt like a bit of a weevil for catching him out with her Vivien Leigh trick question. He was probably just mega-nervous and trying to impress her. That wasn't such a crime! 'Come on,' she said. 'Let's get a Coke and some pick 'n' mix!'

'Great idea,' Paul said.

Cat grabbed a paper bag from the stack and passed it to Paul. 'You choose first.'

He handed the bag back. 'No, please, after you!'

Cat gave up. 'I'll have some shrimps,' she said, digging in the scoop. 'I *love* these.'

Paul smiled – 'Me too!' – and added a few more to the bag.

'And . . . some cola bottles,' Cat said.

'Yep, good idea.' He added some more cola bottles.

Cat picked white mice, flying saucers and sour cherries.

So did Paul.

Now this was getting seriously freaky!

Not having an opinion about the classic film actresses of the mid twentieth century was understandable. Not having an opinion about jelly babies versus strawberry laces was just plain wrong.

Inside the cinema most of the seats were empty, but Cat noticed a couple in the back row. Dressed entirely in black, they were nestled behind a jumbo bucket of popcorn. It looked like an Olympic Snogathon in progress. Then she looked again. Had she *really* caught a glimpse of Lettie Atkins's long chestnut hair?

Yes, now she was sure.

Those two weren't smooching; they were spying!

She half expected a pair of binoculars to poke out above the popcorn.

A few minutes later Cat was lost in the film. She was Marilyn Monroe's character, Sugar Kane, on a train to Florida, in a bar, singing *I Wanna Be Loved by You* . . .

She felt something tickle her shoulder and looked down absently to brush away a fly or a spider. With a start she realized it was Paul's hand, creeping in painful slo-o-o-o-w mo-o-o-o-tion across her shoulder. He was trying to put his arm round her. But as soon he noticed Cat looking, he snatched his hand back, grabbed his Coke and took a slurp.

It was a very loud drain-gurgling kind of slurp.

Right in the middle of a hushed, romantic scene.

An old lady in front turned round and glared at them.

Paul shrank back and hid behind his Coke.

Cat wondered whether Nick and Lettie were taking notes.

On the way back to school Paul asked nervously if she would like to stop for coffee at Café Roma. Cat was about to refuse but decided to give this date one last chance. Maybe it was *her* fault that Paul was afraid to express his opinions. Maybe she'd been too pushy or something. 'That would be nice,' she heard herself saying.

'What can I get you?' Luigi asked.

Cat looked at Paul, letting him choose first in a totally non-pushy way. 'What are you going to have?' she asked.

'What are *you* having?' Paul replied.

'I'll give you a few minutes to decide . . .' Luigi said, glancing around the busy café. 'I'll be back.' He moved away to another table.

'So, did you enjoy the film?' Cat asked brightly.

'Did you?' Paul bounced back.

OK, that's it! Cat decided. *I've tried my best. Paul obviously doesn't have the X-factor. In fact, he has the Y-factor. As in Why-am-I-stuck-here-with-a-boy-who-has-the-personality-of-a-jellyfish?*

It was time to escape! 'Ooh, just remembered! Homework emergency! Science report!' she gabbled. 'Must go the library!'

'Hang on, I'll come with you!' Paul said as Cat stood up.

'*No need! Really!*'

Undeterred, Paul followed her across the café. As they reached the door, Cat spotted a couple sitting at a corner table, their faces shielded by a large menu.

The girl peeped over the top and blushed when Cat caught her eye.

I hope your pretend date is going better than my real one, Lettie, Cat thought.

'I'll come to the library with you,' Paul offered as they crossed the school entrance hall.

'Oh, no, please don't,' Cat said before she could stop herself.

Paul looked at her with a hurt expression in his eyes that you usually only see in charity appeals for mistreated puppies. She desperately searched her brain for a way to stop him following her into the library, 'I can't focus if there's anyone I know in there. I have this, er . . . concentration disorder.'

'That sounds nasty,' Paul said.

Cat nodded seriously. 'Oh yeah, it is.' They'd reached the library and Paul held the door open for her. 'Bye then!' she chirped, ducking inside.

Freedom! At last!

'I'll just wait out here a little while in case it takes you less time than you think,' Paul called through the closing door.

Cat's heart sank. Would she *ever* escape from Jellyfish Boy's clinging tentacles? She opened the door a crack and peered out. He was still there!

She let the door bang shut behind her and darted

over to the furthest set of shelves. *Trapped!* She couldn't go back out how! *But what could she do in the library?* Well, read books, obviously – but for the first time in living memory, she didn't have any homework she needed to read up on. She crept along to the end of the aisle and peeped out. *All clear!* She grabbed a book at random, sat down at a table and sank her head down on her arms.

'Are you OK?'

Cat almost jumped out of her chair. Paul must have followed her after all!

But when she dared look up, the boy she saw sitting on the other side of the table was definitely *not* Paul. He was black for a start, with a wicked grin and slightly sticking-out ears – like a younger, not-quite-as-good-looking Will Smith. The boy – who she vaguely recognized as a Year Nine student called Adam Fielding – was staring at her in a bemused manner. 'You must have some seriously overdue books out!' he whispered.

Cat smiled. *I guess the run-for-cover routine isn't exactly standard library procedure*, she thought.

'Or is there a horde of flesh-eating mutant zombies out there?' Adam asked with a grin, pointing at the book Cat had pulled off the shelf.

She looked at it for the first time – *A History of Zombies in Film and Literature* – and laughed. 'Yeah! They've taken over the whole school – hadn't you heard?'

'Must've missed it! I've been holed up in here all morning,' Adam groaned. 'So, how long do you think we've got before they break the door down? I need to finish this geography essay.'

Cat laughed. She'd almost forgotten why she was hiding in the library. Then she remembered. *Paul!* She glanced fearfully towards the door.

'So what's really out there?' Adam asked.

'A jellyfish.'

'*A jellyfish?*' Adam repeated slowly.

'Yeah, he's called Paul.'

Adam scrunched up his brows. '*A jellyfish called Paul has chased you into the library?* Have you seen a therapist about this?'

Cat laughed again. Then she whispered a speedy explanation of her disastrous date.

'Sounds grim,' Adam agreed. 'D'you want me to go and check whether he's still there?'

Cat nodded gratefully.

'Coast's clear!' he reported back a moment later. 'Apart from the zombies, of course.'

'Thanks!' Cat said. 'I'll take my chances with *them*!'

She waved and headed for the door.

★   ★   ★

Now to tell Holly and Belle exactly *what I think of their matchmaking skills!* Cat thought as she arrived back at her room.

'*Aaaaa, eeeeee, ooooooo . . .*'

It sounded as if a troop of howler monkeys had moved in while she was away.

Cat threw open the door to find Holly and Ruby Drew standing open-mouthed in the middle of the room.

Belle was sitting on her bed, conducting operations. 'Vocal warm-up exercises!' she explained. 'Protects the voice!'

Holly broke off in the middle of an *eeee*. 'Ooooh! How was your date?' she cried.

'Come on, girl, spill!' Belle urged.

Cat threw herself full-length on her bed. 'Er, the *film* was great . . .' she said.

'Oh no! Was he *that* bad?' Holly asked.

Cat nodded slowly and closed her eyes. 'I'm sure Secret Agents Taggart and Atkins will be filing a full report in the morning!'

CHAPTER SEVENTEEN

Holly: Trusting, Timing and Talking

It was Sunday morning! The Big Day! The day of Holly and Zak's first rehearsal of their *Time of My Life* dance routine with Tory King.

Because Tory was currently starring in *Dirty Dancing* in the West End, Sundays were her only free day. The rehearsals were taking place at an incredibly cool dance studio in Covent Garden, which had been hired by the production team for Tory King and the rest of the *Dirty Dancing* cast to use during the run of the show.

Holly was so keyed up she could hardly breathe!

Although that may also have had something to do with being wedged in the back of Miss Morgan's Mini with Zak. Miss LeClair was sitting in the front.

Miss Morgan drove through the narrow streets of central London as if she were in a high-speed car chase. 'Gnarly! It's just like *The Italian Job*!' Zak laughed.

Holly held on tight as they screeched round a corner. 'I can't *believe* we're actually going to be working with Tory King!' she sighed. 'I remember seeing her in *The Lion King*. She was so amazing and I really identified with her – she's from north London, she's black . . . *and* she got into The Garrick through the Steps to the Stars competition just like me—'

'Starting to spook me out here, dude!' Zak teased.

Holly grimaced as Miss Morgan squeezed the Mini into a tiny parking space. 'Sorry! I know I sound like I'm *obsessed*! It's just that it was the moment when I first saw Tory King that I knew that this was my dream – to star in musicals, just like her!'

Holly and Zak followed Miss Morgan and Miss LeClair into the building, which seemed to be constructed entirely of glass. Clear winter light flooded in, splashing across vases of scarlet orchids and huge black and white prints of famous dancers. Feeling as if she was in a dream, Holly followed Zak and her teachers into a huge, airy studio.

Tory King was at the barre doing quad stretches. She was smaller than Holly had expected, and was wearing black footless tights and a wrap-over skirt with a pink lycra top. Her long hair was pulled back under a wide black band.

She smiled her show-stopping smile. 'Ciao!' she

cried, and hurried over to hug Miss Morgan. Holly exchanged a glance with Zak. *Miss Morgan hugged people?*

'Hiya!' Tory said, holding out her hand to Miss LeClair and then to Holly and Zak. Then she giggled. 'Please stop looking so terrified! It seems like only five minutes since I was in Year Eight at The Garrick myself. Is Mr Grampian still there? He used to scare the *socks* off me!'

Holly started to relax. 'Yeah, he's still there!' she said. She was a little afraid of Mr Grampian too, although Cat adored him.

Tory had set up a DVD player, and they started by watching the film version of their number, *The Time of My Life*, with Patrick Swayze and Jennifer Grey playing Johnny and Baby – including the famous overhead lift. 'The "swallow dive", as I call it,' Tory laughed. Then they watched a recording of the stage version. 'So, in the dance I've choreographed for you two, I've adapted things a little because you're younger—'

'We do still get to do the lift though?' Holly interrupted.

'Don't panic! You still get to do the lift,' Tory told her. 'At least, we'll try it. It's a big ask at your age . . . so if it's not working out, we can—'

'Oh, we *know* can do it!' Zak said, holding his hand up for a high-five with Holly. 'We're gonna bust it!'

Tory smiled. 'You guys sound pretty confident . . .'

'Yeah. You see, we already did—' Zak started.

Holly noticed Miss Morgan shooting them a sharp look. 'Er, where do we get changed?' she asked, hurriedly moving on. It was probably best *not* to remind Miss Morgan about their lift at the football match in case she remembered the *Dangerous! Irresponsible!* part.

A few minutes later, Holly and Zak were back in the studio in their dance clothes. They completed their warm-up stretches and started learning their steps. Since it was purely a dance number – they would not be singing as well – they worked in time to the soundtrack. It was a very romantic routine. At first Holly felt awkward about getting quite so up-close-and-personal with Zak, but he was so chilled out about it, she soon got over her qualms.

'Fabulous,' Tory announced as she told them to take a break. 'You two dance beautifully together. Now, who wants to work on the swallow dive?'

'Yay!' Holly cried.

'Bring it on!' Zak agreed.

Tory explained exactly what they had to do and arranged thick safety mats on the floor. Miss LeClair and Miss Morgan took up positions as spotters in case Holly fell. 'Remember, dancing as partners is all about the three Ts: *trusting, timing and talking*!' Tory said.

Holly couldn't wait. She just *knew* they were going to nail it first time.

'*And one, and two, and . . .*' Tory counted her in. Holly checked Zak's position and ran four steps towards him, steadied herself and sprang. Zak grasped her by the hips and lifted. It was working. She was flying high, ready to balance and extend and hold with her stomach muscles . . . but something was wrong. She *wasn't* balancing. She was flying straight over Zak's head. She felt his grip tighten as he tried to slow her momentum, but she had launched herself too hard and it was like trying to hold back a rocket. Holly felt Miss Morgan and Miss LeClair grab her shoulders to break her undignified tumble onto the mats.

'Well done! Good first try!' Tory said enthusiastically.

'Are you all right, Holly?' Miss LeClair asked, pulling her to her feet.

Holly thought for a moment. She was winded, but nothing was hurting.

Nothing, that was, apart from her pride.

Zak was staring at his arms as if they were pieces of machinery that had malfunctioned.

'It was my fault,' Holly apologized. 'I jumped too fast.'

'No, dude. My bad! I was way late!'

Tory beamed at them. 'I can see you two trust each other and you're *definitely* talking. Now we just need to work on that third T: *timing*!'

Miss Morgan clearly thought they were doing *too much* talking. She clapped her hands impatiently. 'Starting positions again, you two! *Allora!* Tory doesn't have all day!'

But on the next try, Holly over-compensated and didn't force herself into the jump with anywhere near *enough* momentum; she slid down Zak's chest. Next time Zak didn't get a good hold. They tried again and again, but it just wasn't happening.

'OK, guys, enough for today!' Tory said finally. 'Good work!'

Zak kicked the edge of a mat. 'Good? We sucked, man!'

'You both lost your nerve a little after over-shooting on that first attempt,' Tory agreed, 'but you'll get there. This is only the first session.'

'Remember, Johnny and Baby didn't get the lift right first time in the movie either!' Miss LeClair said encouragingly. 'It will take time!'

'Not too much time, I hope!' Miss Morgan said, rather less encouragingly. 'We only have a few weeks!'

As they went through their cool-down exercises, Holly felt utterly miserable. She had failed in front of Tory King.

'Noodle-arms!' Zak was groaning, shaking his arms to show how floppy they were. 'Guess I'm not strong enough. Bummed out, man!'

Poor Zak, Holly thought. *It wasn't his fault. I was over-thinking and getting it wrong every time.* 'You *are* strong enough,' she told him. 'Remember at the football match?'

'Yeah, I was pumped with rage!' Zak said. 'Next rehearsal d'you think we could get a bunch of thugs sent in to yell *BALLET DANCERS ARE LAME!*'

Holly smiled. 'I'm sure it could be arranged.'

'Meantime, I'll hit the gym and work on my upper-body strength. We'll nail it *next* time!'

Yes, we will, Holly vowed to herself. *Whatever it takes!*

CHAPTER EIGHTEEN

Belle: Warrior Queens and Prima Donnas

Mr Garcia had decided to hold Monday afternoon's core singing lesson in the Gielgud Auditorium – the huge venue the school shared with the nearby university. This was where the Rising Stars Spectacular was to be staged, and they needed to work with the sound team on the whole-year chorus of *We Will Rock You*.

Belle hummed the first few lines of her solo, *I'm Not that Girl*, as she took a short cut across the sports field through the cold, crisp afternoon with Holly and Cat and the rest of Year Eight.

Her thoughts drifted happily back to the advanced singing class last Friday. Everyone had loved her solo. And she'd been working on it over the weekend so it was sounding even better now. She couldn't wait for the Spectacular to come round so she could perform it on a real stage to a real audience.

It was going to be awesome. It was everything she'd ever dreamed of.

Right now, Belle felt that *anything* was within her reach.

We Will Rock You wasn't *exactly* on Belle's playlist. But she was soon carried along by the big fat over-the-top rock anthem, swept up on the crest of a tidal wave of sound as all sixty students sang together and blocked out the steps they'd learned in Miss LeClair's class.

After an hour, Mr Garcia was so pleased with the results, he decided there was time to start work on another piece. He told the students to take a break while he went back to his office for the song sheets.

Belle sat down at the back of the stage with Cat and Holly and sipped from her water bottle. 'How's your voice holding up, Holly?' she asked.

'Great! Those exercises you taught Ruby and me are really helping. And so are these!' Holly took out a bag of lozenges and offered them round as Nick, Nathan, Gemma, Serena and more and more of their friends came up. 'It's like feeding bread to the ducks! Where *is* Ruby, anyway?' she added.

Belle pointed to the other side of the stage, where Ruby was huddled together with Jack. Every now and then they broke off and sang a few bars. 'Working on their duet by the look of it!' she said, smiling.

Suddenly Bianca appeared at the edge of the group, with a determined look on her face. Belle could tell she was after *something* – and she was pretty sure it wasn't a throat lozenge!

'Yeah . . . so, Belle, I'm going to talk to Mr Garcia when he gets back,' Bianca announced. 'They've put your solo after mine on the programme, but my song *clearly* has a bigger Wow Factor, so it should come *after* yours, not before!'

Cat jumped straight in on Belle's behalf. 'In your dreams, Bianca!'

'*Oh, wake up and smell the coffee!*' Bianca hissed. '*I'm Not That Girl* is just a weedy little I–love–him–but–he–doesn't–love–me number. It's going to be totally over-shadowed by *Popular!*'

Cat was spluttering like a stir-fry but Belle just shrugged. 'Fine by me!' she said. 'I don't care about the order, as long as I get to sing my solo!'

She was so-o-o rising above it today! No way was she going to let Bianca burst her happy-bubble!

Before Bianca could come back with a suitably cutting response, Jack and Ruby approached.

'Got that duet sorted then?' Nick asked.

Jack nodded. 'We're trying some extra harmonies . . . '

'I know! Why don't you try running through it now,

since Mr Garcia's not back yet?' Belle suggested. 'We could all sit in the auditorium and see how it sounds from there.'

'Oh, I'm sure nobody *really* wants to listen to us,' Ruby said modestly.

'Too right! We don't!' Bianca said, smiling spitefully.

'Yes, we *do*!' Holly protested. And everyone else – apart from Mayu and a few of Bianca's other friends – agreed that it was a great idea, and were already making their way down into the auditorium and taking seats in the front rows.

'Oh *puh-leese*!' Bianca scoffed, marching offstage. 'Come on, Mayu. Let's go and get a drink!'

As they began to sing, Belle was struck, as always, by the power and clarity of Jack's voice. It made the hairs on the back of her neck stand up – and that was even *before* she looked into those mysterious hazel eyes. Ruby's eyes, on the other hand, were ringed with thick black eyeliner. Technically, students weren't allowed to wear make-up during the school day, but the teachers must've got so used to Ruby's Goth look that they no longer noticed. She had a sweet, expressive voice and she harmonized beautifully with Jack.

A moment later Belle was distracted by a giggling-chattering-snorting sound. She glanced across and noticed Bianca and Mayu settling down on the other side of the aisle from her. They were noisily opening bottles of mineral water, laughing and pointing at the stage – as if they were watching a pantomime, not a love song.

'Shhh!' Belle whispered.

Bianca's eyes narrowed to shards of pale-blue glass as she turned slowly to face Belle across the aisle. 'And *who*,' she spat, 'put *you* in charge? Jack and Cat and Holly and all the rest of your little entourage might let you boss them about, but don't you dare try it on me.'

'Or me!' Mayu piped up, peeping round from behind Bianca.

'I'm *not* trying to be in charge,' Belle whispered patiently. 'It's just that you'll put Jack and Ruby off.'

Bianca pretended to choke on her drink. '*Put them off!* That's a joke!'

'What do you mean?' Belle whispered.

Bianca laughed. 'Oh, let's face it! Jack thinks he's Mr Cool, but he looks *ridiculous* up there with that Scooby Doo girl—'

'You mean *Ruby Drew* . . .' Belle corrected.

'*Scooby*, *Ruby*, whatever! She *looks* like Kung Fu

Panda! *Skidoosh!*' she added, imitating the podgy cartoon panda. Mayu giggled.

'That's not fair!' Belle was gripping the armrests, feeling angry now. OK, so Ruby was a little over-enthusiastic with the eyeliner and she wasn't exactly cocktail-stick thin, but so what? She was a sweet, shy girl who'd never done anything to hurt Bianca!

'And that *voice*!' Bianca continued, wincing and holding her hands over her ears. 'She has the vocal range of a fire alarm!'

Suddenly Belle noticed two things. One, Jack and Ruby had stopped singing. And two, her whispered conversation with Bianca had somehow escalated into a high-decibel shouting match. Bianca's fire-alarm comment had rung out for all to hear, amplified by the perfect acoustics of the auditorium!

Belle looked up at the stage. Ruby and Jack were staring down at Bianca. Ruby's mouth fell open. Then she burst into tears. Jack bent down and put his arm round her.

Everyone started talking at once.

'Oh, poor Ruby!' Holly gasped.

'The *witch-fiend-rat-snake*!' Cat growled, trying to push past Belle to get to Bianca.

'Who does she think she is?' Nick spluttered.

Belle had the strangest sensation: her friends' voices faded in and out as if she were scrolling through channels on the radio . . . then they were melting away completely. She had tunnel hearing as well as tunnel vision. And the only thing left in that tunnel was Bianca.

'Ah, diddums!' Bianca mocked. 'Little Panda Girl's all upsetty-wetty . . . Good thing your *boyfriend's* there to *comfort* her!' she added slyly.

'Ruby has a lovely voice,' Belle shouted, ignoring Bianca's feeble attempt to make her jealous, 'if you'd just give her a chance!'

'Oh, sure! I suppose next you'll be telling me that *munchkin* Nick Taggart has a "lovely" voice too! Poor Mayu actually has to try to sing a duet with him!'

'He *does*! AND HE'S NOT A *MUNCHKIN*!' Belle knew that she was yelling now, in a totally undignified way, but she no longer cared.

'Oh, excuse me, I forgot Nick's another of your *so-called* friends!' Bianca shot back. 'It's sad, really,' she continued, as if she were talking to Mayu. 'Belle *I'm-So-Superior* Madison over there hasn't even figured out that people are only *pretending* to be her friends because they're so-o-o-o impressed by her big-shot Mommy and Daddy. Why else would anyone want to hang out with a stuck-up, neurotic control-freak?'

Belle felt as if she'd been punched in the stomach.

Bianca had managed to root out her deepest, darkest fear and drag it into the light.

She fought a wave of nausea as a malicious voice inside her head screamed, *Bianca's right. No one likes you! They all think you got into Superstar High just because of your celebrity parents. Everyone you thought was your friend – Cat, Holly, Nick, Gemma, Serena, Nathan, Zak, even Jack . . . they all secretly laugh about you behind your back . . .*

Shakily, Belle rose to her feet. As if looking down the wrong end of a telescope, she was vaguely aware of Holly tugging her arm, Cat shouting, and Ruby still crying onstage . . . but all she could see was Bianca's triumphant face staring back at her across the aisle.

Belle's entire body was now pulsating with white-hot fury. She locked eyes with Bianca in a death-match glare. '*BIANCA HAYFORD*,' she shouted at the top of her voice '*AT LEAST I'M NOT A MEAN, BITTER, TWISTED—*'

'OH, WHAT IS YOUR *PROBLEM*?' Bianca screeched back.

And it was at that precise moment that Belle noticed Mr Garcia standing in the aisle at the front of the auditorium, a sheaf of papers in his arms. She didn't know how long he'd been there, but she knew, she absolutely *knew*, it was long enough to have heard her outburst.

Bianca's face froze as she followed Belle's gaze and saw Mr Garcia.

'YOUR *PROBLEM*, GIRLS,' Mr Garcia thundered, 'is that I have had it *up to here* with this ridiculous, childish *feud*. I go out for five minutes and I return to find the entire class reduced to a *war zone*, and you two in yet another cat fight!'

Belle felt her legs buckling beneath her. Reality started flooding back. There was uproar as everyone tried to give Mr Garcia their version of events. 'Quiet!' he boomed.

There was a long, long silence as he looked back and forth between Belle and Bianca, still standing staring at each other like rival warrior queens.

Then he smiled grimly. 'I *was* going to give you both detentions, but I've just had a much better idea! We've been looking for a way to cut down the Spectacular. It's running a little long. And you two have just made that job *much* easier!'

Belle's heart stopped beating. *He's cutting our solos!* She willed herself not to cry. She heard Bianca gasp.

'That's not fair, it was all Belle's fault,' Bianca muttered. 'You heard her, she said I was bitter and twisted – you can't take *my* number out because of *her*—'

'Enough!' Mr Garcia roared. 'Although neither of you deserve it, you *will* still get a number. And it's still from *Wicked*. But instead of solos, you will sing a duet together. Since you seem to have got into character already, *What Is This Feeling?* should suit you perfectly!'

Giggles and murmurs broke out among the class. 'For any of you who haven't seen *Wicked*,' Mr Garcia added, the anger in his voice giving way to amusement, 'it's sung by two schoolgirls expressing their *loathing* of each other. From what I've just seen, Belle and Bianca will have no trouble with it.'

'Oh no, *please* let us keep our solos,' Belle pleaded. She hated begging, but she hated the thought of losing her beautiful solo even more.

'*I'LL COMPLAIN TO MR FORTUNE!*' Bianca shouted, actually stamping her foot. '*YOU CAN'T DO THIS!*'

'I can, and I have,' Mr Garcia said bluntly. 'Now, it's entirely up to you,' he continued. 'You can either do the duet together. Or we can remove the whole *Wicked* section and you'll both be out of the show! If you are going to work in the real world, young ladies, you're going to have to learn to *get along* with other performers and not act like a pair of prima donnas!'

'OK,' Belle mumbled reluctantly, 'I'll do it.'

'Good!' Mr Garcia said, beaming at her.

'Well, I *won't*!' Bianca snarled. 'No way in a million years will I *ever* sing a duet with Belle Madison.'

'In which case,' Mr Garcia sighed, 'it would appear that this silly power struggle has cost you *both* your parts in the Spectacular. Now, we've wasted enough time on this – let's get *on*!'

CHAPTER NINETEEN

Belle: Hardcore Whingeing

By the time Belle left her room to go and do her piano practice a few hours later, her mood was at an all-time low. She'd lost her solo and – since Bianca refused point-blank to sing with her – she didn't even have the chance of a duet.

And what if Bianca's right? What if I am a stuck-up, neurotic control-freak and everyone hates me? Belle turned the dreadful question over in her mind for the thousandth time as she passed Miss Candlemas on the stairs. The housemistress noticed her bleak expression. 'Tough day, dear?' she asked kindly. 'Nice hot bath, that's what you need to perk you up. And call in for a chat if there's anything you want to get off your chest.'

Belle attempted a smile, but it was going to take more than a hot bath and a chat with Miss Candlemas to help her find her way out of this one.

★ ★ ★

She banged open the piano in the practice room and started crashing through her pieces. At the end of a particularly violent crescendo, she heard the door open behind her.

'I'm busy,' she snapped, without looking round.

'Busy demolishing that piano?'

Belle stopped playing and turned round. 'Oh, sorry, Jack,' she said. 'But if you've come to tell me to cheer up, *don't bother*!'

Jack sighed wearily as he slumped against the wall. 'Do I look like I'm in the cheering-up business?'

'What's the matter?' Belle asked.

'It's all these extra dance lessons. I feel like one of those bees, waggling my butt off all day . . .'

Belle jumped up and gave him a hug.

'I'm sorry!' Jack's voice was muffled by her shoulder. 'I know you've had a terrible day! Why don't we skip dinner and go to Café Roma for pizza? We can both have a really good moan.'

Belle nodded. It was the best idea she'd heard all day.

After signing out at Mrs Butterworth's desk, Belle and Jack hurried through the foggy March evening to the warm glow of Café Roma. The café was empty apart from a table of elderly ladies surrounded by shopping bags. They sat down and ordered pizzas – although neither of them was very hungry.

'You get first moan,' Belle offered, 'as it was your idea.'

Jack slouched in his chair and propped his chin on his palm. 'I'm doing so many catch-up lessons for dance,' he told her, 'that I just don't have time for anything else. I'm getting behind with my homework . . . and, more important, I've had to miss *two* football coaching sessions. I wouldn't mind so much if Miss Morgan and Mr Korsakoff weren't *yelling* at me all the time. If I'm not good enough, why can't I just give it up?' He grinned wearily. 'So, how was that for a bit of hard-core whingeing?'

'I'll give you ten for technical merit,' Belle teased, 'but only a five for originality!' She stroked his hand gently. 'It's only because they see so much potential in you that they're pushing you so hard. Holly told me you're doing brilliantly. Stick with it – at least until Easter.'

Jack nodded and sighed. 'Yeah, yeah, I know you're right. It's only a few weeks. And then I'll be hopping out of that dance class faster than the Easter Bunny!' He smiled at Belle. 'Your turn. What started the showdown with Bianca this afternoon? One minute

Ruby and I were singing *Let's Play a Love Scene*. The next thing, it was all shouting and wailing and gnashing of teeth. I didn't think our duet sounded *that* bad!'

Belle took a deep breath. The shroud of misery had lifted while she was thinking about Jack's problems, but now it enveloped her again as she remembered the afternoon's events. She picked up a straw and began to fiddle with it. 'It wasn't your singing! Bianca was making fun of Ruby, and then she started on Nick. And then, well, you heard the rest . . .'

'You mean the neurotic-control-freak-and-nobody-likes-you bit?'

'Yeah, that,' Belle said, nodding glumly.

Jack grinned. 'Promise me you will *never* listen to anything Bianca Hayford says ever again!' He stared at her for a long moment; so long that she couldn't hold his gaze and looked down at her half-eaten pizza. 'You're the most loyal, genuine, generous person I know,' he said quietly. 'That's what I love about you.'

Belle gulped and wiped away her tears with her napkin. 'Thanks, Jack,' she said simply. She couldn't express how much his words meant to her.

'You're welcome,' he said. Then he picked up his own napkin and wiped her cheek again. 'Er, melted cheese on your face!'

Normally Belle would have *died* if she'd smeared cheese on her face in public, but somehow, with Jack, it was OK.

'But I still don't have a part in the Spectacular,' she sighed. 'There's no way Bianca will sing that duet with me.'

Jack looked thoughtful for a moment. 'I bet deep down she's just as devastated about being out of the Spectacular as you are. But now she's announced – in front of the entire year – that she won't do the duet, her pride will make it hard to get her to back down.'

'Exactly!' Belle said. 'So it's Game Over for me too! You heard what Mr Garcia said!'

'Not necessarily. You just have to think of a really convincing way to persuade Bianca to sing with you.'

'*Persuade? Bianca?*' Belle asked incredulously. 'What d'you have in mind? *Dynamite?*'

'Er, yeah, that could be the tricky part,' Jack admitted, grinning. 'But I know you'll think of something. And I'm with Mr Garcia on this one. You and Bianca doing *What Is This Feeling?* would be amazing. You both have brilliant voices. Bianca's *perfect* as Galinda the Good, all vain and pleased with herself. And you are so right as Elphaba . . .'

'Thanks,' Belle said sarcastically. 'Nice to know my

boyfriend sees me as the Wicked Witch of the West!'

'You know what I mean!' Jack said. 'Elphaba stands up for what's right – just like you.'

Maybe Jack makes sense, Belle thought. 'Although if we do go through with it,' she said, thinking aloud, 'I can't promise not to kill her during rehearsals!'

Jack laughed, and Belle couldn't help laughing too. She looked down and noticed that she'd bent the straw she was fiddling with into the shape of a star. 'For you!' she said, grinning as she dropped it into Jack's hand.

As they got up to leave, they passed the table of elderly ladies. 'Young love!' one of them whispered to Belle. 'You hold onto him, dear!'

I will, Belle thought, slipping her hand into Jack's as they walked back to school.

CHAPTER TWENTY

Cat: The Mind of an Evil Genius

Meanwhile Cat was in her room helping Nathan with the steps for *You Can't Stop the Beat*. At least, she was trying to help, but Nathan's feet still weren't talking to the rest of his body. The friends ended up rolling on the floor, helpless with giggles.

Other than the small matter of Nathan's feet, Cat was really enjoying working on the Spectacular. Her solo was coming on fabulously, and because musical theatre wasn't her Life's Big Dream, she could relax and have fun with it, after the pressure of playing the super-serious Lady Macbeth role last term.

Nathan had just left when Belle returned from her meal with Jack. 'How'd it go?' Cat asked.

'Great!' Belle said, falling onto her bed. 'Jack really cheered me up!'

But despite her smile, her forehead was deeply furrowed. Cat could see that the fight with Bianca and the loss of her solo were still weighing heavily on her.

And when Holly arrived a few moments later, wearing a tracksuit over her dance clothes, *she* looked even worse! Her expression was positively *tragic*.

'Come on, you two!' Cat said. 'Tell Auntie Cat all about it!'

'It's my lift with Zak,' Holly groaned, collapsing onto Cat's bed next to her. 'We're never going to get it right . . . we've been working on it for hours . . .'

Cat had never seen Holly look so wretched. She was pushing herself way too hard. *Time*, Cat thought, *for some Tough Love!*

'Holly Devenish,' she scolded, 'take a reality check! What day is it?'

'Monday?' Holly answered, looking puzzled.

'And which day did you start practising this lift?'

'Er, Sunday.'

'Exactly! Sunday! Otherwise known as *yesterday*,' Cat pointed out. 'You've been working on this lift for *two days*. No wonder you haven't perfected it yet! Did Shakespeare give up on writing *Hamlet* because he'd not finished it in a weekend? I don't *think* so!'

Holly grinned. 'Yeah, I suppose . . . if you put it like that . . .'

'OK, that's you sorted,' Cat laughed, swatting Holly with a cushion. '*Next!*' she called, turning to

Belle, who was lying on her bed staring up at the ceiling.

'You already know what *my* problem is,' Belle said flatly.

'Bianca Hayford!' Cat and Holly replied in unison.

'*I'm* prepared to do the duet with her,' Belle said. 'It's better than not having a part at all. Jack says I just have to somehow talk Bianca into doing it too. But she's so proud it's going to have to be a *really* convincing argument to make her back down!'

Cat closed her eyes and put her palms together. 'This *Jack Thorne* speaks words of great wisdom,' she intoned in a mystical guru chant. 'You would do well to follow the path he counsels.'

'Yeah – just one *tiny* problem with that plan,' Holly pointed out. 'Much as I love Jack – in a totally non-romantic just-as-a-friend kind of way,' she added quickly, grinning at Belle, 'is he completely *off his trolley*? Trying to *talk* Bianca into doing something? You might as well try talking a man-eating tiger into taking up vegetarianism!'

'That's what I told him!' Belle groaned. 'Well, not the bit about being off his trolley, of course . . . But it's impossible . . .'

'Nothing's *impossible*!' Cat said, in her best positive-thinking team-building voice. 'It's just some things are, er, well, a bit less possible than others . . .' She paused, not quite sure where she was going with this. 'The point is,' she went on, 'we're going to have to play Bianca at her own game . . .'

'Which is what?' Belle asked.

'Tricks, lies, schemes . . . all the usual mean-girl weapons of minor destruction!' Cat laughed. 'What we need is a plan!'

'Ooh, I love plans!' Holly jumped up. 'Hang on a minute!' she called as she ran out of the door. Seconds later she was back from her own room with a pack of chocolate-chip cookies. 'You can't plan without the proper equipment!' she said, plonking the biscuits down on the low table in the centre of the room, and knocking several books flying in the process.

Belle reached into her mini-fridge and took out three Cokes. Then she hesitated and looked seriously from Cat to Holly and back again. 'Can I ask you something?' she asked gravely. 'Am I really a control freak?'

'No, of course you're not,' Holly replied instantly. 'Don't take any notice of Bianca!'

'We-e-e-ell . . .' Cat said slowly, as if giving the question serious thought. After all, you couldn't deny that Belle did sort of like to *organize* things . . .

'Ca-a-t!' Holly giggled, throwing a sock at her. 'Stop teasing!'

'OK! No, Belle, you are *not* a control freak,' Cat said firmly – but couldn't resist adding, 'You just have some control-freak tendencies . . .' She grinned at Belle's worried expression. 'But only in a totally constructive and well-adjusted way!'

'Good. Well, in that case,' Belle said, laughing, 'let's get some pencils and sheets of paper. We'll write down potential plans on one side, then fill in the pros and cons in two separate columns. *Neatly!*' she added, summoning Cat to the table and handing her a ruler.

Cat grinned at Holly. This was the Belle they knew and loved!

'*Allora*, girls! One, two, three, and *brainstorm!*' Cat cried, imitating Miss Morgan, rapping the ruler on the table.

They all looked at each other. They all took a biscuit, munched thoughtfully, and then took a drink. Holly held up her pencil, opened her mouth and then closed it again.

Think! Cat told herself. *How to trick Bianca into singing the duet with Belle?* 'Hypnosis!' she shouted. 'I've seen Paul McKenna do it on TV loads of times.'

'*Hyp-no-sis*,' Belle repeated as she wrote it on the

first page. 'Any of us know how that works?' They all shook their heads. She crossed it out.

'Blackmail!' Cat suggested.

Belle simply shook her head. 'I'm not even going to write that down!'

'We could write a letter from Mr Fortune telling Bianca she'll get detention if she doesn't do the duet?' Holly ventured.

'Good thinking,' Belle murmured as she wrote. 'But she still wouldn't agree. Bianca'd rather have a *month* of detentions than back down and sing with me.'

Belle was right. They had to think of something that Bianca would hate *even more* than doing the duet with Belle. Cat racked her brain. Suddenly it came to her! 'What would be Bianca's worst nightmare?'

'Enormous zit on the end of her nose?' Holly suggested.

Cat grinned. 'Even worse than that!' She paused for dramatic effect. Holly and Belle looked at her blankly. She sighed and gave in. 'Belle getting her solo back but *not Bianca*!' she told them. 'We've got to trick her into thinking that that's what will happen *unless she agrees to do the duet*! She'd do anything to stop it.'

Holly grinned. 'Cat Wickham, you have the mind of an evil genius!'

'I know!' Cat uttered an evil *moo-ha-ha*. 'I really ought to give it back!'

Belle didn't look quite so convinced. 'Will Bianca fall for it, though? Why would Mr Garcia suddenly give me my solo back after today's fiasco?' she asked.

But Cat had thought of that too. 'We'll say it's because you so graciously agreed to do the duet when Mr Garcia asked this afternoon. He decided it was unfair for you to lose out completely just because of Bianca being so stubborn.'

Belle nodded. 'Hmm . . . OK, that could work . . .'

'So we're just going to pop into Bianca's room and tell her this story?' Holly asked doubtfully.

Cat laughed. 'Oh no, we won't *tell* her anything!'

'How *are* we going to communicate then?' Belle asked with a puzzled look. 'Telepathy? Appearing in a dream?'

'*Through the magic of acting*, of course!' Cat said. 'We'll arrange for her to "overhear" us talking about it. That shouldn't be hard! Bianca could eavesdrop for England!'

Holly looked nervous. 'You know I'm not very good at acting . . .'

'You'll be fine, Hols,' Cat insisted. 'It's not like you have to go onstage being a fake Lady Macbeth this time! All we have to do is wait for the perfect moment . . .'

CHAPTER TWENTY-ONE

Holly: Seize the Pyjamas

Holly closed her eyes and drifted luxuriously towards sleep. She was exhausted after practising the swallow-dive lift with Zak for two hours earlier in the evening, so as soon as they'd finished hatching the get-Belle-a-duet plan, she'd said goodnight to Belle and Cat and returned to her own room. Gemma wasn't back yet so she left the lamp on.

A moment later, she heard the door open. She opened one eye to see Gemma come in, her hair wrapped up in a towel. Gemma smiled, then turned back to talk to someone behind her in the corridor. 'G'night, Cat. Don't bother trying to get into the bathroom, by the way,' she added. 'Bianca's been ensconced in there for hours. I had to use the one upstairs.'

Suddenly Holly felt someone tugging at the sleeve of her yellow polka-dot pyjamas. Cat had barged in past Gemma and was trying to pull her out of bed.

'Oomph! Cat! What are you doing?' Holly gasped.

'Seizing the moment!' Cat said. 'Let's go!'

'Where?' she squeaked.

'Bathroom! Bianca! Plan! Now!' Cat ordered.

'But I'm asleep!'

'No you're not!'

'I was until you attacked me!' Holly protested. 'Never mind seize the *moment*; this is seize the *pyjamas*!'

'Yeah, sorry about that, Hols, but you only left our room two minutes ago. I thought you'd still be up,' Cat said, still tugging impatiently.

Holly soon realized that resistance was futile. She yawned and rubbed her eyes as Cat bundled her along the corridor until they were outside the bathroom door.

'Come on!' Cat whispered. 'It's show-time!'

'But I don't know what to say!' Holly hissed.

'Yes you do!' Cat hissed back. 'Just act natural!'

'Natural?' Holly repeated slowly. 'I'm wandering around in my pyjamas, half-asleep . . . that's not natural . . .'

But Cat wasn't listening. 'HEY, HOLS, WAIT THERE! YOU'LL NEVER BELIEVE WHAT I JUST HEARD!' she bellowed in an excited, breathless voice.

Holly jumped back. *Had Cat gone bonkers?* Why was she suddenly shouting? 'What? What?' she asked, looking round in a panic. Then she realized Cat was *acting*. She'd started the plan!

'I JUST SAW JACK IN THE COMMON ROOM,' Cat went on, panting as if she'd sprinted up the stairs. 'HE SAID MR GARCIA'S GIVEN BELLE HER SOLO BACK! I CAN'T WAIT TO TELL HER!'

'WOW!' Holly bellowed. She tried to think of something to say next, but her mind was a blank. Thirty seconds ago it had been shutting down for the night; now it was expected to re-boot instantly and improvise something *natural*. It wasn't happening!

'*Wow!*' she said again lamely. Cat was frantically mouthing prompts to her. Holly could lip-read the words – *Ask me why Mr Garcia changed his mind* – but somehow she had lost the power of speech.

But just when it seemed the plan was doomed to failure, Gemma came hurrying back along the corridor. 'Did I hear that right?' she called. 'Belle's got her solo back?'

'Yeah!' Cat replied, her face lighting up with relief. 'It's brilliant, isn't it?'

'Fantastic! But how come Mr Garcia changed his mind?' Gemma asked in amazement.

Cat looked up and did a little *thank-the-Lord* celebration mime. 'It's because Belle agreed to do the duet,' she explained – loudly. 'He didn't think it was fair—'

'For Belle to lose out because of pig-headed

Bianca!' Gemma interrupted. 'Makes sense. I thought it was a bit harsh . . .' Then she turned to greet Ruby, who'd appeared at the top of the stairs. 'Hey, Ruby. Great news! Belle's got her solo back.'

'Hurray!' Ruby shouted. 'I've been feeling terrible about it!'

At that moment the bathroom door flew open and a thunderous – and rather damp – Bianca emerged in a cloud of perfumed steam and a fluffy white dressing gown. She had something that looked like a small blue cushion strapped to her forehead.

'Er, what's that?' Holly couldn't help asking.

Bianca rolled her eyes. 'Herbal cooling pack, if you *must* know! All this stress has given me one of my headaches . . .'

Holly stifled a giggle. Bianca was such a princess – if someone put a pea under her mattress, she wouldn't just be bruised black and blue in the morning, she'd have developed a severe pea allergy.

'Hey, Bianca! Did you hear about Belle's solo?' Gemma asked.

'Hear? How could I *not* hear with you lot yelling outside the door?' Bianca tightened her dressing-gown belt and elbowed her way stiffly past the assembled group. 'That's so-o-o-o Belle Madison!' she muttered.

'*Selfish, selfish, selfish!*' She continued to grumble as she headed along the corridor to her room. '*She's* got her solo back, so *she's* all right! Never mind the rest of us . . . Well, if she thinks she can just push me out of the show by sucking up to Mr Garcia, she's got another think coming! I'll *make* her do that duet with me!'

Holly and Cat exchanged broad, ever-so-slightly smug grins.

I won't be winning any prizes for Best Supporting Actress there, Holly thought.

But somehow it had worked.

Bianca had taken the bait!

By lunch time the next day, *everyone* had heard the news; Bianca and Belle were going to sing together in the Rising Stars Spectacular after all. Apparently, so the gossip went, Bianca had simply marched into Mr Garcia's office and volunteered to do the duet! But what had made her change her mind? No one could understand it! No one, that is, except Holly, Cat and Belle – oh, and Gemma and Ruby, of course. Holly and Cat had filled them in and sworn them to secrecy after they'd unwittingly played their parts in last night's Bathroom Door Conspiracy.

Holly and Belle sat down in the dining room to eat

their salads. Cat was in detention with Mrs Salmon for talking too much in yesterday's science class.

Belle pulled the song sheet for *What Is This Feeling?* from her bag and smoothed it out on the table to study it.

'If I'd told you this time yesterday that you'd be so happy at the thought of singing a duet with Bianca, you'd have said I was crazy,' Holly said, grinning.

Belle laughed. 'I know. But the duet is so much better than nothing – even if it does mean working with Bianca! I wish there was a way to thank Cat for coming up with that awesome plan.'

'There is,' Holly said. 'Operation Romeo . . .'

'But the date with Jellyfish Paul was such a disaster,' Belle groaned.

'All the more reason to start looking for the New and Improved Romeo Mark-Two.' Holly scanned the dining room. Suddenly her matchmaking antennae pricked up on Full Alert. She stared at a rowdy group of boys helping themselves at the baked-potato bar. One of them was juggling with three potatoes and the others were all laughing. 'Wait a minute! Are you thinking what I'm thinking?' Holly murmured.

'Only if you're thinking, *I could do with some French dressing on this salad,*' Belle replied.

'No! Look over there! *Jono Robertson!*' Holly

breathed. Jono was in their year, and he took several advanced dance classes with Holly. She peered over the top of her water glass, analysing him – like that robot-vision thing they always do in films, where computer-text prints out across the scene:

PHYSICAL APPEARANCE: GOOD; TALL, RUGGED, BLOND.
PERSONALITY TYPE: CONFIDENT, OUTGOING, FUN.
NATURAL HABITAT: RUGBY PITCH, DANCE STUDIO,
JOKING ABOUT WITH MATES.
POTENTIAL MATCH FOR CAT: **HIGH**.

Holly looked at Belle. Belle nodded.

'He *can* be a bit loud and cocky . . .' Holly said dubiously, remembering a few incidents when he'd argued with Miss LeClair about the best way to teach a jazz dance class.

'Even better!' Belle said. 'Didn't Cat complain about Paul having nothing to say? She won't have that problem with Jono!'

That's true, Holly thought. She watched him sit down at a table on the other side of the room. He plunged his knife into his potato, pretending it was putting up a fight. His friends all laughed. He did seem fun to be around, even if he *was* a bit over the top.

'Here's Jack!' Belle said, waving to him to join them. 'He knows Jono. I'll ask him to sound him out about asking Cat on a date.'

Belle quickly explained the situation to Jack, who agreed to act as Cupid's messenger. She and Holly watched as he sauntered over to Jono's table. There was a great deal of nodding and laughing.

Moments later Jack reported back. 'Jono says that Cat is *definitely* the foxiest girl at Superstar High. Obviously I had to put him right on *that* point!' he added, winking at Belle.

Belle smiled, blushing slightly.

'But does he want to ask her on a date?' Holly asked impatiently.

'Try stopping him!' Jack laughed. 'He'll send her a text.'

Mission accomplished! Holly thought.

At that point Cat came running into the dining room. She threw her bag down on the table. 'Arggh! That was the longest half-hour *ever*! Just me, Mrs Salmon and atomic compounds! I swear time started running backwards! I'm *starving* and I bet there's no decent food left . . .'

Cat paused, looking suspiciously around the table at Holly, Belle and Jack. 'Why are you three looking so pleased with yourselves?'

CHAPTER TWENTY-TWO

Cat: The Second Chocolate Brownie

But by Thursday afternoon there was still no text from Jono.

Cat and Belle stopped by the common room for tea and toast. Holly had stayed behind after advanced ballet to work on her swallow-dive lift with Zak.

Why *hadn't* Jono contacted her? Cat wondered. According to Belle and Holly, he'd been super-keen when Jack asked him. She couldn't help feeling disappointed. After the jellyfish experience, she'd been looking forward to going out with someone with a bit more *va-va-voom*. Whenever she'd seen Jono around the school, he always seemed to be the centre of attention.

And it didn't exactly do much for her confidence either! *Obviously*, she thought, *Jono's realized his terrible mistake! Oh*, that *Cat Wickham, you mean*, she imagined him saying. *The loud, chaotic Cat Wickham with the bum the size of Russia. I thought you meant the other Cat Wickham; the slim, elegant*, together *one*.

'Be patient!' Belle urged. 'Boys are always disorganized. I'm sure you'll hear by tomorrow.'

'I don't *do* patience!' Cat moaned.

'Boy troubles, dear?' Miss Candlemas asked, bustling into the common room. Her rainbow-coloured bangles and beads clinked together as she placed a huge platter of chocolate brownies on the table. 'Here, have one of these. Just out of the oven. Take your mind off it, eh?'

'*Scrum-a-licious!*' Cat sighed, taking a brownie. *Only one*, she told herself. *Just in case Jono ever gets it together and asks me out, I want to be able to fit into something smaller than one of Miss Candlemas's kaftans.*

'I could ask Jack to *remind* Jono about the date,' Belle offered.

'No way!' Cat protested, almost choking on her brownie. 'I don't want to end up on the bottom of his to-do list – with writing a letter to his granny and washing his socks!'

Cat looked up as Nick, Jack, Mason, Frankie and Nathan joined them at the table, swooping on the plate of brownies like a flock of seagulls.

'I heard you're going on a date with Jono this weekend, Cat,' Nick remarked.

'Thanks for announcing it to the entire world!'

she replied. She wasn't going to admit that it looked as if Jono had dumped her even *before* their date!

Nick bowed modestly. 'You're welcome! It's not a secret, is it?'

'Well, it's not *now*!'

'Let me know where you're going,' Nick said casually. 'I'll check whether Lettie's free and we'll come along and keep an eye on things again—'

'Nick, mate! Can't you just ask the poor girl out on a *real* date?' Frankie said. 'You *know* you want to!'

'Precisely!' Cat turned to look pointedly at Nick.

Nick pretended to be absorbed in the intricate task of surgically dissecting the chocolate brownie on his plate. Everyone stared, awed by the rare sight of Nick Taggart at a loss for words. 'So-o-o-o, anyone worked out who sent Gemma's mystery Valentine card yet?' he blurted eventually.

'Anyone spot the blatant attempt to change the subject?' Mason wondered.

'Leave poor Nick alone!' Belle said, coming to his defence.

'*SO THIS IS WHERE YOU'RE HIDING!*'

The friends all spun round to see Mayu – in a Barbie-pink hoodie and candyfloss-pink dance pants – torpedo into the common room like a heat-seeking fairy cake. '*Nick Taggart!* What are you doing in here scoffing brownies? We're meant to be rehearsing the steps for our duet!'

Nick jumped up immediately, clearly relieved to be spared further discussion of his love life.

But as he followed Mayu towards the door, his pace slowed.

'*Today!*' Mayu snapped.

'I'm on it!' Nick murmured with all the enthusiasm of a man being led to the guillotine. Cat couldn't help grinning. Mayu's constant complaints to Mr Garcia that Nick wasn't good enough to perform *I Am Sixteen, Going on Seventeen* had got her exactly nowhere; it was a like-it-or-lump-it situation, and there was a whole lot of lumping going on!

'*Hurry up, Nick!* It's two minutes past five already!' Mayu yelled.

Suddenly Belle gasped and dropped her chocolate brownie. '*Oh no!* I'm meant to be rehearsing my duet with Bianca with Mr Garcia at five!' She looked down at her watch and shook her wrist. 'It's stopped. I thought I had another ten minutes!'

Belle sprinted out of the common room after Nick and Mayu.

Cat realized that somehow she was halfway through

a second brownie that had jumped onto her plate and begged to be eaten.

Oh well, she thought, *Jono's never going to ask me out anyway . . .*

CHAPTER TWENTY-THREE

Belle: Show Me the Lobsters

Belle raced across the courtyard to the Singing Department.

Wouldn't Bianca just be in heaven *if she was late for their first rehearsal!*

She skidded round the corner to see Bianca standing outside the studio door with an icy smirk on her lips. 'You're late!' she spat.

'Sorry. Watch stopped. Where's Mr Garcia?' Belle panted.

'Not here yet,' Bianca admitted reluctantly.

'So, I'm not *actually* late then?'

Bianca glared at Belle and tossed her sharp blond bob. 'Look,' she said, 'let's get this straight. I don't *want* to do this duet—'

'And you think *I* do?' Belle asked sarcastically.

'Well, you should have thought about that before you had your little meltdown in Mr Garcia's lesson, shouldn't you?'

'Er, *my* little meltdown—?' Belle stopped herself and took a deep breath. If Mr Garcia caught them quarrelling yet again, it really would be curtains for both of them. *It's all about professionalism*, she told herself. *At least, that's what Mom always says.* Belle could hear her mother's voice now, telling her one of her professionalism stories . . . *Like the time I had to model a fake-fur bikini, posing in a giant tank of live lobsters. The guy who was meant to have bound up their claws was drunk and he missed half of them. I've still got the scars to prove it, but I kept on smiling to the end . . .*

'And another thing,' Bianca hissed as Mr Garcia and Mr Piggott, the pianist, approached. 'My name will appear before yours on the programme: *What Is This Feeling? by Bianca Hayford and Belle Madison.* It's *alphabetical*! Don't even *think* about sucking up to Mr Garcia behind my back to try and get it changed.'

Belle considered for a moment. *Bianca Hayford or a tank full of lobsters?*

Just give me the fake-fur bikini and show me the lobsters!

The two girls followed Mr Garcia into the studio. While he conferred with Mr Piggott at the piano, they sat down in opposite corners of the studio and started reviewing their song sheets in stony silence.

Mr Garcia turned round and looked from one to the

other. 'Yes, this number *does* start with the characters facing each other across the stage, but Miss LeClair will work on the choreography with you next week. For now let's just sing through the parts. Come into the middle.'

They stood up reluctantly.

'It won't *kill* you to stand a little closer!' Mr Garcia boomed.

I wouldn't be so sure of that, Belle thought. Slowly she inched towards Bianca. She looked up and caught a smile flickering across Mr Garcia's broad, dark features. She could be wrong, but was he finding this just a little bit *funny?*

Professionalism! Belle reminded herself.

As they began to work on the duet, she tried extra-hard to sing her part as expressively and powerfully as she could. She wasn't going to let Bianca Hayford outshine her! It seemed that Bianca felt the same way. Every time Belle sang her lines beautifully, Bianca raised her game and sang hers even better. Which prompted Belle to redouble her efforts on the next line.

It was more like a duel than a duet!

'Fabulous!' Mr Garcia enthused. 'I *love* the hatred in your voices. I'm really getting that loathing, that contempt. It's absolutely poisonous!'

'It would be better if Belle didn't keep singing off-key!' Bianca grumbled.

'I'm not! It's you!' Belle retaliated.

'No one's singing off-key!' Mr Garcia told them. 'Isn't that right, Mr Piggott?'

The pianist nodded. 'They both have perfect pitch.'

'You see, you two *do* have something in common!' Mr Garcia said, beaming.

Belle forced herself to smile weakly at his joke. At least *he* seemed to be enjoying this! Bianca, on the other hand, glared at him with a wind-chill factor well below freezing.

Eventually they came to the end of the song – where Belle's character, Elphaba, leans forward and shouts 'Boo!' so that Galinda screams and jumps back, afraid. Belle waited for the music to die away, keeping an eye out for Mr Garcia to cue her.

'Boo!' she shouted.

'What?' Bianca muttered, stepping back and tripping over a chair.

'*Boo!*' Mr Garcia said. 'It's in the song sheet, Bianca, if you'd bothered to look at it.'

'I didn't think we'd be doing that bit on the first run-through!'

'Well, we are,' Mr Garcia replied. 'Let's try again. From the last chorus!'

'*Boo!*' exclaimed Belle.

Bianca hesitated. 'Ahh!' she exclaimed feebly.

Mr Garcia groaned. 'You're meant to sound *startled*! Not mildly peeved!'

'It was Belle!' Bianca griped. 'She didn't say it in a very *startling* way!'

On the next attempt Bianca screamed too early. She complained that Belle had missed her cue. 'It's Belle!' she insisted. 'She's booing all wrong *deliberately* to put me off!'

Mr Garcia swallowed hard. He *almost* looked as if he were stifling a giggle. 'Belle's boos are fine!' he said. 'Now, let's try one last time!'

Time for desperate measures, Belle thought. On cue, she leaned in close and shouted, 'Boo!' She also sneakily shot out her hand and pinched Bianca's arm.

'*ARGGHHHH!*' Bianca screamed.

'At last!' Mr Garcia exclaimed. 'That was perfect! This duet is going to bring the house down!'

'If you *ever* pinch me again,' Bianca hissed through her teeth, 'I'll report you for bullying. I bruise easily, you know!'

'Just be thankful it wasn't a lobster!' Belle whispered back.

Bianca looked confused and rubbed her arm.

At the end of the rehearsal they gathered up their music and, without so much as looking at each other, stormed out of the door.

In opposite directions.

Mr Garcia is right! Belle realized as she marched down the corridor. *Our duet is going to sound fabulous. We just have to make it to the Spectacular without strangling each other first!*

CHAPTER TWENTY-FOUR

Cat: Yawnsville

When Cat checked her phone on Friday night and saw that her inbox contained a text from Jono, she was determined to refuse his invitation. How *dare* he ask her out on a Friday and *expect* her to be available at the weekend? For all he knew, her diary was already *crammed* with social engagements.

But then she read the text! DATE TMRW? V&A MUSEUM. MEET HALL 10? JONO.

Cat stared at the message. *The Victoria and Albert Museum!* Only one of the finest museums of art and design in the universe! She'd always wanted to go there.

I'd go on a date with the Incredible Hulk if he asked me to the V&A! she thought as she texted back: Yes. cu@10.

Next morning, Jono insisted they take a taxi to the museum, even though it was only a few stops away on the underground. While he kept her entertained with his impersonations of the Garrick School teachers on the journey, Cat studied him surreptitiously: *Definitely quite good-looking*, she thought, *in a blond, broad-shouldered, rugby-playing Viking way*. She wasn't actually sure whether Vikings ever played rugby – in between all that burning and pillaging – but if they did, Jono would fit right in.

And she'd managed to do up the zip on her slinkiest black skirt – in spite of that second chocolate brownie – so all was hunky-dory in Cat-Wickham World as they arrived at the museum.

When they walked into the beautiful, grand Victorian building, Cat stood in a trance, soaking up the atmosphere, breathing in the refined scent of wood polish and culture.

Meanwhile Jono was poring over the guidebook. 'I've worked out the most efficient route,' he declared. 'We start here and work our way through these galleries, allowing fifteen minutes for each . . .'

Cat bristled a little at Jono's sergeant major tone. *What is this? A military campaign or a leisurely browse around a lovely museum?* But she bit back her objections. They had plenty of time and there was so much to see. This was going to be fun!

But that's where she was wrong! Jono charged

through the galleries like a hyperactive rhino. He hardly glanced at the exhibits. Instead he speed-read the notes out loud and pronounced his opinion on each one, before galloping off to see something he judged to be older, rarer or just generally better round the next corner. Whenever Cat lingered to stare in wonder at a piece of jewellery or glasswork or sculpture, he would drag her away to look at another collection. '*Rather poor example of its type!*' he pronounced as they whizzed past an oriental tapestry; '*Outstanding attention to detail,*' he commented, hustling her past a silver tray.

Eventually Cat could bear it no longer. Her legs were aching from the high-speed route-march and her head was spinning from information overload. She sank down on a bench.

Jono looked at his watch. 'Three-minute break, then on to the photography galleries . . .'

Cat's heart sank. She really wanted to see the theatre and performance collection – especially a first folio of Shakespeare's plays that she knew was on display there. 'Let's go straight to the theatre collection,' she suggested.

Jono consulted his map. He shook his head. 'Ooh, no, you don't want to do that!' he said knowledgeably.

'That would take us way off course. We've got at least ten more galleries first.'

Ten more galleries! Cat wasn't sure she was going to survive that long.

Not on an empty stomach, anyway. 'OK, but let's have lunch first,' she said. 'We just passed the café.'

Jono checked his watch again. 'We'll wait another hour. The queues will have died down by then. That's the *best* time to eat . . .'

Cat ground her teeth. If there was one thing she hated – even more than Mrs Salmon's science lessons and pickled gherkins – it was being told what to do, and she'd been putting up with it all morning. 'No, Jono!' she snapped, unable to hide her annoyance any longer. 'The *best* time to eat is before you pass out from hunger!' With that, she jumped up and headed for the café.

Jono followed her. There *was* no queue and they were soon sitting eating lunch. Jono munched on his sandwich, a sulky look clouding his clear blue eyes.

But revived by a large slice of cake, Cat found her irritation subsiding. She realized that Jono was happy as long as he got his own way on just two minor things: 1) everything he said, and 2) everything he did. Well, he wasn't going to get away with *that*! But he wasn't so bad. At least he had plenty to say for himself! 'Come on then,' she said, smiling brightly as she brushed crumbs off her skirt. 'Photography next, did you say?'

Jono studied the map. 'Yes, there's a history of photography exhibition that's a definite must-see. Then we'll work through the rest of the collection . . .' he said, cheerful again now that they were back on course – *his* course!

Finally they reached the theatre and performance collection. Cat was almost keeling over with exhaustion as she looked around for the Shakespeare folio.

'Oh no, you don't want to *start* with that!' Jono called after her.

'Er, yes I do!' Cat objected.

'There are some costumes we need to look at first!'

Suddenly Cat spotted the folio. Without waiting for Jono, she marched straight over and gazed in awe at the beautiful book with its engraving of William Shakespeare, her hero, on the front. *The first collection of all his plays*, Cat marvelled, *printed in 1623!*

'*Shakespeare . . . blah! First folio . . . blah!*' Jono said, reading over her shoulder. 'I've seen one before in the British Library. *Yawnsville!*'

Shakespeare? Yawnsville? Cat couldn't believe her ears.

'Come on!' Jono grumbled, pulling at her arm. 'Shakespeare exhibits are always so overrated!'

That was the last straw! Cat snatched her arm away. 'I'M STAYING HERE!' she yelled, ignoring the glare from the museum attendant in the corner.

'OK, just for a minute,' Jono agreed, pouting like a toddler.

Cat looked up. She could see Jono's reflection in the glass cabinet. He was standing behind her checking his watch. He was *actually* timing her! *This was mental cruelty!* Cat felt the temperature inside her head soaring out of control, as if she'd bitten into a hot, hot chilli. Another second of Jono and his know-it-all opinions and she was going to explode!

Suddenly she noticed, lurking stealthily on the other side of the gallery, two shadowy figures dressed all in black.

Time to make my escape, Cat thought.

Dragging Jono towards the undercover duo, she called out, 'Nick, Lettie! What an amazing coincidence! You're here too!'

Lettie smiled back at her. Nick shuffled sheepishly. *He thinks I'm going to give him a rocket about stooging in on my date!* Cat realized. *How wrong can you be?* She clapped her hand over her mouth and gasped, 'Oh no!

Seeing you two here has reminded me. We've got that science homework for tomorrow. Sorry, Jono, gotta run.'

Yes, she was relying on the old homework-emergency chestnut again – not exactly original, but it worked every time!

At least it did if Nick Taggart didn't put his foot in it! 'I don't remember any science homework—' he started.

Cat glared at him, trying to convey the words *N-o-o-o, you idiot!* without Jono seeing.

'Oh yes!' Lettie interrupted. 'It's a . . . special project. Mrs Salmon will go ballistic if it's not in tomorrow!'

Cat shot her a look of eternal gratitude. Unlike Nick, Lettie had recognized the international signal for Girl in Need of Assistance Requests Immediate Backup and thrown her a lifeline!

'Yeah, well, I was planning to leave anyway!' Jono declared. 'Best time to go, now! Before the traffic gets bad.'

As the taxi pulled up to the school gates, Jono twisted round in his seat and leaned towards Cat as if he was going to say something. *Probably going to tell me the best way to get out of a taxi*, she thought grumpily. But he didn't speak; he just leaned further. 'Oh, it's OK, I can get the door myself!' Cat mumbled. But still Jono was coming closer, pressing into her shoulder. *OK, personal-space invasion going on here!* He closed his eyes and opened his mouth with a kind of vacant, faraway expression.

Oh no, he's trying to kiss me!

'Off to the library! Thanks! Bye!' Cat shouted, springing out of the taxi as if propelled by an ejector seat.

She didn't stop running until she was safely in the library, where she collapsed into a chair.

'Uh-oh!' came a voice from the other side of the table. 'Jellyfish trouble?'

Cat looked up to see Adam grinning at her. She shook her head, too breathless to speak.

'Or is it zombies again? There's a lot of them about these days!'

Cat laughed. Then Adam's T-shirt caught her eye. It featured a carnival design and the words SAMBA LIKE YOU MEAN IT!

'You admiring my perfectly formed torso, or what?' Adam asked with a grin.

'Er, sorry!' Cat giggled. 'It's your T-shirt. I love samba.'

'Me too!' Adam said enthusiastically. 'Are you taking advanced Latin dance classes?'

'Yeah,' Cat replied. 'Except I had to drop them last term when I was Lady Macbeth. And now I'm doing a solo in the Rising Stars Spectacular, I've had to drop some again to do extra singing.'

'Wow! Talk about multi-talented!'

They were still whispering and laughing when Cat looked up to see Belle entering the library, and waved to her.

'What are you doing in here?' Belle asked. 'I thought you were at the V and A? Anyway, we're throwing a surprise party for Gemma's birthday. Serena and Zak are up in Holly's room now getting it ready. Come and help me find Gemma and delay her a while.'

As they hurried off to search of Gemma, Belle asked her, 'So, how'd it go with Jono? I'm dying to hear all about it!'

Cat thought for a moment. 'Let's just say he thinks Shakespeare is overrated . . .'

'Ooh! That's bad!' Belle groaned. 'I guess Holly and I are going to have to do some target practice. Our Cupid's arrows aren't exactly hitting the bull's-eye!'

CHAPTER TWENTY-FIVE

Holly: The Flying Fish

Holly and Zak were determined that *this time* they would crack that swallow-dive lift.

It was Sunday afternoon and they were warming up for their second lift rehearsal with Tory King at the Covent Garden dance studio.

'Stoked, dude!' Zak replied, bouncing on the balls of his feet, when Tory asked how they were. 'Been working out in the gym all week for this!'

'Yeah! Stoked!' Holly repeated, trying to rally herself into feeling confident.

But no matter how many times they tried, it *still* wasn't happening.

'No problem, guys!' Tory said kindly after their third attempt. 'Don't beat yourselves up over it. Let's work up a simpler lift that we can swap in – just in case.'

Holly's heart went into freefall. She had let Tory King down! Zak was sitting on the edge of a mat, staring disconsolately at the floor. All his bounce had gone.

They soon mastered the simpler lift. Zak bent his knee for Holly to use as a step to boost herself up. Once aloft, she then kept one knee on Zak's shoulder, stretching the other leg out behind her. It was a nice lift, but it wasn't the *real thing*.

It wasn't the swallow dive.

More like the swallow-jumping-in-at-the-shallow-end-holding-its-nose, Holly thought. *And swallows don't even have noses!*

'We're not giving up yet,' she promised Tory. 'We're going to nail the swallow dive next week if it kills us!'

Zak nodded and mustered a brave grin. 'Yeah! Death or glory!'

Holly and Zak hardly spoke on the return journey. Miss Morgan was clearly frustrated too. Although she wasn't *saying* anything, her driving was even more death defying than usual.

Holly leaned her cheek against the cold car window. All the self-doubts she'd felt as she waited to dance her solo in *Nutcracker Sweeties* flooded back: *I shouldn't be here, there's been a mistake . . . I'm not good enough for Superstar High . . .*

Back at school she trudged after Zak into the entrance hall.

'Hey, you guys looking for a cliff to jump off or something?'

The disembodied voice came from the big leather sofa. Holly saw Jack peering over the back of it.

'Dude!' Zak groaned, sinking down into an armchair. 'It's our *Dirty Dancing* lift!'

'Tell me about it!' Jack said with a pained grin. 'I've just survived a two-hour catch-up ballet class with Mr Korsakoff. Feels like I'm in training with the SAS.' He stretched his legs and winced. 'It's dancing, mate! It's bad for your health!'

Holly slumped onto the arm of Zak's chair. She tried to give Jack a sympathetic smile but somehow it came out all wrong and turned into a sob. Zak put his arm round her and patted her shoulder. Holly fought to hold back the tide of tears . . .

'Have you tried doing the lift in the pool?' Jack asked.

'In the pool?' Holly repeated dumbly, so surprised her tears stopped in their tracks.

'Yeah – that's how Johnny and Baby learn the lift in the film, isn't it? In a lake?'

Holly's brain was working so fast she could feel the G-force. *Why didn't I think of it before?*

'Gnarlacious idea!' Zak shouted, high-fiving with Jack.

But then Holly thought of a problem. 'There are no mirrors in the pool. How will we know what we look like?'

'Yeah, point . . .' Zak agreed.

'I'll do it!' Jack offered. 'I can tell you how it looks. I could even help lift Holly into position if you want . . . I know how hard you guys have been working and how much it means to you. There *must* be a way to crack it!'

Holly's heart lifted. 'Jack! Thank you, that would be brilliant!'

Zak leaped to his feet. 'What're we waiting for?'

'What, *now*?' Jack gasped.

'No time like the present,' Holly said. 'Let's get our swimming things and meet at the pool in ten minutes . . . '

Zak held out his hand and pulled Jack to his feet. 'Surf's up, dude!' he cried.

From that moment on, Holly and Zak spent all their free time in the pool, usually with Jack there to assist. Holly was able to try different approaches without worrying about injury if she overshot or if Zak collapsed. By the time they finished their early-morning session the following Thursday, she knew they were almost there . . .

'I think we're ready to try again in the studio tomorrow!' Holly said happily as they left the sports centre.

'Time for a *dry* run!' Zak quipped.

Suddenly Holly looked up and noticed Ethan standing at the bottom of the steps. She felt a pang of guilt. She'd been so busy she'd hardly seen him recently. Even though he was a keen swimmer himself he was probably getting a *little* fed up with having a girlfriend who spent so much time leaping around in the pool; it must be like going out with a performing dolphin! But she needn't have worried. Ethan swept her up in a big hug and kissed her.

'Mmm!' He grinned. 'Chlorine! My favourite!'

Then he presented her with a box of chocolate truffles. 'To keep your energy levels up!' he said.

Holly hugged him back. 'Thank you! I need it.'

'So, where's mine, dude?' Zak demanded.

'What? You want a kiss too?'

Zak grimaced. 'Er . . . I think I'll go for the chocolates!'

Holly and Jack laughed. Suddenly Holly realized she

was starving. 'This calls for a disgustingly enormous breakfast,' she announced.

'So, you guys cracked that lift yet?' Ethan asked as they headed towards the dining room.

Holly nodded. She hardly dared say it but she was finally starting to believe they were going to make it.

'Yeah, we're gonna *own* that move!' Zak said. 'Thanks to our personal trainer here!' He turned to Jack with a we're-not-worthy gesture.

Jack grinned. 'Thanks! I think I'm as psyched up as you two about getting this lift to work. I was even dreaming about it last night! It's like I'm on a mission or something.'

'You mean you've finally seen the point of dance?' Holly asked, smiling.

'I wouldn't go *that* far!'

Holly piled her plate with scrambled eggs and toast and sat down with Ethan, Jack and Zak. Moments later they were joined by Cat and Belle. Belle was looking elegant, as always, in Diesel jeans and Prada shirt, her long blonde hair like a sheet of silk. Cat – in her black dress and boots, auburn curls swept up in a tumbledown twist secured by a pair of pencils – looked ultra-glamorous even though she'd only crawled out of bed two minutes earlier. Holly was suddenly conscious of her ancient comfort-zone jumper and leggings and her damp braids stuffed haphazardly under a hairband. Not to mention the chemical tang of chlorine which was battling it out with the smell of frying bacon, Cat's new Kate Moss perfume and Belle's shampoo.

But Holly was too happy to care as she updated her friends with a swallow-dive progress report.

'Awesome!' Belle said. 'You deserve to succeed after all your hard work.'

Cat agreed. 'But we need to re-name that lift. From now on it's the flying fish!'

They were all still laughing when Felix Baddeley sauntered over to their table, along with a boy Holly didn't recognize. 'Hey, guys,' Felix said. 'This is Orlando Spicer – he's just started in Year Ten. Transferred from Prestige Theatre School . . .'

'And you've got *Felix* to show you the ropes! Good luck, mate!' Ethan joked.

Felix retaliated by snagging a piece of bacon off Ethan's plate, and started introducing everyone to Orlando. But Holly wasn't listening. She was too busy *staring*. Dark wavy hair, cheekbones to die for and smouldering brown eyes. Holly wasn't exactly sure what *smouldering* meant, but whatever it was, Orlando's eyes were absolutely doing it. And those eyelashes! He looked as if he was wearing triple-volume-extra-boost mascara.

In fact, if you looked up *handsome* in the dictionary, you'd find a picture of Orlando Spicer staring back at you.

Holly realized she was pouring orange juice on her toast and quickly put down her glass.

'Orlando's a musical mastermind,' Felix was saying. 'He composed a rock opera *and* staged it at Prestige . . .'

'So how come you left there?' Ethan asked.

'Oh, you know, it was kind of a personality-clash thing,' Orlando said vaguely. Even his voice was gorgeous! 'But I heard they *appreciate* talent at Superstar High, so I should fit right in here!'

Everyone laughed. Orlando flashed a heart-melting smile. His perfect teeth were toothpaste-advert white.

'Hmm, that's nice . . .' Holly murmured vaguely, her mind on other things. Well, one other thing, to be precise: Operation Romeo! *OK, Jono was another wipeout, but third time lucky! Orlando seems to have a good sense of humour, and with those looks . . . he could be perfect for Cat.*

Belle raised one eyebrow – just enough to tell Holly

she was thinking exactly the same thing: *Cupid mode engaged!*

And it seemed that Cat had already caught Orlando's eye. 'Loving that hair,' he said. 'Is it true that redheads are hot-blooded and fiery?'

'Oh, I've been known to sizzle on occasion,' Cat shot back in a super-casual tone.

Holly looked at Belle in amazement. *Wow!* she thought. *That line was straight out of* The Good Flirting Guide. *Maybe Cat doesn't need the Devenish and Madison Matchmaking Agency after all!*

CHAPTER TWENTY-SIX

Belle: Total Warfare

Belle and her friends were lounging listlessly in the entrance hall the following evening. Although it was Friday night, no one had any plans. They'd all been working so hard all week that they didn't have the energy to go out. But they were bored by the thought of staying in! Nick and Zak suggested they play a game of Twister in the common room. No one could quite be bothered. Cat, Nathan and Serena proposed a game of charades. That was too much effort. 'What about a film?' Holly said.

But this just led to an argument. Gemma, Lettie and Ruby wanted to watch *Twilight*, but Jack, Frankie and Mason fancied an old *Star Wars* movie. Belle sighed. *Maybe I'll just go have a bath*, she thought. *If I can make myself get up off the sofa . . .*

Then she heard a clattering sound and looked up to see Bianca and Mayu descending the main staircase like special guests on a TV chat show. Both were wearing designer dresses – last season's John Galliano, Belle thought – and industrial quantities of make-up. Bianca was stunning in shimmering black satin; Mayu, in her trademark pink-with-a-hint-of-pink, was wearing a fishtail skirt so tight she could hardly move her legs. She was having to jump down each step.

They were obviously not planning to spend the evening slouching around on the sofa.

'In case you're wondering,' Bianca announced to the room in general, 'we're off to a charity fashion show in Knightsbridge . . .'

'There are rumours Miley Cyrus will be dropping in . . .' Mayu added.

Belle felt a twinge of jealousy. That sounded like fun. *Who-o-o-oa!* she thought. *I must really be bored if going out on the town with Bianca and Mayu sounds tempting!*

Suddenly the entrance hall was ringing with shouts and yells, and Belle watched in amazement as a raucous group of Year Ten boys, including Ethan, Felix and Orlando, hurtled towards the front doors. Ethan turned and doubled back. 'Come on, you lot!' he called, pulling Holly to her feet. 'Snow!'

Belle was caught up in the excitement as everyone rushed off to put on their coats and gloves and then piled out into the snowy evening.

She stood at the top of the front steps and gazed out in wonder. A thick white duvet covered the broad gravel drive, the stately plane trees of Kingsgrove Square and the Garrick School buildings. There'd been no snow when they'd come out from their afternoon lessons. But it must have been falling steadily ever since, while they were having dinner and sitting around in the hall. There was that special snow-smell and that special snow-hush. A lone taxi swished slowly along Kingsgrove Road, its lights glowing orange in the darkness.

Belle had *seen* snow before, of course, in ski resorts and in New York. But she'd never seen *London* snow.

And she'd *never* been in a snowball fight!

She jumped as the first snowball thudded softly against her shoulder. Nick was standing grinning on the drive, his arm still raised. 'Get him back!' Holly shouted as she aimed. Nick ducked and the snowball hit Jack smack on the nose.

'Revenge!' Jack yelled, firing a snowball at Holly. It missed and hit Ruby.

'Come on! It's girls against boys!' Cat said, charging down the steps.

Before Belle had time to think, snowballs were flying everywhere. It was total warfare!

'No way!' Gemma laughed as Zak grabbed a handful of snow and shmushed it down the back of her neck.

Holly caught hold of Belle's arm and pointed. 'Look at those two!'

Belle glanced up and spotted Bianca and Mayu, ducking to avoid the crossfire as they tottered down the steps and across the drive towards their waiting taxi. She watched as Bianca fended off a snowball, using her sequinned handbag as a shield.

'No, not *those* two!' Holly told her. '*Those* two!'

Now Belle saw that Holly meant Orlando and Cat. Orlando was bombarding Cat with a volley of snowballs. Cat fought back, then they both collapsed, giggling, into a snow-covered laurel bush.

Belle grinned. 'I think we've found our Romeo at last!'

'The love-o-meter is going off the scale!' Holly agreed.

'Now we just need to set them up on a da—' Belle's words were drowned out by a snowball in her face, courtesy of Felix.

She launched a snowball back at him. 'Way to go!' the girls all shouted as it knocked off his hat.

Some time later the friends tumbled back into the entrance hall, feet and fingers tingling and faces glowing. They headed for the common room, where Miss Candlemas was already handing out steaming mugs of hot chocolate, complete with marshmallows. They settled down by the fireplace, happily thawing out in the warmth. Belle sighed contentedly. This was so much more fun than a charity fashion show!

She listened lazily to the conversation around her. Felix was chatting about The Undertow's preparations for the Battle of the Bands. 'I hope you guys will be able to do another gig with us soon,' he said to her. 'Nobody's Angels are one cool band!'

Belle exchanged smiles with Cat and Holly. She couldn't wait to start up their band rehearsals again, and to play some more gigs – and she knew the other two felt the same way. 'As soon as we get back next term!' she promised. 'And I was hoping you might write us another new song,' she said, turning to Lettie.

Lettie smiled modestly. 'Of course! I've had an idea for a love song . . .'

'Lettie is an amazing songwriter!' Cat explained to Orlando, who had settled down on the beanbag next to her. 'Oh, didn't Felix say you'd composed some rock music at your last school? Maybe you and Lettie could work together on something . . .'

Lettie looked pleased.

Orlando leaned back and slowly batted his killer eyelashes. 'Actually, I composed a fully orchestrated three-hour epic rock opera,' he said. '*Slightly* different league to a little pop song!' He smiled self-importantly, seemingly unaware of the uncomfortable silence that greeted his pompous words. 'In fact, to be honest, girls aren't cut out for composing anything *serious*. They just don't have the brainpower . . . the *intellectual capacity* . . .' He paused and looked around, as if waiting for the boys in the group to agree with him. But none of them did. Most of them were just staring in disbelief . . .

He must *be making a joke*, Belle thought, *even if it's a pathetic one!* She waited for Orlando to laugh. But he didn't.

He was deadly serious.

Then it hit her: he'd been serious yesterday when he said his old school didn't appreciate his superior talent. They'd all thought he was joking then too!

The silence dragged on, the dreadful brainpower comment hovering in the air like a flashing neon sign.

No wonder he'd had a 'personality clash' at Prestige. Coming out with comments like that wasn't going to make him popular *anywhere*.

Except, maybe, the Annual Conference of the Obnoxious Sexist Thugs Society!

Cat shrank away from Orlando's side as if he were a giant slug leaving a trail of slime along her arm.

Belle and Holly exchanged horrified looks. Half an hour ago they'd been planning to set Cat up on a date with this guy!

Maybe, Belle thought, *we should keep that fact to ourselves!*

CHAPTER TWENTY-SEVEN

Cat: Through with Frog-kissing

Cat was sitting in her room the next morning staring blankly at a page of maths problems when Belle, Holly and Gemma persuaded her to join them in the art room to help paint the old-fashioned street-scene backdrop which would be used for several of the numbers in the Spectacular, including her solo, *Wouldn't It Be Loverly?*

Not that she took much persuading! *Quadratic equations or chatting with friends while waving a paintbrush around?* Tough decision!

Two hours later they were walking back across the courtyard on the way to lunch when Cat stopped suddenly. '*Yikes!*' she whispered. Jono and his friends were outside the Dance Department building a snowman – or rather snow*woman* – which looked uncannily like Miss Morgan, complete with large stick in her hand.

Cat had been avoiding Jono ever since the museum date. She knew from the stack of texts in her inbox that he wanted to see her again, but she couldn't face another Death by A Thousand Opinions. He was probably holding forth on the best method of snowman construction even now,

Oh no! He was coming towards them.

'In here!' Cat hissed, dragging the other three through an unmarked door.

'What?' stammered Gemma.

'Where?' gasped Belle.

Crash! Thud! Oomph!

'Shhh!' Cat hissed, shutting the door behind them. 'Jono alert!'

'I know this place!' Holly whispered in the darkness. 'It's the kitchen storeroom.'

'It's a secret passageway,' Cat explained. 'You know, like in Cluedo! It comes out in the entrance hall, next to the dining room. I've escaped from Mrs Salmon in here before.'

'Put the light on!' Gemma begged. 'It's creepy!'

Cat fumbled for the switch. Blinking in the glare, she looked down to see Holly spread-eagled in a box of carrots.

'Quick – let's get out of here before Mrs Morecambe finds us!' Cat imagined the look on the cook's face if she opened the storeroom door and found them sabotaging her vegetable supplies.

'OK,' Cat said as they sat down at a table with their soups and salads, 'it's official! You three have taken the last decent boys in this entire school – Ethan, Jack and Gemma's mystery Valentine, whoever *he* is. There's no one left for me!'

'Don't give up!' Holly said. 'We'll find Mr Right in time to use those *Romeo and Juliet* tickets!'

'Yeah,' Belle agreed. 'They say you have to kiss a lot of frogs before you find a prince!'

Cat snorted into her soup. 'Uh-uh! I'm totally through with frog-kissing. And I don't *want* a prince. I just want somebody with a mind of his own who isn't a know-it-all or offensive to women – and who can make me laugh. How hard can it be?'

'Talking about me again, are you?' Nick joked as he and Nathan joined them at their table.

'You wish!' Cat laughed. But the laughter faded on her lips as she noticed the vision of male gorgeousness cruising across the dining hall, tossing his shining hair and smiling his luminous smile.

She tried to hide behind Nick, but it was too late. Orlando was already pulling up a chair and sidling in next to her.

Cat shuddered at the thought of his brainpower

comment in the common room. She'd been so shocked – not to mention mortally *embarrassed* – about flirting with him before she realized what he was really like that she'd made her excuses and gone off to bed shortly afterwards.

'Where did you disappear to last night, Cat?' he asked her. 'You were like Cinderella running away from the ball . . .'

Cat stared at him, her anger sparking. *Cinderella? So he sees himself as Prince Charming, does he? About as charming as a pit viper!* 'I needed some sleep,' she said coldly. 'I was running a bit low on *brainpower* . . .'

'Oh, no, you're not one of those weirdo women's-rights feminist types, are you?' Orlando said, smirking.

If he comes near me with a glass slipper, Cat thought, *he'll be wearing it on his head!*

She was about to explain this point to Orlando when she noticed someone gazing mournfully at her from the salad bar.

It was Paul 'Jellyfish' Zhao.

Cat panicked. *Help! Must escape! . . . Crazy frog-boys . . . everywhere!*

She jumped up from the table, leaving a half-eaten bowl of carrot and coriander soup. 'Library moment!' she blurted to the tableful of flummoxed expressions. 'Just remembered! Must finish essay!'

SANC-TU-ARY! Cat screamed dramatically to herself as she ran across the hall. She should *never* have let Belle and Holly start this stupid Operation Romeo thing in the first place! Now she needed a place to escape from the hordes of failed dates roaming the school . . .

Cat heard the librarian tut loudly as she threw open the door and flew into the library. Without thinking, she made for the table at the far end.

Then she stopped in her tracks.

A familiar figure was poring over a book at his usual table.

A light, happy feeling scampered like kitten paws in Cat's stomach at the sight of him. She couldn't wait to tell him all about Obnoxious Orlando . . .

Adam looked up from his work. Catching her standing staring at him, he grinned his big mischievous grin. Their eyes met. Something happened. It was like looking down a microscope when the blurry image suddenly snaps into focus.

She heard her own words play back in her head: *I just want somebody with a mind of his own who isn't a know-it-all or offensive to women – and who can make me laugh.*

And suddenly she knew! *I'm looking right at him!*

He's funny and interesting and easy to talk to . . . and he's quite nice-looking really . . . his ears hardly stick out at all!

Suddenly Cat heard herself babbling something. 'Maybe we could meet up sometime in a non-library-escape scenario – for a coffee with no jellyfish or zombies or anything?'

Adam stared at her. The moment stretched on and on . . . *Catrin Tara Wickham,* Cat berated herself, *you've really blown it now! One: that sentence made no sense whatsoever, and two: just because a guy cracks a few jokes about zombies with you doesn't mean he likes you . . .*

'I thought you'd never ask,' Adam said, smiling. 'How much homework do you think I actually *have*?'

'You mean you were . . . ?' Cat stammered.

'Coming in here deliberately hoping to meet you again!' Adam said, nodding. 'Well, that and hiding from the zombie legions, obviously!'

'*Obviously!*' Cat agreed, sitting down at last.

'So-o-o . . .' Adam said slowly after they'd spent some time grinning at each other inanely across the table. 'Did someone mention a coffee?'

Cat nodded.

'Sounds great!' he said. 'When?'

'Erm . . . er . . .' She hesitated, suddenly remembering her wall-to-wall schedule leading up to the

Spectacular. She had a technical run-through of her solo this afternoon. Tomorrow, she had costume fittings. And she really did have an essay to do for English! And now Adam was going to think she was changing her mind . . .

But to her relief, he immediately guessed the problem. 'Oh, it's the Rising Stars Spectacular next Saturday, isn't it? You must be swamped this week. Why don't we save that coffee for next Sunday morning, when it's all over and you can relax.'

Cat smiled gratefully. 'That would be lovely!'

Adam smiled back. His deep brown eyes glowed with warmth and understanding and humour.

It was like coming home after a long tiring journey . . .

. . . and remembering your favourite film was about to start on the Movie Channel.

She looked away, suddenly shy, and waved goodbye.

Her frog-kissing days were over!

She didn't need Holly and Belle playing Cupid. She didn't need Nick and Lettie playing secret agents.

She'd found her Romeo all by herself!

CHAPTER TWENTY-EIGHT

Holly: Cod Fillets and Crumpling

The week flew by and suddenly it was Friday, the day before the Rising Stars Spectacular.

The scenery was painted, programmes printed, costumes fitted, sound checks completed, lights positioned.

Now it was all down to the performers!

Afternoon lessons were cancelled and all Year Eight students and their teachers decamped to the Gielgud Auditorium for a full dress rehearsal.

When they weren't performing, students were allowed to sit in the audience; it was a chance to watch each other's numbers, since they would all be cloistered backstage on the night itself. Few of them had ever performed in a venue as big and grand as the Gielgud before – it had none of the familiar cosiness of the Redgrave Theatre – and the atmosphere was electric with excitement and trepidation.

Holly, Belle and Cat had the advantage that

Nobody's Angels had performed here at the gala showcase last term. They knew how it felt to step out onto the wide sweep of the stage and look out into the audience – which seemed to stretch away for ever beneath the elegant Art Deco ceiling.

But for Holly, that wasn't really helping right now.

She felt even more nervous than she had before *Nutcracker Sweeties*! And poor Zak looked even worse! His face was as white as a cod fillet! They'd rehearsed so hard over the last few weeks and – with Jack's help – had perfected the flying fish in the pool. They could even do it beautifully on land.

Most of the time!

The problem was, they weren't consistent. Every now and then, Holly didn't *quite* get the launch right or Zak didn't *quite* get the grip right. The result was an undignified wobble and crumple instead of a soaring overhead lift to crown the show.

To make matters worse, *Time of My Life* was the last number before the finale, so Holly had the whole afternoon to suffer. She tried to put it out of her mind as she watched her friends perform, but then suddenly her blood would turn to ice-water. What if she flunked the lift today? More importantly, what if she flunked it *tomorrow*? She could picture it all too vividly – *crumpling* in front of everyone: her teachers, her friends, her family – Mum and Steve had even invited Gran and Grandad along for the big performance!

And then there was the fact that Tory King was there to watch them today too! She'd come to the dress rehearsal because she'd be on stage herself on Saturday night so wouldn't be able to attend the Spectacular itself.

'Relax.' Tory smiled. 'You've mastered this lift in the studio so many times now. You'll be perfect!'

Holly tried to look convinced.

She danced her ensemble numbers as if being operated by remote control.

Miss Morgan noticed her absent expression. 'Focus, Holly!' she shouted. '*Attenzione!*'

Everyone here is so amazingly talented! Holly thought as she watched the other performers in the first half of the programme. Nick and Mayu were so sweet together in *I Am Sixteen, Going on Seventeen*, you almost believed Nick *was* in love with Mayu and wanted to spend the rest of his life with her! What an actor he was! Holly couldn't help smiling when she saw Lettie watching from a few seats away – almost pea-green with jealousy! Cat played the part of the poor flower-seller Eliza Doolittle so powerfully as she sang *Wouldn't*

It Be Loverly? that Holly longed to run onstage to give her a hug and some money for something to eat. Frankie's *Razzle Dazzle* brought her out in goosebumps.

Why do they all *have to be so fabulous?* Holly caught herself wondering. Even Nathan Almeida had finally nailed his steps in the dance choruses! She *almost* wished someone would trip over, or fluff a line or miss a note . . .

. . . *anything* so long as she wasn't the only one to let the whole year down.

CHAPTER TWENTY-NINE

Belle: Moon Landings and Royal Weddings

As Belle and Bianca sang the last notes of *What Is This Feeling?* Belle knew they'd *rocked* it! Everyone was standing up, shouting and applauding. Mr Garcia, Mr Grampian and Miss Morgan were at the side of the stage, all clapping and cheering.

'Boo!' Belle said, leaning towards Bianca.

'*Arggh!*' Bianca screamed.

There was laughter and more applause.

'Bravo!' piped Miss Morgan.

'Brilliant!' boomed Mr Garcia.

'Exemplary characterization,' said Mr Grampian.

Belle and Bianca looked at each other, grinning jubilantly, their eyes shining with shared triumph. Their hands started to fly up for a victory high-five . . .

Then they remembered who they were!

Bianca snatched her hand back.

Belle's dropped to her side.

Bianca glared at her. 'You *kicked* me when you said

boo!' she hissed. 'Don't you *dare* do that tomorrow! This isn't *The Itchy and Scratchy Show*, you know!'

'I'll try to remember that,' Belle said coolly, turning on her heel and marching off stage left.

Bianca stalked off stage right.

'Come back!' Mr Garcia called. 'Starting positions for *One Short Day*!'

Belle and Bianca had been so keen to see the back of each other they'd forgotten they had to remain onstage for the second number from *Wicked*. They were joined by the rest of the advanced singers as the music started and the stage was flooded with the green light of the Emerald City.

Belle hurried into the dressing room, pulled off her dark wig and switched Elphaba's dowdy black jacket and skirt for her *Flashdance* grand-finale costume. Still giddy with the thrill of the duet, she ran back out into the auditorium and took a seat next to Cat – just in time to catch the last minute of the advanced dance group performing *Disco Inferno*. Belle scanned the stage for Jack. She couldn't wait to see how he was getting on in the big dance number.

Cat nudged her. 'Not bad!' she whispered. Belle watched, enthralled. It was true – Jack was a natural!

You'd never have guessed he'd only been moved into advanced dance a few weeks ago.

'I don't think he's quite seen the *point* of dance yet, though!' Cat added. Belle knew what she meant. Jack wore a slightly bored expression – as if he'd rather be home polishing his football trophies.

After Darya Petrova's beautiful solo *As Long as He Needs Me*, Jack was back on again in his duet with Ruby Drew.

For a moment Belle thought that the wrong two students had come out onstage. The shy boy who hunched his shoulders and peeped through his fringe looked more like Nathan than Jack! And Ruby Drew was almost unrecognizable without her Goth make-up; suddenly she was a short, plain girl in an unflattering orange blouse and brown skirt. They were playing their parts perfectly!

As they started singing *Let's Play a Love Scene*, an awed silence fell over the audience. Even Bianca and Mayu stopped discussing their next appearance on the London social scene for several seconds. Jack and Ruby wove their harmonies gradually closer as they declared their characters' love for each other. It was a stellar performance.

Belle looked at Cat and grinned.

'I think he sees the point of *singing*!' Cat said.

A few minutes later Jack and Ruby tiptoed out from backstage and joined Cat and Belle in the audience. 'You were awesome!' Belle whispered, giving them both a thumbs-up as they sat down to watch a spine-tingling performance of *Empty Chairs at Empty Tables* by Danny Adu – one of Jack's friends from the football team.

At last it was time for the *Dirty Dancing* routine. It was the moment everyone had been waiting for. Holly and Zak were known to be the best dancers in the year, and expectations were sky-high. The fact that rumours had been flying about for weeks about whether or not they would master the big lift only added to the frisson of excitement crackling round the auditorium like an electric storm.

Belle felt as if they were about to witness a momentous event – like a moon landing or a royal wedding. 'I'm more nervous for Holly than I was for myself!' she whispered.

Cat nodded. 'Me too! She and Zak have looked petrified all day, poor things!'

'I know the feeling!' Jack said with a grimace. 'I almost feel as if I'm up there with them!'

Belle squeezed his arm. He'd spent so much time

helping Holly and Zak in the pool, she knew how much the lift meant to him too.

The music started to play *Time of My Life* . . . Slowly the lights went up, revealing Holly alone in the middle of the stage, in a floaty pale pink dress. She looked to one side and smiled. Everyone followed her gaze to see Zak, dressed in black shirt and trousers, his sun-streaked hair slicked back, sashay towards her.

They looked into each other's eyes and began to dance the sexy steps, closer and closer . . .

'Not sure you should be watching this!' Cat put her hand over Belle's eyes. 'It's not got a PG rating!'

Belle laughed. The moment of the big swallow-dive/flying-fish lift was almost upon them. The music was growing louder, more intense . . .

Go on, Holly, you can do it! Belle urged. She could hardly bear to watch as Holly paused, exchanged a special smile with Zak, and then ran across the stage to meet him. She jumped . . .

There was a gasp as Holly flew up into the air. Zak held her high above his head for one long perfect moment. Arms and legs beautifully extended, Holly soared high above them all, as if carried on a wave of emotion.

'Ye-e-e-s!' Jack shouted, punching the air. Belle

hugged him, and then Cat, in pure relief. Then she saw Tory King get to her feet to lead a standing ovation. Everyone stood, and the auditorium rang with applause.

After they'd all returned to the stage and performed the closing *Flashdance* number, the students lingered in small groups, comparing notes and congratulating each other. Everyone was on a high. Tory King and Miss Morgan joined the friends in showering Holly and Zak with praise. Both dancers had tears of joy in their eyes as they thanked everyone – and especially Jack – for their help.

'Totally stoked!' Zak said, his voice slightly trembly.

'Go and get some rest!' Tory told him. 'You look shattered!'

Finally Belle put her arms around Cat and Holly and led them off to their dressing room. There were so many performers in the show that they were sharing with at least ten others, but everyone else had already changed and left. The three of them sank down on stools in front of the large wall mirror and grinned cheerfully at their reflections. It was such a relief to see Holly her usual sunny self again. *And Cat has seemed extra-bubbly the last few days too*, Belle suddenly realized. She sneaked a look at her friend. Yes, there was definitely some kind of dreamy, space-cadet smile going on there. 'Cat, is there something we should know?' she asked.

Cat just looked mysterious.

'You're not planning to elope with Orlando, are you?'

'Hey! I may be crazy but I'm not *that* crazy!' Cat giggled. 'OK, I'll fess up,' she added, holding her hands up in surrender. 'Operation Romeo has *worked*. Just not *quite* how you two planned it!'

Belle and Holly listened in amazement as Cat told them about Adam Fielding and the Library of Love. 'That is so-o-o romantic!' Holly sighed.

'So,' Belle asked, pretending to be cross, 'when exactly *were* you planning to tell us about Adam? Your wedding anniversary?'

'Yeah, sorry about the top-secret thing!' Cat said. 'I just have this funny feeling that saying anything might jinx it and make something go wrong before we even get to the first date — knowing my luck with boys lately . . . But, well, I've been bursting to tell you the whole time!'

Belle and Holly laughed. 'But nothing will go wrong!' Belle said reassuringly. 'This is going to be the best weekend ever!'

She looked back at their three shiny happy faces in the mirror. They were still wearing their 1980s dance outfits from the *Flashdance* number: purple headbands, lurex leotards, lime-green leg-warmers and ripped sweatshirts.

'Come on!' said Belle with a shudder. 'Let's get changed before we're arrested by the fashion police.'

CHAPTER THIRTY

Holly: Maybe, Just Maybe

Holly was swooping gloriously through the air. But all at once her wings were melting; she was growing heavier, plummeting . . .

She hit the ground and jolted awake.

The alarm clock was ringing. It was only 6.30, but she was meeting Zak before breakfast for one last rehearsal to make sure their big lift was absolutely *perfect*. Then they could spend the rest of the day relaxing ahead of the Spectacular in the evening.

Holly was so excited! The dress rehearsal had been fantastic and she couldn't wait to do it again tonight *for real*. It was going to be even better! All the nerves she'd felt yesterday were behind her now.

She pulled on her tracksuit, trying not to wake Gemma, eased her dance bag from its hook and tiptoed to the door.

There was a rustling of pages and a thud behind her. Cursing her clumsiness, Holly turned to see that she'd knocked Gemma's diary off her bedside table. Gemma stirred in her sleep but didn't wake as Holly bent to pick it up.

Holly *really* and *truly* didn't mean to snoop . . . but the diary had fallen open . . .

Doodled all over the centre pages, among hearts and flowers, was the name *Zak Lomax*.

Guiltily Holly dropped the diary on Gemma's bedside table as if it were radioactive. *I had no idea Gemma was keen on Zak*, she thought. *It must have been horrible for her seeing me working so closely with him all this time, but she's too nice to say anything.* Holly felt awful. *How could I not have noticed?* Tomorrow, she vowed, she would see if Gemma wanted to talk about it. Maybe she could even help things along with a little matchmaking.

But all that would have to wait.

I need Zak all to myself for just one more day!

Zak was late. Holly waited in the dance studio, working through her third set of hamstring stretches, running through the lift in her mind – she was confident that she could get the jump even smoother, find a little more extension . . . *Where is he?* Holly glanced at the clock. Surely he couldn't have overslept?

The door banged open. 'Zak, there you are—' Holly started. But it wasn't Zak. It was Nick Taggart.

Nick's face wasn't cut out for looking grim. It was a goofing, spoofing, clowning-around kind of face, which made it even scarier that this morning, beneath its thatch of uncombed sandy hair, it had BAD NEWS written all over it.

'Sorry, Holly,' he said, crossing the studio and gently placing his hand on her shoulder. 'It's Zak. He's been awake all night barfing his guts up. I took him over to the nurse. She says there's no way he's going to be fit for the Spectacular tonight . . . Mr Fortune's already told his family to save them coming all the way from Cornwall . . .'

'Oh no, poor Zak!' Holly murmured. 'He's worked so hard and now he's going to miss the show!'

Nick was staring at her as if she'd suddenly started speaking in fluent Vietnamese. 'I don't think you've quite got it,' he said slowly. 'If Zak's not there, you can't . . .'

Suddenly it sank in! No Zak meant no *Dirty Dancing*, no *flying fish*! Holly felt the studio blur at the edges. Her knees gave way and she folded to the floor. *Just when they'd finally mastered the lift, their chance to shine had been snatched away!*

All at once Holly needed to be alone. She staggered to her feet and dashed out of the dance studio. Blindly she ran along the corridors until she came to a halt in the basement laundry room.

She curled up on a pile of sheets in Miss Candlemas's linen cupboard and cried until she had no tears left to cry . . .

Which is where Cat and Belle found her half an hour later.

'We've been looking for you everywhere!' Cat said gently. 'Nick told us about Zak. I'm so sorry, Hols!'

'You need some camomile tea to calm you,' Belle said, taking charge. 'You're shaking!'

Too miserable to resist, Holly allowed herself to be led along to the dining room, where breakfast was still in progress.

By this time, the Garrick grapevine had carried the news of Zak's illness to every corner of the school. Everyone crowded around, bombarding Holly with sympathy and suggestions as she sipped her tea. She felt hollowed out and brittle. Nothing mattered any more.

'Could someone else take Zak's place?' Nathan suggested hesitantly.

'*Oh, get real!*' came a sarcastic voice from the next table. Bianca had been pretending to ignore all the commotion but clearly couldn't resist weighing in. 'It's obvious you know *zilch* about dancing! She's *barely* getting the lift right after six weeks' practice with the best dancer in the year – she's not going to magically *ace* it with a last-minute stand-in!'

For once, Holly agreed with Bianca.

'I could do it.'

Everyone turned to see who was heartless enough to make a joke of Holly's misfortune. But the person who'd spoken wasn't laughing.

It was Jack Thorne.

'I've seen you do that lift a million times in the pool,' he said, stepping up to the table and speaking directly to Holly. 'I know it inside out. The rest of the routine could be a bit tricky, but I've had so many extra dance lessons lately, most of my brain has re-programmed itself to learning steps. I'm sure I could pick it up . . .'

'Oo-ooh, Jack! My hero!' Bianca mocked.

Holly stared at Jack. There was no way he could learn the whole routine in a single day. She shook her head. 'Thanks, but—'

'Come on, Holly!' Jack persisted. 'Don't you *want* to do it?'

Holly shook her head again – *He must be crazy!* – but

219

now Cat and Belle were joining forces with Jack.

'At least give it a try!' Belle was saying.

'You can't turn a boy down when he's *begging*!' Cat added.

Holly closed her eyes. *Maybe*, she thought . . . But suddenly she remembered something. 'What about Zak? How will he feel if I dance with someone else while he's in his sick bed?'

'Oh no,' Nick laughed. 'You're not getting out of it *that* easily. I know for a fact that Zak's feeling *totally bummed out* about ruining your big moment. If you can go ahead without him, he'll feel a million times better!'

'I could go and ask him first . . .' Holly said doubtfully.

Nick shook his head. 'Nurse Patel's put him in quarantine, in case it's something infectious.'

Then Holly thought of another problem. 'But you have a football match this morning, Jack. It's the semifinal.'

For a moment he looked torn, but then he smiled. 'It's OK, I'm on the sub bench anyway because I've missed so much training. I'll clear it with Ethan.'

Finally Holly gave in. *Maybe, just maybe* . . .

She nodded slowly. 'OK, Jack, what are we waiting for?'

★ ★ ★

Holly felt as if she'd been caught in the path of a tornado.

She had never worked so hard in her life!

First she and Jack ran over to the Dance Department to explain their master plan to Miss Morgan and Mr Korsakoff. Both were sceptical, but they were persuaded to see what Jack could do – first in the pool and then in the dance studio. What they saw was nowhere near perfect, but there was enough promise for both teachers to agree it was worth a shot. But they *insisted* that Holly and Jack spend the morning working on the rest of the routine before moving on to the lift.

Wary at first, Holly soon found that she really enjoyed dancing with Jack. He didn't have Zak's technical ability or experience, of course, and they had to cut out some of the more complicated sequences, but his natural languorous manner was perfect for the part of the rebellious Johnny.

After a quick lunch, they began work on the lift, aided by Miss Morgan and Mr K. Jack was taller than Zak. It took more energy to jump into his arms, but she didn't have to worry so much about over-shooting. And, being stronger, Jack was able to stabilize her more easily.

The first time they tried, Jack almost bounced her off the ceiling. The next time was a little better, but

Holly was flying at such an angle it looked as if she was banking round a hairpin bend on a racetrack.

'*Mamma mia!*' Miss Morgan shrieked, holding her head in her hands.

'Try again!' Mr Korsakoff barked.

We must both be total fruit-loops, Holly thought as they capsized on their third attempt.

There was so little time to get this right!

But as long as they still had even the tiniest chance to shine in the Spectacular, Holly was going to grab it with both hands!

She seized Jack by the arm and helped him up off the mat. 'Come on, we'll get it next time!' she said, hoping she sounded *way* more optimistic than she felt.

CHAPTER THIRTY-ONE

Belle: A Snow-white-unicorn Moment

Belle hadn't known a day drag by so slowly since Christmas Eve when she was four years old and she'd asked Santa to bring her a snow-white unicorn.

(He didn't! *And where would you keep a unicorn in a New York apartment anyway?* Mom had pointed out reasonably.)

On top of her own nervous excitement about her duet, Belle couldn't help worrying about Jack and Holly. She'd been so proud when Jack volunteered to stand in for Zak – but as the day wore on, she began to wonder: could he *really* do it? Or were he and Holly doomed to disappointment of snow-white-unicorn proportions?

Belle was so wired that even an extra-long yoga session couldn't quite restore her Inner Peace.

But at last it was time to dash through the rain to the Gielgud Auditorium.

The dressing rooms were bursting at the seams:

all sixty Year Eight students were getting ready for the opening number, *You Can't Stop the Beat*, assisted by students from the fashion college who'd been drafted in to help with all the hairstyling, make-up and costume changes.

Belle stepped into her pale blue dress with its swirly skirt and stiff petticoats, and sat down to have her hair backcombed into a 1960s bouffant style. In the mirror, she could see the other girls – Cat, Gemma, Serena, Ruby, Darya, Lettie, Bianca and Mayu – all bustling about. Holly was sitting quietly in a corner. Belle caught her eye and shot her an encouraging smile. Belle and Cat had tried pumping Holly and Jack for information about how their rehearsals had gone, but they'd both refused to give anything away.

The call for the starters for the first number came over the Tannoy. Excitedly the girls all crowded out into the corridor and up to the wings, where the boys were already waiting for them.

The Garrick School Rising Stars Spectacular was about to begin!

Belle jostled to the front and peeped round the thick midnight-blue curtain. Mr Fortune was onstage, welcoming the audience to the show.

Looking into the packed auditorium, Belle caught a

glimpse of her mother in the front row. And surely that couldn't be . . . yes, it was – *Dad*! Belle had no idea he was coming – she thought he was still in Hong Kong. Even more of a shock was the fact that *Dad was sitting next to Mom*! Since their divorce they'd mostly avoided being in the same hemisphere, let alone the same *building*!

Suddenly the music started. Miss Morgan was counting them in – '*Uno, due, tre* . . .' and then Belle was running onstage.

It was *thrilling* to be performing again, dancing in the big whole-year numbers and singing in the advanced singer ensemble pieces, *Seasons of Love* and *The Circle of Life*. The audience loved it, and each performance received more applause than the last. Belle was backstage while Cat sang her solo, but she could tell it had gone fabulously when Cat came running into the dressing room.

The high kicks, whoops of joy and bear-hugs were kind of a giveaway!

Then it was Act Two. After the opening chorus of *We're All in This Together*, Belle dashed back to the dressing room to change into her Elphaba costume and have her face painted an attractive shade of Wicked-Witch-of-the-West green.

She sat down at the mirror and closed her eyes while Anna – a fashion student who sported cropped pink hair and six nose piercings – layered on the thick green make-up.

When Belle opened her eyes, it was to see a Human Avocado staring back at her from the mirror. 'I'm *loving* it! Just what I wanted!' she joked to Anna.

'Ha! *That's* a major improvement!' Bianca commented as she sat down at the mirror to have her silver-blonde hair fashioned into glamorous waves. As Galinda, she was wearing a pretty white dress and her face was beautifully made up.

'Thank you,' Belle said, refusing to be rattled by Bianca's remark as she pulled on her ugly black wig. 'Green is so-o-o in this season!'

'*You think!*' Bianca sneered. 'Anyway, hurry up – we're on in a minute.'

Grrr! What I wouldn't give to be a real *witch for five minutes,* Belle thought. *Just long enough to turn Bianca into something small, harmless and without the power of speech . . . like a woodlouse . . .*

'And don't you dare kick me this time!' Bianca hissed as they reached the wings. 'My shin's still swollen where you attacked me last night . . .'

And then they were onstage. Belle was in paradise!

The combination of singing to the vast audience *and* telling Bianca *exactly* what she thought of her was a dream come true! A double dose of adrenaline spiked through her body.

'Boo!' she shouted at the end of the song.

'*Arghhhh!*' Bianca shrieked.

And this time Belle hadn't even needed to resort to physical violence! Bianca was so jittery about what Belle *might* do that she screamed right on cue anyway!

The two girls turned and bowed to the audience. The applause swelled to a deafening roar. People were on their feet, whistling and shouting, '*Bravo!*'

Swept up in the glorious moment, Belle suddenly found that she and Bianca were clamped together in a celebratory hug!

It was the shortest hug in history! Bianca leaped back. 'Eughh!' She grimaced. 'Your face has ruined my dress!'

There was a smudge of green on her white collar. 'You look as if you're going mouldy!' Belle laughed.

'*It's not funny!*' Bianca snarled, shoulder-barging Belle as they turned to walk offstage. Then Belle remembered they had to stay on for the next number and yanked Bianca back. There was a roar of laughter from the audience. *They think this is part of the act!*

Belle realized. She gave Bianca another little tug for good measure while she could still get away with it.

After *One Short Day*, Belle ran to the dressing room to change. She hurried back and crowded into the wings with the rest of the cast to watch Holly and Jack's dance. The atmosphere was even more highly charged than it had been at the dress rehearsal. Everyone shared a single thought: *Can Holly and Jack really pull it off?*

Belle found Cat and held her hand tightly. 'Good luck!' they whispered to Holly as she squeezed past to take her position centre stage. Her look of determination mixed with terror tugged at Belle's heart. *If only I could help!* But there was nothing anyone could do but watch. The deep voice on the soundtrack began to croon the familiar words . . .

Suddenly Jack was dancing across the stage. Belle gasped. He was *amazing*. He looked seductive and breathtakingly dangerous in his black costume. He locked his X-ray eyes onto Holly, stepped closer and pulled her into his arms. Belle shivered. She could hardly bear to watch. Jack and Holly were dancing as if they were hopelessly in love.

The audience was silent, transfixed by the spellbinding performance.

'I think he's finally got the *point* of dancing,' Cat whispered.

Belle gulped. Jack certainly didn't look bored any more! Maybe she liked it better when he *did*!

'And he's such a great *actor*!' Cat added, nudging Belle in the ribs as she stressed the word *actor*.

Belle took the point. *Jack's not in love with Holly any more than he was in love with Ruby in* Let's Play a Love Scene, she told herself firmly.

And then, suddenly, Holly was running across the stage towards Jack for the lift.

The entire audience held its breath, then screamed in delight as Holly floated high into in the air in a soaring, if very slightly wobbly, flying fish.

They had done it!

It was a snow-white-unicorn moment.

CHAPTER THIRTY-TWO

Holly: Doodles Never Lie

The Spectacular was over!

Time of My Life had gone better than Holly could possibly have hoped!

And the lift had been *utterly, completely, totally magical.*

It was like her flying dream – but without the melting wings.

Now, in a state of euphoria, she joined her friends among the crowds of students thronging the corridors backstage in a flurry of hugs and high-speed chatter.

'Whoa!' Jack breathed. 'That was *amazing.* I feel like I just got an Oscar for Best Actor *and* scored the winning goal for England in the World Cup Final at the same time! I didn't know dancing could be like *that!*'

'I think you've converted him, Hols,' Cat said, giggling.

'*I be-lie-e-e-e-v-e in the power of dance,*' Nick chanted in a gospel-preacher voice. '*I have s-e-e-e-n the light!*'

'Well done, everyone! *Fantastico!*' Miss Morgan exclaimed as she hurried over. She showered Jack with air-kisses. 'I knew the moment I saw this boy on the football field that he was *born* to dance! Was I right or was I right?'

Jack blushed and shook his head modestly.

'OK, OK!' Mr Garcia's deep laughter reverberated around the corridor as he joined the group. 'Drusilla Morgan's proved right again! But the boy can sing too!'

'And Holly was *bravissima* as well, of course!' Miss Morgan said.

Holly smiled and thanked her. The dance teacher had worked tirelessly all day helping her and Jack.

'Now, go and get changed, all of you!' Mr Garcia said eventually. 'You don't want to be late for the—'

'*Par-tay!*' everyone chorused.

Everyone except Belle, Holly noticed. 'What's wrong?' she asked as the girls reached their dressing room. Abandoned garments, wigs and coat hangers were strewn everywhere, as if there'd been a riot in a department store.

'Nothing,' Belle murmured.

Holly looked at her friend. Belle's face was as sphinx-like as ever, but there was a shadow in her eyes that told Holly it was a *something* kind of a nothing.

'OK,' Belle admitted. 'I know this is pathetic, but I feel a bit left out now Jack's got the dancing bug! I'd love to be able to dance with him the way you did on stage – not the flying-fish part, obviously . . .'

'Just the smoochy, luvved-up bits at the beginning, you mean!' Cat teased.

'But you *shall* go to the ball, my dear!' Holly said, in her best fairy godmother voice – relieved that that was the only thing bothering Belle. 'I'll show you a few of the steps.' She grabbed Belle round the waist and walked her through the moves.

Meanwhile Cat was pulling off her *Flashdance* costume. 'Ooh, that's better,' she gasped. 'That headband was cutting off the circulation to my brain!'

'Well done, Holly! You and Jack were brilliant!' Holly looked up to see Gemma coming into the dressing room with Serena and Lettie.

Holly smiled. Then something tugged at a corner of her memory. Seeing Gemma had reminded her of something . . .

Oh yes, it was Gemma's diary! *Hearts, flowers and Zak Lomax!*

Poor Zak was lying in the sick bay missing out on all the fun. Holly wished she could do something to cheer him up . . .

And suddenly she had a last-piece-of-the-jigsaw moment!

Zak being so keen to know whether Gemma had a boyfriend in Australia; Zak helping Serena organize Gemma's surprise party; Zak stuffing a snowball down Gemma's neck!

'I'll meet you guys at the party,' she said, hastily pulling on her jeans and boots, grabbing a bouquet from the pile of flowers she'd been given and bolting for the door. 'Something I've got to do . . . ' Everyone was staring at her with bemused expressions but there was no time for explanations.

Holly sprinted across the sports field back to school.

'Yes, he's allowed visitors now,' Nurse Patel confirmed. 'Must've been something he ate. Nothing contagious.'

Holly knocked and entered the sick bay. She'd never been inside before and was surprised to find it looked just like a cosy bedroom. She'd imagined it to be more like something out of *Casualty*, complete with machines going *beep*. Only the faint whiff of disinfectant hinted at the room's medicinal properties.

Zak was propped up on the bed zapping things on a Nintendo DS. He looked pale, but he smiled brightly when he saw Holly.

'Dude!' he said.

'Dude!' Holly replied, tapping her knuckles to his outstretched fist.

'How'd it go?' Zak asked, patting the bed for her to sit down. 'I heard Jack was subbing for me.'

'Oh, you know, it was *OK*,' Holly said carefully, trying to play it down.

Zak grinned and held his hands up. 'Hey, you can tell me! I won't break!'

'OK, it was amazing!' Holly conceded. 'It wasn't the same as dancing with you though,' she added quickly. *Which was true.* For all Jack's passion, Zak was technically a much better dancer.

'Rad!' Zak said. 'Stoked for you!'

'Anyway, I didn't come here just to gloat!' Holly said. 'I've got to run back to the party – my family and Ethan are waiting for me. But if you'd like someone to come and sit with you for a while, I could ask around, see if there's someone without a load of relatives to entertain – like . . . oh, I don't know . . . maybe . . . *Gemma* . . . or . . .'

She peeped at Zak out of the corner of her eye to gauge his reaction. His pallid face was blushing a furious tomato-ketchup red . . .

She was right!

'Zak Lomax!' she said, laughing. '*You* sent Gemma that Valentine's card, didn't you?'

Zak's face flushed another three shades of scarlet.

'No point trying to hide it from *me*!' Holly chided. 'We're partners, remember – timing, trusting, *talking*!'

'Do you think I, like, stand a chance?' Zak blurted.

'I'm sure of it!' she said with a smile.

After all, she thought, *I've seen the doodles – and doodles never lie.*

'Leave it to me!' she said, reaching over to give Zak a quick hug.

Holly knew that Cupid was on a roll when she caught sight of Gemma and Serena hurrying across the courtyard on their way to the party in the dining room. She put on a burst of speed and caught up with them.

'Hey, Gemma!' she called. 'Glad I caught you. I just saw Zak. He asked if you'd call in and see him about something.'

A rapturous smile lit up Gemma's pretty face. Then she hesitated and looked at Serena. She wasn't the kind of girl who deserted her best friend on the way to a party! 'It's OK!' Serena said. 'You go. My mum's brought half the population of Manchester with her and I'll have to talk to all of them!'

'If you're sure!' Gemma called, already halfway to the sick bay.

'What was that all about?' Serena asked as she and Holly continued towards the party.

'Put it this way,' Holly told her. 'I don't think Gemma's mystery Valentine will be a mystery for much longer!'

Serena grinned. 'You mean Zak? Wow! Good work, Miss Marple.'

Holly went across the courtyard to the entrance hall. Music, chatter and laughter were spilling out from the dining room. Photographers from several society and stage magazines were stationed around the doors, snapping the performers and their guests as they arrived.

As she drew closer, Holly smiled briefly for the cameras. Then she spotted Ethan, obviously looking around for her. She took his arm and they went in. Now she was smiling even more.

She'd spent enough time sorting out everyone else's romances.

It was time to concentrate on her own for a while.

CHAPTER THIRTY-THREE

Cat: Watch Out for Those Zombies

Maybe I should*'ve kept that purple headband on*, Cat thought. *It'd stop my head swelling up too much with all this praise!*

She'd been at the after-show party for twenty minutes – and people *still* hadn't stopped telling her how marvellous her solo had been!

True, most of them were members of her family who were probably a *little* biased, but there had been others too.

Like, incredibly, *Mrs Salmon*! She'd come to watch the show with her husband. Yes, not only did she *have* a husband, but he was actually rather handsome in a clean-cut, sporty kind of way. And Mrs Salmon looked disconcertingly glamorous out of her usual lab-coat and sensible shoes, and in a blue silk dress. 'Well done, Cat!' she said warmly. 'You were superb!'

You were superb! Cat repeated to herself. Not *Where's your homework!* Or *You're in detention!* Now Cat knew her solo must've been something *really* special!

The only problem was that it had started Mum off on her Cat's-career-in-musical-theatre campaign again. 'She was born to it, Brian!' she was telling Dad. Dad was nodding vaguely, more interested in studying the dining room's ornate Regency ceiling mouldings. 'I see her in *Oliver!, The Sound of Music . . .*' Her voice trailed off as Mr Fortune approached. Mum had a serious crush on James Fortune! Cat could hardly bear to look as she cornered him. 'Catrin is an all-rounder, she gets it from me . . .' she began.

'Ah! Catrin, I do trust that your triumphant foray into musical theatre won't entice you away from classical acting,' Mr Grampian said, appearing at her shoulder. 'We would be devastated to lose your prodigious talents.'

'Could you say that again so my mum can hear?' Cat asked him.

She blinked as a storm of blue flashes went off near the door. She looked up just in time to see Bianca and Mayu turn instinctively towards the photographers and switch on their red-carpet smiles. But the cameras weren't pointing at them. They were all trained on Belle, who was walking into the room with her mum and dad – alias Zoe Fairweather, the super-model, stunning in a simple long black velvet dress, and Dirk Madison, famous Hollywood film director. Cat laughed as all three of them jumped away from the cameras as if they'd been caught shoplifting! Belle hated any kind of publicity, and her parents surely didn't want to appear in *Hello!* magazine *together* when they'd spent the last decade avoiding each other!

Cat beckoned Belle over. After their respective parents had been introduced, the two girls slipped away to the side.

'Where's Holly?' Cat asked.

'Last sighted running towards the sick bay!' Belle reported. 'Hope she's not— Oh, look, here she is now!'

Cat turned round to see Holly at the door giving Ethan a hug. Then there were more hugs with her family.

Holly herded her group of guests to join Cat's and Belle's, and once everyone had been thoroughly hugged and/or air-kissed, Cat and Belle listened in surprise as she gave them the run-down on her Gemma-and-Zak mission.

Was there no end to Holly's talents? Cat wondered. Not only was she the Dancing Queen, she was the Queen of Hearts too!

Her thoughts were interrupted as a familiar song

started to play out over the speakers. It was *Time of My Life* . . . Suddenly the DJ was fading the music and announcing, '*This one is for Belle Madison!*'

Belle gasped. Cat looked around, wondering who had made the request. Then she saw Jack sauntering casually towards them, a wicked grin on his face.

'May I have this dance?' he asked, pulling Belle up onto the dance floor.

Cat looked suspiciously at Holly. 'Did you set this up too?' she asked.

Holly winked, then turned to Belle with a thumbs-up. 'Remember those moves!'

Belle and Jack made a beautiful couple – even if they did step on each other's toes occasionally. 'Ah!' Cat sighed. 'How romantic!'

Then Ethan came over to ask Holly to dance.

She smiled at him. 'I didn't think I'd ever hear myself say this, but I think I've had enough dancing for one day. Can we just *stand still* for a while?' She leaned against him, suddenly looking exhausted but very happy as she snuggled into his arms.

'You were amazing!' Ethan said.

'So were you, I heard,' Holly replied. 'Didn't you score the winning goal in the football match today?'

Another perfect couple! Cat thought.

'Can *we* dance, Cat?'

Cat grinned as she looked down to find her own dance partner. Not a super-gorgeous boyfriend for her, but her eight-year-old sister, Fiona, gazing up from her wheelchair.

'Thought you'd never ask!' Cat teased, wheeling her to the back of the dining room, away from the main dance floor, to spin her round in their special wheelchair boogie.

Within moments, they'd been joined by Nick, Lettie, Nathan, Serena, Frankie, Mason, Ruby . . . and now Belle and Jack and Ethan and Holly also deserted the main dance floor to take turns spinning the wheelchair round. Fiona giggled as she became more and more dizzy.

'Don't look now!' Belle laughed, nudging Cat's elbow and tipping her head towards Nick and Lettie, who were dancing together in a rather unconventional style, 'but the Dancing Bees are back!'

Cat laughed and paused for breath. She looked out through the open door into the entrance hall. Someone was loitering just outside, watching her.

It was a familiar figure with very slightly sticking-out ears.

He caught her eye, smiled and stepped forward

hesitantly – the party was only for Year Eight students and their guests.

Cat's heart flipped right over like a pancake. She stepped forward to go and invite him in.

'*ADAM FIELDING!*' came a shout from the entrance hall, accompanied by the unmistakable high-velocity rattle of Mrs Butterworth's chair. 'Don't just stand there gawping! I need a big strong lad like you to come and shift these boxes of photocopier paper . . .'

At the same moment, Cat felt her mother at her side. 'Come on, Catrin, you need to come and *network*. There's an agent you *have* to meet . . .'

She looked at Adam. They both grinned and shrugged. There was no resisting the combined force of Mrs Butterworth and Mrs Wickham!

'Coffee tomorrow at eleven!' he mouthed.

'See you then!' Cat whispered.

Adam was saying something else but she couldn't catch what it was.

'*Watch out for those zombies?*' Fiona asked. 'Cat, why did that boy say that?' Being in a wheelchair most of the time, she was used to people talking *about* her rather than *to* her and had become very good at lip-reading.

'Never you mind!' Cat laughed.

'Ooh, is that your boyfriend?' Mum asked, poised to rush out and introduce herself as his future mother-in-law.

'He's just a boy I know from the library,' Cat said hurriedly, pulling her mother back into the party.

She looked around the crowded room. Life at Superstar High was bursting with dreams and excitement and promise. She couldn't wait to tell Adam all about the Spectacular tomorrow morning. And maybe she *would* be needing those spare *Romeo and Juliet* tickets of Belle's after all!

As long as those two don't find out we're going out for coffee and decide to stalk us! Cat thought, watching Nick and Lettie waggle-dancing together. *It's about time they got their own date and stopped gate-crashing mine.*

Perhaps I'll get Holly to work on that tomorrow!

The Garrick School for the Performing Arts
RISING STARS SPECTACULAR

ACT ONE

You Can't Stop the Beat (Hairspray) Full cast

Good Morning Baltimore (Hairspray) Willow Griffiths

Sixteen Going on Seventeen (The Sound of Music)
Nick Taggart and Mayu Tanaka

Greased Lightning (Grease) Male advanced dancers

Wouldn't It Be Lovely (My Fair Lady) Catrin Wickham

Seasons of Love (Rent) Advanced singers

America (West Side Story) Female advanced dancers

Razzle Dazzle (Chicago) Frankie Pellegrini

All That Jazz (Chicago) Advanced dancers

Can You Feel the Love Tonight? (The Lion King)
Alex Armstrong and Sophia Khan

The Circle of Life (The Lion King) Advanced singers

We Will Rock You (We Will Rock You) Full cast

ACT TWO

We're All in This Together (High School Musical) Full cast

Get Your Head in the Game (High School Musical)
Male advanced dancers

Holding Out for a Hero (Footloose)
Female advanced dancers

Bring on Tomorrow (Fame) Advanced singers

What Is This Feeling? (Wicked) Bianca Hayford and Belle Madison

One Short Day (Wicked) Advanced singers

Disco Inferno (Saturday Night Fever) Advanced dancers:
led by Gemma Dalrymple and Philippe Meyer

As Long as He Needs Me (Oliver) Darya Petrova

Let's Play a Love Scene (Fame) Ruby Drew and Jack Thorne

Empty Chairs at Empty Tables (Les Misérables)
Danny Adu

Time of My Life (Dirty Dancing)
Holly Devenish and Zak Lomax

What a Feeling (Flashdance) Full cast

Read on for the next book in
this fantastic Superstar High
double bill!

KEEP THE
DREAM ALIVE

Isabella Cass

For E and W

CHAPTER ONE

Belle: Walking on Sunshine

Belle Madison was walking on sunshine.

OK, she was *actually* walking on carpet tiles – striding through Arrivals at Heathrow Airport in her new white leather jacket, her long blond hair in a single plait, pushing her matching Louis Vuitton suitcases on a trolley in front of her. But she was singing along with the super-cheerful Katrina and the Waves track on her iPod.

She spotted a silver-haired man holding up a placard with her name on, dropped her bags and smiled, still singing to herself. The driver her dad had booked to take her back to school was looking at her as if trying to figure out whether she was a harmless lunatic or someone he needed to worry about letting into the back of his car.

Maybe she was singing a little *too* loudly!

'The Garrick School for the Performing Arts, please,' Belle announced as he took her bags and led the way to the waiting limousine.

Then she said it again just to hear the delicious words. '*The Garrick School . . .*'

'Heard you the first time, love! Kingsgrove Square. I know it.' The driver shook his head in amusement.

Belle sank back into the seat and took a deep breath. She couldn't *wait* to get back to school for the new term. Dad was on a world tour to promote his latest film, and Mom was in Paris as the new face of Glamelle cosmetics, so Belle had spent the Easter holidays with her grandmother in Los Angeles. It had been fun, although Mimi (*no one* was allowed to call her Grandma!) clearly hadn't read *The Good Granny Guide* – Belle didn't think she'd ever baked a cookie or told a bedtime story in her life. But she had driven Belle round all the beauty parlours and designer boutiques in Hollywood in her red Ferrari, happy to have someone to spoil instead of her poodle, Cherub. Cherub, on the other hand, had been less impressed. She hadn't had the pink highlights in her fur retouched or a new rhinestone leash for at least a week!

But there was only so much shopping a girl could do, and Belle had missed her friends from school. She was aching to see them again. She pulled out her phone and fired off a quick text to Holly and Cat to let them know she was on her way.

Catrin Wickham was Belle's room-mate. Warm-hearted and hot-tempered, the word *dramatic* had been invented for Cat. And she was a fantastically gifted actress. Belle's other best friend, Holly Devenish, was an awesome dancer. She was also the sweetest, kindest person you could imagine – the kind of girl who'd persuade Harry Potter and Lord Voldemort to sit down and make friends over tea and biscuits.

Belle gazed out of the window as they approached central London. The wet Tarmac road was glittering in the sunlight. She sang along softly, still plugged into her iPod.

'They call the Garrick School *Superstar High*, don't they?'

Belle realized the driver was talking to her. Hastily, she stopped singing and removed her headphones. 'Oh, er, yes.'

'You a superstar then, love?' he asked.

'Not yet!' Belle laughed.

'You will be,' the driver chuckled, glancing at her in the rear-view mirror. 'Got that look about you. I can spot it a mile off. I've driven hundreds of Garrick students in my time. That Tory King was one . . . She's big in the West End now, her picture's on all the buses . . .'

Belle nodded but she was only half listening. Soon she would be back with the two loves of her life. Number One: her gorgeous boyfriend, Jack Thorne, another Year Eight student at the Garrick. She couldn't *wait* to see him again. And the other love? The one she thought about when she woke up in the morning and when she fell asleep at night and every second in between?

Singing!

A stage, a microphone and a song. Those were Belle's ingredients for Happily Ever After.

There was so much to look forward to this term. Rehearsals for the school's end-of-year musical, *Anything Goes*, would be starting the moment she got back. The Year Eleven students who would graduate this year were taking all the leading roles, but there would be plenty of smaller ensemble parts for younger students like Belle and her friends. And she couldn't wait to start working on some new songs with Nobody's Angels, the group she'd formed with Holly and Cat just a few weeks into their first term at Superstar High. There would be lots of school work too, with end-of-year tests coming up in all their subjects. And if that wasn't enough to keep her busy, Belle was planning to take her Grade Seven singing and piano exams before the summer holidays.

She was going to have to work very hard to keep on top of it all. But she didn't mind. Belle loved every minute at Superstar High. She felt like the luckiest girl alive.

And now at last familiar landmarks were starting to come into view; the trees along Kingsgrove Avenue all bursting into leaf; golden daffodils crowding the borders in Kingsgrove Square; Café Roma, the students' favourite meeting place. And then her heart was jumping for joy . . . they were gliding through the ornate iron gates, tyres crunching on the sweeping gravel drive as they swept towards the grand eighteenth-century building.

Before the limousine had stopped moving, Belle leaped out and ran up the broad stone steps past the pots of trees clipped into star shapes. She threw open the double doors into the entrance hall. Cat and Holly hurried towards her, arms outstretched – Cat in her favourite rock-chick mini-dress and boots, her tangle of red curls loosely pinned up with what looked like a pair of chopsticks; Holly petite and sporty in her skinny jeans and striped top, her long micro-braids in a ponytail – to sweep her up in a joyous group hug.

Then Belle noticed Jack hanging back behind them

in the busy entrance hall, his shaggy-but-in-a-cool-way brown hair flopping over his laser-beam eyes. A pulse of electricity shot through her as their eyes met. And then he was running towards her too.

This must be how wild birds feel when they're released from captivity, Belle thought as she flew into Jack's arms.

This was where she belonged.

And it was going to be the best term yet.

CHAPTER TWO

Holly: Message from the Mangrove Swamp

After dinner the following Friday, Holly and Belle made a beeline for their favourite sofa in the common room. It was the end of the first week of term – which had been as busy and exciting as always with its jam-packed routine of academic subjects in the mornings and performing arts in the afternoons. From Monday to Wednesday all students took core lessons in singing, dancing and acting, with Thursday and Friday afternoons spent on their advanced options. For Holly these were jazz, tap, Latin dance, musical theatre and her favourite, ballet.

The two girls sat down near an open window. Early evening sunlight played across the photographs of famous ex-students that lined the walls, and birdsong flooded in from outside. Belle was sipping the Slippery Elm tea she drank to protect her singing voice. Holly preferred to stick to hot chocolate!

Holly gazed across the courtyard. Groups of friends

were stopping to chat or heading out for the evening. *Only two more days until Ethan gets back*, she thought happily. Her boyfriend, Ethan Reed, along with several other Garrick students, had small parts in a new movie and they'd been away for several weeks now, filming on location. The film was a romantic comedy called *Sinking Feelings*, set on a distant waterlogged planet a hundred years in the future.

Holly had been delighted that Ethan had landed the part. Becoming a film actor was his dream and appearing in an Alistair Reagan movie could be his big break — even if he *was* only playing the hero's mutant second-cousin from Mars. *Sinking Feelings* had everything — aliens, vampires and snogging — and it was predicted to be a major blockbuster. Holly just wished the location in question was *slightly* nearer London than the mangrove swamps of the Everglades in southern Florida. What was wrong with Kent? They had marshes there, didn't they? OK, Florida wasn't *quite* a distant planet, but it was so far away it might as well be.

'You're really missing him, aren't you?' Belle asked gently.

Holly suddenly realized she'd been staring dreamily out of the window. She'd stirred her hot chocolate for so long it had turned into a brown whirlpool and was splashing over her lap. She snapped herself back from imagining Ethan knee-deep in a mangrove swamp.

'Oh, look,' she whispered, changing the subject (after all, there was no point going into a mega-mope when Ethan would be back in less than 2,880 minutes – not that she was counting, of course!). 'There's Owen Mitchell and Tabitha Langley. I wonder if they're working on their scripts already.' The two older students were sitting on the other side of the room, their heads bent together as they conferred over a sheaf of papers.

Owen and Tabitha were most popular boy and girl in Year Eleven. They'd won the school talent competition earlier in the year – and probably every other year since the dawn of time. And now they were playing the leading roles of Billy and Hope in *Anything Goes*. The cast list for the major roles had gone up earlier that day, and the whole school had been abuzz with feverish excitement ever since.

'I heard all the Year Elevens screaming and shouting around the notice board this morning,' Belle said. 'It reminded me of us last term when we got our solos in the Rising Stars Spectacular!'

Holly nodded. She'd been thinking about that too.

'Don't tell anyone, but I'm sort of glad Year Eights only get small parts in this production,' she admitted. 'It was exciting doing the big *Time of My Life* dance finale last term, but I'd be heading for Nervous Breakdown Central if I had to go through anything *quite* that exciting again just yet!' She grinned, remembering how her dance partner, Zak Lomax, had fallen ill just when they'd finally mastered the swallow-dive lift and Jack Thorne had heroically come to the rescue at the last minute. 'I'm happy to be tucked away in the chorus-line with the rest of the advanced tap class, well clear of the spotlight. Specially as I have my Intermediate ballet exam at the end of term.'

'Snap,' Belle agreed. 'I'm singing in the ensemble in *Bon Voyage*. No solos this time. And *definitely* no duets!'

Holly laughed. In the Rising Stars Spectacular, Belle had ended up singing a duet with her arch-enemy, Bianca Hayford. Holly always tried to See The Good in People, like her mum had taught her, but if Bianca had any good bits, she kept them *extremely* well-hidden. Bianca was the undisputed Queen of Mean at Superstar High. But luckily they'd had a week off from Bianca's spiteful comments; she was with the same talent agency as Ethan, and was also in the mangrove swamp filming *Sinking Feelings*.

Holly looked up as she heard someone singing *You're the Top* – her favourite number from *Anything Goes*. It was Cat, sashaying into the common room, singing in a throaty, over-the-top nightclub-singer voice.

'That's the part I'd want if I was in Year Eleven,' Cat announced, flopping down onto the arm of the sofa. 'Reno Sweeney! She's so slinky and glamorous.'

Cat was looking pretty slinky and glamorous herself, in her black mini-dress, red leather jacket and boots. She told them she'd just got back from a romantic date at Café Roma with Adam. Cat and Adam Fielding had only been going out together since the end of last term, but already it seemed like a match made in heaven. Or at least, in the *library* – which is where Cat had found him.

Holly smiled. 'Good time?'

Cat grinned. 'Yeah. Adam's so funny. We were laughing so much I thought Luigi might throw us out for putting the other customers off their food! Then Adam started singing *You're the Top*, except we changed it to You're the Topping – you know, like pizza toppings . . . *You're the sundried tomato, you're the parma ham*, and, er . . .' Cat's voice trailed off as Holly and Belle looked at her doubtfully. 'You had to be there!'

Holly laughed. 'I love *You're the Top*,' she said. 'In fact, I love all the songs in *Anything Goes*. And the tap-dance routines are amazing – all that nineteen-thirties style and glitz. But the plot's so complicated. All I know is it happens on a big ship and there's a load of mix-ups and mayhem all over the place. But the girls all get the right guys in the end!'

'Just like an average day at Superstar High, really!' Cat joked. 'Well, not the ship part, obviously.'

'And just like us,' Belle added. 'We all got the right guys in the end too. Jack and me, Ethan and Holly, Adam and Cat.'

'Oh yeah, we've so nailed this whole romance thing.' Cat did a little celebration shimmy and high-fived Belle and Holly. 'There's nothing to it!'

The subject of *romance* lured Holly's thoughts back to Ethan. *Only two more days*. Or 2,867 minutes (not that she was counting, of course!). She was already planning her outfit for meeting him on Sunday evening . . . her new pink and black top, grey shorts, silver ballet pumps . . .

Holly's Ethan-greeting-outfit plan was interrupted by the sound of Beyoncé singing *Halo*. She pulled out her phone from her jeans pocket and checked the screen. Her heart skipped a beat.

'Yes! It's a text from Ethan!' She sighed with relief. She hadn't heard from him for days.

'If he wants to know what present you'd like him to bring back,' Cat said, 'tell him a big box of chocs to share with your friends. We've nearly finished the ones Belle got in duty-free!'

But Holly could barely hear her. Reading the first few lines of the message, the words began to swim out of focus as her eyes filled with tears. Wordlessly, she passed her phone to Cat and Belle.

She'd seen enough.

Eight more weeks!

She couldn't even begin to count how many minutes that was!

CHAPTER THREE

Cat: What Would Mary Poppins Do?

Cat was almost choking with impatience to see Ethan's message.

You could see from the tears welling in Holly's big Malteser-brown eyes that it was something truly catastrophic. Possibilities bounced around Cat's mind. *He's been mortally wounded during filming.* No, he wouldn't be able to send a text if he was dying. *He's met another girl and is dumping Holly?*

Cat grabbed the phone and began to read out loud. '*Lead actor, Josh Kelso, bitten by alligator. They want me to take his place . . .*'

It was OK! Ethan wasn't gasping for his last breath. And he hadn't ditched Holly. In fact, this wasn't just *OK* – this was *full-on fantastic*! Ethan Luck-Monster Reed had just walked into the leading role in an Alistair Reagan movie! Cat felt a tiny pang of jealously. Not that she was planning a career as a film star – at least, not in films like *Sinking Feelings*, which sounded like a cross between *Star Wars* and *Enchanted*. *I am a serious actress*, Cat reminded herself. *The Royal Shakespeare Company is more my style . . . or at least, important French films with subtitles . . .*

'But this is *brilliant*, Hols,' she enthused. 'Wow! Ethan's just fast-tracked his way to superstardom. Start planning your dress for Oscar night, girl!'

Suddenly Cat noticed Belle glaring at her with one of her special eyebrow-twitching warning looks. *Uh-oh. What have I done now?* Then she looked at Holly and realized she wasn't sharing the joy. What was wrong?

Belle took the phone from Cat and read out the next line of the message. '*So I have to stay in Florida eight more weeks* . . . Oh, no!' Belle put her arm round Holly and handed her a tissue.

'Eight whole weeks? But that means he's away all term!' Cat spluttered in outrage. Holly gulped and made an odd strangled noise, like someone sitting on a set of bagpipes. Belle frowned and made a zip-it gesture, her arm still round Holly's shoulder. *Oops*, Cat thought, *I've done it again*.

'I'm sure Ethan's just as upset as you are about having to stay longer,' Belle was saying.

Holly shook her head. 'He'll be so busy and excited

about the new part, he won't have time to be upset!' she wailed.

Cat hated seeing Holly so miserable. She wished she could find a silver lining in the cloud somewhere to cheer her up. What would Mary Poppins do? *A spoonful of sugar wouldn't solve this one!* It didn't even have to be a solid-silver lining. Silver-*plated* would do! Then, suddenly, she thought of something.

'If the filming is delayed by eight weeks, the whole term will be a Bianca-free zone!' Cat declared triumphantly. She looked at Holly, waiting for a smile. Surely the prospect of no Bianca *all term* would be enough to pull her back from the Swamp of Despair . . .

'Only part of it,' Holly sighed. 'Ethan says the others come back in a couple of weeks as soon as they've re-shot their scenes with him.' She leaned back against the sofa cushions and closed her eyes. 'Oh, why couldn't that stupid alligator have bitten the leading *girl* – *Violet Dubarry*, or whatever her name is – instead of Josh Kelso? Then Ethan would be coming home, and it might even be Bianca staying in the Everglades . . .'

Holly suddenly clapped her hand over her mouth. 'Sorry, I can't believe I said that. I wouldn't *really* want anything to happen to Violet . . .'

Cat exchanged glances with Belle. Sometimes Holly was just too nice for her own good! Knowing Bianca, she was probably thinking the exact same thing. In fact, Cat could imagine her training up a crack team of attack alligators right now to ambush Violet Dubarry and nibble off a few chunks so she could step into the starring role!

'I'm being so selfish, aren't I?' Holly was saying glumly. 'I know you're right, Cat. Getting this part is a dream come true for Ethan. And I'm *trying* to be happy about it. But I was so looking forward to seeing him on Sunday—' She broke off in a sob.

Cat wrapped Holly in a big sympathy-hug.

She was all out of silver linings.

Even silver-plated ones!

CHAPTER FOUR

Cat: Friends Who Are Boys

Cat looked on in astonishment as Belle jumped up from the sofa with a rousing battle cry.

'This calls for Drastic Action!' She stood in a heroic hands-on-hips pose, like a warrior princess. 'I was going to wait and tell you about this tomorrow, when I'd printed off all the details, but we need something to cheer Holly up *now*, so . . .'

Cat stared at her. What did Belle have up the sleeve of her immaculate white Chanel T-shirt? *Please don't let it be something that would count as 'exciting' only in Belle Madison World*, Cat prayed. *Like a hundred-page history project, or a new set of yoga-inspired voice exercises. This needs to be good!*

'It's a music-video competition for new artists,' Belle went on. 'I saw it on the PopTV website. You have to film a video of your band performing an original song, and the five winners get to record their video professionally and have it played on PopTV. The deadline's less than a month away. What do you think?'

'What do I think?' Cat shouted. 'I think, *Why aren't we filling in our entry form already!*' She sprang off the sofa, took hold of Belle's shoulders and jumped up and down. 'This is going to be so much fun!'

In her head she was already in an amazingly cool recording studio – headphones clamped to her ears – singing with Belle and Holly. Now Lady Gaga was coming in and asking if she could jam with Nobody's Angels on the next track . . . OK, so they had to actually *make the video* and *win the competition* first, but these were minor details. Suddenly remembering she was meant to be on cheering-up duty, Cat glanced anxiously at Holly. Surely no one could stay sad for long with something so awesome to look forward to?

Yes! Holly was smiling! It was a bit of a thin, watery smile, but it was the first one since Ethan's text arrived.

'That sounds great,' she said, wiping away her tears. 'This is just what I need to keep my mind off Ethan being Missing in Action.'

'And with Ethan away doing his mangrove thing, you'll have tons of time to concentrate on the video!' Cat said triumphantly, finding that silver lining at last. 'We'll need you to choreograph a dance routine for us, of course, and with *Anything Goes* and your ballet exams, you'll be so busy . . . in fact, it's a *blessing* that Ethan's not around. I'm starting to think maybe we should dispatch Jack and Adam off to a swamp too, because we definitely won't have time for *boys* this term!'

Holly laughed and held her hands up in surrender. 'OK, OK, don't overdo it!' She jumped up and joined Cat and Belle in their Happy Dance.

'It's a deal then?' Belle asked, her blue eyes sparkling with excitement. 'Nobody's Angels are GO?'

Cat nodded. 'Look out, world – here come the girls!'

'Boys need not apply!' Holly laughed as they linked arms and flopped backwards onto the sofa in perfect formation.

'Boys need not apply for what?'

Cat looked up to see their friend Nick Taggart striding across the common room, followed by Nathan Almeida carrying a plate of biscuits.

'Now, correct me if I'm wrong,' Nick continued, putting on a pompous official voice and pretending to make notes on a clipboard, 'but this sounds like a case of *blatant* sex discrimination! Haven't you ladies *heard* of equal opportunities?'

Cat laughed as Nick plonked himself down on Belle's knee. Belle shoved him off and he settled on a beanbag. Nathan perched on the corner of a coffee table.

Nick and Nathan were total opposites. Nick, a stocky sandy-haired boy from Edinburgh, was a talented comedian and singer. Nathan, who'd come all the way from Mexico City to study at Superstar High, was tall and skinny with straight black hair and wire-framed glasses that gave him a borderline geeky look. He was very a gifted actor, but very shy and quiet in real life. And Nick? Well, Nick definitely wasn't! They were Cat, Holly and Belle's closest boy friends. *Friends Who Are Boys, that is*, Cat thought as she watched Nick dunking custard creams in Holly's leftover hot chocolate. *Definitely not to be confused with boyfriends!*

'Did I hear something about a competition?' Nick asked. 'I luuuurve competitions. What is it? Girls only, you say? Miss World? Wimbledon Ladies' Triples?'

Belle rolled her eyes and smiled. 'It's for Nobody's Angels.' She explained the PopTV competition to the boys. 'The judges will be looking for the best song and the most original video.'

'Sweeeeet,' Nick whistled. 'This is a brilliant opportunity for us!'

'Us?' Cat exclaimed. 'What's with the *us*?'

'Hel-lo!' Nick retorted in mock-surprise. 'You'll

need a director for the video. And I *am* your manager!'

The girls looked at each other. It was true that Nick had helped Nobody's Angels prepare for a big talent competition in their first term, but Cat wasn't sure this qualified him as their *manager*.

'Well, I don't know,' Belle was saying uncertainly. 'I guess we *could* use a director . . .'

Holly nodded. 'I think Nick would be great.'

'You got it!' Nick pronounced enthusiastically. He'd now switched to a cheesy transatlantic show-biz accent. 'You just made the most important decision of your career, baby! Having the right director is a make-or-breaker!'

'And the right cameraman,' Nathan added quietly. 'I could help with that. I did a course on film-making back home last summer. I made a short film for my final project.'

Cat smiled at her friend gratefully. Nathan was so clever and his calm influence might help to keep a lid on some of Nick's wilder ideas. She couldn't wait to get started.

'Was it a music video?' Holly asked.

Nathan bit his lip shyly. 'Er, no, it was more of a documentary really. On the life cycle of the Mexican dwarf tree frog.'

Belle looked doubtful. 'Do we *look* like tree frogs?'

'Camera skills are transferable,' Nick asserted. 'Welcome on board, Nathan. Now, we need a team brainstorm.' He closed his eyes and threw back his head. 'Oh yeah! I can feel the creative spirits coming to me, baby! You'll be doing *Done Lookin'*, right? That's got Latin rhythms, yeah? I'm being drawwwwn towards a South American *concept* . . . I'm seeing carnival in the background, then a tracking shot on the girls wearing red flamenco dresses . . . no, maybe that's too much. Help me out here, Nathan . . .'

'Whoa there!' Belle told him. 'We haven't even decided on the song yet!'

Nick looked disappointed. Then he held up his hands, 'Yeah, we're getting waaay ahead of ourselves here. I'll go and book a rehearsal room for tomorrow morning so we can have a play and decide on *material*.'

'And I'll borrow a video camera from the ICT department,' Nathan offered.

'Good man,' Nick said, patting him on the back as they turned to leave. 'Now, get an early night, ladies, we've got a lot of work ahead!'

'Excuse me,' Belle protested. 'I thought you were our *director* now, not our *manager*!'

'Or our *nanny*,' Cat added.

'Oh, I can multi-task, baby,' Nick quipped over his shoulder. He tripped on a rug and bumped into Nathan. They both tumbled over the back of an armchair.

'Yep, so we can see,' Holly whispered, grinning.

'What have we let ourselves in for?' Belle sighed. But she was smiling and shaking her head fondly.

'That was totally *meant* to happen,' Nick said loudly, picking himself up off the chair.

Cat grinned. This was going to be a fabulous term.

And she was *really* looking forward to recording that track with Lady Gaga when they won the prize!

CHAPTER FIVE

Belle: Figments and Footprints

As they climbed the elegant sweeping staircase from the entrance hall to their bedrooms on the first floor, Belle was deep in thought. Nobody's Angels had several original songs in their repertoire, all written by their friend, Lettie Atkins, but which one would work best for the video competition?

Done Lookin' was a great song. But would a romantic ballad like *Opposites Attract* showcase their voices better?

'I'm not sure which would work best either,' Holly said as they reached the top of the stairs.

Belle jumped. 'How did you know what I was thinking?'

'Telepathy,' Holly told her. 'That and the fact you've just hummed your way through the entire Nobody's Angels playlist!'

Belle smiled. 'Maybe we need to come up with a brand-new song.'

'Uh-oh!' Cat laughed. 'Belle Madison, please tell me

you are not *seriously* suggesting that we write something ourselves. You *do* remember the Great Original Material Incident of the winter term?'

'How could I ever forget?'

Before Lettie, a talented musician, came to their rescue, the girls had tried to write their own song. To say that they weren't terribly good at writing songs would be like saying penguins weren't terribly good at flying.

'No, I'm not *that* crazy!' Belle assured them. 'When I said, *we* should come up with a new song, what I meant was that we should ask *Lettie* to come up with a new song . . . if she has time, of course.'

'I'm sure Lettie will *make* time,' Holly said mysteriously. 'Considering who else we have on our team, *baby*!'

Belle instantly knew what Holly was talking about. Nick and Lettie were really into each other. It'd been obvious to everyone at Superstar High for months now. Everyone, that was, except Nick and Lettie. Last term he had even asked her on 'pretend dates' – supposedly to keep an eye on Cat when she went out with a new boy – but he still hadn't plucked up the courage to ask her out for real.

'Asking Lettie to join the team would be perfect,' Holly said. 'We'll have a new song, *and* we get to do a bit of matchmaking on the side. If Nick and Lettie are working on this video together, they won't fail to fall for each other's charms!'

'And Nick's charms are *what*, precisely?' Cat asked, with a grin.

'*Beauty is in the eye of the beholder!*' Holly quoted.

Belle smiled. Holly was almost back to her old self again after the shock of Ethan's message. And there was nothing Holly liked more than a spot of matchmaking.

'No time like the present,' Belle said.

They were standing right outside Lettie's room. Belle knocked and poked her head round the door. Normally she would have hesitated since Lettie shared with Bianca Hayford – but with Bianca safely ensconced in a swamp in Florida, the coast was clear.

The bright, cosy study-bedroom was identical to the rooms that Cat and Belle shared next door and that Holly shared with Gemma Dalrymple on the other side of the corridor, except that each had a different colour scheme. Cat and Belle's was blue and turquoise, Holly's was all lilacs and lavenders. Lettie's was decorated in pretty shades of yellow and orange.

Lettie was sitting on her bed in her pyjamas pencilling notes on a musical score. Her beloved cello was leaning against the wardrobe. She looked up and waved the girls into the room, her brown eyes thoughtful behind her reading glasses and her long chestnut hair pulled back in an elastic band.

Belle went to sit down on Bianca's bed. Then she leaped up. Something had moved! She lifted the duvet to see Shreddie, the school cat, snuggled on the pillow.

'Lettie! Bianca'll go ballistic if she finds out Shreddie's been in the room,' Belle gasped in horror. 'Let alone in her bed!'

'I know,' Lettie said with a giggle. 'But I can't keep him out of there. I'll just have to sneak the bedclothes into Miss Candlemas's laundry pile before Bianca gets back.'

They all laughed. No one could figure out *why*, but Shreddie was truly, madly, deeply in love with Bianca, despite the fact she didn't even *like* cats. She said she was allergic to them, although it was hard to be sure since Bianca said she was allergic to most things.

'You weird, confused little creature,' Belle murmured fondly, stroking his golden fur. Shreddie leaped down and stalked away, obviously disgusted that Belle, Cat and Holly had defiled the Sacred Bed of Bianca by daring to sit on it!

Belle quickly filled Lettie in on the music-video competition, with plenty of interruptions from Holly and Cat.

'Sounds great!' Lettie said excitedly. 'Count me in! I'd love to see one of my songs on PopTV!'

'Awesome! Welcome to the team,' Belle said, smiling.

'Team?' Lettie asked.

'We've got a couple of other people helping,' Holly explained. 'Like Nathan. He's the cameraman. Oh, yeah'- she added in a super-casual voice - 'and Nick Taggart, of course. He's directing.'

At the mention of Nick's name, Lettie blushed – so slightly that it was almost invisible to the naked eye. But Belle, Cat and Holly's eyes were far from naked; they were fully equipped with Low-Level Blush-Detection Devices. They all saw the telltale pink tinge.

'Oh yes, Nick'll be very involved,' Cat added. 'You'll be working *closely* with him all the way . . .'

Belle grinned at Holly. Cat's idea of a *subtle hint* was about as subtle as a sumo wrestler with a sledgehammer! Not surprisingly, Lettie's blush now had deepened to a glowing shade of crimson.

'Oooh! I think I have the perfect song,' she said, changing the subject. She rummaged in a desk drawer. 'I started working on something for you over the Easter holidays . . . ah, here it is.' She pulled out a sheet of paper. 'It's called *Keep the Dream Alive*.' She started humming a soft, haunting melody.

'It's so sad,' Holly said. Then she grinned apologetically. 'I mean, *beautiful-sad*, not *pathetic-sad*, obviously!'

Belle murmured her agreement. 'Wait a minute!' she said, and ran next door to fetch her electronic keyboard. She propped it on the low table in the middle of the room and knelt on the floor. She took the handwritten musical score and picked out the tune.

'*I'm loving it!*' Cat started humming along. Holly joined in.

'Have you written some lyrics for this, Lettie?' Cat asked. 'I'm not sure the world is ready for my deeply meaningful *La-la dooby-doos . . .*'

Lettie took another sheet of paper from the drawer and passed it over. Belle, Cat and Holly began to sing the first few lines.

'You walked past me in the street,
But when I turned round there was no one there.
I saw your smile and the look in your eyes,
But then nothing but thin air . . .'

'How lovely,' Holly sighed. 'So, is it about anyone special?' she added with a smile.

Lettie blushed again. 'No, of course not. It's just something I made up.'

'So, not even the *tiniest* bit about someone with the initials N.T.?' Cat asked, with a wicked grin.

'Don't tease her.' Holly batted Cat on the head with a pillow. 'If Lettie wishes to remain a Woman of Mystery, that's fine with us.'

'Yes, after all, she was our very own Mystery Songwriter,' Belle added, remembering how Lettie had written songs for them anonymously in their first term.

'OK! Come on,' Cat declared. 'Let's sing the chorus.' The girls gathered round Belle at the keyboard, while Holly held up the lyric sheet for them all to see.

'Everyone tells me you're not for real
That you're a dream, you're in my mind
But one day we'll find each other
I will keep the dream alive.'

As they finished they all beamed excitedly. Belle's mind was already buzzing with ideas for developing the vocals and adding harmonies. She couldn't wait to get into the rehearsal room tomorrow and start working on it.

They all enveloped Lettie in a huge thank-you hug.

Their dream of winning the video competition was very much alive!

CHAPTER SIX

Holly: Just Someone from School

Holly was running through allegro combinations. They were going to have to be perfect in time for her Intermediate exam at the end of term. *Keep it strong, floooowing* . . . eyelids closing . . . *Must stay awake* . . . Her bed was just too comfortable!

She wasn't *actually* in ballet class, of course. There would be no chance of nodding off there. The merest suspicion of a stifled yawn and Miss Morgan would be poking her in the ribs and yelling '*Attenzione!*' No one knew why she delivered her most urgent instructions in Italian; she was no more Italian than a frozen mini-pizza. In this afternoon's advanced class, Miss Morgan had worked them even harder than usual.

'We need to step it up a gear now, girls,' she'd cried, banging her stick on the floor, 'if we are to be ready for the Intermediate exam. *Rapidamente!* Get out of the slow lane!'

Having been a passenger in Miss Morgan's mini,

Holly was surprised she even knew that there *was* a slow lane!

Holly didn't go in for All-Night Virtual Ballet Marathons as a rule. But tonight she had A Plan. She was going to call Ethan at two o'clock. She couldn't set the alarm clock, for fear of waking Gemma – who was snoring peacefully in her bed on the other side of the room – so she had to stay awake for another two hours until she could lock herself in the bathroom and make the call.

Not that two a.m. was an *obvious* time for a romantic chat, but Holly was desperate. Florida was five hours behind London time, so if she called before lessons in the morning Ethan would still be in bed, and when she'd tried at lunch time or in the afternoon, he was always on set filming. But two a.m. was nine in the evening in Florida. Ethan would be safely back in his hotel room after dinner, on his own, with plenty of time for a lovely long talk.

Which is exactly what Holly wanted. It was now Thursday, almost a week since Ethan's Eight-Week bombshell, but they'd only exchanged a few short text messages since. She was dying to tell him all about the PopTV competition and their brilliant new song. She'd been rehearsing it with Belle and Cat all week and it was sounding better and better. They'd not started on the video itself yet, but Holly had been busy working out a dance routine for it.

Must stay awake . . . It was no good. She kept sinking into sleep and having to shake herself back to consciousness. *I know, I'll sneak down to the common room and do some real ballet practice. May as well make use of all this extra time . . .*

Holly pulled on her dressing gown and put her phone in the pocket. Holding her breath, she crept along the dark corridor. If she was caught wandering around the school at night she would be in deep trouble. Slowly, Holly felt her way down the stairs leading to the entrance hall. She paused at the bottom to get her bearings. The hall was in shadows, lit only by a glowing emergency light over the front door. There was something eerie about the emptiness – during the school day the huge cavernous space was always teeming with life. Even more spooky was the sight of Mrs Butterworth's unoccupied desk; the school secretary was always at her post between the pigeon holes and the notice board, keeping tabs on the entire school from her swivel chair.

Holly tiptoed into the common room. Silver moonlight threw strange shadows across the carpet.

Using the back of an armchair as a makeshift barre, she began to run through her *tendus*. Soon she was in her own world, with no idea of time or place, as always happened when she was dancing. So when something soft and furry brushed against her leg she almost jumped out of her skin.

Holly only just managed to stop herself letting out a scream. Her heart racing, she peered nervously down at the floor where she was standing and spotted . . .

'*Shreddie!*' she groaned. 'You nearly scared me to death! And is that a *mouse* you're eating? Gross!'

Taking deep breaths to bring her galloping heart back under control, Holly checked the time on her phone. She'd been dancing for over an hour and it was now two o'clock precisely. She curled up in the comfiest armchair and as she scrolled down to Ethan's name in her contacts list, she pictured him in his hotel room, watching TV or reading a book, after a tough day of filming . . . He was going to be so pleased to hear from her. Excitement mounting, she listened to the ring tone . . . and listened . . . and listened . . .

Just when Holly was about to hang up she heard a reply.

'Hello? Yes?' Ethan's voice sounded oddly muffled.

'Hi, Ethan, it's me!' Holly blurted out. She was so

eager to tell him *everything* she had thought, felt or done over the last week that she could hardly get the words out fast enough. 'I'm missing you so much! I know it's a brilliant opportunity for you, though, and I'm really happy for you. Is everything OK there?'

'Yes, everything's . . . er . . . fine . . .' Ethan whispered.

'You'll never guess what! We're entering a video competition! Belle and Cat and me, that is. If we win, we'll be on PopTV!'

'That's great, Holly. I'm really sorry but I can't talk right now . . .'

All of a sudden, Holly realized that Ethan wasn't sounding very pleased to hear from her at all. His voice wasn't just muffled, it was strained and . . . distant. And not just the 4,500-miles-away kind of distant, but the I've-got-other-things-on-my-mind-right-now kind of distant too.

He doesn't want to talk to me! Holly felt as if a trap door had opened in the seat of the armchair. She was being sucked down into a bottomless pit of disappointment.

'It's just that we're filming right now,' Ethan whispered, 'doing a night scene. I shouldn't even have my phone on but I forgot to turn it off.'

'Oh, sorry, I didn't know,' Holly began. But then

she heard a girl saying something to Ethan and a giggle down the line. She caught a few words of Ethan's reply, '*Just someone from school in London . . .*'

'Ethan?' Holly quavered.

'Sorry, Holly. I'm being called on set – gotta go. Speak soon, I promise. Bye!'

The connection was broken. She stared at the lifeless phone, her thoughts spinning. *Who was that girl Ethan was talking to? Why was she giggling? 'Just someone from school.' Is that all I mean to him?*

Holly felt totally deflated. She'd been so looking forward to a long, romantic moonlight chat. She'd kept herself awake, even though she was exhausted, and all she got in return was a measly two minutes and a *Just someone from school*. She dragged herself out of the chair, and trudged miserably back upstairs, hardly caring whether anyone heard her or not.

As she climbed back into bed, the chorus of Lettie's new song floated into her mind.

I will keep the dream alive . . .

Right now it seemed her dream was barely even breathing.

CHAPTER SEVEN

Cat: The Leotard That Time Forgot

The next day found Cat lying on her bed reading *Much Ado About Nothing*, with half an hour to spare before her afternoon class. She was planning to audition for the part of Beatrice for a production in Cambridge in the summer holidays. Although the audition was still weeks away, she had already started making notes. She loved the character of Beatrice – she was so feisty and funny. She just *had* to get the part! She closed her eyes and she was *there*, cycling through the cobbled streets of Cambridge to the theatre every day, looking very much like an auburn-haired Kate Winslet, waiting in the green room, joking with the other actors, stepping onto stage . . .

She opened her eyes again and glanced at her watch. *1.25!* She stared in disbelief. Advanced Latin dance started in five minutes! And she wasn't even changed yet. She was going to have to break the land-speed record to get to there on time – not to mention the dressing-speed record!

In one Houdini-like movement, she stripped off her jeans and jumper and reached out to grab a leotard from her specially designed storage solution; otherwise known as the-gigantic-heap-of-clothes-on-the-bed.

But her leotard wasn't there.

Frantically Cat burrowed into the clothes mountain. *No leotard!* Then she tried the smaller foothills on the floor. Still no luck. *Why, oh why can't I be more like Belle?* Cat thought glancing enviously across at Belle's half of the room. Belle always had her clothes laid out in advance, washed and ironed (she'd even been sighted in the laundry room once *ironing a pair of footless tights!*).

Then suddenly Cat remembered. On Wednesday afternoon, she'd been seized by an uncharacteristic fit of tidiness and taken all her dance clothes to the laundry.

Which is where they were now.

Her three leotards, two dance skirts and five pairs of tights.

Hanging on the drying rack in the laundry room.

But there was no time to retrieve them.

Turning up to dance class in her bra and knickers was not an option. She reached down the back of the radiator and pulled out a pair of purple tights.

'Yes!' she shouted, brushing off the dust balls and pulling them on. They were so full of holes they could almost pass for fishnets. Then she rummaged in the back of the wardrobe and found an old leotard scrunched so tightly into a little grey ball that it made a creaking noise when she prised it open. It didn't smell too great either, but she wriggled into it, trying to ignore the crusty feel of the fabric. She stepped into a short red ra-ra skirt. It wasn't actually a dance skirt and the hem was coming down but it would have to do. She completed the look with a baggy beige sweatshirt – so ancient, only carbon-dating could reveal its true age.

Glancing into the mirror, she couldn't help giggling at her reflection.

She couldn't have done any worse if she'd covered herself in glue and rolled through a jumble sale!

'Girl, you are lookin' gooood!' she laughed.

She hurtled out of her room and sprinted across the school like Usain Bolt with a train to catch.

Cat barrelled into the dance studio as Miss LeClair was calling everyone to gather round. She slipped in behind Holly and Gemma, planning to keep a *very* low profile. Gemma – looking as wholesome as ever with her bouncy blond hair and a leotard so clean it could've played a starring role in a washing-powder advert – did a double-take at Cat's dishevelled outfit. Holly smiled, but it was one of those fragile smiles that's somehow sadder than no smile at all. Cat had hardly seen Holly all day, and for the first time she noticed her cappuccino-coloured skin was blotchy and there were dark shadows under her eyes. Cat made a mental note to have a Serious Talk with her after the class and find out what was wrong.

Cat looked up at Miss LeClair, enviously admiring her raspberry-pink and slate-grey dancewear combo. Her wavy primrose-blond hair was tucked neatly under a co-ordinating pink hairband.

'We have a very exciting opportunity . . .' she was saying to the class. 'We want to show off everyone's talents in *Anything Goes*, so we've taken some liberties with the direction, while staying true to the 1930s setting. We've choreographed a new dance routine, a slow tango in the shadows as the backdrop to Tabitha and Owen singing *All Through the Night* . . .'

Cat's heartbeat quickened. She loved all forms of Latin dance, but the tango was her all-time favourite. And the dance routine sounded so romantic and atmospheric. The urge to shoot her hand in the air, shouting, '*Pick me! Pick me!*' was almost irresistible!

That's when she caught sight of Adam, sitting at the front of the group with two other Year Nine boys.

I know Adam's into Latin dance, but what's he doing gate-crashing the Year Eight class? Cat wondered. *And, did he have to pick the day that I look as if I'm entering a fancy dress competition as a scarecrow?*

She didn't have to wait long to find out.

'We'll be working on our tango all afternoon,' Miss LeClair continued, raising her voice over the excited whispers rippling around the group. 'I will then select the best three couples to dance in *All Through the Night*. And because there are more girls than boys in this class, these gentlemen from Year Nine have kindly agreed to join us to balance out the numbers.' She gestured to Adam and the other two.

'And I've another surprise for you,' Miss LeClair announced. 'We have a visiting expert with us this term. He'll help me select the couples today and then work with them over the next few weeks to perfect the routine. He's from Argentina, the home of tango, *Miguel Silva*!'

Cat couldn't believe it! Miguel Silva was *only* one of the most famous Latin American dancers in the entire universe. He was currently starring in a Samba Spectacular in the West End *and* he was one of the judges on *Dance-Factor* on TV.

Now I'm really glad I dressed up specially for this class,

Cat thought despairingly. *I'm bound to impress Miguel Silva looking like this!*

Everyone applauded as Miguel Silva appeared from the side door. Tall and olive-skinned with sleek dark hair, he moved with a soft, dangerous stealth, like a panther stalking its prey. He grasped Miss LeClair and kissed her on both cheeks. She blushed and giggled as she told the class to get into pairs and start warming up.

Cat was in a major tailspin. She'd been about to run over and grab Adam for her partner. They'd never danced together before and it would be so much fun. They might even get selected to dance in *Anything Goes*. How cool would that be? Then she remembered the Leotard That Time Forgot. Adam obviously wasn't going to come within a ten-mile radius of her, looking – and smelling – like this, let alone *dance* with her.

But she was wrong. She was still lurking at the back of the class when Adam marched right up to her.

'Would you care to be my partner?' he said formally, doing that special lopsided grin she liked so much. Then he took a step back and looked her up and down.

'Er, *interesting* outfit!' he laughed. 'Is this some hot new fashion-trend I've missed out on?'

Cat grinned with relief. She should have known Adam was too laid-back to body-swerve a girl just because she looked like she'd got dressed in a skip.

'Yeah, where've you been?' she joked back. 'It's called Retro Garbage Chic. It's all over the catwalks!'

'And that *divine* perfume you're wearing?' Adam whispered, sniffing, as they embraced for the *salida*, or opening steps, 'What is it? Hmm . . . I'm getting compost heap . . . Perhaps a hint of old sock?'

Cat giggled, then concentrated on following his steps.

The students all knew the tango, of course. But Miguel pushed them further, working on precision and fluidity, and teaching them complex steps like double *ganchos*, or leg-wraps, and *ochos* – a series of dizzying pivots and spins. He walked amongst the couples, stopping to adjust their positioning, shouting instructions in a sultry Antonio Banderas-style Spanish accent. 'Guys! You must lead. Be *macho*, no? Ladies, you must follow. With attitude and energy!'

Cat instantly forgot all about her whiffy leotard and her holey tights and threw herself into the lesson. She was having the time of her life! Adam was an amazing dancer. He led confidently but was flexible enough that she could improvise her own adornments. It was as if they were reading each others' minds – this was Dance Heaven!

After two amazing hours of nonstop tango, Miguel Silva clapped his hands. 'Everybody rest!'

Adam's dark eyes were shining, 'They've *got* to pick us,' he breathed fervently. Cat nodded. She wanted this more than anything!

'We've been watching you all very closely,' Miss LeClair announced. 'And we've decided on our three couples.

'First, Zak Lomax and Gemma Dalrymple!'

Everyone clapped as Zak and Gemma high-fived, beaming at each other in delight. Gemma had been going out with Zak since the very end of last term – when Holly worked her Cupid magic on them – and they were both superb dancers.

'Totally gnarlacious, dude!' Zak exclaimed.

Cat held her breath. She and Adam *had* to be the next couple called! *Please, please* . . .

'Next, Philippe Meyer and Sophia Khan!'

There was a round of applause as Philippe and Sophia took a bow.

Cat glanced across at Holly. Holly attempted a smile. She was the best dancer in the year, and usually she'd have been the favourite to be chosen, but today, even Cat had to admit that Holly's dancing had seemed tired and lacking in sparkle.

Cat's heart was trying to crawl out through her mouth. *We're not going to be selected* . . . She closed her eyes and mentally adopted the brace position, ready to bear the disappointment. She felt Adam squeeze her hand.

'But there has been one stand-out couple today,' Miguel Silva was saying. 'In a league of their own!'

Cat opened her eyes. He was looking straight at her. And he was smiling . . .

'Adam Fielding and Cat Wickham!' Miss LeClair shouted.

Cat thought she would explode with joy! She jumped into Adam's arms and hugged him as if she would never let go. 'Yes, we did it!' she yelled. Adam laughed and spun her round in a victory twirl. But as she was being twirled, Cat spotted Holly sloping off towards the door of the studio, looking dejected. *Oh no!* she thought, *I hope she didn't think we were being insensitive. Maybe I was a bit loud in my celebrations . . .*

'I'm just going to check on Holly . . .' Cat began saying to Adam, but she was interrupted by a loud, slow clapping sound coming from across the dance studio. Miguel Silva strode forward to congratulate them.

'Cat, you dance with your heart,' he said. 'I believe you must have Argentinean blood in your veins!'

Cat was so overwhelmed by the compliment she couldn't speak.

'Ah, when I started dancing, I was just like you,' Miguel continued, glancing at Cat's saggy beige sweatshirt and threadbare leotard. 'I couldn't afford expensive clothes, either. I had to work three jobs to pay my way through dance school. But talent will shine through. You will *find* a way to overcome your humble origins!'

Cat stared at her feet, and mumbled something she hoped sounded suitably poverty-stricken.

Then Miguel smiled at Adam. 'And you danced beautifully too, my friend. But you must be careful' – he laughed – 'this girl has *fire* in her soul. If you cross her you will be in bi-i-ig trouble!'

Adam and Cat laughed. *As if Adam could do anything to make me angry!* Cat thought.

Miguel air-kissed them both goodbye. Then he wrinkled his nose. He looked around as if searching for a gas leak.

'Just off for a shower!' Cat muttered, darting away before Miguel realized where the pong was coming from and changed his mind.

Being too poor to buy new dance clothes was one thing.

Smelling like the bottom of a dustbin was quite another!

CHAPTER EIGHT

Holly: Alien Death-beasts and Low-flying Condiments

At dinner that evening Holly picked at her fish pie. Ever since her non-conversation with Ethan, she felt as if a giant brick had lodged in her chest.

'OK, Hols!' Cat said firmly, sitting down next to her. 'You're not leaving this table until you've told me what's wrong! I could tell you weren't really trying in tango class and you left before I could talk to you. Is everything OK? No offence, but you look awful . . .'

'Thanks!' Holly retorted. 'You weren't exactly a fashion goddess yourself earlier!'

Cat grimaced. 'True. But I'm not talking about clothes. I'm talking about *you*. I hope you don't mind that Adam and I, y'know . . .' she began falteringly.

'Of course not!' Holly gave another of her sad smiles. 'I'm really happy for you guys – you danced amazingly today.' She sighed and decided to tell Cat the sneaking-down-in-the-night-to-phone-Ethan story.

'. . . then I heard Ethan say that it was *just someone he knew from school!*' she groaned, coming to the end of the sorry tale. 'Is that all I mean to him?'

Cat smiled reassuringly. 'He was probably just dead embarrassed that his phone went off in the middle of filming. Imagine,' she went on, helping herself to mashed potato from Holly's plate, 'it's a really tense, spooky night-scene. Our hero's creeping around the snake-infested swamps of Planet Xargon, pursued by blood-crazed alien death-beasts. He crouches behind a mangrove tree; he peers out into the darkness – all is silent – and then you hear . . . What's Ethan's ring tone these days?'

'*Queen*, I think. *We Are the Champions.*'

'You see my point?'

Holly giggled. Cat was right. The misery-brick felt a little lighter in her chest. She felt much better after talking to her friends. Nothing was ever too dull or grim for Cat not to see the funny side . . . If Snow White's stepmother had had a friend like Cat to talk to after the magic mirror told her she wasn't number one in the looks department, she'd have probably just had a good laugh about it instead of going down the whole poisoned-apple-revenge route!

Holly and Cat were still laughing when Nick and Nathan joined them at their table. Nick was wearing wraparound sunglasses.

'What's wrong with your eyes?' Holly asked, concerned. 'Is it hay fever?'

'It's his Important Film Director image!' Nathan whispered as Nick got up to fetch the tomato ketchup.

'OK!' Nick announced, shaking the bottle in the direction of his chips. 'Lettie tells me your vocals on *Dream* are coming on well . . .'

Holly nodded. 'Yeah, we've squeezed in three rehearsals already this week.'

'And we are sounding amaaazing!' Cat enthused, 'though I say so myself!'

'Cool!' Nick leaned back in his chair. 'I think we're ready to *go visual* . . .'

'Go visual?'

'Yeah, storyboarding the video, you know? I've booked a practice room. We'll run through your vocals, throw some ideas around . . . get my creative sparks flying . . .'

'When?' Holly asked.

'Soon as we've finished eating,' Nick replied, now thumping the bottom of the ketchup bottle.

'OK,' Cat said. 'Belle and Lettie will be back in a minute. They've gone to see Mrs Butterworth about times for their cello and piano exams next week.'

Nick looked at his watch impatiently. *Wow! He's really taking this director thing seriously!* Holly thought. But all of a sudden he leaped out of his seat. A tidal wave of ketchup had splurged from the bottle, splattering him all over with red goo. Holly looked at Cat and Nathan, trying her best not to giggle. This was not exactly the super-cool image Nick was trying to project.

He grinned broadly. 'OK, that went *rather* well!' he joked, slowly peeling the ketchup-speckled sunglasses from his face. 'I knew there must be a reason why people wore shades indoors. They protect the eyes from low-flying condiments!'

They all laughed. Holly was relieved that the old joke-a-minute Nick still lurked beneath the new serious-director Nick!

'Here's Belle and Lettie now,' Holly said, handing Nick a napkin to wipe his face with.

Just as they reached the table Jack Thorne ran in behind them, put his arm round Belle and whispered something in her ear. Belle smiled up at him.

'Got to get to football practice! See you later!' Jack

called, giving Belle a kiss on the cheek before hurrying away.

Holly swallowed a lump in her throat. Jack and Belle were such a perfect couple and she was happy for them. But seeing them together just reminded her how much she missed Ethan. *If Ethan were here now he'd be rushing off to football practice too*, she thought. She could almost *feel* his kiss on her cheek. Then she remembered the phone call. *That's if he still even wants to kiss me* . . . Holly rubbed her cheek as if to scrub away the memory, and tried to focus on what was going on.

'Wow, Lettie's just had the best surprise!' Belle was saying as she pulled up a chair. 'She's *only* been invited to see the London Philharmonic play Mahler's Second Symphony at the Royal Festival Hall next week! The tickets arrived in the post just now.'

'Sooo, who's the invite from?' Cat asked,

'Just a friend from my old school . . .' Lettie said casually.

'This *friend*,' Cat teased, 'wouldn't happen to be of the *male* variety, would they?'

Lettie blushed a little. 'Well, yes, it is a boy actually. Callum. His dad plays violin in the London Philharmonic. That's why he gets tickets.'

Cat cupped her hand to her ear. 'Ooh, do we hear

the sound of an old flame crackling back into life? We didn't know you had such a steamy romantic past, Lettie!'

Holly smiled. Then she caught sight of Nick. He'd gone quiet since Callum was mentioned. *Very quiet.*

'Come on, we're wasting time here!' he said gruffly. 'We've got work to do.'

'To the practice room!' Cat heralded as they all piled out of the dining room.

As they walked across the courtyard, Holly noticed that Belle was a little quiet too. She didn't seem as fired up about starting work on the video as she'd expected.

'Are you worried about Nick getting carried away with his creative sparks?' she asked.

'It's not that,' Belle sighed. 'It's just . . . this!' She took an exercise book from her bag and opened it. Holly looked down to see a six-page essay entitled 'The River Amazon' in Belle's ultra-neat handwriting. *B+* had been written in red ink below it.

'B plus,' Cat said. 'That's pretty good. I got a C for mine!'

'That's just it,' Belle said anxiously. '*Pretty* good's not good enough! Not for my dad anyway.'

Holly hugged Belle sympathetically. She knew how

serious this was. Mr Madison had only allowed Belle to come to a performing arts school like the Garrick on condition she scored A grades in all her work. He was determined she should get a 'proper' education and become a rocket scientist or brain surgeon.

'I'm sure he won't notice one tiny little B plus,' Holly said encouragingly. 'It's your first one, isn't it?'

'Yeah.' Belle nodded. 'It's just that I went for a walk with Jack on Sunday instead of studying and I ran out of time . . .'

'Hmmm . . . you chose a romantic walk in the sunshine with your boyfriend over sitting in the library slaving over a geography essay!' Cat laughed. 'Shocking!'

Belle smiled. 'I guess I just have to work twice as hard on the next one to make up for it.'

They reached the practice room, and found Nick perched on the piano seat very close to Lettie – who was playing the accompaniment.

After warming up, Holly, Belle and Cat all launched into the version of *Keep the Dream Alive* they had perfected over the last week. When they finished, Belle rushed over to the piano and started discussing the musical arrangement with Lettie. They were planning to record a backing track with Belle on piano and Lettie on cello.

'Let's ask Mason Lee and Felix Baddeley if they'll put down a drum and guitar track for us,' Belle suggested.

'Brilliant idea!' Holly said as she and Cat joined them. Their friends Mason and Felix played in a rock band called The Undertow and were both excellent musicians.

'Er, people, who's directing this movie?' Nick asked, holding up his hands. 'Any changes in musical score will need to gel with the visual narrative!'

Cat laughed. 'Nick, this is a pop video. The music comes first. It's not *Lord of the Rings!*'

Holly stepped in quickly to smooth things over. 'Nick, you're so good at the technical stuff. I'm sure you'll have no problem synchronizing the soundtracks with the video on the computer . . .'

'Yeah, well, obviously!' Nick blustered.

'We want this video to be really cool and edgy,' Cat said.

'But mysterious and romantic too,' Belle added.

'And I've got loads of ideas for the dance sequence . . .' Holly said.

'Don't worry, it's all in here!' Nick said, tapping his

head. 'Now, from the top, daaahlings!' he drawled.

The girls went back to the microphones and began to sing. But every few bars, Nick waved his arms, yelled '*Cut!*' and scribbled on large sheets of paper. At last, he seemed satisfied.

'OK, here's the *concept*. I'm thinking six different locations around the school. I'm visualizing this really cool aerial scene over the intro—

'Aerial? As in *flying*?' Cat said. 'What, like on broomsticks, or something?'

Nick tutted. 'No, we'll use those invisible flying wires, of course!'

'Hel-lo? Health and Safety?' Belle said, shaking her head. 'I'm not dangling on a bit of wire.'

'Belle, Belle, Belle! Just trust me on this,' Nick said breezily. 'Then we'll cut into a moody, atmospheric scene as Cat walks across the courtyard in the pouring rain . . .'

'Pouring rain?' Cat snorted. 'The forecast says it's going to be sunny for weeks!'

'Leave it with me!' Nick said rather impatiently. 'Let's not get bogged down with *details* . . .'

'Ceasefire!' Holly interjected quickly. A three-way pitched battle between Nick, Belle and Cat was not going to be pretty. 'You've got some great ideas there,

Nick, but we only have a couple of weeks . . .'

Holly looked questioningly at Cat and Belle. She could see that Belle was worried about whether they'd be able to carry off Nick's complicated plans and that Cat was already bristling at Nick bossing them about. But Nick did have some interesting ideas – mixed up among the weird stuff. And he was certainly enthusiastic.

'OK,' Cat said eventually. 'Let's just go for it and see what we can do.'

Will we ever be able to agree on anything long enough to make this video? Holly wondered.

CHAPTER NINE

Belle: Salt, Vinegar and Pistachio Swirl

Panic was rising through Belle's body like flood water.

It was Monday morning's double science class.

Next to her, Cat was fishing around in her bag for a pen. 'Chemistry test,' she grumbled. 'The perfect way to start the week.'

Usually Belle enjoyed tests. But usually she'd have revised the subject thoroughly, with the aid of alphabetically organized note cards and coloured highlighters. After last week's Geography B+ Crisis, she'd planned to get her study schedule back on track – they had important tests in all their school subjects ahead of them over the next couple of weeks – but somehow recording the soundtrack for *Keep the Dream Alive* with Lettie, Mason and Felix had got in the way. How many times had she told Cat it was all just a question of time management? Now she knew what it felt like when Time didn't want to be managed!

'Question One: What is H_2O?' Mrs Salmon strolled around the class, hands in the pockets of her white lab coat, glaring over her glasses at anyone who wasn't writing.

Water, Belle wrote. *OK, that was easy.*

And she knew the answers to the next few questions. Maybe this wouldn't be so bad, after all.

'Question Fifteen: *As what household substance*,' Mrs Salmon asked, '*is the compound NaCl more commonly known?*'

Belle closed her eyes and tried to think. But her mind was blank. Holly, Cat and Nathan were all writing. She couldn't believe she was *actually* tempted to sneak a peek at Cat's answer sheet.

Her heart sinking faster than the Titanic, Belle guessed wildly and wrote: *Vinegar.*

'Swap your papers with the desk behind you,' Mrs Salmon instructed at the end of the test.

Belle turned, hoping to give her paper to Jack, but Mayu Tanaka snatched it out of her hand. Mayu was Bianca Hayford's best friend. Her long black hair was in bunches and she was wearing a frilly T-shirt and polka-dot shorts in her trademark pink-with-a-hint-of-pink. Bianca's place, between Mayu and Jack, was empty, of course, as Bianca was still away in Florida.

Mrs Salmon read out the answers. '*The common name for NaCl is . . . now, who can tell me?*'

Belle cringed as Mayu put her hand up.

'It's salt, miss,' Mayu lisped in her icing-sugar-sweet voice. 'But Belle Madison's written *vinegar*! I think she's been eating too many crisps!'

Belle felt her face flame as a giggle rippled round the classroom. She wished she could crawl under the lab bench. How could she have let this happen? And, even worse, what was Dad going to say when he found out?

'Oh dear! Only eighteen out of twenty,' Mayu gloated as she handed Belle back her test. 'Little Miss Perfect's standards are slipping!'

Belle snatched her test back. *Looks like Bianca's promoted Mayu to Acting Head of Mean Girl Operations Ltd (London Area) in her absence*, she thought. *The perfect choice for the job.*

Belle worked extra-hard for the rest of the week, getting up even earlier than usual and continuing even later at night.

By Friday afternoon's advanced singing class she was exhausted, but happy to be working on something she really enjoyed – the chorus of *Bon Voyage* for *Anything*

Goes. Neither Cat nor Holly took advanced singing – they were both in dance classes on Friday afternoons – so Belle sat with Jack, Nick Taggart and Ruby Drew, who was modelling her usual any-colour-as-long-as-it's-black Goth-girl look.

Belle was delighted when Mr Garcia, the singing teacher, asked her to come up to the front to show the others how to sing the words *Bon Voyage* in a perfect French accent.

'Excellent work, Belle,' Mr Garcia boomed, his voice so deep he sounded like film-trailer voiceover man. 'Well done!'

Belle couldn't help smiling, and seeing Jack beaming at her made her feel even happier. At least her singing wasn't going downhill! And although her grades in her school subjects were important, because they were what allowed her to stay at Superstar High, in her own heart, singing was what *really* mattered.

'Thank you, Mr Garcia,' she said politely as she took her seat again.

'Ooh, *thank you, Mr Garcia!*' Mayu mimicked in a babyish voice from the other side of the class. 'How d'you say *teacher's pet* in French?'

Jack glared at Mayu and squeezed Belle's hand.

Rise above it, Belle told herself. *Fighting with Bianca*

got me in so much trouble last term, I'm not going to make the same mistake with Mayu!

'Lettie, could you lead us in the next chorus,' Mr Garcia asked. Lettie jumped up, but she caught her foot on a chair leg. She landed in a heap, surrounded by sheets of music. Nick rocketed out of his chair to help her up. Lettie smiled and blushed and thanked him.

'Aw, how sweeet!' Mayu mocked. 'It must be luuurve!'

Mayu was right for once. Nick and Lettie *were* sweet together. But although they'd been working closely on the Nobody's Angels video for weeks, they still hadn't stepped over the line marked Just Good Friends.

By the time those two get it together they'll be going on a date to the post office to pick up their old-age pensions! Belle thought. *It's definitely time to step up our matchmaking efforts . . .*

After dinner, Holly suggested a girls-only outing to Café Roma to take Belle's mind off the Chemistry Test Disaster. The three girls linked arms and set off across Kingsgrove Square. The late-spring evening was still light and warm. 'Warm enough to sit outside,' Cat declared, 'and pretend we really *are* in Rome!'

They settled down at the small table on the

pavement outside the café and ordered their ice creams. 'We've got to do something about Nick and Lettie,' Belle said, tucking into her Pistachio Swirl.

'I know,' Cat agreed, through a mouthful of Death By Chocolate. 'It's getting painful!'

'So, any ideas?' Belle asked. 'Holly, you're our matchmaking expert.'

Holly licked Strawberry Sundae from her spoon and looked thoughtful. But it was Cat who spoke first. 'It's obvious!' she said. 'We have to play the Monster Card . . .'

'Monster?' Holly asked. 'As in Loch Ness?'

'No! As in Green-Eyed! *Beware the green-eyed monster which doth mock the meat it feeds on* . . . It means jealousy. From Shakespeare – you know, *Othello* . . .'

'Well, Nick's definitely jealous of Lettie's friend Callum and the concert tickets,' Belle told them. 'He looks as if he's swallowed a whole grapefruit every time it's mentioned!'

'Right, so . . . we just need to give the monster a little more *meat* to feed on and Nick will be spurred into action,' Cat said.

'Brilliant!' Holly laughed. 'We'll big up the Callum Factor so Nick starts thinking Lettie's in danger of getting back together with him.'

'But Lettie says this Callum guy is just a friend,' Belle pointed out.

Cat laughed. 'I'm sure he is! But the more Lettie insists there's nothing going on, the more Nick will think she's covering something up!'

Belle had to agree it was a great idea. 'OK, Operation Monster it is then! What about sending Lettie some flowers? From "A Secret Admirer"?'

'Ooh, yes,' Holly said, her dark eyes glowing at the prospect of a matchmaking plan. 'Red roses, of course!'

'Naturally! And we need to make sure that Nick is there when they arrive,' Cat added.

Belle nodded, happily switching into Organization Mode. 'OK, so tomorrow morning, Holly brings Lettie to the entrance hall at ten o'clock – tell her we want to have an urgent meeting about the video, or something. Cat, you find Nick and do the same. And I'll sort out the flowers' – she pulled her phone out of her bag and started scrolling through her contact list – 'to arrive at ten-o-five a.m. precisely . . .' She looked up and noticed Cat and Holly both looking at her doubtfully.

'But all the florists will be by shut now,' Holly said.

Belle smiled. 'Have you heard of Sasha Mulholland?'

'You mean the celebrity florist?' Cat asked. 'She does

flowers for footballers' weddings and stuff! We can't afford *her*!'

Holly looked at Belle suspiciously. 'Sasha Mulholland wouldn't happen to be a friend of your mum's by any chance?'

Belle grinned. She didn't like cashing in on her parents' celebrity status, but she had to admit it did sometimes come in handy to have a super-model like Zoe Fairweather for a mother. And this *was* for a Friend in Need.

'You guessed it!' Belle laughed. 'They worked together on some photo shoots a few years back. I've got her home number here. I'm sure she'll sort something for us.' She shivered as she waited for the phone to connect. It was starting to get chilly. 'Brr! I could do with a . . .'

'Hot chocolate?' Luigi announced, placing a tray of mugs on their table. 'On the house! For my favourite customers!'

Belle picked up her mug and gratefully inhaled the sweet steam, just as she heard Sasha Mulholland pick up the phone.

She'd forgotten all about the chemistry test and the B+ in geography.

For now, at least!

CHAPTER TEN

Cat: Just a Normal Saturday

Next morning Cat snuggled under her duvet, trying to ignore her alarm clock. It was Saturday, the first week of school tests was over and she deserved a lie-in. In fact, she *owed* it to herself. Her brain had been seriously overworked!

She reached out and switched the alarm off. *Don't forget to bring Nick to the entrance hall for ten.* Those were Belle's parting words when she went out at six o'clock for an early homework and revision session before her morning run. But it was only half past eight. *Plenty of time*, Cat thought. *I'll just have a few more minutes!*

Cat dozed contentedly, thinking back over yesterday's tango class. She and Adam, along with the other two chosen couples, were working separately with Miguel Silva on the *All Through the Night* routine. Cat loved everything about the class: dancing with Adam *and* the chance to learn from a world-expert like Miguel Silva. The only not-quite-so-fabulous thing was having to keep wearing her shabby old leotard and laddered tights to every lesson. She couldn't very well turn up in the lovely new matching Capezio dancewear Mum had treated her to in the Easter holidays and shatter Miguel's belief that she was a poor, homeless orphan, dancing her way out of the ghetto . . .

Cat opened her eyes and peered at the clock again. Then she bolted out of bed in a single bound. *Twenty to ten!* She must've drifted back to sleep. *Uh-oh.* She'd be up in front of Belle's firing squad if she didn't report for duty in the entrance hall at ten hundred hours precisely, with the correct quantity of Nick Taggarts about her person!

She grabbed a pair of black jeans and a blue fluffy jumper from the floor and pulled them on, then flew downstairs to the dining room. Holly – her hair still damp from an early morning swim – was eating breakfast with Gemma and Lettie. But there was no sign of Nick. *Probably still in bed – like most normal, sane people*, Cat thought.

She dashed across the sunny courtyard towards the boys' rooms at the back of the school. Taking a corner at speed, she crashed headlong into Mr Grampian, head of the Drama Department – and her favourite teacher.

Mr Grampian brushed down his cord jacket, smiling in a no-harm-done kind of way. 'It would appear,' he said, 'that your excessive haste is hampering your endeavours. But now I have bumped into you, Catrin, this proves to be a most serendipitous encounter!'

Seren-dippy-what-i-puss? Cat thought, but she didn't ask. With Mr Grampian, it was best not to.

'Looking for one thing and finding another,' Mr Grampian explained. 'I was searching for a prospective student for next year. Two, actually – twins. Exceptionally interested in the dramatic arts. They're visiting our noble establishment today and wished to have a quick word with me . . .'

Cat stifled a grin. Mr Grampian didn't *do* quick words!

'. . . but instead I have found you, Catrin! I've arranged an appointment for you to select your *Much Ado About Nothing* audition speech with Simon Steele. He's our Shakespearean specialist, after all, and he was terrifically impressed with your Lady Macbeth last year.'

Much as Cat would have loved to stay and chat

about the audition, she was on a mission. 'Great! Thank you,' she mumbled, backing away.

'Ah, there you are, Mr Grampian!'

Cat turned to see Miss Candlemas, the housemistress, bustling across the courtyard. Her purple zebra-print kaftan billowed around her and strings of beads bounced on her large bosom. Two tall, pretty girls with strawberry-blond hair were jogging along in her wake, trying to keep up. 'This is Abbey and Libby,' Miss Candlemas announced. 'Applying to join our merry band at the Garrick for next year.'

Mr Grampian shook the girls' hands. 'Delighted to make your acquaintance!' They smiled back shyly. 'And this is one of our exceptionally promising young actresses, Catrin Wickham,' Mr Grampian added.

Miss Candlemas started to leave, then turned back. 'Oh, Cat, would you take Abbey and Libby under your wing for a couple of hours this afternoon? Show them what a normal Saturday at the Garrick is all about?'

'Yes, sure,' Cat mumbled. *A normal Saturday? There's no such thing at Superstar High!* But she'd have agreed to anything if it meant she could get on with her Nick-finding mission! She waved to the twins, then darted off.

★ ★ ★

Cat finally found Nick in Mr Woolfox's shed, tucked away at the back of the school next to the sports fields. Mr Woolfox, a man so old he probably dated from the eighteenth century along with the original school buildings, always sported the jacket and waistcoat of a black three-piece suit set off by a pair of mud-coloured cord trousers tied up with string. Right now he appeared to be demonstrating to Nick the merits of various watering cans and sprinkler attachments.

'Nick! What *are* you doing?' Cat panted. 'No, on second thoughts, I don't even want to know!' she added. 'Come with me. Quickly!'

Nick stared at her blankly, water dripping from the watering can in his hand. 'What? *Now?*'

'Urgent summit meeting about the video. The others are waiting in the entrance hall!' Cat tugged at his sweatshirt. It was now one minute to ten!

'Better be off then, lad,' Mr Woolfox chuckled. 'Doesn't do to keep the ladies waiting!'

At two minutes past ten, Cat dragged a rather bemused Nick into the hall. Panting, she headed for the big sofa. 'Phew!' she breathed. 'Just made it!'

But the sofa was empty. Where was Belle? Where

was Holly with Lettie? What had happened to Operation Monster?

'Thought you said the others were waiting for us,' Nick grumbled. 'What's going on?'

If I knew that, Cat thought, *I'd tell you!*

CHAPTER ELEVEN

Cat: Special Delivery

The entrance hall was empty.

Even Mrs Butterworth was missing from behind her desk between the pigeon holes and the notice board.

Had there been a fire drill? Or a mass alien abduction?

Suddenly there was a rattling noise as Mrs Butterworth scooted into view on her swivel chair. In a cream safari-style trouser suit, she looked as if she were about to go out lion-hunting.

Mrs B was followed by Belle, Holly and Lettie. Cat hurried across to see what was going on. 'Let me guess,' she joked. 'You're throwing a surprise party for me in Mrs Butterworth's office?'

Holly smiled and held up her hands, which were cupped together.

Belle laughed. 'It's a mouse! When we got here a few minutes ago, we heard Mrs B screaming in her office. We went to see—'

'I simply cannot bear rodents, in any shape or form!' Mrs Butterworth said, wrinkling her powdered nose and shuddering. 'But luckily these three girls came to the rescue. Holly caught the mouse and Belle made me a nice cup of tea to calm my nerves . . .'

'I bet Shreddie brought that mouse in,' Holly said. 'I think he's missing Bianca. It's making him go a bit weird.'

'No, that cat's *always* been weird,' Nick laughed. 'The missing-Bianca part is a bit of a giveaway!'

There was a buzz at the front door and Mrs Butterworth pressed the entry button to admit a delivery man, weighed down by a colossal bunch of red roses.

'Special Delivery for a Miss Lettie Atkins!' he announced, placing the bouquet on Mrs B's desk.

For a moment Cat was surprised. She'd been so distracted by the mouse episode she'd forgotten that the whole point of the gathering in the entrance hall was for Nick to witness Lettie's roses arriving. She glanced across to see his reaction.

Nick was definitely doing some serious *witnessing*. His eyes were tracking back and forth between Lettie and the bouquet as if he were watching a tennis match.

'Who are they from?' Holly asked as they all crowded round to see.

Lettie reached in and pulled out a card. '*From one passionate music-lover to another,*' she read, blushing so violently that her face was now colour coordinated with the roses.

'They must be from Callum,' suggested Holly.

'I suppose so . . .' Lettie mumbled, frowning doubtfully. 'We both love music and we did go to the Mahler concert last night.'

Cat grinned. Belle's message was a masterpiece; technically it wasn't even a lie. Belle *was* a passionate music-lover and the flowers were from her!

'So, Lettie,' Cat said, nudging her in the ribs, 'I guess you and Callum had a pretty good time last night then!'

'The concert was amazing,' Lettie agreed. 'But I've no idea why Callum would send me flowers. Especially as he knows stargazer lilies are my favourites.'

'Whoa! Take a look at those gorgeous flowers!' Gemma and her best friend Serena Quereshi gasped, detouring on their way to the dining room.

'Lettie, you lucky thing! This is a Sasha Mulholland arrangement!' Serena pointed to the logo on the back of the card. 'This guy must be super-keen.'

'And super-rich. They must have cost a fortune!'

'So, when are you seeing him again?' Serena asked.

'Well, we might go to a couple more concerts while he's in town,' Lettie mumbled. 'But it's really not a big deal.'

'She's so modest,' Gemma laughed. 'If I got flowers like this, I'd be shouting it from the rooftops!'

'If *you* got flowers like this, I'd be checking whether Zak had robbed a bank!' Serena teased. 'What do you think, Nick?'

Everyone turned to look at Nick. Since the flowers arrived he'd been silent – a word that had probably *never* been used to describe Nick before in his entire life. Cat glimpsed a tormented expression flicker across his face. *Yup! One hundred per cent green-eyed monster!* For a moment, she felt a bit of a slime-weasel. Maybe they should own up and tell him the flowers weren't really from Callum? *No way!* she told herself firmly. *It's for his own good!*

Suddenly Nick realized everyone was staring at him. He forced a grin.

'Well, he can't be *that* amazing a guy, if he didn't even check what Lettie's favourite flowers were before sending them,' he joked, putting on a mock-horrified voice. 'I mean, red roses! So predictable! Now, if you'll excuse me, I have some important business to attend to with Mr Woolfox.' He turned dramatically on his heel and walked away. 'Don't forget. We're shooting the courtyard scenes for the video this afternoon. Two o'clock sharp!' he called back.

It was a pretty convincing why-would-I-care-if-a-boy-sends-Lettie-flowers? act. He was, after all, a very good actor. But Cat wasn't fooled. Nor, she could see, were Belle or Holly. They all knew Nick too well. Not to mention the fact that he was obviously so upset he'd totally forgotten to ask why they'd called an emergency meeting about the video in the first place. Lettie seemed to have forgotten they were meant to be having a meeting too. She was busy gazing at the flowers, looking puzzled.

'Come on, gang,' Cat said, laughing. 'I smell pancakes. We can't film a music video on an empty stomach!'

CHAPTER TWELVE

Holly: The Cure for a Sprained Heart

Holly followed Cat, Belle and Lettie into the dining room. She'd already had breakfast after her early swim – but there was always room for Mrs Morecambe's yumalicious pancakes.

Gemma and Zak were sitting at the next table, deep in conversation. Holly was especially proud of having figured out that Zak had sent Gemma's anonymous Valentine's card last term and bringing the two of them together. *After that triumphant success*, she thought, *I'm sure we can do the same for Nick and Lettie*. Operation Monster was off to a flying start. Nick looked so jealous when Lettie's flowers arrived, Holly was sure he'd ask her out soon.

Lettie balanced the bouquet of red roses in the middle of the table – it was so enormous the girls could hardly see round it.

'Can you pass the maple syrup?' Holly called to Cat through the foliage.

'Ooh, who's been getting flowers, then?' Mayu's voice piped up from behind Holly's chair, making her jump and drop the jug, spilling syrup all over the roses.

'Sorry, Lettie,' Holly mumbled, trying to mop up the mess. 'I'm such a klutz!'

Lettie smiled. 'Don't worry. It's only a bunch of flowers.'

'Oh, so they're *Lettie's*. They wouldn't be from *Nick Taggart*, would they?' Mayu asked with a smile like sherbet-coated barbed wire.

'No,' Lettie replied hurriedly. 'They're just from a friend.'

'Oh yeah, they are a bit classy for Nick,' Mayu sniggered. 'A droopy old bunch of daffodils from the petrol station would be more *his* style!'

Holly was about to protest on Nick's behalf when Mayu shot her a sly little look. 'At first I thought the roses might be *yours*, Holly, from Ethan, but then I remembered, of course . . .'

'Remembered what?' Holly asked, her mind suddenly working overtime. Did Mayu know something about Ethan that she didn't?

Mayu picked up a spoon and checked her reflection. 'Oh, it's just something that Bianca mentioned on Facebook.'

'What?' Holly demanded, her voice rising in despair.

'Well, I wasn't going to say anything, but as you're *forcing* it out of me. Apparently, Ethan's been spending a lot of quality time with Violet Dubarry, so he's probably been far too busy for sending flowers—'

'Oh yeah?' Cat butted in angrily. 'He is playing her boyfriend in the film, so they *have* to spend time together. It's called *acting*!'

Mayu shook her head in amusement. It was obvious she was sooo enjoying being Head Mean Girl while Bianca was away. 'You think? Well, Bianca says the whole cast are talking about it. Happens all the time, you know, co-stars and their off-screen romances! Look at Zak Efron and Vanessa Hudgens!'

Holly's head was spinning. *Of course, that explains it* – the giggle she'd heard on the phone, the *just-someone-from-school* line . . . Ethan had found someone else!

'I'm sure that's not true,' Belle was saying. 'Ethan's not like that.'

'I'm only telling you what I heard,' Mayu said innocently.

'Yeah! As in, *heard from Bianca*!' Cat yelled, glaring at Mayu across the roses. 'Like *that's* a reliable source!'

'Come on, Holly, don't listen to Mayu,' Belle coaxed.

But Holly *had* listened. And what she'd heard made perfect sense.

Her heart was breaking into a million pieces. 'Got to go,' she mumbled, pushing back her chair and stumbling blindly out of the dining room. Somehow she found herself in the computer room next to the library. She slumped down at a terminal.

She needed to see the face of the girl who had stolen Ethan from her.

Violet Dubarry.

Holly clicked on the web browser and typed the name into the search box.

Then she wished she hadn't.

Violet Dubarry had her own website crammed with publicity photos. She was utterly everyone-else-might-as-well-give-up-and-go-home-right-now stunning. She smiled into the camera; perfect teeth, porcelain skin, sky-blue eyes. Here she was at a film premiere in a glittering red dress, her golden hair piled on top of her head in an elaborate up-do. Here she was scampering along a California beach in shorts and T-shirt, *Taking time out*, the caption read, *from her hectic filming schedule with her two Irish setters, Max and Pookie.* She looked gorgeous. Even the dogs were more groomed than normal dogs.

How can I ever compete? Holly despaired.

Tears running down her cheeks, she bolted for the toilets. She stared at her reflection in the mirror. Her braids were wonky and damp from her morning swim. She reeked of chlorine. People always told her she had lovely clear caramel-coloured skin. *But let's face facts*, she thought. *Basically, it's a dull light brown. And my eyes? Boring dark brown.*

Ethan had told her she was beautiful. He said she was sweet too, and funny and kind and special, and the most graceful dancer he'd ever seen. He even said he *liked* the smell of chlorine!

But Violet Dubarry was in a different league. She was beautiful and elegant and tall and sophisticated and famous.

I bet Violet's never crashed into a boy at high speed, fallen flat on her behind and then squeaked, 'Don't kiss me, I'm alive!' A giant sob escaped Holly's throat as she remembered her first meeting with Ethan – and how much they'd laughed about it ever since.

It was such a loud sob she almost missed Beyoncé singing in her handbag. She pulled out her phone and stared glumly at the incoming message symbol. It was from Ethan. Was this the Big Goodbye?

But as she started to read, it slowly dawned on her. This wasn't goodbye at all . . .

THINKING ABOUT U 24/7. MEGA–BUSY HERE BUT WILL CALL TMRW 4 ++LONG TALK. LOVE U ALWAYS, ETHAN XXXOOOXXX

Holly stared at the phone in wonder. *Six kisses and three hugs!*

Ethan can't be in love with Violet Dubarry. He's too busy missing me!

Dizzy with happiness, she blew her nose and headed out of the toilets, where she met Cat and Belle coming out of the library.

'Hols! We've been looking everywhere for you!' Cat cried, running up to give her a huge hug.

'Are you OK?' Belle asked, putting her arm round her.

'Never better!' Holly said, grinning as she held up the text for her friends to see. 'Do you think there are any pancakes left? I'm starving. Mayu put me off my first attempt at second breakfast!'

'We'll have to see if there's any maple syrup left after you tried watering the roses with it,' Cat teased.

'And after that we need to go and get ready for filming the video this afternoon,' Belle said. 'Nick wants to start at two. I can't wait!'

'Ah yes,' Holly said as they headed down the library stairs back towards the dining room. '*My hectic filming schedule!*'

'What?' Cat and Belle asked.

'Oh, nothing!' Holly laughed. 'Just something I was reading.'

My heart isn't broken, she thought happily, throwing her arms around her friends. *It was just a minor sprain.*

And everyone knows that the cure for a sprained heart is good friends and a generous helping of pancakes!

CHAPTER THIRTEEN

Belle: How to Hip-hop in a Kirtle

Belle scanned the bedroom, making sure that everything was ready for Nobody's Angels to transform themselves into super-glamorous pop divas for their video shoot.

Outfits laid out on the bed (washed and ironed). *Check!*

Make-up on the coffee table (eye pencils sharpened). *Check!*

Mirrors in place (polished). *Check!*

Getting-ready music (*I Gotta Feeling* by the Black-Eyed Peas). *Check!*

Perfect. Now all she needed was Holly and Cat.

'Sorry we're late!' Cat shouted, hurtling into the room. 'I was washing my hair.' She swept the three outfits off Belle's bed, flopped down and started drying her hair vigorously with a towel.

'Oops, sorry,' Holly said as she tripped over a hairdryer cable and landed on the coffee table. She crawled around the floor after the eye pencils she'd scattered. 'I was just making a few last-minute changes to the dance routine . . .' She reached up to Belle's laptop on the desk, switched off the Black-Eyed Peas and fired up the backing-track to *Keep the Dream Alive*.

Belle closed her eyes and took a deep breath. Sometimes, being friends with Cat and Holly was like hanging out with a couple of tornadoes! But then she smiled. It was also fun and action-packed. Life would be soooo boring without them!

'OK!' She extracted a skirt from under Cat's soggy towel. 'Let's get changed and then work on the new steps.'

They'd decided on co-ordinating outfits in black and white with bright red accessories. 'Argggh!' Cat screamed as she pulled on her black satin skirt. 'Call the fire brigade!'

'What is it?' Belle asked, panicking.

'I've squeezed my way *into* this skirt,' Cat groaned, 'but I'll need heavy-duty cutting equipment to get out again! I must've eaten too many Easter eggs in the holidays.'

'You look lovely!' Holly said.

'I look like Humpty Dumpty in a fat suit!' Cat complained, puffing out her cheeks.

Belle giggled. 'Only when you make that face.'

A few moments later they were all dressed. They were running through Holly's changes to the dance routine – a short hip-hop-style sequence – when there was a knock at the door.

Nick, Nathan and Lettie piled into the room.

'We've just had a wicked idea!' Nick blurted. 'Tudor costumes for the video! Loving it!'

'Tudor?' Cat gasped. 'You mean sixteenth century, Henry the Eighth, and all that?'

'What do you think, Lettie?' Belle asked doubtfully. 'It's your song.'

Lettie smiled adoringly at Nick. 'I think it's a brilliant idea. It'll be like the girl goes back in time trying to find the guy she loves . . . and then maybe she's trapped there . . .'

'We could use a soft-focus lens to give it a historical feel,' Nathan added.

'Sounds like you guys have got this all worked out!' Belle laughed. In fact, she was starting to like the idea too. She loved everything about the Tudor period. And the heavily embroidered, bejewelled dresses were gorgeous . . .

'I've already asked Serena if we can borrow costumes from the wardrobe department,' Nick announced. 'They're on their way now.'

'Well, I guess we'd stand out from the crowd,' Holly said. 'I can't imagine there'll be that many videos of girl bands kitted out in full Tudor costume!'

Nick, Lettie and Nathan high-fived as Serena and Gemma staggered into the room with the heavy costumes.

'Nick! Nathan!' Gemma ordered. 'All boys outside while we get them into these dresses.'

Belle, Cat and Holly pulled off their black and white outfits and Serena – who was an expert on costume design – helped them into the elaborate long underskirts or *kirtles*, stomachers and embroidered over-gowns.

'*Kirtle*,' Belle exclaimed. 'Don't you just love that word!'

'This is worse than my black skirt,' Cat said as Serena laced her into her stomacher. 'Breathing was obviously an optional extra for Tudor girls!'

'I've got an idea!' Lettie cried, rushing next door and coming back with a handful of roses from her bouquet. 'Red roses pinned to the bodices will look really romantic.'

'Looking good!' Nick whistled as he and Nathan returned moments later to find the girls practising their dance steps. Cat had giant curlers in her hair and Belle was using her hairdryer as a microphone.

'Whoa! These kirtles weren't made for body popping!' Holly said as she tripped over her long skirt. 'I'm going to have to make some big changes to the choreography, unless we do the dance sequence in modern dress.'

At that moment Belle heard Miss Candlemas's cheerful voice in the corridor. 'Here we are, dears,' she was saying. 'This is Catrin's room. She and her friends will show you the ropes! And you'll get to see a typical student rooo . . .' Her voice trailed off as she put her head round the half-open door. 'Goodness! What the dickens is going on in here?' she gasped, sounding more amused than angry.

Belle looked around slowly. She could see Miss Candlemas's point! For a start, with eight of them in the room, it looked as if they were attempting to break the world record for the Most Crowded Bedroom. Then there was the fact that three of them were busting hip-hop moves in full Tudor dress, the floor was strewn with clothes and make-up . . . and red rose petals were stuck to every surface with a fine layer of maple syrup!

'Well, Cat, I'm sure Abbey and Libby won't mind joining in your fancy-dress karaoke party, or whatever it is!' Miss Candlemas said.

Belle looked questioningly at Cat. *Abbey and Libby?*

'Oh, er, yeah I promised to look after them for a while this afternoon.' Cat waved to the two girls who were now peering round the door frame behind Miss Candlemas, their eyes wide with amazement.

'But we're about to start filming the video for PopTV,' Belle pointed out.

Holly smiled kindly. 'They can come and watch.'

'Wow,' Abbey sighed. 'PopTV? That's so cool!'

'Yep! It's just one of those normal old days,' Cat laughed, 'in a typical student room!'

'We have sooo got to come to this school!' Libby breathed.

CHAPTER FOURTEEN

Belle: Plastic Drainpipes and Tudor Underwear

The film production team gathered in the courtyard to start work on the video. Nick was equipped with CD player, ladders, and a fold-out chair with DIRECTOR printed on the back. He'd also brought along an enormous box of props, and kept Libby busy handing them out. Nathan, meanwhile, was adjusting his video camera and muttering about light diffusion and contrast. Abbey volunteered to carry light meters and screens. The twins were so pretty and helpful, the boys seemed more than happy with their new assistants!

Lettie, Gemma and Serena sat on a bench and watched.

'No dangling from invisible wires, remember?' Belle warned.

Nathan grinned. 'Total no-fly zone!'

'OK, people!' Nick shouted, back in director-mode. 'We're working on the second verse here. Positions for starting, please! Belle, you go into the common room and lean out through the window. You're looking sad and singing, "*I see you from my window*", then we cut to Holly opening the door for "*But by the time I reach the door*", fading out with a tracking shot of Cat walking across the courtyard holding a lantern, *searching* left and right, then breaking into a run, through "*You have gone and all that's left is a footprint on the floor . . .*" '

Belle thought it sounded a bit complicated with so many shots in one verse, but it would bring the story of the song alive and she was excited to finally be working on the video. This was going to be fun!

They began to rehearse, miming to the backing track to make sure the timing was accurate. Belle went inside to the common room, perched on the windowsill and leaned out.

'Look to the side, no, more to the front, hold your head higher . . .' Nick commanded. 'You're sad, remember! Cry, baby, cry!'

Belle composed her face into a wistful expression. *Gotta feel tragic here . . .* But all she felt was pins and needles in her leg. *Must think of something sad. What if Dad makes me leave Superstar High because my grades aren't good enough?* Belle had been suppressing the terrible thought for days, but now it bubbled to the surface. *It could really happen . . .*

All of a sudden, tears were rolling down her face.

'Yep, yep, yep! Lovin' it!' Nick called, giving her the thumbs-up sign. 'Don't overdo it, we don't want snot in shot . . .'

At last Nick was satisfied – they were ready to shoot!

'And *action*!' Nick shouted. 'Cameras!'

'Take One,' Libby announced importantly, snapping down the clapperboard.

Nathan whispered something to Abbey, who passed the message to Nick.

'Cut!' Nick yelled. 'Plastic drainpipe!'

Plastic drainpipe? Belle wondered. *Is that some kind of technical film-director jargon?*

'There's a drainpipe in shot,' Nick complained. 'Not exactly a Tudor period feature. We need to move windows.'

Belle positioned herself at the next window. At last they were ready.

'Take Two!' Libby shouted.

Her words were drowned out by the roar of a jumbo jet flying overhead.

'I don't think Heathrow had been built in the

sixteenth century,' Cat called from her position on the other side of the courtyard.

'Cut!' Nick yelled.

'And Take Three!' Libby shouted.

Belle tried to get into the tragic zone again by dredging up another miserable moment. *Like when Bianca tricked me into thinking Jack was really in love with her? Yes, perfect!* Tears were flowing again and she began to sing her line with extra feeling, '*I saw you from my . . .* eeeekkk!'

Belle screamed as a large marmalade cat jumped off the sideboard into her lap and started batting at a tassel hanging from her bodice. 'Shreddiiiie!'

'Cut!' Nick yelled.

'Take Eighteen,' Libby shouted hoarsely.

At last! This time nothing went wrong. No drainpipes, no planes, no kamikaze cats. Belle sang her line perfectly and waited for Nick to shout 'Cut'. But then a shower of freezing water poured down on her head. 'Arggh!' she shrieked. 'What d'you think you're doing?'

There was a ripple of laughter. By this time the film shoot had attracted quite a crowd.

'It's rain, of course.' Nick was standing on a

stepladder holding up a watering can with a long sprinkler attachment. 'It's meant to be all gloomy and atmospheric. We can adjust the light on the film, but we needed some real rain.'

'This is crazy!' Belle shouted. 'I've been leaning from this window crying my eyes out for over an hour. I've got cramp and I'm soaking!' She pushed her sodden hair out of her eyes. 'And there's no way I can do any more filming looking like this!'

'But we have more scenes—'

'Get that dress off!' Serena screamed, running over to Belle, her long black hair flying behind her. 'It'll be ruined if I don't get it dry!' Horrified at the thought of damaging the costume, Belle let Serena pull off the heavy gown. *Great! I'm standing in the middle of the school, dripping wet and in my underwear.*

But at least it was Tudor underwear – the blouse, corset and long kirtle weren't exactly revealing!

Holly came to the rescue, draping a cardigan round Belle's shoulders. 'You need to go and get warm,' she said. Then she turned to Nick. 'We'll just have to work on mine and Cat's scenes for the rest of the shoot.'

'But if you even *think* about coming anywhere near me with a watering can, you're toast!' Cat added.

Belle couldn't help laughing. She spotted Jack

coming towards her from his position in the crowd. He was laughing too as he scooped her up into a massive hug. She was already starting to feel a bit better.

'I have an idea,' Nathan said quietly. 'Why don't we film the girls from inside looking out through the window – with rain dripping down the glass.

'Nate, you are a genius! Cat laughed, hugging him. 'You're the next Steven Spielberg!'

Nick looked doubtful, but then Lettie smiled. 'Great idea! We could cut to a mysterious boy walking past outside in the rain . . .'

Suddenly Nick was on board! 'Sounds good! OK, Nathan, you've just got yourself a starring role. You can be Mysterious Boy in the Rain!'

Nathan shook his head. 'I'm needed *behind* the camera on this one.'

'Well, this won't work without a boy!' Nick groaned dramatically. '*Someone find me a boy!*'

Belle shivered with the cold and Jack held her tighter. She looked up and smiled at him. He winked and did that x-ray thing with his eyes. *Jack would really fit the part*, she thought. *He's gorgeous and a little mysterious-looking . . .*

Suddenly she realized everyone had gone quiet.

'Er, why are you guys all staring at me?' Jack laughed nervously.

Nick pointed dramatically. 'Jack Thorne,' he intoned in a deep voice. 'You are the Perfect Boy.'

'Gee, thanks, Nick!' Jack grinned and pretended to be embarrassed by the compliment. 'You're not so bad yourself!'

'So you're in?' Nick asked. 'Good! I'll write in your part and we'll start again tomorrow afternoon.' Then he paused and turned to Belle. 'Er, sorry about half-drowning you by the way . . .'

Belle smiled, blinking the drips out of her eyes. 'It's OK. Just warn me next time so I can put my waterproof mascara on!'

Nick clapped his hands. 'OK, people! It's a wrap for now!'

A wrap in a big fluffy towel after a hot bath for me! Belle thought as she trailed back to her room.

It wasn't the most promising start to her music-video career!

CHAPTER FIFTEEN

Cat: A Very Serendipitous Morning

Cat gazed out of her bedroom window the next morning. The sun was shining in a radiant blue sky. The trees in Kingsgrove Square were frothy with blossom. It was a day made for running barefoot through the long grass, making daisy chains and watching baby lambs frolicking in the meadows.

The only problem was she had a pile of homework the size of Mount Everest.

And she had to finish it before starting work on the video again this afternoon.

So much for Sunday being the day of rest!

Then she had a brainwave. *Why not take our books and do our homework sitting under the trees in Kingsgrove Square!* OK, there were no lambs, but they could get the rest of the sunshine-blossom-daisy-chain experience and work through those essays and worksheets at the same time. What could be better?

An hour later, the three girls settled down in the

345

perfect spot under a cherry tree. Dappled sunlight filtered through the branches. Bees were buzzing in the blossom, considerately staying just far enough away that you didn't have to worry about being stung.

Cat spread out a blanket. Holly emptied several packets of biscuits out of her bag and Belle arranged the drinks neatly.

Now to get down to some serious study! Cat opened her maths book, and ran her eyes over the first worksheet: *Multiplying fractions . . .*

She lay back, propping her head on her bag, and admired the blossom. It was so pretty. Maybe they should film some of their video for *Keep the Dream Alive* here. But that wouldn't exactly fit with Nick's dark, mean-and-moody concept. Still, it would work with the Tudor costumes: girls must've sat around under trees on beautiful spring days in the sixteenth century too. Not that they'd have been saddled with worksheets on fractions, of course. Girls weren't allowed to learn stuff in those days, in case their brains exploded or something. *They were so lucky!* Cat imagined herself as Beatrice, her audition character in *Much Ado About Nothing*. Although Beatrice wasn't exactly a typical Tudor girl – she was really clever and independent; she'd probably have *wanted* to study maths! – it'd be better than all that boring needlework.

Cat's thoughts meandered back to the video. Holly had persuaded Nick they needed to change into modern clothes for the hip-hop dance routine, but he wanted the rest all in Tudor Dress. *But is that really going to work?* she wondered. She glanced across at Holly who was sharpening a pencil. Belle was writing in her history book. Surely they were allowed a few minutes' break from work now and then.

'I've been thinking about our video,' she said, helping herself to a chocolate biscuit, and picking a few daisies to get a chain started. 'D'you think the Tudor look is the right image for us? We might end up looking more like a trailer for a new historical drama on BBC Two than a music video!'

'Historical drama? *Hysterical* drama, you mean!' Holly giggled, putting down her pencil. Cat laughed, remembering the unfortunate incident in which Nick had mistaken Belle for a hanging basket and watered her.

'I'm starting to like the Tudor thing,' Belle said, passing over a handful of daisies. 'It's so romantic and it'll be really original.'

'True, but I can't help thinking we should be doing something more up-to-date and edgy,' Cat insisted.

'And why film the whole thing inside the school? We're right in the middle of London, the coolest city in the world. We should get out there and find some different locations.'

'Maybe we could combine the two,' Holly said diplomatically. 'What about going back and forth between modern and Tudor times . . . it'd be like, *hundreds of years have passed but nothing has changed . . .*'

Cat clapped her hands and jumped up, scattering her books and her daisy chain – which was now the length of a skipping rope. 'Hols, that's brilliant! Girls have been falling in love with boys who totally ignore them since the beginning of time. There were probably girl stegosauruses pining away over boy stegosauruses in the Jurassic period . . .'

To Cat's delight, Belle seemed to like the idea too. 'That's awesome!' she said, getting to her feet. 'And I agree, we should use some of the amazing locations in London too. We could even find some Tudor buildings.'

Cat and Belle reached down and pulled Holly off the grass to join their celebration dance. They held arms and jumped up and down. *Now we can really make a competition-winning video*, Cat thought excitedly.

But suddenly Holly frowned. 'What about Nick? He's not going be too happy if we suddenly want to go off on a totally different tangent after all his work.'

Cat's first instinct was that Nick should *just deal with it*. Were they going to let a *boy* tell them what to do? But then she hesitated. Holly was usually right about these things. And Nick had put a lot of effort into helping them.

'OK, let's discuss it with him,' she said. 'If you do the talking, Hols, I'm sure you can win him round with your tact and charm!'

'We have to do it straightaway,' Belle said. 'Before he does any more work on the script . . .'

Cat started to pack her books in her bag and wound her daisy chain round her curls like a tiara. So much for conquering the homework mountain!

She hadn't even reached base camp.

They found Nick in the computer room with Lettie and Nathan, looking over yesterday's footage.

The girls crowded round the screen, eager to see the results of their film shoot.

'How's it looking?' Holly asked.

Nick shook his head. 'There's a few seconds here and there,' he said. 'Like this bit . . .' He fast-forwarded, then played a snippet of Belle gazing out of the window. Her beautiful face was sad in a tragic-but-brave kind of way. A tear glistened on her cheek.

'Wow,' Cat said, 'that's amazing! Belle looks like Anne Boleyn about to be taken off to the chopping block or something!'

'But there's nowhere near enough,' Nick groaned. 'We've only got about twenty seconds of good stuff.'

'So, it's lucky we've decided to go in a new direction then!' Cat said, smiling. 'We can ditch all this lot!' *This is so lucky*, she thought. *We needn't have worried about Nick's feelings − since he didn't like what we got from yesterday anyway. So why*, she wondered a few seconds later, *has everyone suddenly gone quiet? And why's Nick looking at me like a grizzly bear with a migraine?*

Belle shook her head. 'Cat, I thought we were letting Holly do the talking?'

'The thing is, Nick,' Holly said gently, sitting down next to him, 'we really love what you've done so far. But we think we can build on your ideas and carry your vision to the next level . . .'

'Isn't that what I just said?' Cat asked indignantly.

Holly explained their Tudor-and-modern mix-and-match locations concept. 'And you're so clever, you'll be able to edit all the different scenes together perfectly,' she finished. 'It'll really showcase your talents as a film director!'

Cat had to admit it. No one did tactfulness like Holly!

Nick, Nathan and Lettie listened carefully. There was another tense silence as Nick digested the idea. Then, all of a sudden, he leaped out of his chair.

'Brilliant!' he shouted. Then he paused. 'But what do you think, Lettie? You're the musical director . . .'

Lettie smiled. 'Love it!'

'Me too!' Nathan added.

The six of them high-fived.

Nick started making plans. 'We'll need to get a pass to go out next weekend and film on location. We'll have to get it all done in a day to make the deadline.'

'I'll start researching some of the best Tudor London landmarks,' Belle said. 'I'll go straight to the library.'

'I can't wait to Email Ethan and tell him all about it!' Holly said.

'So, I'll go and finish my maths homework, I suppose,' Cat said grimly. It was about as thrilling a prospect as having a wart removed. But so far today her progress on the homework mountain was precisely zero. At least they'd found the perfect idea for the video. And made a daisy chain. *What was that word Mr Grampian used . . . when you're looking for one thing but you find something else? Oh yes . . .*

'Well, this has been a delightfully *serendipitous* morning!' she said as they all trooped out of the computer room.

Holly giggled. 'Seren-what?'

Cat smiled and waved.

Multiplying fractions, here I come!

CHAPTER SIXTEEN

Holly: UFOs and Puffed-up Pants

A week later, Holly met with the rest of the team in the entrance hall on Saturday morning, ready to go out on their film shoot. They were quite a crew – Cat and Belle, of course, plus Nick, Nathan, Lettie and Jack, playing the Perfect Boy, Serena, who was helping with the costumes and make-up, and finally Adam Fielding, who'd volunteered to help. 'General dogsbody reporting for duty!' he proclaimed, joining the group.

'We've got you down as head fetcher and carrier,' Cat told him. 'All this kit weighs a tonne!' She pointed to the pile of equipment stacked by the front door. Bulky bags containing the Tudor costumes – the girls were wearing their black and white outfits for the modern-day film sequences and planned to change into their kirtle ensembles for the Tudor sections later – were piled up with Nathan's camera and lighting equipment, Serena's make-up supplies and a random assortment of UFOs, otherwise known as Unidentified Filming Objects.

It had been a busy week. Miss Morgan was still driving the advanced ballet class at breakneck speed in preparation for their Intermediate exam, and had now added extra practice sessions in the evenings. And their end-of-year tests were still in full flow, which meant even more homework and revision.

In her spare moments, Holly had been reworking the dance routine for *Keep the Dream Alive*. She'd adapted it so that the hip-hop steps gradually morphed into a slow, courtly Tudor dance called a pavane. She was so pleased with the new sequence, and she couldn't wait to film it on location.

At last everyone was ready. After signing out at Mrs Butterworth's desk, the nine of them set off along Kingsgrove Road, each carrying a load of equipment, like worker ants on a food-finding mission. To Nick's delight, the weather was overcast and atmospheric. At the corner, they all piled onto a double-decker bus bound for the Tower of London. With the help of their history teacher, Miss Chase-Smythe, Belle had identified the Tower of London as the best Tudor location; she was carrying a large folder, stuffed with maps and in-depth historical notes.

But before they'd been on the bus five minutes, Nick leaped up and announced that he'd had another Creative Eureka Moment.

'I'm seeing Belle sitting on the bus, doing her dreamy-gazing-out-of-window thing again,' he said, framing the scene with his fingers and thumbs. 'Then she sees Jack walking past on the crowded street – we'll add in a camera shot at street-level later, Nate. She gets off the bus to run after him. But he's gone . . .'

Everyone agreed this would make a great scene. Even the other passengers got into the spirit; they all crowded onto one side of the bus leaving a space around Belle, so that Nathan could film her.

'But if I see anything *remotely* like a watering can, the whole thing's off!' Belle warned.

'Artistic temperament! What can you do?' Nick laughed, playing to the audience.

They all got off the bus at the next stop – Nick pausing to hand out his card to the other passengers. 'Nick has a card?' Cat giggled. Holly took one. NICK TAGGART: FREELANCE FILM DIRECTOR, she read. Underneath were the words, IN A CLASS OF HIS OWN!

'In a *world* of his own, more like!' Belle laughed, shaking her head.

Nathan set up his camera while Belle and Nick ran

back to the previous bus stop and boarded the next bus. When the bus arrived, Nathan filmed Belle getting off and running along the street looking anxiously for the boy.

After they'd finished filming the scene, they all climbed back on the next bus to continue their journey to the Tower of London. Nathan played back the footage on the camera screen. Holly crowded round with the others, all jostling to get a glimpse.

'Wow!' Nick said. 'This is solid gold! Look at Belle's face against the grimy streaks on that bus window. It's brilliantly moody!' He was so swept up in the moment, he put his arm round Lettie and kissed her on the cheek. Then he pulled away and glanced round sheepishly to see if anyone noticed. *Result!* Holly thought. *If all goes well, those two will be in full smooch-mode by the end of the day!*

'I love those pigeons!' Lettie exclaimed, blushing and straightening her glasses, but looking terribly pleased at the hug-and-kiss incident. Holly peered over Lettie's shoulder at the camera screen and saw what she meant. As Belle ran along looking for Jack, she'd disturbed a flock of pigeons and they'd all fluttered up around her. It made an amazing image.

At the Tower of London, the filming continued to

run smoothly. First they shot their scenes in modern dress, using the White Tower, the execution site on Tower Green and the Chapel Royal as their backdrops. Then it was time to squeeze into the toilets and change into their Tudor outfits.

Changing and doing hair and make-up in the ladies' room was a little cramped, to say the least.

'I bet Keira Knightley doesn't have to put up with these working conditions!' Holly laughed as she bumped against the hand dryer and blasted her bottom with hot air while Serena tried to lace up her stomacher.

Eventually they emerged and met up with the boys. 'These puffed-up Tudor pants are a nightmare!' Jack complained, trying to pull his tunic down over the velvet knickerbockers. 'I feel as if I've got watermelons stuffed up there!'

Belle giggled. 'I have to say, it's not your best look!'

Suddenly they were surrounded by a crowd of tourists all taking photographs. 'Are you doing a historical re-enactment?' they asked eagerly.

Adam grinned. 'Yeah, he said. 'We're the court of Henry the Eighth. If you come back in half an hour we will be chopping off Cat's head!'

Cat stuck her tongue out at him.

The tourists checked their watches. 'Ooh, time for a cup of tea first, then!'

'Let's shoot our scenes and get out of here,' Holly laughed. 'Before we're *thrown* out!'

'Come on, people!' Nick called. 'All in position for Cat running across Tower Green. Can you get those ravens in shot, Nate?'

Nathan gave a thumbs-up and they got to work.

After filming modern scenes at the London Eye and Piccadilly Circus, the team finally made their way to Hyde Park for the dance routine. They staked out a good spot near the Serpentine Lake and filmed under the trees while Jack rowed around in circles behind them being Mysterious Boy. Adam set up the CD player so that the girls could dance to the soundtrack. They recorded the first half of the hip-hop-to-pavane sequence in their modern clothes and the second part in their Tudor costumes, so that Nick could edit it together on the computer later.

Nick was in his element. He'd brought his director's chair with him, and sat slurping from a large polystyrene cup of cappuccino that Adam had fetched him, wearing his shades, even though the sky was now darkening from grey to black.

'Girls! Girls! *Work* those kirtles!' he yelled.

Finally Holly was satisfied that the dance routine was perfect and Nathan had caught it all on film from every possible angle.

'And it's a wrap!' Nick shouted. Everyone cheered. There was a flurry of hugs and high-fives all round. Holly, Belle and Cat thanked everyone for all their help.

'When Nobody's Angels win the competition, you're *all* coming up with us onto the stage to collect the prize!' Holly told them. 'Nick, Lettie, Nathan, Serena, Jack . . . and Adam, of course! We couldn't have done it without his superior costume-carrying skills!'

Adam grinned and flexed his biceps in a strongman pose. 'Ow!' he winced. 'My arms are aching!'

'And don't forget Mason and Felix for their cool soundtrack,' Belle added.

'And Abbey and Libby for helping last week!' Cat said. 'This is going to have to be a *biiiig* stage!'

Suddenly there was a flash of lightning.

Holly held her bag over her head and ran with the others through the pouring rain to the café by the lake for a well-earned and very late lunch.

Nick pulled up his chair next to Lettie and began discussing the editing he would do tomorrow. Belle and Jack were swapping memories of their previous visit to the Tower of London – on their very first date – and debating which film they would go out to see later. Cat and Adam were engrossed in a flirtatious argument about whether they should share a burger if Adam promised to eat the pickled gherkin. It was like a scene from Noah's Ark: everyone two-by-two. Even Serena and Nathan were chatting happily about Tudor hairstyles.

Suddenly Holly felt very alone. If only Ethan were here to share the fun of the film shoot with her. Ethan had never got in touch, despite promising to in his last text – and she hadn't heard from him all week. The pain of missing him was as sharp as a splinter.

'Hey, Hols, look,' Cat whispered, winking in the direction of Nick and Lettie. Nick had casually put his arm round the back of Lettie's chair. She was leaning against his shoulder.

Holly smiled. They made such a sweet couple.

And, she reminded herself, Ethan would be back in four weeks.

Only 40,300 minutes to go.

CHAPTER SEVENTEEN

Belle: Bursting with Total Awesomosity

Belle had closed down all non-essential functions.

She'd been in the library all day and had left her post only for lunch and dinner (fifteen minutes each) and three visits to the bathroom (seven minutes, total).

She studied her exam-revision schedule – a fold-out chart colour-coded with highlighter pen. This was catch-up time.

She'd lost a day's studying yesterday due to the video film shoot. And then she'd gone to see *Moulin Rouge* at the Arts Cinema with Jack. *What was I thinking? I knew I had piles of revision to do!* But somehow, in all the excitement of finishing the video shoot, when Jack had asked her out and looked so intensely into her eyes, her brain had turned to syrup and she'd said yes. *And it was worth it!* Belle's thoughts drifted back over the perfect evening – sharing popcorn . . . holding hands . . . the film was so romantic and the soundtrack so amazing . . . Belle had wished the evening would never end. But when it did, that parting kiss was like . . .

Belle Madison! Come back down to earth this minute! she scolded herself. *Focus on this French vocabulary. The library closes at nine. You have precisely one hour left to revise.* Most of their end-of-year tests had taken place last week, but they still had French and maths tomorrow. Belle sighed, adjusted the wall of books she'd constructed around her desk to make sure she wasn't disturbed, and returned to work.

But moments later, her mind was wandering again – this time, wondering how Nick was getting on with editing their video. He'd locked himself in the computer room all day, refusing to let anyone see it until it was finished, apart from Lettie, who had special permission as musical director. Belle hated the fact that the video was out of her control, but she had to face reality: she didn't know how to use the editing software and she didn't have time to learn. The deadline was Tuesday so they had to get it in the post tomorrow morning. And she did trust Nick. *Well, sort of!*

Belle forced her attention back to the screen. The list of French adjectives swam before her eyes, *magnifique . . . difficile . . . petite . . .* What if Nick messed up the video? There'd be no time for second chances now!

Suddenly Belle's book wall came cascading off the desk as Cat and Holly hurtled into the library.

'Come on!' Holly panted. 'Nick's ready. We can see the video!'

For a moment Belle was paralysed with indecision. She still had two pages of vocabulary to memorize. But if she didn't see that video within the next thirty seconds she was going to explode! *I have to go! I have to stay!* Cat made the decision for her. She reached over, clicked on SAVE FILE and closed the laptop.

'What about my revision?' Belle began.

But she was the first one out of the library and into the computer room!

They all crowded round Nick and Lettie at the computer screen. Grinning manically, Nick handed out headphones. Belle's hands trembled with anticipation as she put them on.

'And, now, the moment we've all been waiting for,' Nick declared dramatically. 'The first official viewing of . . .'

'Get on with it!' Cat laughed. 'There are people dying of suspense here!'

With a flourish, Nick clicked PLAY.

Belle watched spellbound as the video unfolded.

It was all there: the Tudor scenes at the Tower of London, gazing out of the window in the courtyard, seeing Jack from the bus and running after him with the pigeons flying up round her, the dance sequences in Hyde Park where the girls magically morphed from hip-hop to Tudor pavane and back again. Jack could be seen coming and going as a ghostly presence in the background. The soundtrack and vocals sounded fabulous too; their three voices harmonized perfectly on the haunting melody.

Jack, Adam and Nathan arrived and they watched the video again. They watched it a third time with Serena and Gemma, then a fourth with Mason Lee and Felix Baddeley who'd come to see how the drum and guitar tracks had worked out.

'It gets better every time I see it!' Belle exclaimed.

By now there was a full-scale celebration party going on in the computer room.

'It's brilliant,' Holly gasped. 'Thank you, Nick! Thank you, Lettie!'

'Amazing!' Cat agreed.

They were running out of words to say how much they loved it, so they started inventing some new ones.

'Megarific!'

'Fabtasticacious!'

'*C'est magnifique! Formidable!*' Belle threw in. *No harm practising my French vocabulary at the same time*, she thought.

'If this video doesn't win the competition, I'm a tree frog!' Nathan piped up, grinning at everyone shyly through his thick fringe.

Next day, Belle, Holly and Cat asked Mrs Butterworth for permission to run out to the post office before breakfast.

They had a very important parcel to post. One DVD and one entry form, addressed to the PopTV offices.

They all gave the package a kiss for good luck before handing it over to the lady behind the counter. 'Something special?' she asked, smiling at their obvious excitement.

'Something bursting with total awesomeosity!' Belle replied.

She linked arms with Cat and Holly and skipped back across Kingsgrove Square. 'We did it!' she said proudly.

Now all they could do was wait.

CHAPTER EIGHTEEN

Belle: The Dvořák Fan Club

The three girls skipped all the way back to school. But when Belle stepped into the entrance hall, she stopped so abruptly that Cat and Holly shunted into the back of her.

'Could you give some kind of warning signal next time you do that!' Cat said. Then she fell silent.

In the middle of the floor was a set of matching luggage. Very familiar, last-season Louis Vuitton luggage.

Belle's heart sank.

'Uh-oh!' Holly breathed.

'Of course, it's soooo refreshing to work with professionals . . .'

Belle knew that voice. Slowly she turned to look. She didn't really *want* to see, but, like watching a gruesome operation on *Grey's Anatomy*, she couldn't resist. Draped across an armchair, dressed in a silver jumpsuit, high-heeled boots and Dior sunglasses, ice-blond bob wrapped in a tiger-print scarf . . .

. . . Bianca Hayford was back from the swamp.

She was holding court to a small crowd of admirers. Mayu Tanaka was there, of course, perched on the arm of Bianca's chair in official best-friend/sidekick position. Belle also recognized Orlando Spicer, a Year Ten boy who had one thing going for him: he was stop-and-swoon gorgeous. Unfortunately, that was the *only* thing he had going for him: he was obnoxious and big-headed, as Cat had discovered to her cost when he took a liking to her last term.

'I don't know what Al's going to do without me in Florida,' Bianca was saying. 'That's Al Reagan, of course, the director. He *totally* relied on me for advice on how to handle the younger cast members. They weren't all as *professional* as me, especially after poor Joshy was bitten . . .'

'Ooh, did you see it?' Mayu asked. 'Was it dead gory?'

'Of course. I was first on the scene. In fact, he'd probably have died without my first-aid training . . .'

'Yeah, what you really *want* to do when an alligator attacks is wedge its mouth open with a large stick,' Orlando chimed in, as if he fought off wild alligators on a daily basis.

'So, what's Violet Dubarry like?' Mayu asked.

'Oh, Viles? Absolute *sweetheart!*' Bianca gushed, wiggling her hand impatiently for Mayu to pass her a diet Coke from the table. 'We're like sisters! We're so tuned in to each other. Sometimes we'd open our mouths and say *exactly* the same thing! Mayu, I need a straw for this!'

Mayu got up to fetch a straw from the water-cooler station in the corner of the hall. Judging by the pout on her face, it was clear she wasn't too happy that Bianca had found a new 'sister'.

'Bianca! Could you move your luggage to one side?' Mrs Butterworth shouted from her chair. 'It's a trip hazard.'

'Oh, here we go!' Bianca scoffed, chuckling coldly. 'Back to the real world! I didn't have to lift a finger in America. They really know how to look after their talent there. It was VIP treatment all the way . . .'

'VIP? That'd be *Very Irritating Person*,' Cat whispered.

Belle couldn't help giggling.

Bianca must have heard her. She looked up and narrowed her pale blue eyes. 'As I was saying,' she went on loudly, 'being a film star can get quite tedious, with so many boys throwing themselves at your feet. Like Ethan Reed. He was totally into Viles — they were inseparable.' Bianca glanced up and pretended to notice Holly for the first time. She smirked. 'Oops, didn't notice the three little pigs lurking over there!'

Belle gasped. She'd almost forgotten how spiteful Bianca could be. She was sure Bianca had invented the entire Ethan–Violet affair. She ground her teeth and turned to Holly. 'Rise above it,' she whispered. To her relief, Holly was still smiling. She didn't seem to have taken Bianca's lies to heart.

'Come on, we don't need to listen to this rubbish,' Cat growled, marching towards the common room.

As they left, Belle could still hear Bianca going on . . . and on . . . and on . . .

'Ooh, the jet lag is really catching up with me! I've hardly slept for weeks. The heat there is terrible. It was like *I'm a Celebrity Get Me Out of Here!* And don't get me started on the mosquitoes. I'm sure I've contracted malaria . . . I'm going for a bath. Orlando, bring my bags! Mayu, get that cat away from me, you know I'm allergic . . .'

Bianca Hayford was well and truly in the house.

'Go on, admit it,' Cat teased. 'You've missed her really!'

Belle looked at Holly. They both shook their heads. 'Nope!' they said, with one voice.

After lunch, Belle collected her dance kit and walked with Holly and Cat to the dance department for a core dance lesson with Miss LeClair.

'I think it's time for Phase Two of Operation Monster,' Holly said. 'Nick and Lettie just need one more little push!'

Belle agreed. Nick and Lettie were as cute together as the little plastic bride-and-groom figures on the top of a wedding cake, but still hadn't quite reached Love Central.

'Next time we've got them both together,' Cat said, 'let's have another guest appearance from Callum and the concert tickets!'

They didn't have to wait long for their chance. After an hour working on their tap combinations, Miss LeClair told them to take a short break. As Belle sipped from her water bottle, she spotted Nick sitting on a bench chatting with Zak and Nathan. Lettie was leaning against the wall behind them adjusting the screws in her tap shoes. Belle nudged Holly and Cat and they sidled over – their tap shoes clip-clopping on the wooden floor.

'Yeah, I'm thinking of going to a classical concert next weekend,' Belle said casually as if they were midway through a conversation. 'I'll check out what's on after class . . .'

'Oh, that reminds me!' Cat said loudly. 'Lettie, have you seen Callum again since your Mahler date? Got any more concerts lined up?'

Lettie looked up from her shoe. 'It wasn't a date! But yes, he did ask if I wanted to see Dvořák's cello concerto in a couple of weeks.'

Belle peeked at Nick to make sure he was listening. *Yep!* He was listening so hard you could almost see his ears quivering!

'So, are you going to go?' Holly asked.

Lettie laughed. 'How can I refuse? It's my all-time favourite!'

Nick stood up from the bench and moved closer. 'Would that be Dvořák's Cello Concerto in B Minor, Op. 104,' he said in an offhand couldn't-help-overhearing tone, 'written in 1895, first performed by the London Philharmonic in 1896?'

Lettie stared at him open-mouthed. 'Wow! I didn't know you were such a Dvořák fan, Nick!'

Belle was just as surprised. Nick had always shown about as much interest in classical music as in Hawaiian nose-flute music. She grinned at Holly and Cat as the newly formed Garrick School Branch of the Dvořák

Fan Club (membership: two) wandered off, deep in conversation.

Zak pushed himself up lazily from the bench and grinned. 'Dude's been speed-reading *The Encyclopaedia of Classical Music* every night for weeks,' he whispered. 'Says he's just *broadening his mind. Getting down with some culture . . .*'

'Not trying to impress Lettie at all, then?' Belle joked.

Zak danced a perfect little *shuffle-spring-wing* combination. 'How could you even *think* such a thing?' he laughed.

It seemed that Phase Two of Operation Monster was on target!

CHAPTER NINETEEN

Holly: Core Abdominals and Xargoid Claws

'*Mamma Mia!* Holly Devenish! Where *are* your core abdominals?' Miss Morgan scolded.

In my stomach? Where I usually keep them? Holly thought grumpily. But she kept it to herself. Tiny, wizened and very fierce, Miss Morgan did not tolerate lip or cheek. And Holly wasn't a talking-back kind of girl anyway.

'Sorry, Miss Morgan!' she mumbled, pulling in her wayward stomach muscles.

They were halfway through Thursday afternoon's advanced ballet class, and although it was Holly's favourite lesson of the week she felt thoroughly fed up. She wasn't concentrating on her barre work, and it clearly showed.

She hadn't had a text or call from Ethan all week. Not even a message in a bottle or by carrier pigeon. He wasn't answering his phone. He'd completely fallen off the radar. And although Holly refused on principle to believe anything that Bianca said, she was starting to have her doubts. *What if Ethan really has fallen for Vile Violet's blond and blue-eyed charms?*

'Now, the *fouettés*. One more time! They must be *perfecto* for your Intermediate exam!' Miss Morgan shrieked. Hopping from foot to foot in her black leotard, she reminded Holly of a raven in the Tower of London. '*Attenzione!* Holly, I said *fouettés* not *tendus*! Where is your head today?'

'On my neck!'

Gemma and Serena froze mid-step and stared at her in horror.

Oops, did I say that out loud?

'*Excuse me?*' Miss Morgan screeched.

Holly felt her ears flaming with embarrassment. She'd never said anything so rude to a teacher before. 'Er, I said I've got a *crick* in my neck,' she mumbled.

By Friday night, the misery brick in Holly's ribcage was back with a vengeance. She'd been trying to forget about Ethan, but the world wouldn't let her. In the first class of the day, Mrs Jeffries, the English teacher, brought in photographs of her grandchildren at Disneyland. *Disneyland is in Florida!* Then, in their French lesson, the first sentence she had to translate was: Yesterday, I received a letter from my boyfriend. *In my dreams!* Holly thought. In art, Mr Potter asked them to sketch natural landscapes. *Like mountains, deserts or . . .* swamps.

She trudged upstairs after dinner to find that Gemma was throwing a slumber party in their bedroom. At least that's what it looked like. Gemma, Belle, Cat, Lettie, Serena and Ruby were all lolling around on the beds and beanbags. Their conversation instantly faded to a guilty silence.

'What's up?' Holly asked. 'Are you guys figuring out how to tell me I've got bad breath or something?' Just when she'd thought her day couldn't get any worse!

'Hols, don't look so worried!' Cat laughed. 'It's not a personal-hygiene issue.'

'It's just that we know how *down* you've been . . .' Belle added.

'And we couldn't quite afford to fly Ethan back from Florida . . .' Gemma added.

'So we're having a Girl's Night Out to cheer you up!' Serena interrupted.

'One of your favourite films,' Lettie said.

'And we're leaving in five minutes!' Ruby held out Holly's jacket and bag.

Holly stared at her friends' smiling faces and tried to

take in what they were saying; not easy when all six of them were speaking at the same time. She laughed and hugged them all.

'Thanks, guys – this is just what I need.' Then she hesitated. 'As long as the film doesn't have *anything* to do with swamps, alligators or missing boyfriends!'

'*It's* The Sound of Music*!*' her friends chorused.

'I should be safe there then!' Holly laughed.

'*The swamps are alive with the sound of music!*' Cat sang as they all they bundled down the stairs like the Charge of the Girl Brigade.

Holly loved *The Sound of Music*. She laughed, she cried and she sang along with her friends.

When they came out of the cinema, Belle announced that she had another treat in store: they were going to a new restaurant she'd read about.

'But we've eaten dinner already,' Gemma pointed out.

Undeterred, Belle marched them along the road, turned the corner and pointed to a restaurant, with pastel pink and green paintwork as pretty as icing on a cupcake and fairy lights twinkling in the windows. 'Ta da! Just Desserts!'

'Oh, *puddings*,' Cat said, 'Now we're talking!'

Holly could hardly move by the time they waddled out of Just Desserts. They'd felt it their duty to sample the entire menu to check it was up to their exacting standards.

They awarded it five Garrick gold stars!

Soon they were all back in Holly and Gemma's room.

'Time to play No-Mirror Makeover!' Cat announced. 'The rules are simple. We all empty our make-up bags into this box.' She waited while the girls all ran to their rooms, fetched their make-up and deposited it into a shoebox in the middle of the room. Lettie didn't wear make-up, but that was more than made up for by Ruby's collection of black eye pencils.

'Now, everyone take out ten items at random,' Cat continued. 'Then all you have to do is put your make-up on. Only catch is, you don't get a mirror!'

Five minutes later they were all rolling on the floor, laughing at each other's faces. Serena had a clown-smile of red lipstick, while Gemma had managed to apply perfect rings of eyeliner. To both nostrils.

'Argghh!' Holly laughed, holding her sides in agony as she gasped for air. 'This game should come with a health warning,' she groaned. '*Do not attempt immediately after consuming sticky toffee pudding and banoffee pie!*'

'Side effects include uncontrollable giggles and stomach pains,' Cat panted.

Her face looked like a map of the London Underground, but Holly hadn't felt so happy in weeks.

Ethan? Ethan who?

The next day was Saturday. After a morning of homework, Holly's afternoon was taken up with a costume fitting for *Anything Goes*. The Year Eight advanced tap class were dancing in the title song, and they were all wearing sailor outfits. This was followed by a long rehearsal of the main dance numbers with the Year Eleven students. It was less than two weeks until the show now. Owen Mitchell and Tabitha Langley were fabulous as Billy and Hope. Holly watched them admiringly, wondering how it must feel to be rehearsing for your last ever performance at Superstar High.

Still humming *Anything Goes*, Holly headed for the common room to meet Cat and Belle.

As she entered, Holly noticed a crowd of people gathered around the table. *Miss Candlemas must have baked a batch of her famous chocolate brownies*, Holly thought. But it was soon obvious that the main attraction was *not* a plate of brownies. Unless the brownies had brought their laptop and were entertaining the crowd with photos of a recent trip to Florida . . .

'And here's me with Violet Dubarry in the hotel pool. And here's me with Al Reagan on set. And here's me . . .'

Holly hurried to the other end of the room where Cat and Belle were sitting, and tried to block out the sound of Bianca's running commentary.

No chance! They could probably hear her in Florida!

'. . . and here's me in the hot tub! Oh, and here we are at a hu-u-u-g-e celebrity bash in Miami. You won't believe this, but me and Viles *almost* turned up in the *same* off-the-shoulder Versace dress! We were always doing things like that. It was *spooky!*'

Cat held her hand over her mouth and pretended to be shocked. 'Oh my God!' she whispered. 'Not *the same dress*! Is this the end of civilization as we know it?'

Holly giggled. She wasn't going to let Bianca's all-about-me brag-fest bother her.

But suddenly Bianca turned up the volume. 'Ooh look, Violet with *Ethan* sunbathing by the pool . . . Violet and Ethan sharing a hot dog at the food trailer . . .'

Holly closed her eyes and tried to shut it out.

'. . . Violet and *Ethan* goofing around with the alien costumes . . . that's a Xargoid claw he's chasing her with . . . Violet and Ethan . . . Ooh, now *this* is a *very* interesting one.' Bianca paused tantalizingly.

As if drawn by an invisible magnetic force, Holly got up and crossed the room. She could hear Cat and Belle calling her back, but took no notice. She pushed past Mayu Tanaka and Orlando Spicer and stared at the screen.

Against a background of twisted roots and lush green vegetation, a couple were clinging together in a passionate embrace.

You couldn't see their faces.

But Holly didn't need to. She knew who it was.

Ethan was kissing Violet Dubarry.

This time her heart really *was* breaking.

CHAPTER TWENTY

Cat: Do My Feet Look Big in These Socks?

Cat watched in horror as Holly took one look at Bianca's laptop and fled the common room.

She stormed over to the group at the table. 'Bianca? What have you done?'

Bianca smiled a sly alligator-smile. 'It was just a picture . . .'

Cat reached across Mayu's pink-frilled shoulder and clicked back to the previous photograph. Ethan Reed was locked in the arms of a beautiful blond girl. Either they were demonstrating a new wrestling hold or they were doing some serious snogging.

'Is that your best-buddy Violet attached to Ethan's face?' Cat demanded.

Bianca smirked. 'She's *kissing* him, if that's what you mean.'

'As in *pretending* to kiss him!' Cat yelled. 'They're obviously on the film set. They're acting!'

Bianca shrugged. 'Did I say it was real?'

'You didn't say it *wasn't* either. You *knew* what Holly would think when she saw that picture.'

'Oh, boo hoo,' Bianca sneered. 'Holly needs to get over herself. Ethan's an A-list player now. He's not going to want some little Z-list excuse for a girlfriend tagging along. She may as well get used to the idea!'

Cat felt the flames of rage flicker through her body like a forest fire. And Bianca Hayford was a tanker full of petrol sitting right in her path. There were going to be fireworks! 'You, you . . . *slimy hagfish!*' she yelled. 'What's Holly ever done to *you?*'

'Uh-oh! Tantrum in progress,' Mayu simpered, doing her usual impression of a sugar-coated scorpion.

Orlando flicked back his floppy dark hair. 'Seems Cat has some serious Anger Management Issues,' he said in a stage-whisper. He rolled his gorgeous eyes under their impossibly long lashes and put his arm around Bianca's shoulder protectively.

Yeah, like Bianca needs *protecting. About as much as a great white shark!*

'Just look at this!' Cat seethed, turning to Belle, who was now at her shoulder. 'This is what Holly saw!'

Belle examined the photo. 'But that's just a screen kiss. Ethan would never wear a ridiculous blue leather tunic like that for real!' She drew herself up to her full height and glared down at Bianca. 'Do you have to *practise* to be this mean or does it come naturally?' she asked in a lethally quiet voice.

All of the above, Cat thought as she followed Belle out of the door.

Cat and Belle ran upstairs to find Holly lying on her bed, staring at the ceiling as if expecting a message from outer space.

'OK, Hols, listen up!' Cat said, flopping down on the bed next to her. 'One: that photo *wasn't* Ethan and Violet kissing. Well, it was, but they were just acting. It was a pseudo-snog. Two: Bianca was doing that whole Ethan-and-Violet thing *deliberately* to wind you up . . . And three . . .' Her voice trailed off as she tried to think of a third rallying point.

'And three,' Belle chimed in, sitting on the other end of the bed, 'Ethan would never cheat on you like that. He's too nice a guy.'

'Yeah, that's right!' Cat said.

'Well, even if that wasn't *real* kissing – although it looked pretty realistic to me,' Holly muttered in a flat voice, 'it still doesn't explain why he's not bothering to reply to my messages.'

Cat shook her head. 'I'm sure there's a perfectly

logical explanation!' She *wanted* to sound convincing, but secretly she was starting to agree that Ethan's behaviour was bordering on Decidedly Dodgy. He'd always been a model boyfriend in the past, so why the sudden Silent Treatment? Cat knew communications could be unreliable in remote parts of the Everglades, but had he suddenly lost the use of his thumbs, so he couldn't send text messages? Or had an alligator eaten his mobile phone?

Whatever the reason, Cat knew they were going to need another emergency Girls' Night Out to perk Holly up again. She pulled out her phone and called Adam to cancel their date.

'Don't you dare!' Holly snatched Cat's phone from her just as Cat started speaking. 'Ignore her, Adam. Cat will meet you as planned,' she said firmly. Then she turned to Cat. '*My* love life might have gone down the toilet but it doesn't mean yours has to as well.'

'Yeah, you should go,' Belle said. 'You've not been out with Adam for ages. Holly and I can have a pamper session. My nails are in dire need of a manicure.'

Cat was in a quandary. She knew that Belle had been planning to go to the library to catch up on her homework. But she'd been looking forward to dinner with Adam at Café Roma all week.

'Well, if you're sure . . .' she said.

'Sure we're sure!' Belle laughed. 'Now hurry up, or you'll be late.'

Cat darted into her room to change. She grabbed a red lipstick rescued from the No-Mirror Makeover shoebox in one hand and her favourite black skirt from under her bed in the other. She wriggled the skirt over her hips and tugged at the zip. It seemed to be stuck. *Oops*, now it had completely broken. She searched around and found a safety pin at the back of a drawer.

Cat stared at herself in the long mirror. The skirt was even tighter than before! Surely vast new wodges of flab hadn't sprouted on her hips overnight? *Or had they?* With a overwhelming sense of doom, she remembered the visit to Just Desserts.

She examined her figure from all angles. She couldn't see any telltale passion-fruit-pavlova-shaped lumps or trifle-shaped bumps. In fact, if she pulled her top down a little, she looked pretty sleek and slinky really.

The zip just broke because I was yanking on it too hard, she told herself firmly.

★ ★ ★

'You look great,' Adam said as they sat down at a corner table in Café Roma.

Cat smiled. Adam looked pretty good too, with his wide cheekbones, clear brown skin and wonky grin. If she was being picky she'd have to admit his ears still stuck out slightly more than necessary, but this was A Good Thing. Without those ears Adam would be too handsome (not without *any* ears, of course, that would just look *weird*), and Cat's in-depth research had revealed that boys who were ultra-gorgeous were usually lacking in the Decent Human Being Department. Obnoxious Orlando was a case in point.

'You don't think my bum looks big in this skirt, then?' Cat asked. She knew she was fishing for compliments in a big way, but after the zip malfunction she needed reassurance.

'No way! It's just good to see you out of that disgusting old leotard you've been wearing to tango lessons,' Adam teased as he perused the menu. 'How long are you going to keep up the ragamuffin act?'

'D'you think I *enjoy* looking like a tramp's laundry basket?' Cat asked. 'But Miguel thinks I'm a poor little street urchin with fire in my soul . . .'

'. . . and Argentinean blood in your veins!' Adam joked, mimicking Miguel Silva's sexy Spanish accent.

'Fiery and tempestuous. *Be careful not to cross this girl!*'

They ordered their meals and continued to chat about their tango routine for *Anything Goes*. The rehearsals were going fabulously and Miguel was really impressed with their progress. They couldn't wait to perform for real.

'You're so macho when we dance together,' Cat giggled, tucking into her spaghetti carbonara. 'I love it!'

'So do I!' Adam said. 'It's the only time I get to be the boss!'

Cat poked his arm with her fork and made a face. 'Just don't get too used to it!'

Adam laughed and pulled away. As he did so, his foot slipped and caught Cat on the shin.

'Ouch!' she cried. Adam was wearing heavy Doc Marten boots under his jeans. And he had very large feet.

'I'm so sorry!' he said. 'Me and my macho tango feet!'

'Just keep those humungous size ten monsters under control,' Cat joked. 'It's like sitting next to Bigfoot!'

Adam grinned. 'Hey, you'll give me a foot complex! I'll be all *Do my feet look big in these socks.* Like you with your bum!'

Cat froze, staring at him, her fork midway to her

mouth, as if she'd been stunned with a taser-gun. The silence was broken by the sound of her fork clattering to the table.

'Are you saying I've got a big bum?' she asked, so softly it was almost a whisper.

'No! Of course not.' Adam shook his head, smiling.

Cat didn't hear him. The blood was rushing in her ears and deafening her. 'You think I'm fat, don't you?' she snapped. 'And if you even *think* the words *big-boned*, I promise I'll never speak to you again!'

Adam stared at her with a bewildered look on his face. 'Of course I don't think you're fat!' he protested. 'Or big-boned. Don't freak out on me!'

Cat couldn't even look at him. She scowled down at her spaghetti carbonara. *Pasta, eggs, cream, cheese and bacon. Five of the scrummiest foodstuffs known to man. Or girl.* But all she could see now were three million calories jeering at her from the plate. She pushed it away. 'I'm not hungry any more. I want to go. Now.'

Adam reached out to take Cat's hand but she snatched it away. He shook his head sadly. 'This is insane! You *know* I'm not into that size-zero lollipop-head look.'

Cat stomped back to school three paces ahead of Adam, barricaded in cold, flinty silence.

How dare he say I'm fat! she fumed. *And I thought he was different. I should have known he was a loathsome slug-beast like every other boy on the planet. He's worse than Orlando!*

How had their lovely evening ended like this?

It had all gone pear-shaped.

And she didn't just mean her figure!

CHAPTER TWENTY-ONE

Belle: Deeper Than Paper

Belle examined the array of nail varnishes she'd laid out on the dressing table. She plumped for Fabulous Fudge Frosting and picked up the bottle.

'Give me your hand and don't fidget this time.'

Singing along to Leona Lewis on her iPod speakers, Belle carefully applied the brush to Holly's nails. *Poor Holly.* She was doing her best to be cheerful but that stupid photo of Ethan and Violet was clearly tormenting her; Belle could almost see the image projected on a giant screen behind Holly's eyes. Which is exactly what Bianca had intended, of course. Belle was furious. She was used to being Bianca's Public Enemy Number One herself, but she couldn't bear to see her lashing out at someone as sweet as Holly. It was like watching a rattlesnake attacking a fluffy little duckling.

Bianca's spiteful antics were even more infuriating because everything else was coming together so well.

She'd received a confirmation note from PopTV to say that their video had arrived safely. The end-of-year tests were finally over and she was nearly back on top of her homework schedule. The rehearsals for *Anything Goes* were great fun and were now ramping up to fever pitch. Things were going wonderfully with Jack, and Cat was getting on well with Adam . . .

If they could just sort out the Ethan situation for Holly, everything would be perfect.

There was a crash and the bedroom door flew open.

'Cat! You're back early. Did you have a lovely time?' Holly asked, tucking a braid behind her ear and totalling an entire hand's worth of nail varnish in a single move.

Belle groaned, reached for the nail-varnish remover again, and waited for Cat to belly flop onto her bed and start entertaining them with the edited highlights of her evening with Adam. But to her surprise, Cat slammed the door and stormed round the room, knocking a pile of papers from Belle's desk. Belle put down the bottle and started gathering the landslide of pages off the floor.

'Cat, what's the matter?' Holly asked. 'Has something happened?'

'I don't want to talk about it!' Cat said flatly.

'Come on. Sit down and tell us the whole story,' Holly coaxed.

Cat fell onto her bed, grabbed a tissue and blew her nose loudly. 'He said I was fat!' she wailed. 'He said my bum looked big in this skirt. Why did he have to ruin everything? We were chatting and laughing and eating and then he just came out and said it. I thought he didn't care that I wasn't super-skinny, but he does . . . I hate him!'

Belle and Holly looked at each other in dismay. They knew how sensitive Cat could be about her figure – even though she looked fantastic. When Cat paused to blow her nose again, Belle interrupted. 'I just can't believe Adam would say that.'

'Well, he did!' Cat sniffed. '*And* he said I was freaking out and being insane!'

Belle was deeply confused. Why were all these great guys suddenly turning to the Dark Side? Kind, honest Ethan was turning into some kind of Dastardly Scoundrel who couldn't be bothered to send Holly a text message, and now Adam – funny, good-natured Adam – had started dishing out personal insults. It made her realize how lucky she was to have someone as lovely as Jack.

Holly hugged Cat and found her a new supply of

tissues. Belle was still kneeling on the floor, clearing up the paper-avalanche. She glanced down and noticed an unopened letter in the pile of papers in her hands. It must have been in with the rest of the mail she pulled out of her pigeon hole this morning.

Without really looking, she tore open the envelope and pulled out the letter. She started reading – then she stared in disbelief:

Darling Belle,
Your school report arrived today. Your teachers say you
could do better and I'm seeing a bunch of A-minus grades
in there, and that B+ in geography. Like we said at the
start, 'No A, No Stay.' Sorry, kid, a deal's a deal. You will
transfer to the Girls' Elite Science Academy in Switzerland
at the end of term. This is a tough call, but one day, when
you have achieved your true potential, you will thank me.
Your loving father

Belle let the letter drop through her fingers.
No, Dad, I will never *thank you for ruining my life.*
Still on her knees, her head sank until the weave of the carpet pressed into her forehead.

'What's wrong? Belle?'
'Did you get a paper cut on that letter?'

Belle could hear Cat and Holly's voices drifting towards her as if across a vast, empty ocean.

The letter had cut her. But it was deeper than paper. Deeper than a knife, even.

Her dream was over.

CHAPTER TWENTY-TWO

Cat: I Will Survive

The next day was Sunday. Cat usually loved Sundays but this morning she felt as if the mojo had been squeezed out of her by a giant steamroller.

She lay on her bed with The Killers turned up to brain-melting volume on her iPod. It wasn't so much like listening to music as being inside a washing machine of sound. The curtains were still closed and the usually cheerful blue and turquoise room was shrouded in gloom, like the bottom of a murky pond.

She had replayed the fight scene with Adam so many times, it was starting to feel unreal, as if it was something she'd seen in a film. How had everything suddenly gone so spectacularly wrong? It was like that Chaos Theory thing she'd read about somewhere; a butterfly flaps its wings in Brazil and causes a tornado in Texas. There must have been some major wing-flapping going on last night.

Belle was upside down on her yoga mat in the middle of the floor. She was balancing on her forearms, her long legs pointing up to the ceiling in a feathered-peacock pose. According to Belle, it helped to calm the mind. But the look on Belle's face didn't exactly suggest Inner Peace. She was totally devastated by yesterday's letter from her dad. It was a massive shock. The girls hadn't even known their school reports had been sent out yet.

Heralded by a waft of chlorine, Holly trailed into the room.

'Welcome to the Misery Dome!' Cat said grimly. 'It's just nonstop fun and jollification in here. What's the matter, Hols?' she added, noticing that her friend was limping slightly. 'With your leg, I mean, not life in general, which we all know is a total train wreck all round.'

'Banged my knee in the pool,' Holly sighed. 'I was thinking about stuff and I turned too late at the end of a length.' She flopped down on a beanbag, rubbing her bruised knee. 'Miss Candlemas gave me some ice for it. If it's still swollen when I do my Intermediate ballet exam, it'll be a nightmare.'

Belle lowered her legs and sat cross-legged on the yoga mat. 'It's no good,' she groaned. 'I just can't get my head in the zone. I keep thinking about leaving . . .' Her voice faded away.

Cat removed her iPod ear-buds. Her head was throbbing from having the music way too loud. She sat up on her bed, grabbed a cushion and gave it a good therapeutic thump. *We can't go on like this*, she thought.

It was time for action.

'OK, ladies,' Cat said briskly. 'We need some Positive Thinking here. Are we going to lie down and give up? Or are we going to start fighting back? Show them what we're made of?'

Belle and Holly gazed up at her. Neither of them spoke but the defeated looks in their eyes said that what they were made of was very similar to wet tissue paper and they actually quite liked the sound of the lying-down-and-giving-up option.

But Cat was made of stronger stuff. 'Come on! We'll grow strong, we'll learn how to get along!' She realized she was sounding like the old Gloria Gaynor disco anthem. She starting singing *I Will Survive* at the top of her voice. Now she was strutting around the room, shaking her booty like a true disco diva. At last, Holly and Belle were laughing.

'Can we go and do our positive thinking over breakfast?' Holly asked. 'I'm starving.'

'You got it,' Cat replied. 'You can't triumph over adversity on an empty stomach.'

Or with a stomach that your boyfriend thinks is fat. But in the interests of positive thinking, Cat kept that thought to herself.

Pouring skimmed milk on to her small bowl of cereal, Cat addressed the troops with a morale-boosting speech. 'If we work as a team, we can help each other through this . . .'

'OK, you first, Cat. How can we patch things up with Adam?' Belle asked.

Cat almost choked on her orange juice. 'No way! Adam can go and live in a swamp for all I care, and not bother coming back. I'm going to ask Miguel Silva if we can swap partners. I don't even want to be in the same *room* as Adam Fielding, let alone dance the tango with him.'

At that moment Cat looked up to see Adam walk into the dining room carrying his breakfast tray. From the look on his face, like a puppy whose beloved owner has just hit him on the nose with a rolled-up newspaper, he'd clearly overheard her outburst. Her conscience jabbed her as if she'd swallowed something sharp. *Maybe my meltdown was a bit of an over-reaction?*

But the uncomfortable emotion instantly fed into her own wounded feelings. *Serves him right! He's the one who'd insulted me; he's the one who said my bum looked big . . .*

Adam turned and walked away to sit with a group of boys at the far end of the room.

Holly sighed. 'I'm sure he didn't *mean* to hurt you, Cat. At least he's here and you *can* talk to him. I just wish I could talk to Ethan . . .'

Cat snatched at the chance to change the subject. 'Right! That's our first mission. We'll get in touch with Ethan somehow.'

Belle nodded and smiled. 'Yes. After all, he's only in Florida. It isn't really a different planet!' She looked up from tearing her toast into tiny little pieces. 'I'll help you two any way I can . . . while I'm still here. But there's nothing you can do to help *me*. My dad's made up his mind. End of story! I'll be locked away doing a life sentence in some maximum-security boarding school by next term . . .'

Suddenly she pushed aside her plate of shredded toast and jumped up. 'I'm going to find Jack,' she sobbed. 'He doesn't even know I'm leaving yet.'

Cat felt like crying as she watched Belle run out of the dining room. She looked at Holly. Tears were running down her face.

For the first time since Belle received her letter, it really sank in that Belle was leaving. Superstar High wouldn't be the same without her. They were the Three Musketeers. They were Nobody's Angels. They couldn't let the PopTV video be the last time they ever sang together. They couldn't let *Anything Goes* be their last show together at the Garrick. They'd all dreamed of graduating and going out to conquer the world . . . *together*.

They *had* to keep their dream alive.

'We've got to think of a way to change Belle's dad's mind,' Cat said. 'If it's the last thing we ever do!'

Holly nodded and sniffled into her napkin. 'I couldn't bear it if Belle had to leave!'

'Ooh, Belle Madison is *leaving*, is she?'

Bianca's cold voice sliced across the table. She and Mayu had appeared out of thin air, attracted by the scent of gossip like sharks to a drop of blood in the ocean.

'Sorry, did someone *invite* you to join this conversation, Bianca?' Cat retorted sharply.

'Oooh, so it's *true*, then!' Bianca chuckled. 'Her little friends are getting all *stressy* about it too . . .'

Bianca sashayed to the middle of the dining room. 'Wow! So Belle Madison is being thrown out of

The Garrick,' she remarked to Mayu. Mayu was right behind her, but Bianca projected her voice as if she was addressing a crowded stadium. 'They must have finally twigged that she can't really sing!'

'Or dance!' Mayu giggled.

'That she only got in in the first place because of her famous *Mommy and Daddy*,' Bianca went on.

A buzz of excited whispering began to spread through the room. The Garrick Rumour Factory was at work! Who knew what the story would be by lunch time . . . that Belle was being expelled for putting superglue on Mrs Butterworth's chair, or arrested for stealing the Oscar from Mr Fortune's office . . .

'Come on, let's get out of here,' Cat groaned.

Before I lose my temper and get expelled for assaulting Bianca with a sawn-off Weetabix.

CHAPTER TWENTY-THREE

Holly: Cuckoo Clocks and Pig Farmers

Holly and Cat wandered out of the dining room and into the courtyard. In contrast to their sombre moods, it was a bright morning. Everything was sparkling as if freshly washed by last week's rain.

They slumped down on a bench. Holly leaned back and let the sun warm her face.

Cat sighed. 'We have to come up with a plan to stop Belle's dad taking her away and locking her up like Rapunzel in her tower!'

Usually Holly loved making plans. But it was different without Belle there with her charts with action points and columns for pros and cons. And it was different when it was a matter of Life and . . . well, maybe not *Death*, but *No Life at All*.

Cat looked as if her battery was running out of charge, Holly thought. Her red curls were limp and there was no spark in her grey eyes. She was also wearing the baggiest, grottiest T-shirt and leggings

Holly had ever seen. Then again, Holly had to admit that she wasn't exactly a *fashionista* herself today, with her prehistoric trackies and swimming-pool hair.

'What are we going to do?' she wailed.

Cat shrugged. 'I guess hiding Belle in the kitchen store cupboard when Mr Madison comes to pick her up wouldn't work?'

Holly couldn't help grinning. 'What about disguising Bianca as Belle so that Mr Madison takes *her* to Switzerland instead!' Holly suggested.

'Oh, no, we couldn't inflict *that* on the Swiss nation. After all, they gave us all that lovely chocolate,' Cat laughed.

'And those cute little cuckoo clocks,' Holly added.

They fell silent. The jokes had cheered them up for a moment but now they were at rock bottom again. They were no nearer a solution.

Then Holly had a brainwave. 'We could ask Belle's mom to talk to her dad!'

Cat shook her head. 'I asked Belle about that already but she says her dad is in charge of her education – it was in the divorce settlement or something, like who got the private plane and the apartment in Manhattan. It's all just so unfair! Belle's report couldn't have been *that* bad. She's the smartest in our year.'

'Yeah,' Holly agreed. 'I bet the teachers just wrote something about Belle having to be careful not to let her high standards drop. I know from when my mum does reports that she writes stuff like that about the brainy ones, just to make sure they don't start coasting.'

'So, let's just write to Mr Madison and explain. Tell him that Belle really is a world-class genius,' Cat said, brightening at the thought.

'No, he wouldn't buy it from us,' Holly replied thoughtfully. 'But maybe if we got the *teachers* to write something, he'd listen. I remember how impressed he was when he took us out to the Ritz and I told him my mum was a teacher. He *really* respects them.'

'So, it's a plan!' Cat stated decisively. 'We'll ask all the teachers to write something about Belle being the next Stephen Hawking. You'd better do the talking, Hols. I'm not exactly Student of the Year with most of them!'

'OK,' Holly agreed. 'Come on then. There's no time to waste!'

Suddenly Cat leaped up. 'I can't!' she gulped. 'I've just remembered, I've got a meeting with Mr Steele to work on my audition speech for *Much Ado About Nothing*. I completely forgot!'

'Well you can't go like that,' Holly said, looking at Cat's shapeless black T-shirt. It wasn't even clean!

'I'll have to. He hates it when people are late. You remember what he was like on the set of *Macbeth*!'

Holly laughed, remembering the deeply embarrassing incident in first term – she'd disguised herself as Cat playing Lady Macbeth when Cat was running late. It seemed such a long time ago now.

Cat started to hurry away. Then she paused and looked back over her shoulder. 'One thing!'

'What?' Holly asked.

'I think we should keep our plan a secret from Belle. She'll only try and talk us out of it. She thinks it's hopeless trying to change her dad's mind.'

Holly nodded. Deep down, she suspected Belle was right.

But they wouldn't give up without a fight!

Holly went directly to Mrs Butterworth to make an appointment with Mr Fortune. She knew they couldn't start asking the teachers to write to Belle's father without clearing it with the principal first. In her mint-toothpaste-green linen trouser suit, Mrs Butterworth looked as if she was about to scrub up and perform major surgery. She smiled at Holly over her gold-rimmed glasses and shook her head.

'I'm afraid Mr Fortune is away at a conference until

Tuesday, dear. I'm holding the fort until then. Can I help you?'

Holly shook her head sadly and made an appointment to see Mr Fortune on Tuesday morning.

After lunch Holly was at a loose end. She couldn't settle to her homework and wandered aimlessly around school. As she drifted through the music department, she heard piano music coming from one of the practice rooms. She peeped through the glass window in the door. Lettie and Nick were sitting on the piano stool. Giggling, Lettie slapped Nick's hand gently and guided his fingers to the correct notes on the keyboard. She was teaching him to play, and it definitely looked like a *private* lesson.

Holly swallowed the tennis-ball-sized lump that had suddenly appeared in her throat. They looked so happy together. Like her and Ethan. At least, how they were once.

She was sure it was all over now.

Half an hour later Holly found herself doing what she'd always done when life was going downhill faster than an avalanche.

Dancing.

She stood at the barre in one of the practice studios

in the Dance Department, gazing at her reflection in the wall mirror as she worked through her *frappés*.

Her bruised knee was fine now. But the pain in her heart was almost unbearable.

I've lost Ethan and now I'm losing Belle too . . .

But gradually, as she worked through the exercises, the repetition began to soothe her. Just as it had when she was a little girl dancing in her bedroom when Mum and Dad were having one of their rows, before Dad left. Dance had always been her refuge.

Holly looked into the mirror again and noticed a figure standing behind her.

A small figure, all in black.

Miss Morgan was watching her, head on one side, beady eyes glistening, like an inquisitive crow studying a worm.

Uh-oh, Holly thought, *here comes the lecture about how off-beam I was in the last lesson . . . get ready for* 'Mamma Mia! *Where are your core abdominals!'*

But for once Miss Morgan didn't want know the location of her abdominals or any other muscles for that matter. She stepped forward and put her hand gently round Holly's shoulders.

'You remind me of myself at your age.' She smiled at their reflections in the mirror.

Holly blinked, not knowing what to say. The idea of Miss Morgan ever being young was beyond her imagination; she was ancient and timeless – like the pyramids.

'I can tell something is wrong . . . it is boy trouble?'

Holly nodded mutely.

'I have been there too,' Miss Morgan continued. 'In Italy, many years ago. Oh, he was *bellissimo* . . . a pig farmer. I gave up my chance to join La Scala theatre ballet in Milan to be with that boy.'

'What happened?' Holly asked, finding her voice at last.

'He married another girl a month later. I came back to London.'

'I'm so sorry.' The lump was back in her throat. *As a pep talk, this really isn't working*, Holly thought.

'Don't be,' Miss Morgan said. 'He would have been a pig of a husband too!'

Holly smiled weakly.

'You have a great future ahead of you, Holly. If you stay focused you can achieve a Distinction in your Intermediate exam. I know you've got your heart set on musical theatre, but you have the talent to apply for any ballet company in the world – the Royal, Rambert, even the Bolshoi. Don't let a broken heart hold you back like I did. Use the pain and it will make you stronger.'

With that, Miss Morgan stepped back from the mirror. 'And pull up that core!' she scolded, poking Holly in the ribs. Then she marched back out of the studio.

Holly stared into the mirror. *Did that really happen or did I imagine it?*

Suddenly she felt she could do anything.

She *would* get a Distinction. She *would* find a way to stop Belle leaving.

And as for Ethan?

The pain will make me stronger!

CHAPTER TWENTY-FOUR

Cat: Bad Hair Day

Next morning Cat was in double science. At least, her
body was in double science. Her mind was all over the
place. She was worried about Belle leaving, and about
Holly and Ethan. On top of that she was planning to
go and see Miss LeClair at lunch time and ask her to
tell Miguel Silva she wanted to switch partners for the
Anything Goes tango routine. It was heart-breaking –
dancing with Adam had been so wonderful – she could
almost feel his hand on her waist, the sensation of
whirling into his arms . . . Before she could stop
herself, she'd wrapped her arms dramatically around
her shoulders, and dropped her head back – her final
pose in the doomed tango . . .

'*Cat! You're on fire!*'

'Thanks, Hols. Yeah, I know – we made such good
partners. But there's no way I can dance with him now,'
Cat mumbled, her thoughts still with Adam.

'No, Cat, you're *really* on fire! Your hair caught my

Bunsen burner!' Belle shouted in a voice spiked with panic.

What's that horrible burning smell? Cat wondered. Suddenly Holly was batting at her head with a science book.

'Keep still,' she yelled. 'I'm trying to smother the flames!'

'Ow! You're going to give me brain damage with that book,' Cat protested.

'It's OK, Holly, I think you've put it out now,' Nathan said, patting Cat's curls.

The smell was appalling. People were coughing and holding paper towels over their noses.

'Catrin Wickham! *What the blazes is going on here?*' Mrs Salmon was striding towards them, her face flushed with anger.

'Er, nothing, miss,' Cat said, turning away to hide the singed back of her head.

'I didn't know they still burned *witches* . . .' Bianca was laughing.

Then the fire alarm went off.

Standing outside in the designated fire evacuation area on the front drive, Cat spotted Felix Baddeley with some of the other Year Ten boys. They were throwing a cricket ball around while they waited to be counted.

Suddenly Cat had a Lightbulb Moment. She'd been trying to think of a way to get in touch with Ethan all morning – before setting herself on fire, that is. *Felix was Ethan's best friend*. Surely he'd have been in contact . . .

But Felix was no use. 'Hardly heard a peep from him in weeks. Guess he's too busy wowing the American chicks with those green eyes and his cute British accent!'

'Thanks. Big help,' Cat muttered. *Not!*

'Sorry. Wish I could help.' Felix laughed. 'Your Spontaneous Combustion Act got me out of a maths test!'

'How did you know it was me?'

Felix grinned. 'You've not looked in a mirror yet then? If you *wanted* cool black dreadlocks like mine, there are safer ways of doing it!'

Cat laughed too. She watched as Felix loped away to join his friends. He threw the cricket ball to Duncan Gillespie. Duncan caught Cat's eye and waved. They'd been friends since Cat had starred in *Macbeth* when Duncan was the assistant director. Cat remembered hearing a rumour that he'd started going out with Lucy Cheng last term, but Lucy was away in . . .

Of course! Cat remembered, almost bursting with excitement. *Lucy's part of the group who've gone to Florida to film* Sinking Feelings *too!*

'Duncan!' she cried, hurrying towards him. 'You have a number for Lucy in Florida, right? Could you call her and let me ask her some questions about Ethan?'

Duncan shrugged and raked his hands through his thick brown hair. 'Sure. I'll do it now.'

He pulled out his mobile phone and made the call.

Cat's heart was racing as she tried to work out a tactful way to say: *Tell that Ethan Reed to stop being such a prize maggot and call Holly!*

But Duncan was shaking his head. 'Sorry, I can't get through. Reception is terrible there.'

Defeated, Cat turned on her heel and walked away.

At lunch time Cat sat grumpily on her bed. It was so unfair; Miss LeClair had *refused* to let her swap partners for the tango number. Now Belle was kneeling in front of her trying to prune away the worst of her char-grilled hair. This gave Bad Hair Day a whole new meaning!

Cat told Belle about her failed attempts to get in touch with Ethan via Felix and Duncan. 'The whole of

Florida's *unobtainable*,' she sighed. 'It's like the Bermuda Triangle! The only way we're ever going to get through to Ethan is a personal hotline to Al Reagan himself. I bet he has one of those fancy satellite phones.'

Suddenly Belle leaped up from the floor. Cat threw herself back on the bed to avoid having her ear cut off by the scissors that were now waving about in the air.

'Aaarghh!' Belle screamed. 'I can't believe I didn't think of it before. I've been so taken up with my own problems, my brain hasn't been working! I'm such an *idiot*!'

'What?' Cat asked, frantically trying to imagine what imbecilic thing Belle could possibly have done. '*What?*' she shouted again.

'We'll call Al Reagan, of course!'

'Like a famous Hollywood director's really going to take a call from two random girls on the other side of the world,' Cat snorted. Maybe Belle's brain really wasn't working.

'That's just the point,' Belle said. 'We're not random! At least, *I'm* not. Al's one of my dad's best friends. In fact, he's my godfather.'

Cat stared at Belle in amazement. 'Al Reagan is your godfather! And you didn't mention this before *because* . . .'

Belle frowned sadly. 'I know, I'm sorry. Like I said, I've had a lot on my mind.'

Now Cat felt mean for snapping at her. 'OK, never mind. Let's call him.' She sprang on to the bed and jumped up and down. 'Now!'

'I'm on it,' Belle said. 'I'll call his secretary and ask for his number on set.'

Moments later, Belle had Al Reagan's number and was dialling. She put her phone onto speaker so Cat could hear.

Cat could hardly contain her excitement when the call was answered.

'Al Reagan.'

'Oh hi, Uncle Al, it's Belle here,' Belle said.

'How you doing, kid? Long time no speak! How's that father of yours, the old devil?'

Cat fidgeted impatiently as Belle spent several minutes small talking with 'Uncle Al'. '*Ask him! Ask him!*' she chanted, still jumping on the bed.

Finally Belle explained that she was trying to get in touch with Ethan Reed. 'He's a friend . . . we're worried as we haven't heard anything from him in ages . . .'

'Yeah, communications down here in the 'glades are pretty flaky,' Al Reagan said. 'We've had some big storms lately that've taken a lot of lines out. But don't worry, you'll be seeing your boyfriend soon enough. We've got through the filming faster than we expected!'

Belle started to explain that Ethan was not her boyfriend, but Cat was too impatient. She grabbed the phone. 'How soon is soon?' she asked.

'Couple of weeks. We finish filming on Thursday. Ethan and Violet go straight to Miami for some publicity shoots. Then he'll be on a flight home. Ethan's a great guy, by the way. He really stepped up to the part!'

Belle thanked him and rang off.

Almost bursting with the wonderful news, they ran across the corridor to Holly's room to tell her.

'Ethan's coming home early! Only two more weeks!' Cat shouted.

Cat waited for Holly to run around with her T-shirt over her head, doing victory back-flips.

Instead she barely smiled. 'That's good,' she said grimly, 'I'll be able to find out the truth about him and Violet at last – and move on.'

Cat looked at Belle. It seemed they were too late.

CHAPTER TWENTY-FIVE

Holly: May We Respectfully Ask You

At break on Tuesday morning, Holly and Cat knocked on the door of the principal's office. They entered the comfortable wood-panelled room to find Mr Fortune leaning back on his chair, feet on the huge desk, reading an important-looking document. He'd been a famous actor in the 1970s and 80s, and with those twinkly blue eyes and white designer stubble, he looked like a cross between Michael Caine and Sean Connery.

'Ah, Catrin and Holly. What can I do for you two?' he asked, gesturing for them to sit down.

Holly perched on the corner of the leather chair. Shreddie was taking up most of it, curled up washing his paws. She began to explain their plan to try and stop Mr Madison taking Belle away from the Garrick.

'I appreciate your concern,' Mr Fortune said thoughtfully. 'We will all be sorry to lose Belle – she's an exceptional pupil, star quality at every level. But it is up to the parents, of course.'

'What? Even when the parent is being a totally unreasonable, short-sighted *thug?*' Cat objected.

Holly silenced her with a zip-it look.

'We wondered if he might change his mind if we got every one of her teachers to write something about how brilliantly Belle's doing in all her school subjects, and how perfect she is for The Garrick.'

'He might actually see sense!' Cat interrupted.

'Well, you have my permission to try,' Mr Fortune said with a smile. 'But I don't hold out much hope. I made a couple of movies with Dirk Madison back in the day, and he's a tough cookie!'

Leaving Mr Fortune's office, Holly couldn't help feeling optimistic. It was a long shot, but at least they were doing something positive.

'We'll have to start at lunch time,' she said as they passed Mrs Butterworth's office. 'It'll take us ages to track down all the teachers . . .'

Mrs Butterworth – in a pale-apricot trouser suit – scooted out of the open door and intercepted them. 'Ah, girls, I couldn't help overhearing you.'

Holly started to apologize. 'Sorry if we were making too much noise.'

But Mrs B cut her off. 'I heard you talking about trying to keep Belle Madison at the Garrick. Such a *lovely* girl. No airs and graces and always so thoughtful . . . and she was an absolute angel, making me cups of tea when Shreddie brought that dreadful *mouse* into my office. I'll do what I can to help.'

'Er, thank you,' Holly mumbled. Although she wasn't sure that telling Mr Madison about Belle's ability to make a cup of tea in a rodent crisis was going to convince him that The Garrick was the perfect place for his daughter.

'There's a staff meeting at lunch time,' Mrs Butterworth went on. 'To save you going round all the teachers individually, I'll arrange for you to be allowed to come and address them at the end of the meeting. Now, off to your next lessons!'

After their lunch, Holly and Cat entered the staff-room. At one end of the room, Belle's teachers had pulled up their armchairs in a circle. They were all balancing mugs of coffee and packed lunches on their knees.

Nervously, Holly explained the keep-Belle-at-the-Garrick plan.

Cat assisted with constant motivating interruptions!

Then there was a silence as the teachers looked at each other.

It was Mrs Salmon who spoke first.

'We certainly don't wish to lose Belle Madison. We need hard-working students to keep our academic standards high. It makes up for the rather *less* motivated students.' She looked pointedly at Cat, who was due for a lunch-time detention directly after this meeting, following yesterday's Human Olympic Torch incident. 'I, for one, would be happy to write in support of Belle staying here,' Mrs Salmon continued. 'I must admit I feel partially responsible for Mr Madison's reaction. I mentioned in her report that Belle's science results had slipped a *little* since last term. Of course, they are still the best in the year by far.'

'Oh golly!' Miss Chase-Smythe wailed, clutching at the pearl necklace under her frilly collar. 'I've done the same! I said that her essay on the French Revolution was a *tiddly* bit disappointing after her outstanding work on the Tudors last term.' Miss Chase-Smythe had an accent so posh she sounded as if she was practising to do the voiceover for the Queen's Speech, right now she looked about to burst into tears.

Dr Norris cleared his throat and smoothed down his combed-over hair. 'Ah, yes, I fear I may too have made a similar point. Her maths test score was down this term from ninety-five per cent to ninety-two per cent. Of course, most students *never* get above ninety per cent.'

Holly grinned at Cat. Her theory was right. All the teachers' reports had made a big deal of Belle's schoolwork being a teensy bit worse than her usual advanced genius level.

'I think we're all in agreement,' Mrs Salmon stated eventually. 'We may have been a little harsh. We will all write personal letters to clarify that Belle is an outstanding student and that her work is still of an exceptionally high standard.'

Thanking the teachers, Holly and Cat left the staffroom.

They closed the door behind them and high-fived.

Things were looking up!

That evening, Holly sat at the laptop in her room, composing a letter to Mr Madison to accompany the teachers' reports.

Dear Mr Madison, she wrote. *May we respectfully ask you to reconsider your decision . . .*

Cat leaned over her shoulder, making less-than-useful suggestions: 'And stop trying to run Belle's life for her, like she's some kind of *halfwit . . .*'

'No, I'm not going to write that!' Holly laughed, pushing Cat away. She continued typing. *The Garrick is the perfect place for Belle's unique combination of academic brilliance and singing talent . . .*

'So get over it. Stop acting like a medieval tyrant and let her stay!' Cat said, tapping on the screen.

'I think I've got this, Cat,' Holly sighed. *Please find enclosed some letters from Belle's teachers . . .* she wrote.

'You pig-headed bully!'

Holly put her fingers in her ears. 'Cat, I am *so* not listening to you. La la la!'

At last Holly finished the letter and slid it into the envelope, leaving it open to add the teachers' letters which they'd arranged to collect from Mrs Salmon in the morning.

But would it be enough to keep Belle at Superstar High?

CHAPTER TWENTY-SIX

Belle: Intensive Care for Dreams

Almost a week later, Belle was walking hand in hand with Jack across the sports fields. It was a beautiful summer evening and the rose-coloured brickwork of the school buildings was glowing softly in the evening sun. On the tennis court, Zak and Gemma were playing doubles with Nick and Lettie, who were spending a lot of quality time together these days, although still officially *just good friends*. The gentle *thwack* of ball on racket could be heard above the drone of Mr Woolfox's lawnmower on the football pitch.

It couldn't be more perfect.

It couldn't be more heart-breaking.

It was Monday. *Anything Goes* would be opening on Wednesday and playing for four nights. The end of term was only a week after that and Belle would be leaving Superstar High for ever. She'd be saying goodbye to Holly and Cat – the best friends a girl could possibly have. Goodbye to singing. Goodbye to Jack.

'We'll still talk to each other every day,' Jack said, trying to cheer her up. 'And we can see each other in the holidays.'

'I know,' Belle sighed. *But we'll be in different countries*, she thought. *You'll find someone else. Look what's happened with Ethan and Holly, and that was after only a few weeks apart.* She was going to miss him so much.

Jack squeezed her hand. They wandered along a winding path under the stately oak trees behind the main building.

'It's my singing exam tomorrow morning,' Belle murmured. 'But it's hardly worth even taking it now. I don't suppose there's much singing on the syllabus at the Girls' Elite Science Academy . . .'

They stopped walking. Jack turned and gazed into her eyes. 'Never stop singing, Belle! You can sing even if there aren't proper lessons. And Switzerland won't be for ever.'

'I guess,' she said. 'But—'

Her words were silenced by Jack leaning close and kissing her. She kissed him back, clinging tightly to his arms.

She could taste the salt of her own tears.

If only this moment could last for ever.

Next morning, Belle walked into the main studio in the Singing Department for her exam. Usually she was nervous and excited when she took her singing grades, but today she felt only a hollow sensation. It didn't matter how well she did today.

Nothing mattered any more.

Her dream had died.

The examiner welcomed her in and asked her to begin her technical work. Mr Piggott, the accompanist, smiled at her from the piano and played the first chord.

Suddenly Belle was alive again!

She sang the series of vocal exercises, concentrating on her pitch, pace and vocal control, and the examiner nodded approvingly.

By the time she started on Purcell's *An Evening Hymn*, the first of her four songs, Belle had almost forgotten about leaving Superstar High. It was such a beautiful, restful song.

She was back in her element, doing what she loved.

Maybe her dream hadn't died, after all.

It was just in intensive care.

After lunch the students gathered in the huge Gielgud

Auditorium on the edge of the school grounds for the dress rehearsal of *Anything Goes*. Or rather the *stress* rehearsal, Belle thought as she watched Owen and Tabitha and the other Year Eleven students pacing anxiously up and down, and the teachers shouting about missing props and fluffed lines.

'Starters for *Bon Voyage!*' Mr Garcia yelled.

Belle took her position with the rest of the chorus, which included Nick, Ruby, Lettie, Mayu and Frankie Pellegrini. The stage had been transformed into a huge ship with beautifully painted backdrops and platforms. The school big band began to play the exuberant tune. In spite of her worries, the excitement of performing again suddenly pulsed through her. Dressed in her stylish 1930s dress and hat, she was suddenly in character, waving goodbye to the ship from the dock, and singing *Bon Voyage!* She was determined to make the most of her last dress rehearsal at Superstar High and she loved every minute of it – even Mayu trying to crowd her out of position and the three false starts when Owen Mitchell missed his cue.

After her number, Belle sat down in the auditorium with Nick, Lettie and Ruby. They watched Holly, Jack and the rest of the Advanced Tap group strutting their stuff in their sailor outfits while Reno Sweeney, brilliantly played by a Year Eleven girl called Ella Cross, sang the title number, *Anything Goes*.

Suddenly Nick produced an ear-splitting wolf-whistle. '*Arriba! Arriba!*' he cooed in a cartoon Spanish accent.

Belle looked up and saw Cat marching towards them. She'd changed into her costume ready for her tango number. In a low-cut black ruffled top and swirly black skirt, her hair swept up in a dramatic up-do, one red curl slicked to her cheek, she looked stunning – and every inch the tempestuous Argentinean Tango Diva! She threw herself down next to Belle with a proud, angry expression on her face.

'What's up?' Belle asked.

'Nothing,' Cat mumbled. She clamped her jaw so tight, it made Belle's teeth hurt just to look at her.

'Nothing?' Belle asked. 'So you don't want to talk about it then?'

'No, I don't!' Cat said, folding her arms and staring fixedly at the stage.

'OK, fine,' Belle waited patiently. She knew Cat couldn't do Suffering in Silence.

'Yeah, well,' Cat blurted a few seconds later. 'I tried telling Miss LeClair and Miguel Silva *again* that I couldn't dance with Adam Fielding in *All Through the*

Night because of artistic differences – i.e. he's a total pig and I can't bear to even look at him any more – and they said I couldn't let my personal problems interfere with the performance. I could either dance with Adam or not dance at all . . .'

At last Cat paused for breath.

'Well, I'm sorry, but I agree with them,' Belle said. 'You have to be professional and go on with the show.' Then she smiled, remembering her feelings when she found out she was going to have to sing a duet with Bianca in the Rising Stars Spectacular last term. 'If Bianca and I could do it, I'm sure you and Adam can.'

'Hmmph!' Cat fumed. Belle was worried she'd pushed her friend too far and that there was about to be a Cat Wickham volcanic-eruption special. But suddenly Cat shrugged her shoulders and sighed. 'Yeah, I guess you're right. It's just that every time I see him I can't get those horrible words he said out of my head . . . and I really thought he liked me.'

'There you are, Cat!' Holly said, running up to join them, having changed out of her sailor costume. 'Gemma's looking for you. *All Through the Night* is starting in a minute.'

'Don't suppose *Adam* was looking for me though,'

Cat mumbled, not showing any sign of leaving.

Belle gave her a stern look. 'Go on. You can do it.'

'Yeah, yeah, I'm going!' Cat said, trudging reluctantly off towards the wings.

Belle, Holly and Nick watched as Owen and Tabitha began their duet. The three tango couples appeared in the background, building up the romantic atmosphere of the soulful ballad. The stage lighting was designed so that the dancers were in silhouette for much of the time, highlighting the elegance of their movements, but every now and then one of the couples would be caught by a spotlight, throwing their faces into relief. Everyone in the auditorium was spellbound. All the dancers were fabulous, but Cat and Adam had a special extra *something*. They had passion and grace and *buckets of attitude*.

When the light played across them, Adam's face was contorted with raw emotion while Cat was stormy, proud and passionate.

It was impossible to tell whether they were bound together by pure love or pure hate!

But whichever it was, it was impossible to take your eyes off them.

Belle leaned back in her seat, remembering the times she'd performed in this theatre before; the gala showcase in first term when Nobody's Angels had sung *Done Lookin'* and *Opposites Attract*. She and Holly and Cat had been so new then, and so excited about everything! Then there was the Rising Stars Spectacular last term when she sang *What Is This Feeling?* with Bianca. Belle smiled, remembering the enormous battle they'd had right here, almost in these very seats . . .

And now here she was again.

Her last ever show at Superstar High.

At least she would go out singing.

CHAPTER TWENTY-SEVEN

Cat: Little White Lies

The whole school had been a-tingle with first-night nerves all day. But now the opening performance of *Anything Goes* was underway.

So far, everything was going spectacularly well.

The Gielgud Auditorium was packed and the audience were loving every minute of the show.

Now Cat was waiting in the wings with the rest of the tango dancers. The band was striking up with the opening strains of *All Through the Night*.

Zak and Gemma were holding hands, their faces glowing with excitement. Sophia and Philippe were whispering together.

Cat glanced at Adam. The straight black trousers and white shirt suited his tall, slim build. He looked romantic and heroic, but his forehead was furrowed and he was chewing his lip. He was obviously nervous.

For a moment Cat longed to reach out and put her arm round him, but she stopped herself. Miguel Silva had forced her into dancing with Adam Slime-Mould Fielding, but no one could make her *like* it! She wasn't talking to him, and that *included* non-verbal communication.

Onstage, Owen was beginning to sing. Cat counted the beats, her stomach suddenly quivering like a jelly. This was the first time she'd felt nervous. She'd been too busy being angry and upset to feel anything else until now.

Then suddenly she was on stage in Adam's arms, swept up in rhythm of the dance. He was pulling her close, pushing her away. Cat threw her head back as she followed his lead. But each time she moved away she hung on to the very last shadow of the beat before snapping back into Adam's arms like a bungee cord.

'Stop *fighting* me all the time!' Adam whispered in her ear as he dipped her to the floor.

Cat treated him to her most scornful glare. *I am so not talking to you*, she thought.

'How long are you going to keep up the silent treatment?' Adam hissed in her ear a few moments later.

Until you stop being such a rude, insensitive pig, Cat thought, clenching her teeth to stop a single word escaping as she stamped out of the close embrace into a *barrida* – sweeping Adam's foot out with her own so fiercely he almost fell over.

The last few dramatic steps and then they held the pose as the music died away, caught in the spotlight like moths in amber.

Cat's heart was beating double time. In spite of Adam, the dance had been electrifying.

'And I can't *believe* you asked Miguel to swap partners!' Adam whispered as they ran offstage to the sound of wild, uproarious applause.

'I thought you might like to dance with someone whose bum wasn't quite as big as mine!' Cat snapped as they bundled into the corridor behind the stage. *Argggh! I spoke to him.* She slapped her forehead in frustration, while all around her the other dancers were hugging and high-fiving.

Adam shot her a hurt look. 'Well, if *that's* how you feel . . .' he started.

'A triumph!' Miguel Silva enthused, hurrying over to congratulate them. 'Catrin! Adam!' he added. 'You two were sensational! Loving that *tension* between you.'

Back in the dressing room Cat ripped the combs and grips out of her hair and yanked off her false eyelashes.

'Ouch!'

She was furious. Furious with herself for breaking

her silence, furious with Mr Madison for not having replied to the begging letter to let Belle stay, furious with Gemma for that dreamy look she had whenever she saw Zak, furious with Sophia for asking her if she was OK, furious with her hairbrush for snagging in her hair . . .

Most of all she was furious with Adam for . . . for what? She couldn't quite remember now why she was so furious with him.

She just was!

Cat was still fuming when she joined Holly, Belle and Jack and made her way through to the foyer of the Gielgud Auditorium to meet up with the guests who'd come to the first-night performance. Belle's parents were both overseas and Jack's were away on a business trip to Singapore, but Holly's mum and stepdad were there, and so were Cat's parents with her eight-year-old sister, Fiona. The two families had met before and were chatting together as they waited. They greeted the girls warmly and congratulated them all on their parts in the show.

Suddenly Cat noticed Miguel Silva coming across the crowded room.

'Quick, hide me!' she gasped to Belle and Holly.

'What?' they asked, looking round for the cause of the panic.

'Miguel Silva can't know these are my *parents*!' Cat whispered.

'I know they're *weird*, but they're not *that* bad, are they?' Fiona had been eavesdropping. As always.

'It's *complicated*, OK!' Cat hissed as she ducked down behind Fiona's wheelchair. Miguel Silva was now only inches away!

She hadn't exactly told Miguel a lie about being a penniless street urchin. But she hadn't exactly *untold* it either. She could easily have explained that the ancient leotard was a simple laundry disaster, but instead she'd kept up the little-orphan-girl act all term. He wasn't going to be impressed if he suddenly found out she had a perfectly serviceable set of parents. Not that Mum and Dad were millionaires or anything – Dad was a history professor and Mum'd spent most of her time at home looking after Fiona since the accident – but, dolled up in their best clothes for the show, they didn't exactly look *destitute* either!

And they definitely didn't look *deceased*.

'What *are* you doing down there, Catrin?' Mum asked.

Oh, no! Cat could see Miguel Silva's shiny black shoes on the other side of the wheelchair. 'Look, Mum!

There's Mr Fortune!' Cat whispered in desperation.

'Where? Where?' Immediately Mum was beetling off in search of James Fortune, her all-time heart-throb. 'Come on, Brian,' she said, dragging Dad behind her. 'We must go and say hello!'

'Phew,' Cat breathed, standing up. She smiled at Miguel Silva. 'I was just, er, checking my sister's wheels!'

'And you look after your disabled sister too!' Miguel said, shaking his head in awe. Cat was sure there were tears in his eyes. 'You are one in a million!'

'Er, thanks,' Cat mumbled, deeply embarrassed.

To her relief, Fiona provided a distraction. 'Hey, isn't that Adam over there?' she asked.

Adam was the last person Cat wanted to speak to right now, but before the big-bum episode she'd told Fiona all about how lovely he was in her letters and E-mails. She'd even sent some photographs of them together, which is how Fiona must have recognized him.

'Oh, I'm sure he's busy! He probably has family here too,' Cat muttered.

'No he's *not*!' Fiona insisted. 'He's on his own. I've been dying to meet him!'

Cat stalled. Somehow she hadn't got round to mention that she'd broken up with Adam and she hated to shatter Fiona's image of her big sister's True Romance with the Boy of Her Dreams.

Anyway, it was too late now . . .

'Adam! Over here!' Fiona was yelling.

Adam looked up and approached hesitantly.

'Hi! I'm Cat's sister!' Fiona said enthusiastically. 'I know *everything* about you. She *really, really* likes you!'

'Oh, er, that's cool!' Adam mumbled, looking massively confused. *Really really liking him* wasn't *exactly* the message Cat had been giving him the last few weeks! But he shrugged and grinned at Fiona. 'Good to meet you too,' he said shaking her hand. Fiona beamed with delight as if she'd been introduced to royalty. Cat was sideswiped by a sudden twist of pure love for her little sister – with her long ginger plaits and her freckled, trusting face – so fierce it almost took her breath away.

'Soooo, yeah, Adam,' Cat muttered, 'I expect you've got loads of things to get on with . . .'

'Not really,' Adam replied happily.

'Awww! He just wants to be with you, Cat!' Fiona said.

'Let's go and see if we can find some drinks!' Holly said, stepping in gallantly. Belle was talking to Jack and hadn't noticed that the situation was spiralling into Extreme Awkwardness.

'Cat told me you're a dead good kisser too!' Fiona giggled.

Cat felt herself blushing. This was embarrassing on so many levels.

'Fiona!' she warned.

Luckily her parents were returning. Cat had never been so relieved to see them in her life!

'Who fancies Café Roma for late-night hot chocolates?' Mum asked.

'What a great idea, Terri!' Holly's stepdad, Steve, joined them too. 'I was just about to suggest the same thing!'

'And Belle and Jack as well, of course,' Holly's mum said, putting her arm round Belle and pulling her into the family group.

'And Adam!' Fiona piped up.

Everyone looked at Adam and then at Cat. They were all smiling in a warm-and-welcoming, one-big-happy-family kind of way.

Cat's heart sank. She couldn't bear playing nicey-nice with Adam any longer.

'What a shame, Adam can't come,' she said. 'He, er, has to go and' – she scanned around desperately for an excuse. Looking down, her eyes lit on Adam's feet; those stupid great big feet that started off their whole row in the first place – 'er, see the nurse. About his foot.'

'His *foot*?' Mum asked.

'Yeah! The, er, left one.' Cat crossed her fingers firmly behind her back. 'I stepped on his foot when we were dancing.'

'No, you didn't . . .' Adam said. 'I'm fine!'

Cat shook her head and laughed. 'Adam, it's OK, you don't have to cover up for me. I *stamped* on your foot like a big clumsy elephant! I wouldn't be surprised if your toe's broken.'

If Adam had been looking confused before, he was now baffled beyond belief. 'Really. There's nothing wrong with my—' he started.

Steeling herself, Cat cut off his words with a quick kiss on the lips. Then in one swift move, she spun round, grasped the handles of Fiona's wheelchair and started to push purposefully towards the door, barging her way through the throng of people.

'Come on!' she called to the rest of the group. 'We won't get a table if we don't hurry!'

'Why didn't you want Adam to come with us?' Fiona asked.

'I did,' Cat protested. 'I just wanted him to get his foot sorted first.'

'Yeah, right! So how come he wasn't he limping? And how come you've got your fingers crossed?' she asked.

Not for the first time, Cat realized her little sister was far too smart for her own good.

'What is this, a police interrogation?' she joked. 'I have the right to remain silent!'

She wasn't going to admit *anything*.

Especially not how good that kiss felt!

CHAPTER TWENTY-EIGHT

Belle: A GCSE in Pure Bliss

As they left the Gielgud Auditorium, heading back across the sports field towards the main school buildings, everyone was laughing and talking about the great success of *Anything Goes*.

But Belle's heart wasn't in it.

That was her last opening night at Superstar High.

She dawdled, dropping back behind the group, wishing she could somehow slow down time itself. But it was all fast-forwarding out of control.

Only nine days left.

As they walked through the archway to the central courtyard, Holly and Cat hung back to wait for her. Without saying a word, they both put their arms around her in a big we-know-how-you-feel hug. There was nothing they could do, but she felt a little better knowing that her friends were there for her. She tried to smile. Jack took her hand as they crossed the cobbled courtyard, now prettily lit with twinkling lamps.

Going into the entrance hall, it was all so familiar. The elegant high ceiling, the wood-panelled walls, the gleaming floorboards, the sweeping staircase up to their rooms, the comfortable leather sofas and armchairs, Mrs Butterworth sitting at her desk, the smell of lavender polish . . .

Belle was going to miss it all so much.

Bianca and Mayu were lounging on one of the sofas, poring over *Hello!* magazine, debating loudly which swanky star-studded red-carpet events they would be attending over the summer.

I can hardly believe it, Belle thought, *but I'm even going to miss those two!*

'Ooh, look,' Mayu lisped, noticing Belle and the rest of the group. 'A little family outing. How sweet!'

'Of course, I'll be flying out to the States for the premiere of *Sinking Feelings*,' Bianca continued, pretending she hadn't noticed that Holly was in earshot. 'Then I'm going to stay with Violet at her parents' beach house in Malibu. *Ethan* will probably join us, of course . . .'

On second thoughts, maybe I won't miss them that *much*, Belle thought.

Then Belle heard a voice she thought she recognized. A silver-haired, broad-shouldered man in a perfectly tailored charcoal-grey Armani suit was leaning against the pigeon holes, talking to Mrs B over the desk. Belle's heart pole-vaulted into her mouth. For a moment that man looked just like . . .

'Dad?'

The man turned round.

'Dad!'

'Belle!' He smiled and pushed his sunglasses onto his forehead. 'Darling!' He opened his arms wide for a fatherly hug.

But Belle was glued to the spot by raw panic.

Dad's come to take me away from school already! The room was swaying like a ship on a stormy sea. The light was fragmenting into tiny sparkles. She clutched Jack's arm.

'But I *can't* go yet,' she gulped. 'I still have four more shows to do. And term's not over till next Friday. *Please* let me have these last few days!'

By now Holly and Cat were at her side. Holly's stricken face looked as if it was about to crumple in tears. Cat's pale complexion was flushing an angry shade of red.

Dad smiled and put his hand up in hold-on-a-minute gesture.

'I haven't come to take you away, Belle,' he said.

'I flew in from Morocco to see the show. I was sitting on the back row. You were all excellent, by the way.'

Everyone was staring. Dirk Madison seemed to be enjoying the moment. 'A few days ago I received a letter from your friends here . . .' he said, pausing dramatically and smiling in turn at Cat and Holly.

What's he talking about? Belle looked at her friends, searching their faces for clues, but both of them were staring uncomfortably at their feet as if they'd been caught scrawling graffiti in the girls' toilets.

'We were only trying to . . .' Cat stammered.

'We didn't mean to . . .' Holly mumbled.

'. . . telling me how well you are doing,' Dad continued, ignoring Cat and Holly's interruptions. 'They sent me personal letters from all your teachers assuring me that you *are* reaching your full intellectual potential.'

Belle knew he was speaking English but she could hardly understand a word. *Personal letters? From teachers?*

'So . . . and these are not words you will often hear me say' – Dad's monologue was still in full flow – 'I am prepared to reconsider my original decision. It seems that the Garrick School of the Performing Arts is where you belong!'

Belle looked at Holly, Cat and Jack. *Did Dad just say what she thought he said?* They were all grinning and nodding. *That I can stay at Superstar High?*

In a move worthy of a world-champion gymnast, Belle sprinted across the floor and leaped into her father's arms. She hugged him and kissed his expensively cologned cheek over and over. 'Thank you, thank you, thank you!'

And then she was caught up in a whirlwind of embraces from her friends.

Even Mrs Butterworth wheeled out from behind her desk, resplendent in a lemon-sorbet-coloured trouser suit. She scooted to a halt, stood up and hugged Belle.

'I'm so pleased you are staying, dear!'

'I don't know which is more amazing,' Cat laughed. 'That your dad's letting you stay at Superstar High or that Mrs B actually *got out of her chair* to hug you!'

Belle shook her head. It was *all* amazing!

'Do join us for hot chocolates, Dirk,' Cat's mum said brightly, stepping forward from near the front door, where she and the rest of Cat and Holly's family group had witnessed the entire scene. Mrs Wickham took Dad by the elbow – she was so tiny she couldn't reach any higher. 'We can have a *lovely* chat about the crazy old world of showbiz. Have I told you that I was an actress myself in my younger days?'

'Love to,' Belle's dad said graciously. 'OK, people, where are we going? The Ivy? Quaglino's? The Ritz?' He pulled out his phone. 'I'll call my limo driver, make some reservations.'

There was a flurry of excited chatter. 'Oooh! The Ritz!' Holly gasped.

'The Ivy!' Cat's mum's eyes were shining with anticipation. 'We might run into the Beckhams—'

'Or Kate Moss!' Fiona interrupted.

'Who's Kate Moss, love?' Cat's dad asked, looking up from inspecting the fine Georgian carvings around the door frame. 'Is she a friend of yours?'

Cat laughed. 'Come on, Dad! Keep up!'

Holly's mum was checking her watch. 'I'll ring the baby-sitter and say we'll be late back.'

'I've always wanted to go to Quaglino's!' Jack said, squeezing Belle's hand.

Suddenly Belle was engulfed by a wave of exhaustion. She longed for the cosy comfort of Café Roma. 'Er, Dad,' she said quietly, tugging at his sleeve. 'There's this great place we go to, just down the road . . .'

'Sure,' Dad said. 'It's your night, sweetie.'

'Café Roma would be great,' Cat whispered.

'Why are we whispering?' Holly whispered.

Cat grinned. 'I just caught sight of Bianca and Mayu's faces when they heard us talking about The Ivy. *Their eyes were popping out with jealousy!* They think we're being chauffeur-driven to the hottest celebrity hang-out in London, *with* Dirk Madison, internationally famous film director. *Please* let's work this moment!'

Belle grinned. She glanced back at Bianca and Mayu to make sure they were listening. 'OK, WHERE'S THAT LIMO? WE'RE OFF TO THE IVY!' she pronounced at top volume as she pushed open the front door.

'*Not!*' she added under her breath.

Belle linked arms with Jack and Holly, while Cat took charge of Fiona's wheelchair. They skipped along Kingsgrove Road – towards the buzz of voices and the delicious aroma of coffee, chocolate and pizza emanating from Café Roma's open door.

Belle looked back to see Mrs Wickham telling Dad about her *Star Wars* days. Cat giggled. 'That's Mum's big claim to fame. But your dad's not even listening!'

Which was true. Dad was far more interested in talking to Holly's mum.

'So, Jackie, as a *teacher*, what GCSE options do you think Belle should take to get a place to study medicine at Oxford or Cambridge?' he asked seriously.

Holly laughed. 'Mum teaches seven-year-olds. She's not usually called upon for advice on university applications!'

Meanwhile Belle could hear Holly's stepdad and Cat's dad deep in conversation about different types of gas boiler.

'Is Café Roma the place you always go?' Fiona asked.

'Always,' Jack said, sharing a special smile with Belle.

'I'm so glad we're going there instead of one of those posh restaurants then,' Fiona said.

'Me too!' Belle laughed.

The moon was shining brightly above the orange street-lamp glow of the summer night.

'*Walking on Moonshine*,' Belle hummed to herself.

If there was a GCSE in Pure Bliss, I'd get a double A-star right now!

CHAPTER TWENTY-NINE

Cat: Gladiators and Mixed Doubles

The following evening Cat took her position on stage
for the tango.

Let battle commence!

Relations with Adam had sunk to an all-time low
since she'd brushed him off with the injured-foot fib.
Now *he* wasn't speaking to her either.

They glared at each other as they locked in a lethal
embrace.

We're more like gladiators than dance partners, Cat
thought, *and I'm not talking about the TV programme. I
mean the Ancient-Roman-blood-and-guts-fighting-to-the-death
type.*

Miguel Silva clapped his hands in delight as they
came offstage. 'Fabulous! What fire! What spirit!'

'But you might want to rein it in just a fraction,'
Miss LeClair said quietly when Miguel wasn't
listening. 'You're in danger of upstaging Owen and
Tabitha's duet!'

Cat swished her skirt and marched off to the dressing room, the *click-clack* of her high-heeled dance shoes resounding all along the corridor. *Rein it in?* she fumed. *What I am, a carthorse?*

She scowled at herself as she scraped off her thick stage make-up and brushed out the reinforced-concrete-strength hairspray. She'd worked out a new way to part her hair so the patch where Belle Scissorhands Madison had snipped out the burned section was hardly noticeable.

Which reminded her. Belle's not leaving! For the millionth time, she replayed the fabulous moment that Mr Madison said Belle could stay. Just thinking about it made her happy again.

Things weren't *all* bad!

The next day was Saturday, the last day of *Anything Goes*, which meant two shows: an afternoon matinee and the grand finale in the evening. Cat was leaving the dining room with Holly, Belle, Gemma and Lettie after a late breakfast. Belle and Holly were planning to go to the library to pack in a few hours' homework before getting ready for the matinee.

'I'm off to play tennis with Zak,' Gemma said. 'Do you and Nick want to play mixed doubles, Lettie?'

Cat was starting to feel a little sorry for herself. She wished she had someone to play tennis with. Not that she even *liked* tennis, but that wasn't the point. She'd blown her chance of playing mixed doubles with Adam ever again. *Maybe I'll go and see if Nathan wants a game of table tennis*, she thought glumly. *It's the closest I'm going to get.*

As they crossed the entrance hall, Mrs Butterworth looked up from her desk.

'Ah, just the girl I was looking for! Some flowers have arrived for you, dear.'

For one magical moment Cat thought Mrs Butterworth was talking to *her*; that the enormous confection of exotic flowers on the desk – waxy white petals bursting open to show deep pink and crimson speckled centres – was from Adam.

'For Lettie Atkins!' Mrs Butterworth announced.

What was I thinking? Cat reprimanded herself. *I don't want his smelly flowers anyway!*

And they did smell! The entire hall was filling up with the heady perfume. It was like a tropical garden at nightfall.

'Stargazer lilies – my favourites!' Lettie gasped.

'Ooh look, they're Sasha Mulholland ones again,' Gemma commented, checking the label.

Cat glanced at Holly and Belle. 'I didn't know we were planning another Callum express delivery?' she whispered.

'We weren't,' Belle hissed. 'This is nothing to do with me!'

'Nor me,' Holly mouthed. 'Open the card, Lettie,' she urged. 'They must be from Callum? You're going to that cello concert tomorrow night, aren't you?'

'Yeah, but I'm sure Callum isn't sending me flowers . . .' Lettie muttered as she fished around in her bag for her reading glasses. 'They're probably just from my mum, to wish me luck for the last night of *Anything Goes*.' She put on her glasses and studied the card. From the way she blushed – exactly the same shade as the lilies' cherry-red throats – Cat guessed the note was not from her mum.

Or anyone's mum for that matter!

'What does it say?' Gemma asked, craning her neck to look over Lettie's shoulder.

'*I see you everywhere I go*,' Lettie read hesitantly. '*Maybe you don't even know. But one day we'll find each other. I will keep the dream alive.*'

'But those words are from our song!' Cat said. 'That's so weird. Does Callum know about *Keep the Dream Alive?*'

'Not unless he's psychic,' Lettie laughed. 'I've never told him about it.' Then she frowned. 'You don't think this is some kind of a joke, do you?'

'No, it's not a joke.' The voice came from behind them.

The five girls and Mrs Butterworth, who had obviously been following the proceedings with great interest, all turned round in perfect time.

It was Nick Taggart.

'How do you know?' Cat asked. 'Unless *you* sent them, of course?' She waited for Nick to deny it but instead there was a Very Awkward Silence.

Suddenly Cat had a Cluedo Moment. *It was Nick Taggart, in the entrance hall, with the stargazer lilies!*

Not that she needed finely honed powers of detection to work it out. Nick's face was traffic-light red. He shuffled. He cleared his throat. He thrust his hands in the pockets of his jeans. Then he took them out again. Cat had never seen him so far out of his comedy comfort zone.

'*You* sent them, Nick?' Lettie whispered.

Nick nodded. Slowly he pulled an envelope out of his back pocket and held it out.

Lettie took it uncertainly, gazing up at Nick with her serious brown eyes. He nodded encouragingly.

Lettie pulled two tickets out of the envelope. 'They're for the Dvořák concert tomorrow!' she said. 'But I'm meant to go with . . .'

'Callum. I know,' Nick replied. He said the name *Callum* with a slight wince in his voice, the way people usually say *mouth ulcer* or *cold sore*. 'But I don't want you to go to your favourite concerto with some random Callum-guy. I want you to go with *me*!'

Cat realized that she and the rest of the onlookers had all fallen silent, and were hanging on Nick and Lettie's every word – as if they were watching an episode of *EastEnders*. With bated breath, they all waited for Lettie's response . . .

'I'd much rather go to the concert with you too,' she said, smiling shyly.

Nick grinned. Then he cleared his throat again. 'But what about Callum? Won't he be mad if you stand him up?'

Lettie shook her head. 'Callum really is just a friend. I'll call him and explain. I've no idea why he sent me those red roses in the first place.'

'Er, well, *we* might have had something to do with that . . .' Holly stammered.

'We're really sorry, we were only trying to . . .' Belle started to explain.

'. . . make me think Lettie had this really cool boyfriend so I'd get dead jealous?' Nick interrupted. His face was unsmiling and his voice was gruff.

Cat felt terrible! They'd never meant to hurt Nick's feelings. 'No! Well, not *exactly*. Er, sort of, kind of, OK . . . *yes* . . .' she mumbled, gearing herself up for a full grovel-on-the-floor-and-beg-for-forgiveness apology.

Suddenly Nick cracked a huge grin. 'Well, it worked!'

Cat laughed with relief.

Then Nick gazed at Lettie. As if hypnotized, Lettie took off her glasses and looked into his eyes. Slowly they leaned towards each other.

And kissed.

Cat, Holly, Belle, Gemma and Mrs Butterworth all clapped and cheered. So did several other people who happened to be passing. Including Zak Lomax, who'd come to find Gemma. He punched the air and played an air-guitar riff on his tennis racket. 'Way to go, dude! Catching that wave!' he yelled.

Nick made a shooing gesture at Zak over Lettie's shoulder.

Then he and Lettie turned and walked away, hand in hand.

At last, Operation Monster was complete!

CHAPTER THIRTY

Holly: A Rush of Blood to the Head

Holly's world was upside down.

She was in the corridor outside the dressing rooms in the Gielgud Auditorium shortly before the start of the matinee performance of *Anything Goes*. Using the wall for balance, she bent over from the waist, hands on the floor, stretching out her hamstrings and her back — which felt as stiff as a broom handle after sitting in the library all morning working on her English homework with Belle. Or *trying* to. Every few minutes Belle, who was *usually* the one telling everyone else to concentrate on their work, would look up from her book and say, 'I can't believe it! I don't have to leave!' And now she was even more excited than ever, because she'd received a message from Larry Shapiro, the vocal coach who'd worked with the advanced-singing students at the Garrick for the two previous terms, inviting her to attend the international opera summer school he was running in New York.

Holly sighed as she stretched. She had an exciting summer holiday lined up too; she'd got a place on Tory King's musical theatre summer workshop, which was staging a production of *West Side Story* in the West End in August. But try as she might, she couldn't shake off the shadow that Ethan's sudden exit from her life was casting over everything. Before he went to Florida they'd talked about her going to visit him in Yorkshire for a few days before the workshop started; she'd been so looking forward to meeting his family and long walks together on the moors. Like that was ever going to happen now! He'd probably be hanging out at Violet's beach home in Malibu instead.

She was about to straighten up when she noticed movement at the end of the corridor. She did a double-take. Was she imagining things or was a huge bunch of white roses coming towards her. Accompanied by a boy . . . who looked very like Ethan!

Maybe it was an optical illusion – something to do with being upside down.

She stood up and turned to face the apparition.

It still looked a lot like Ethan!

Was she seeing a ghost – like in their *Keep the Dream Alive* video? But this boy wasn't wearing Tudor costume. He was in jeans and T-shirt and he looked just like

Ethan. In fact, exactly like Ethan did when he brought her white roses after the gala showcase back in first term, when they first got together. Feeling dizzy, Holly put her hand on the wall to steady herself. Her thoughts were chasing each other round her brain. *This can't be right! Ethan's in Miami doing publicity shots with Violet. I'm seeing things. Must be a rush of blood to the head from standing up too quickly . . .*

'Holly!' he said.

It was Ethan's voice.

It was Ethan!

Holly felt as if a hand had reached into her ribcage and squeezed her heart to bursting point. She'd forgotten how *gorgeous* he was! His dark hair was a little longer, the sculpted jaw that even Robert Pattinson would be proud of, his sea-green eyes − even more striking now his skin was tanned.

Ethan dropped the flowers, ran towards her and scooped her up in his arms. 'Oh, I've missed you so much!' he murmured. 'It's so great to see you.'

Holly pulled away, reeling in confusion. 'But I thought you were . . . you didn't . . .'

'I know. I'm sorry. It's been a nightmare trying to keep in touch. The internet connections were always down, and then there were these storms, and my mobile phone stopped working . . . Remember that day you phoned and I was on set? We were on a boat at the time. I was so flustered I dropped the phone in the water. We managed to fish it out but it was never the same again. I know it sounds like I'm making excuses, but . . .'

Holly stared into his green eyes. She knew he was telling the truth. 'So we're not over?' she asked.

Before Ethan could reply, someone pushed past him, carrying a box of wigs. It was Bianca. Because she'd been away for most of the rehearsals she didn't have a part in *Anything Goes*, so Mr Garcia had put her to work helping in the wardrobe department – much to Bianca's annoyance! Her face was scrunched up in irritation like a pampered Persian cat who has just been offered a tin of no-brand cat food instead of fresh line-caught tuna.

But when she caught sight of Ethan, Bianca smiled and air-kissed him extravagantly. 'Oh, *Ethan*, welcome back, honey! We weren't expecting you yet,' she gushed, slipping into an American film-star accent.

'Yeah, the publicity tour was cut short,' Ethan said. 'Violet had had enough! Which was fine by me! I couldn't wait to get home either,' he added, smiling at Holly. 'I've come straight from the airport.'

Bianca glanced at Holly and her eyes flickered as she saw a perfect chance to get out her wooden spoon and start stirring. *Or, knowing Bianca-level stirring,* Holly thought, *one of those cement-mixer machines, so huge it needs its own lorry to carry it.*

'So, Ethan, darling, how's our *friend* Violet getting on in Miami?' she asked.

Ethan shrugged vaguely. 'Happy now she's with Josh again, I guess. That's why she axed the publicity in Miami. So she could get back to spending some quality time with Old Peg Leg!'

'Old Peg Leg?' Holly asked.

'Yeah, Josh Kelso, the original lead actor. He got the nickname Old Peg Leg after the alligator bite.' Ethan paused and laughed. 'Don't look so worried, Hols, he didn't *really* lose the whole leg. Only a tiny little chunk of it. But he and Violet were all loved up and she was not a happy bunny when he had to pull out of the film . . .'

'Josh Kelso is *Violet's boyfriend*?' Holly asked slowly.

'Yeah. They've been an item for months,' Ethan said. 'I don't know how they managed to keep it out of the gossip columns. I'm surprised Bianca hasn't already told you all about it . . .'

Holly looked at Bianca. Bianca narrowed her cold

blue eyes and tried to stare her out. But she couldn't. She looked down and pretended to be busy smoothing the hair on one of the wigs.

'No,' Holly said, still looking pointedly at Bianca. 'She must have *forgotten* to mention it!'

Ethan shrugged in surprise. 'When I first took over Josh's part, Violet hated the idea of working with a different guy. She almost walked out, and then the whole film would've gone down the pan. I had to work really hard to earn her trust. In the end, we got to be quite good friends, really.'

Holly could feel happiness frothing up inside her like bubble bath under the taps. But first she had to be absolutely, totally sure she'd got this right. 'So, *you're* not going out with Violet?'

Ethan laughed and shook his head. 'No way! Whatever gave you that idea?'

Holly looked at Bianca. 'Oh, nothing important!'

'*BIANCA HAYFORD!*' Mr Garcia's thunderous voice echoed down the corridor. 'Serena needs those wigs in dressing room three NOW!'

Bianca jumped and dropped the box. Assorted hairpieces spilled out. Ethan and Holly stooped to help pick them up. Bianca snatched them and bundled them into the box. 'I shouldn't have to be doing this,' she muttered. 'I'm suffering from nervous exhaustion. *And* I've got suspected malaria.'

Ethan grinned and shook his head slowly as they watched Bianca flounce away down the corridor. 'There hasn't been a case of malaria in the Everglades since nineteen forty-eight!' He turned to Holly. 'Now, where were we?'

'About here,' Holly whispered, reaching up and putting her arms around him.

'Oh yes, I remember!' Ethan pulled her close and kissed her.

That melting-chocolate feeling was unmistakable. Now she *really* knew Ethan was back!

But all too soon Holly became aware of people bustling back and forth in the corridor. She pulled away. 'I've got to go. The show is starting in a minute and I'm not even changed!'

Ethan grinned. 'I think I can wait another couple of hours.'

'Another hundred and twenty minutes, you mean!' Holly laughed. 'Not that I'm counting.'

Ethan laughed. 'I'll wait for you here after the show.'

Holly nodded, kissed him again, picked up her roses and walked, in a dreamy bluebirds-singing-and-bells-ringing daze through the nearest door.

Which would've been fine, if it hadn't been one of the boys' dressing rooms.

'Can we get some privacy here, dude!' Zak laughed, throwing a T-shirt at her.

Holly giggled and backed out.

Her dreams were alive again!

CHAPTER THIRTY-ONE

Belle: The Language of Love

Belle was in the dressing room in her silky blue 1930s dress for the *Bon Voyage* chorus.

Most of the other girls from their dressing room had gone to the green room to wait for their onstage calls already. Holly was out in the corridor doing some stretches. *She must be as flexible as a bungee cord by now*, Belle thought. *She's been gone for ages.* She was about to go investigate when the door swung open and Holly appeared.

One look told Belle that *something* had happened.

Maybe it was the glazed look in her eyes. Or the fact that she was clutching a bouquet of white roses.

It was either something very, very good or something very, very bad.

Holly spun round in a series of pirouettes, holding the roses aloft like a trophy.

Something good! Belle thought, with a sigh of relief. And she was starting to suspect it was more than just a stretch; getting the knots out of your hamstrings could be kind of satisfying, but *this* good? She didn't think so!

Only one thing – or rather, one person – could have put the twirl back in Holly's step quite so dramatically.

'Ethan's home?' Belle asked.

Holly grinned and hugged her.

'And I'm taking a wild guess here – but are things OK with you two by any chance?'

Belle listened in amazement as Holly recounted the scene in the corridor. As she spoke, Holly grabbed garments off the costume rail at random. She pulled her white skirt on back to front. Belle twisted it round. She buttoned her sailor jacket up the wrong way. Belle unbuttoned it and started again. She tried putting her tap shoes on the wrong feet. Belle changed them round. It was like trying to dress a three-year-old on Christmas morning.

'Don't even think about it,' Belle said as Holly picked up her lipstick. 'I'll do it for you.'

She took the lipstick but Holly couldn't stop talking long enough for her to apply it. 'I should've known! All the time Ethan was just being *nice* to Violet because she was missing her boyfriend. I should *never* have listened to Bianca.'

'Yeah, we should all have learned that little life-lesson

by now,' Belle laughed. It was awesome to have the old happy Holly back again.

Belle tried again with the lipstick, but Holly suddenly did another twirl so she ended up with a red stripe across her cheek. 'I've been thinking,' she said. 'Our problems are all sorted. You're staying at Superstar High. I've got Ethan back. That only leaves . . .'

'Cat and Adam,' Belle groaned.

'We've got to help them get back together. And as soon as possible, so that Cat can enjoy the last few days of term.'

'But if Adam *really* said she was fat,' Belle pointed out, reaching for a tissue to wipe off the smeared lipstick, 'he doesn't deserve her.'

'But I'm *sure* he didn't really use the F-word,' Holly said. 'He obviously adores her. Why would he suddenly look up from his pizza one day and say, *Oh, by the way, I've just noticed, you're a bit fat, aren't you?*'

Belle laughed. Thinking about it like that, she was sure Adam hadn't used the F-word either. And Cat *did* sometimes jump in at the deep end.

'It's not going to be easy,' Belle said. 'Even for an advanced matchmaking duo like us. We might need a magic wand as well as our Cupid's arrows!'

'We've got to try at least,' Holly said. 'Like you

and Cat tried to help me with getting in touch with Ethan.'

'And you and Cat helped me by getting my dad to change his mind.'

'That's what friends are for,' Holly cried, jumping up with a flourish. 'One for all and all for one!'

Belle grinned. She gave up on the lipstick. 'We've got to get to the green room. We'll talk to Adam straight after the show.'

But as they walked along the corridor, Holly stopped outside one of the boys' dressing rooms. 'This is the room the tango boys are sharing, isn't it? Their dance is quite near the end of the show. We could talk to Adam now!'

Belle nodded reluctantly. She hated being late for anything. 'OK, but we have to be quick. I'll be called in a few minutes for *Bon Voyage*. It's the third number.'

Holly knocked and entered.

'Hey, Holly! You back for more?' Zak asked.

Puzzled, Belle looked at Holly.

'Oh, I just, er took a wrong turn earlier,' she said.

Adam, Zak and Philippe Meyer had changed into their tango outfits. They looked like off-duty waiters in their white shirts and black trousers. Zak was piling discarded clothes onto a chair while Adam was sitting in the corner cleaning his shoes and chatting to Philippe.

'Adam, we wanted to talk to you about something,' Belle explained.

Adam held his hand up and smiled sadly. 'If you've come to persuade me to apologize to Cat, don't bother. Read. My. Lips. *I didn't say she was fat.*'

'Yeah, we know,' Holly said gently. 'But Cat's got it in her head and she's sooo miserable. You *do* want to get back together with her, don't you?'

'Of course! If she'd give me half a chance.'

'Well, *something* you said must've upset her,' Belle added. 'So maybe you could just say sorry, even if you're not saying sorry for what she thinks you should be saying sorry for.'

'Right.' Adam laughed, making a no-idea-what-you-just-said face. 'Sounds dead simple when you put it like that! But I can't apologize anyway. We're not even *talking* to each other.'

'OK, so you need to tell her *without* words . . . some kind of over-the-top romantic gesture that'll sweep her off her feet,' Belle said, thinking aloud.

'Yeah, like flags, dude,' Zak chimed in.

'Er, flags?' Belle echoed.

'Yeah, I learned all about it on a sailing course last

summer. They use them on ships to tell each other stuff. Like *I am on fire and carrying dangerous cargo*. It's gnarlacious!'

Holly laughed. 'I know *Anything Goes* is set on a ship, but if Adam starts waving flags at her, Cat's going to think he's bonkers as well as rude!'

Belle checked her watch. She was dangerously close to being late for her call. They had to come up with something fast! 'Philippe, you're French, that's the language of luuurve,' she said. 'Any brilliant ideas? Preferably *not* involving flags.'

'I'm *Belgian*!' Philippe pointed out, bristling slightly.

'Even better. The language of *chocolate*,' Belle said. 'A big box of Belgian chocs would be the perfect peace offering!' Then she thought about it. Given the fat content of the current dispute, chocolate *could* be seen to be in bad taste. 'No, maybe not,' she added weakly.

Suddenly Holly's face lit up. 'Don't move . . . Back in a second!' she shouted. With that, she darted out of the room. Belle exchanged bemused looks with Adam, Zak and Philippe. Moments later, Holly returned, waving a white rose. 'The language of *flowers*. That's the real language of love!'

'Awesome!' Belle said. 'Adam could present this to

Cat during the dance. Hold it in his teeth. They're always doing it in movies.'

Adam looked doubtfully at the rose. 'I'm not putting it in my mouth. It's got thorns.'

'You gotta commit, dude,' Zak said. 'No pain, no gain!'

'Here,' Holly said, tucking the stem through Adam's belt.

Adam grinned. 'I guess it's got to be better than waving a flag!'

Belle jumped as an announcement came over the tannoy: 'Starters for *Bon Voyage!*' Heart pounding, she catapulted out into the corridor – straight into Nick.

'Oh, that's where you're hiding,' he said urgently, grabbing her arm and pulling her along the corridor. 'Come on! We're on. *Now!*' Then he looked at the door Belle had just shot out of. '*Boys'* dressing room four? Is this something you want to talk to the school counsellor about?'

Belle laughed and punched his arm as they hurried to the wings.

After *Bon Voyage*, Belle waited impatiently for *All Through the Night*. At last she and Holly were huddled in the wings, watching anxiously as Adam and Cat whirled round in their furious, feisty tango. Would Adam give Cat the rose? And would the rose work its magic and bring Cat to her senses?

The number was almost over. Adam and Cat glared at each other. They stamped and swirled and spun as if they were dancing a duel to the death. There were only a few more seconds left for Adam to make his move. *Oh no*, Belle thought, glancing at Holly, *he's chickened out* . . .

But as the last chorus began, Adam took the rose from his belt. He placed it in Cat's hand as they stepped into a close embrace.

Belle held her breath, her eyes locked on Cat's face.

Cat took the rose. She stared at it lovingly for a moment. She lifted it to her nose and smelled it.

It was all going so well! Belle gripped Holly's arm in trepidation.

And then Cat swept out her arm majestically and dropped the rose to the floor.

Belle watched in horror as she ground it to a pulp under her toe.

The audience loved it! There were whistles and screams of 'Bravo!' Owen and Tabitha faltered slightly in their duet, unsure what all the applause was for.

Moments later, Adam trailed off the stage looking

thoroughly dejected. 'Do you think Zak has a flag for *This ship is fed up — stop sulking and give me a break,*' he grumbled.

Cat stormed offstage after him. 'A stupid rose? Does he really think he can get round me with a bit of old vegetation!'

'I thought I said try *not* to upstage Owen and Tabitha!' Miss LeClair called after them.

Belle exchanged a despairing look with Holly.

If this was the language of love, Adam and Cat were in serious need of a translator!

CHAPTER THIRTY-TWO

Cat: Guilty as Charged

Cat was still fuming as she marched back across the courtyard after the matinee show. *A rose? If Adam thinks I'm falling for that predictable old cliché he has another think coming.*

'Catrin!' came a shout from behind her.

Cat whirled round. 'Oh, *now* what?' she snapped. 'Oh, sorry, Mr Grampian, I was just, er, immersing myself in a character part, like you always tell us to. I was being this really grumpy girl who . . .'

'Highly commendable! Developing your character acting,' Mr Grampian replied, puffing a little as he jogged to catch her up. 'I just received a rather pleasing telephone communication from the casting director in Cambridge. Apparently he saw your Lady Macbeth last term and he was so impressed he wishes to see you *before* he auditions anyone else for the part of Beatrice. I would dare to wager the part is yours for the taking!'

Cat stared at her Drama Teacher. She'd been so

absorbed in being angry with Adam, she'd totally forgotten about the upcoming audition for *Much Ado About Nothing*.

'You *are* still aspiring to attain the part, I trust?' Mr Grampian asked, frowning with confusion at her unenthusiastic response.

'Yes,' Cat laughed, pulling herself together. 'Of course! Thank you!'

What's the matter with me? Cat puzzled, as she walked away. *This is fantastic news. I should be jumping for joy. If only . . .*

If only what . . .

What was this hollow feeling in her stomach?

Cat drifted back to her bedroom and slumped on her bed. Holly and Belle had gone for a walk with Jack and Ethan. *If only . . .*

There I go again, she thought. *If only . . .*

. . . if only I could go for a long walk with Adam and tell him all about the audition.

There, I've said it!

Catrin Tara Wickham. What you need is a Really Good Think!

Belle would get out her yoga mat. Holly would swim up and down in the pool. But for Cat the perfect thinking place was a Long Hot Soak in the Bath. She jumped off her bed, grabbed her towel and bubble bath and headed for the bathroom.

She sank luxuriously into the scalding hot water. *Now, I'm going to get straight to the point. I have not been very impressed with your behaviour recently.* The voice she was using to give herself a Good Talking To sounded remarkably like Mrs Salmon. *Now I want you to think very carefully before you answer this question. Do you really cross-your-heart-and-hope-to-die think that Adam said you were fat?*

Cat closed her eyes and thought back to that evening in Café Roma. Suddenly she heard Adam's exact words replaying in her mind. *I'd be all 'Do my feet look big in these socks, like you with your bum!'*

'No,' she squeaked in a tiny voice.

Aha! Now the truth comes out! She pounced on her own confession. So, *Adam was merely referring to your own concerns about having a large posterior. I put it to you, ladies and gentlemen of the jury* (Mrs Salmon had somehow turned into a blustering courtroom lawyer), *that the defendant seriously over-reacted to her boyfriend's perfectly innocent comment and is guilty of first-degree pig-headedness and grievous bodily sulking.*

Guilty as charged! Cat groaned as she slid down

under the jasmine-and-watermelon-scented bubbles and let the hot water wash over her. I was so worried about not being skinny I didn't even listen to what Adam was saying. And then it all got out of hand and I didn't know how to back down.

I've been mean to Adam. And I've been cranky with Holly and Belle. I marched right past them when I came offstage this afternoon and hardly listened when Holly told me about Ethan being home. Then I nearly snapped Mr Grampian's head off. Worst of all, I'm not even focusing on my acting. Playing Beatrice in Much Ado About Nothing *has been my dream for months. How could it have slipped my mind?*

Cat re-surfaced and turned the on hot tap with her toe for a top-up. *Well, it's time to do something about it. Tonight is the final show, my last tango with Adam. There are only a few more days left at school and then we'll all be going our different ways for the summer – Belle to New York, Holly to the West End, Adam to . . . where?*

Cat realized she didn't even know what Adam was doing for the holidays. It was so long since she'd talked to him. Now she knew what that hollow feeling was. *She missed Adam!* She missed talking and laughing and sharing their stories and hopes and dreams. She wanted to talk to him about Beatrice. She wanted to know what he was planning to do, whether they would see each other in the summer . . .

Then an awful thought turned her stomach to water. *Maybe he won't even want me back now? I wouldn't blame him after I stepped on his rose.*

There was a hammering noise at the door. 'Has somebody *died* in there?' Bianca's voice rang out. 'Because if they have, this is a very inconsiderate time to do it. If I don't have my aromatherapy bath soon I'll get one of my headaches . . .'

Cat emerged from the depths and opened the door.

'Argggh!' Bianca screamed, recoiling in horror and almost leaping out of her designer silk kimono.

'What?' Cat asked. 'I know my dressing gown's a bit tatty but it's not *that* bad, is it?'

'What happened to your *face*?'

Oh no! Just what I need! Some kind of hideous skin disease . . . Cat turned in dread to the mirror and wiped off the steam with her sleeve.

She looked as if an army of pre-schoolers had been using her face for finger-painting practice.

Top tip for aspiring young actresses, Cat thought as she reached for the cotton wool. *Remove your stage make-up before you get in the bath!*

★ ★ ★

Hardly even aware of Gemma and Sophia chattering at the dressing-room mirror next to her, Cat's hand shook as she drew her thick black eyeliner back on for the evening show. She was dry-mouthed and jelly-legged with nerves – not about the tango performance, but about talking to Adam. How was she going to start the conversation? Could she just dive in with, '*So, about this total meltdown I've been having? What d'you say we pretend it never happened?*'

Would Adam even listen to a crazy rose-crushing maniac?

A rose! That was it! She could return the gesture and give Adam a rose. It would the prefect symbol that she'd repented her old flower-murdering ways. But where was she going to get a rose now? Then she remembered. Didn't Holly say Ethan had brought her a bouquet? Maybe they were still in the dressing room Holly shared with Belle and the other Year Eight girls.

Eye pencil still in hand, Cat sprinted down the corridor. Holly was sitting at the mirror. On her dressing table was a bouquet of white roses in a pint glass of water.

'Oh yes!' Cat shouted, punching the air.

'What?' Holly asked, looking up with a puzzled smile. Belle hurried across to join them.

'Wait a minute,' Cat said. '*White roses?*' She looked suspiciously from Holly to Belle. They were both looking a little sheepish. 'Adam gave me a *white rose* . . .' She clasped her hand to her forehead and pretended to be thinking very hard. 'And Holly has a whole bunch of *white roses*. Could there *possibly* be a connection here?'

'We were only trying to . . .' Holly and Belle both started to babble at once.

Cat laughed at their worried faces. 'It's OK! I just wanted to ask if I could have one. I'm going to give it to Adam . . .'

Now Holly and Belle were looking even more aghast! *What do they think I'm going to do with the rose?* she wondered. *Stick it up his nose or something?* 'Don't worry,' she giggled. 'I'm going to play nicely now!' She looked down at the floor for a moment. 'And I'm sorry I've been such a pain lately . . .' she mumbled.

Holly and Belle jumped up and engulfed her in a hug.

Lettie, Ruby and all the other girls in the dressing room cheered.

In a list of Things That Are Way More Difficult Than They Sound, Cat thought, *presenting a boy with a rose while dancing the tango is definitely in the Top Ten.* First, there's the thorny question of where to put the rose (she eventually opted for tucked down the front of her blouse) and then there was the problem of picking the right moment to whip the rose out (scratches and unfortunate blouse-coming-undone incidents were potential hazards here) *and* the fact that you hardly ever had your hands free!

But somehow, Cat overcame the obstacles, and halfway through *All Through the Night* she presented Adam with the rose. He stared at her, almost forgetting to step backwards as she leaned in for a dramatic *volcada*.

'I'm really sorry,' she whispered into his ear.

Adam grinned and pulled her close. 'Me too. I didn't mean to say the wrong thing!'

'You didn't,' Cat replied, smiling. 'I was just being a ridiculous drama queen!'

Adam kissed her cheek as he dipped her low. He lingered, smiling and staring into her eyes so long they almost missed a beat.

Suddenly Cat felt as light as thistledown floating in the breeze. She came back to earth with a bump as she found herself backing into Gemma. Zak quickly compensated by taking an extra step and leading Gemma further downstage.

'Oops!' Cat giggled. 'Must focus!'

'You look gorgeous when you focus,' Adam whispered. 'And so-o-o-o slim too!'

'What on earth was happening out there?' Miguel snapped as Cat and Adam ran offstage. 'You two were all over the place! Where did the passion go?'

Cat and Adam looked at each other. 'Sorry. Just a bit tired,' Cat mumbled, trying not to laugh. Then she took Adam's hand and they flew down the steps into the corridor.

'All over the place!' Adam said sternly, imitating Miguel Silva.

'Where did the *passion* go?' Cat giggled.

'Um, I think this is where it went,' Adam said, smiling as he scooped her up in his arms and kissed her.

'I think you're right!' Cat murmured happily.

CHAPTER THIRTY-THREE

Holly: Keep the Dream Alive

The final number of the show was coming to a close.

The audience rose in a standing ovation as Holly ran back on stage with the rest of the singers and dancers to take their bows. She grinned at Belle and nodded towards Cat and Adam, standing hand in hand. They couldn't take their eyes off each other.

Holly peeped round the Year Eleven students in front of her and saw Ethan waving to her from the audience.

Everything had worked out perfectly. Cat and Adam were together again and Cat was almost guaranteed her part in *Much Ado About Nothing*. Belle was staying at Superstar High, and had her place at the opera summer school in New York. And now Ethan was back, Holly was looking forward to her Intermediate ballet exam on Monday and the musical theatre workshop in the summer. And they should be hearing about the PopTV video competition any day now . . . it was almost too exciting to think they might actually win!

Mr Fortune strode out onto the stage and made a long, emotional speech, bidding the graduating students farewell and wishing them luck in their future careers. The Year Eleven students were all hugging and crying and laughing together.

One day that will be us, Holly thought. *But we have three more amazing years at Superstar High ahead of us first!*

After they'd changed out of their costumes, Holly, Cat and Belle gathered with a huge crowd of friends outside the dressing rooms, chatting noisily about the show. They were even joined by the twins, Abbey and Libby, who'd come to watch the show with their parents.

'We just came backstage to say we'll see you next year,' they shouted joyfully. 'We found out today – we've both got places!'

'Welcome on board!' Holly said warmly.

Cat and Belle joined her in congratulating them. 'Now you're officially part of Superstar High,' Cat said, 'you should come and join us. There's a big party in the dining room.'

'Wait up!' Nick Taggart was pushing his way through the crowd, waving a purple and orange envelope. He was followed at a run by Nathan Almeida. 'Belle, this just came for you!' Nick was panting as if he'd run a marathon. 'I just went over to school to check the DJ had arrived for the party and Mrs Butterworth was putting this in your pigeon hole!'

Holly knew what it was immediately. Bright purple and orange were the trademark colours of PopTV.

So did Cat. 'Open it!' she yelled. '*Open it!*'

'*Open it! Open it!*' By now everyone was joining the chant. Then they fell silent, watching breathlessly as Belle tore open the envelope.

Holly clutched Cat's arm. She could hardly bear the tension.

Belle looked up with a serious look on her face. 'It looks as if . . .' she said gravely.

Oh no, Holly thought, *we haven't made it through*.

'. . . WE'VE DONE IT!' Belle screamed, waving her arms in the air. Holly had never seen her so ecstatic. 'We're one of the five chosen groups! We're going to have our song recorded and our video filmed professionally. We're going to be on PopTV!'

Now they were all jumping up and down and hugging each other.

'Nobody's Angels will be famous!' Cat shouted.

Holly took the letter from Belle. '*Highly original . . .*' she read, '*excellent vocalists . . . imaginative choreography, superb camerawork and direction . . .*'

'Yeah, baby!' Nick crowed. '*Su-perb* direction! Read it and weep!' He high-fived everyone, ending with Jack.

Belle smiled at Nick. 'Yes, you're right. You did brilliantly. Thank you!' She ran to Jack for a celebratory kiss.

'And thank you to Nathan for the superb camerawork too,' Cat added, patting him on the back. Nathan shuffled awkwardly but looked delighted.

Holly continued to read the letter aloud: '*Outstanding melody and lyrics* – that's all thanks to Lettie, our genius songwriter, of course. Where's she gone anyway?' she asked, looking around.

'I'm here!' Lettie called, pushing her way towards them. 'There's someone I want you to meet. He came to see the show with his dad. This is Callum.'

Nick looked as if the rug had been pulled out from under his feet. *What's Lettie doing?* Holly wondered. *I thought she and Nick were doing Happily Ever After now?* And where was this Callum guy anyway? Lettie just seemed to have a cute little boy with her . . .

'Everyone, meet Callum Foster,' Lettie said. 'An eight-year-old child prodigy! He's such a musical genius he used to join in with our class at my old school.'

'But he's a *kid*!' Nick spluttered. 'Why didn't you say?'

'I did *try* to say when those red roses arrived,' Lettie said. 'But you weren't listening. Then I thought maybe it wouldn't hurt to let you think I had this really cool secret admirer . . .'

Cat threw back her head and laughed. 'Lettie! You mean you were playing the green-eyed monster card as well!'

Lettie just smiled shyly.

Nick high-fived with Callum. 'Good to meet you, mate!' Then he turned to Lettie and laughed. 'What a sneaky, devious, low-down trick to pull on a poor, innocent Scotsman!' He pulled her towards him and planted a big smoochy kiss on her lips.

'Euugh! Yuck!' Callum grimaced, putting his hands over his eyes. 'I'm going to find my dad!'

Everyone laughed.

Suddenly Cat grabbed hold of Adam and struck up a dramatic tango pose. 'Did someone say something about a party?' she purred in a sultry Spanish accent.

'I believe it was mentioned,' Adam laughed, spinning her round.

'Come on, let's go,' Ethan said, taking Holly's hand and pulling her out through the stage door into the warm summer evening. Soon the others were all following.

'Last one on the dance floor has to lead the Macarena!' Belle laughed, starting to run across the sports field.

'Ooh, me please!' Cat shouted, chasing after her.

Holly knew she had a big day of ballet practice ahead of her tomorrow, ready for her Intermediate exam on Monday, but she was going to make the most of tonight. She looked into Ethan's eyes and smiled. Then she pulled off her shoes and sprinted after Holly and Cat.

Soon Holly, Cat and Belle were holding hands, racing through the twilight towards the twinkling lights of the school buildings. Holly could hear the music spilling out from the party already. She looked back and saw the others running behind them . . . Ethan, Jack, Adam, Nick and Lettie hand in hand, Gemma and Zak, Serena, Ruby, Nathan, Mason Lee, Frankie Pellegrini, Felix Baddeley, Philippe and Sophia and many, many more of their friends. Friends who would be leaving, like Owen and Tabitha, and new friends who were only just starting out, like Abbey and Libby.

Holly was brimming over with happiness. She wished this night, and this term, would never end.

But, she thought, *we'll be together at Superstar High again next year and who knows what even bigger dreams and surprises and adventures the future holds?*

One thing's for sure though – until then, we'll keep the dream alive!